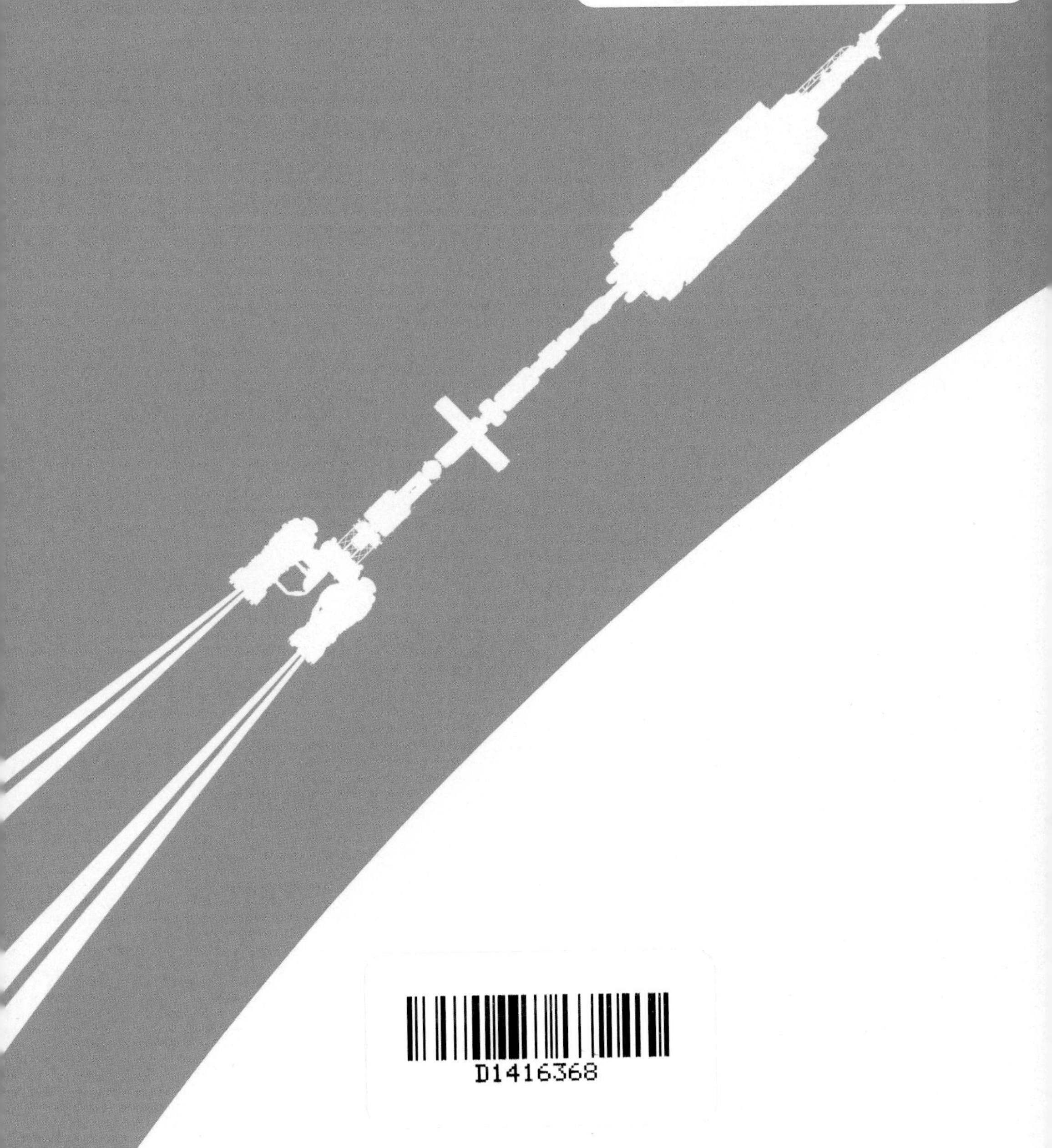

FASTER THAN LIGHT™

 **COMICS PRESENTS** A *Shadowline*® PRODUCTION

FASTER THAN LIGHT

Created by
BRIAN HABERLIN & SKIP BRITTENHAM

 for **ANOMALY** PRODUCTIONS

Story & Illustration
BRIAN HABERLIN

Colors
DAN KEMP

Lettering & AR Data
FRANCIS TAKENAGA

Programming
DAVID PENTZ

Assists
DIANA SANSON
KRISTIAN NEE &
SAM TODHUNTER

Editor for Anomaly Productions
SALLY HABERLIN

for *Shadowline*®

Editor
LAURA TAVISHATI

Communications
MARC LOMBARDI

Publisher
JIM VALENTINO

THE COMIC IS ONLY PART OF THE STOR
Download the FREE companion app to: Watch the captain's l
interact with aliens, read the encyclopedia and much more.
Visit ExperienceAnomaly.com/ftl on your device to download

VOLUM
"LEARNING TO RUN": Issues

Cover
BRIAN HABERLIN &
GEIRROD VANDYKE

Captain's Log
VINCE CORAZZA (#'s 7-10)
ALLYSON RYAN (# 6)

IMAGE COMICS, INC.
Robert Kirkman – Chief Operating Officer
Erik Larsen – Chief Financial Officer
Todd McFarlane – President
Marc Silvestri – Chief Executive Officer
Jim Valentino – Vice-President

Eric Stephenson – Publisher
Corey Murphy – Director of Sales
Jeff Boison – Director of Publishing Planning &
Jeremy Sullivan – Director of Digital Sales
Kat Salazar – Director of PR & Marketing
Branwyn Bigglestone – Controller
Drew Gill – Art Director
Jonathan Chan – Production Manager
Meredith Wallace – Print Manager
Briah Skelly – Publicist
Sasha Head – Sales & Marketing Production D
Randy Okamura – Digital Production Designe
David Brothers – Branding Manager
Olivia Ngai – Content Manager
Addison Duke – Production Artist
Vincent Kukua – Production Artist
Tricia Ramos – Production Artist
Jeff Stang – Direct Market Sales Representat
Emilio Bautista – Digital Sales Associate
Leanna Caunter – Accounting Assistant
Chloe Ramos-Peterson – Library Market Sale
IMAGECOMICS.COM

First Printing: November, 2016
ISBN: 978-1-6321

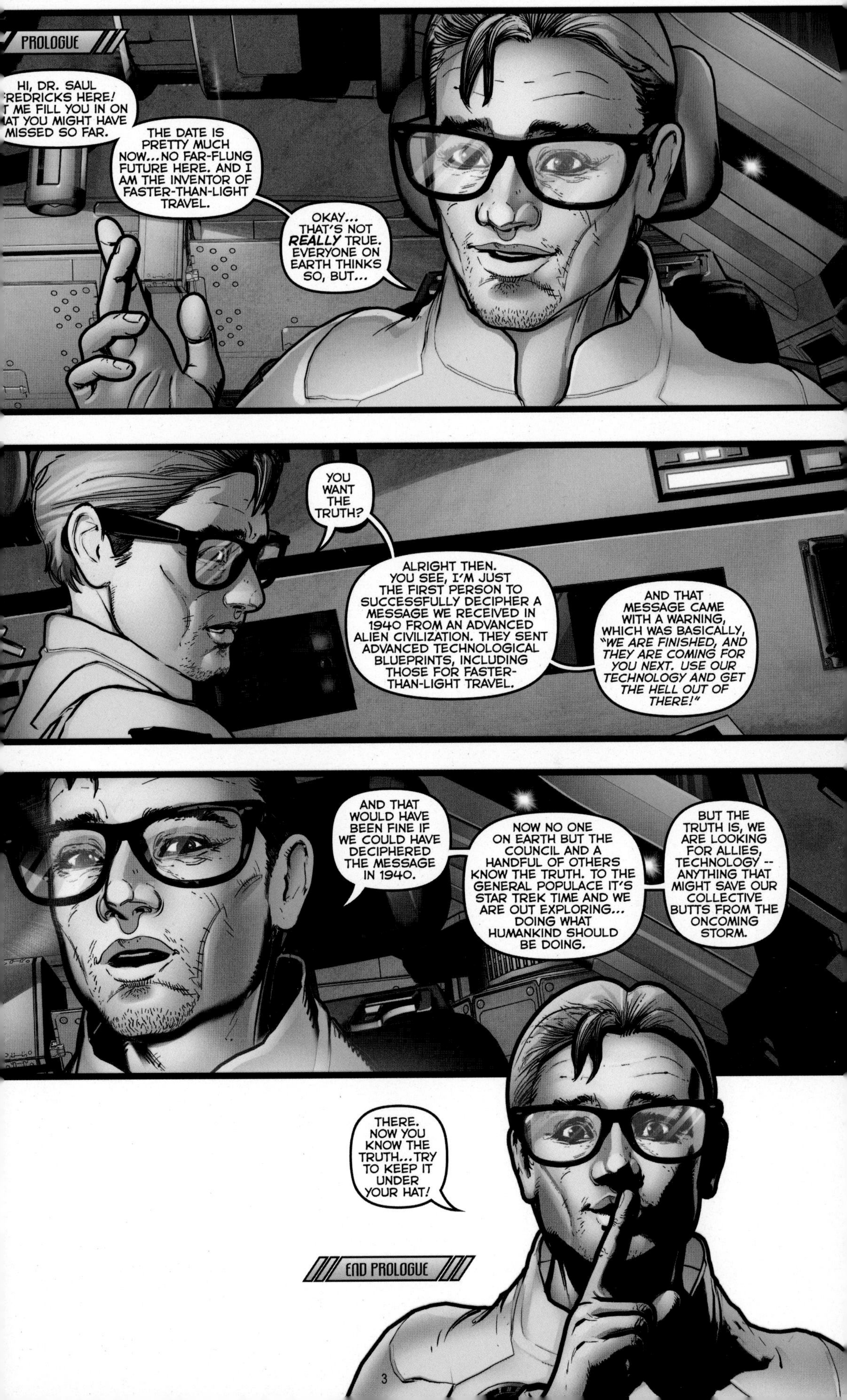
PROLOGUE
HI, DR. SAUL FREDRICKS HERE! T ME FILL YOU IN ON AT YOU MIGHT HAVE MISSED SO FAR.
THE DATE IS PRETTY MUCH NOW...NO FAR-FLUNG FUTURE HERE. AND I AM THE INVENTOR OF FASTER-THAN-LIGHT TRAVEL.
OKAY... THAT'S NOT ***REALLY*** TRUE. EVERYONE ON EARTH THINKS SO, BUT...
YOU WANT THE TRUTH?
ALRIGHT THEN. YOU SEE, I'M JUST THE FIRST PERSON TO SUCCESSFULLY DECIPHER A MESSAGE WE RECEIVED IN 1940 FROM AN ADVANCED ALIEN CIVILIZATION. THEY SENT ADVANCED TECHNOLOGICAL BLUEPRINTS, INCLUDING THOSE FOR FASTER-THAN-LIGHT TRAVEL.
AND THAT MESSAGE CAME WITH A WARNING, WHICH WAS BASICALLY, *"WE ARE FINISHED, AND THEY ARE COMING FOR YOU NEXT. USE OUR TECHNOLOGY AND GET THE HELL OUT OF THERE!"*
AND THAT WOULD HAVE BEEN FINE IF WE COULD HAVE DECIPHERED THE MESSAGE IN 1940.
NOW NO ONE ON EARTH BUT THE COUNCIL AND A HANDFUL OF OTHERS KNOW THE TRUTH. TO THE GENERAL POPULACE IT'S STAR TREK TIME AND WE ARE OUT EXPLORING... DOING WHAT HUMANKIND SHOULD BE DOING.
BUT THE TRUTH IS, WE ARE LOOKING FOR ALLIES, TECHNOLOGY -- ANYTHING THAT MIGHT SAVE OUR COLLECTIVE BUTTS FROM THE ONCOMING STORM.
THERE. NOW YOU KNOW THE TRUTH...TRY TO KEEP IT UNDER YOUR HAT!
END PROLOGUE

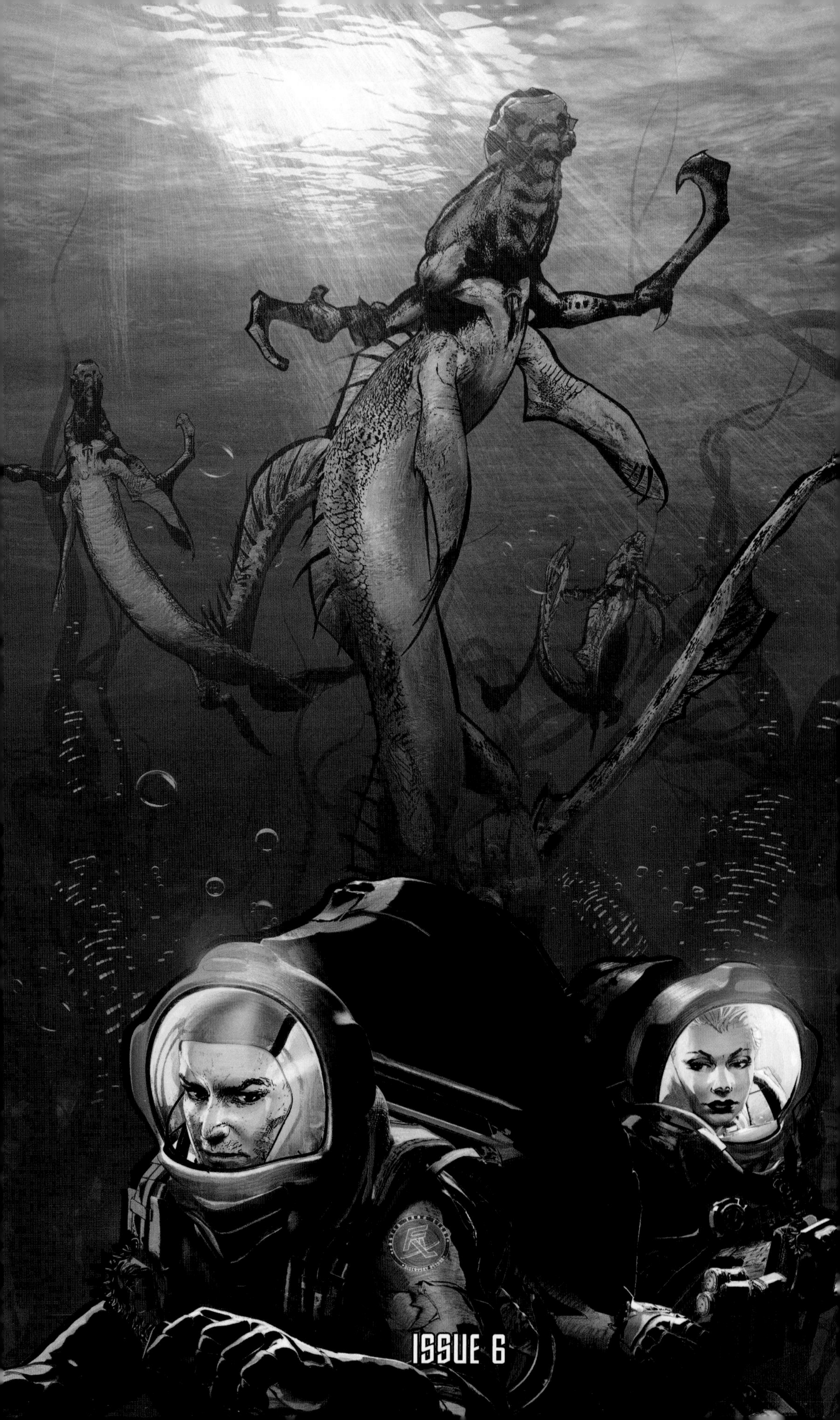
ISSUE 6

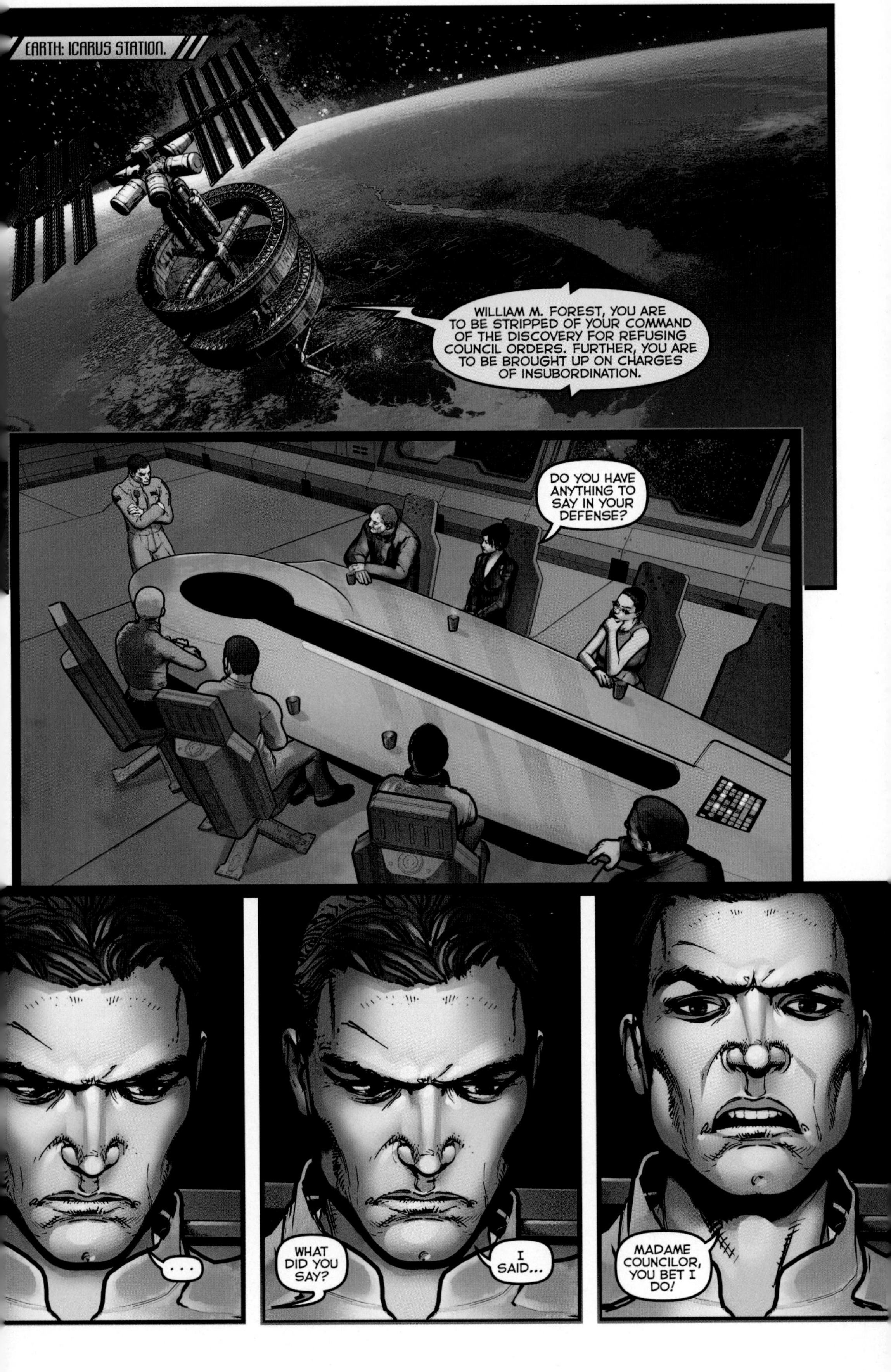
EARTH: ICARUS STATION.
WILLIAM M. FOREST, YOU ARE TO BE STRIPPED OF YOUR COMMAND OF THE DISCOVERY FOR REFUSING COUNCIL ORDERS. FURTHER, YOU ARE TO BE BROUGHT UP ON CHARGES OF INSUBORDINATION.
DO YOU HAVE ANYTHING TO SAY IN YOUR DEFENSE?
...
WHAT DID YOU SAY?
I SAID...
MADAME COUNCILOR, YOU BET I DO!

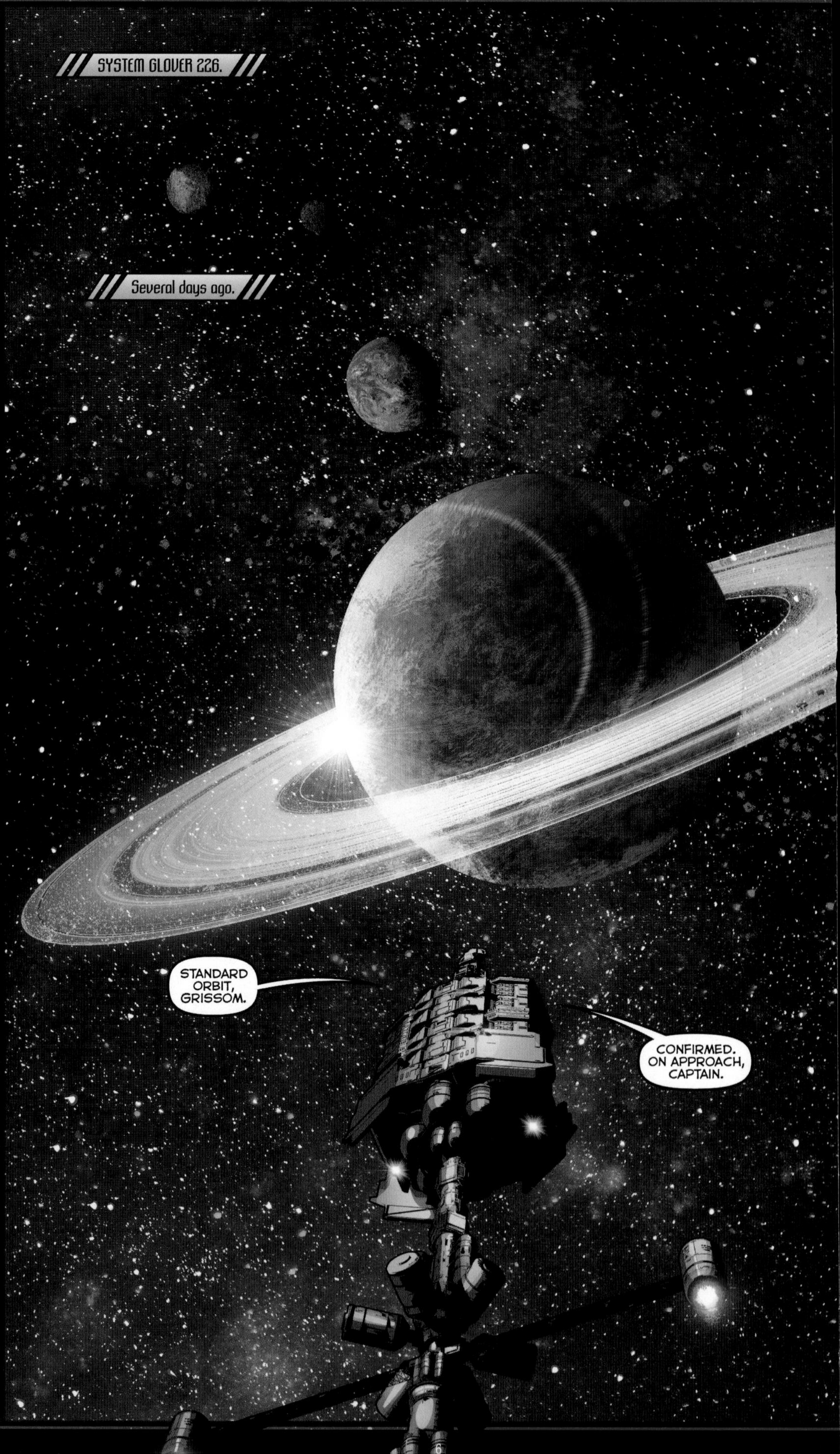
SYSTEM GLOVER 226.
Several days ago.
STANDARD ORBIT, GRISSOM.
CONFIRMED. ON APPROACH, CAPTAIN.

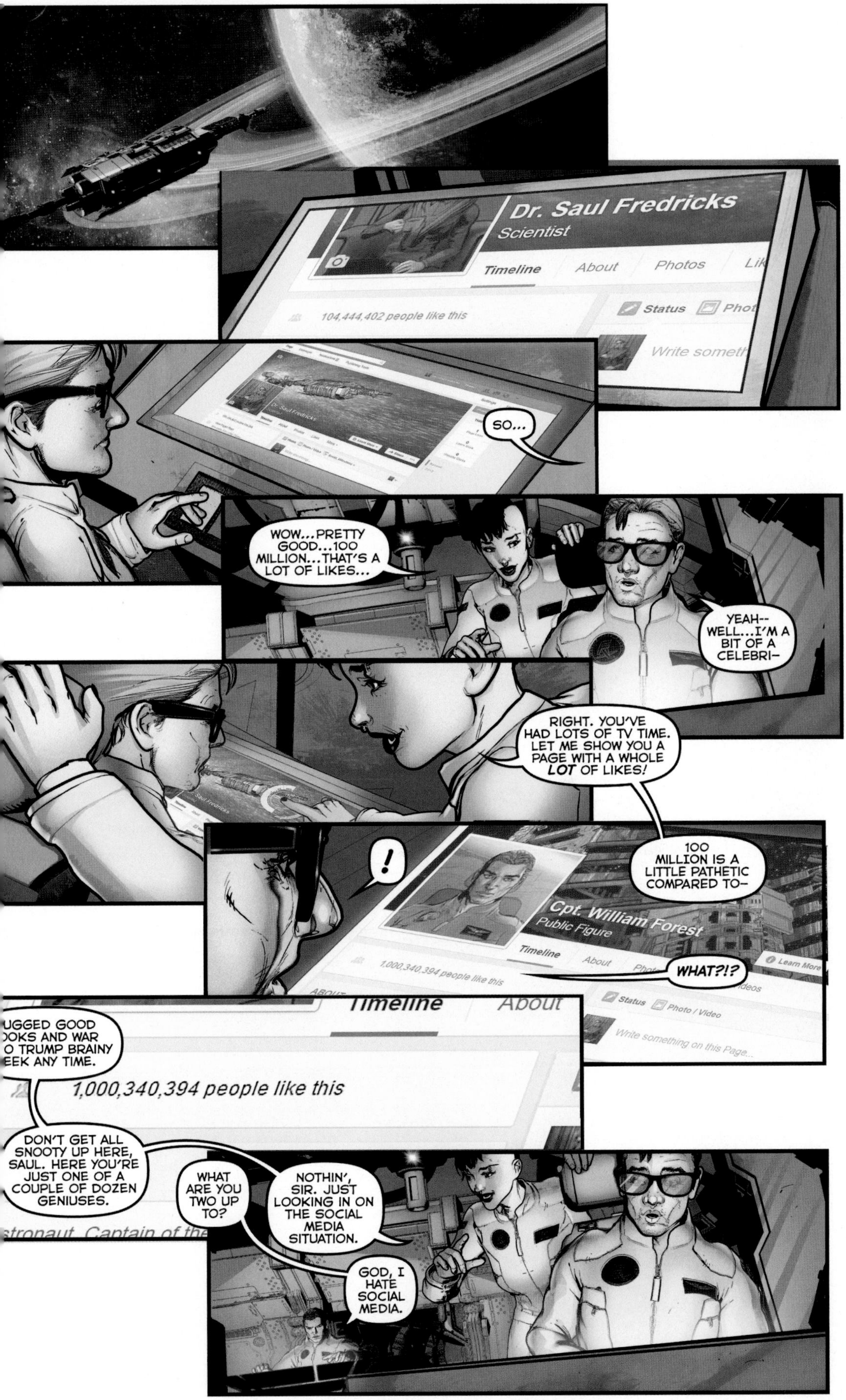
Dr. Saul Fredricks
Scientist
Timeline
About
Photos
104,444,402 people like this
Status
Write someth
SO...
WOW...PRETTY GOOD...100 MILLION...THAT'S A LOT OF LIKES...
YEAH-- WELL...I'M A BIT OF A CELEBRI–
RIGHT. YOU'VE HAD LOTS OF TV TIME. LET ME SHOW YOU A PAGE WITH A WHOLE LOT OF LIKES!
!
100 MILLION IS A LITTLE PATHETIC COMPARED TO–
Cpt. William Forest
Public Figure
Timeline
About
1,000,340,394 people like this
WHAT?!?
Status
Photo / Video
Write something on this Page...
UGGED GOOD OOKS AND WAR O TRUMP BRAINY EEK ANY TIME.
Timeline
About
1,000,340,394 people like this
DON'T GET ALL SNOOTY UP HERE, SAUL. HERE YOU'RE JUST ONE OF A COUPLE OF DOZEN GENIUSES.
WHAT ARE YOU TWO UP TO?
NOTHIN', SIR. JUST LOOKING IN ON THE SOCIAL MEDIA SITUATION.
GOD, I HATE SOCIAL MEDIA.

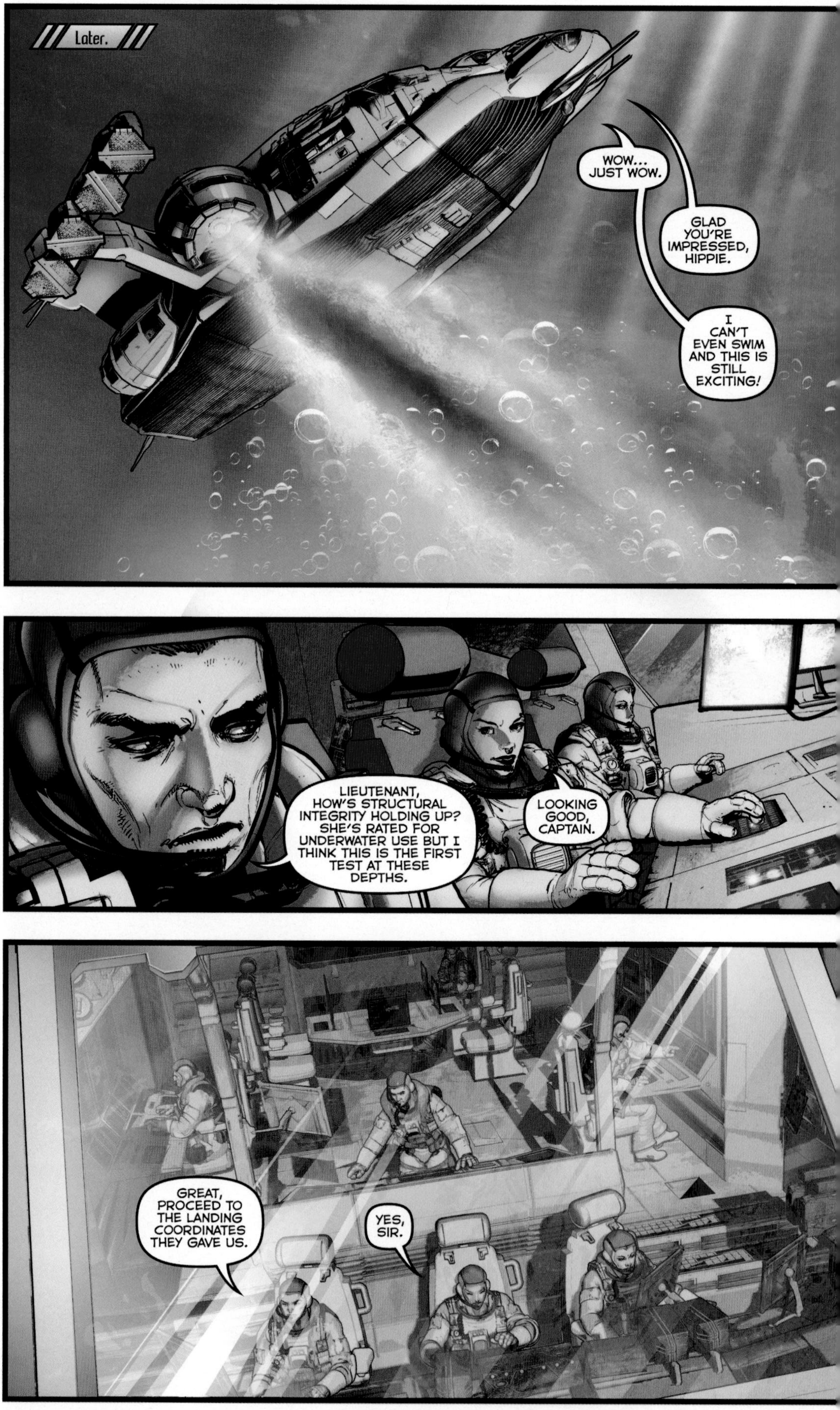
Later.
WOW... JUST WOW.
GLAD YOU'RE IMPRESSED, HIPPIE.
I CAN'T EVEN SWIM AND THIS IS STILL EXCITING!
LIEUTENANT, HOW'S STRUCTURAL INTEGRITY HOLDING UP? SHE'S RATED FOR UNDERWATER USE BUT I THINK THIS IS THE FIRST TEST AT THESE DEPTHS.
LOOKING GOOD, CAPTAIN.
GREAT, PROCEED TO THE LANDING COORDINATES THEY GAVE US.
YES, SIR.

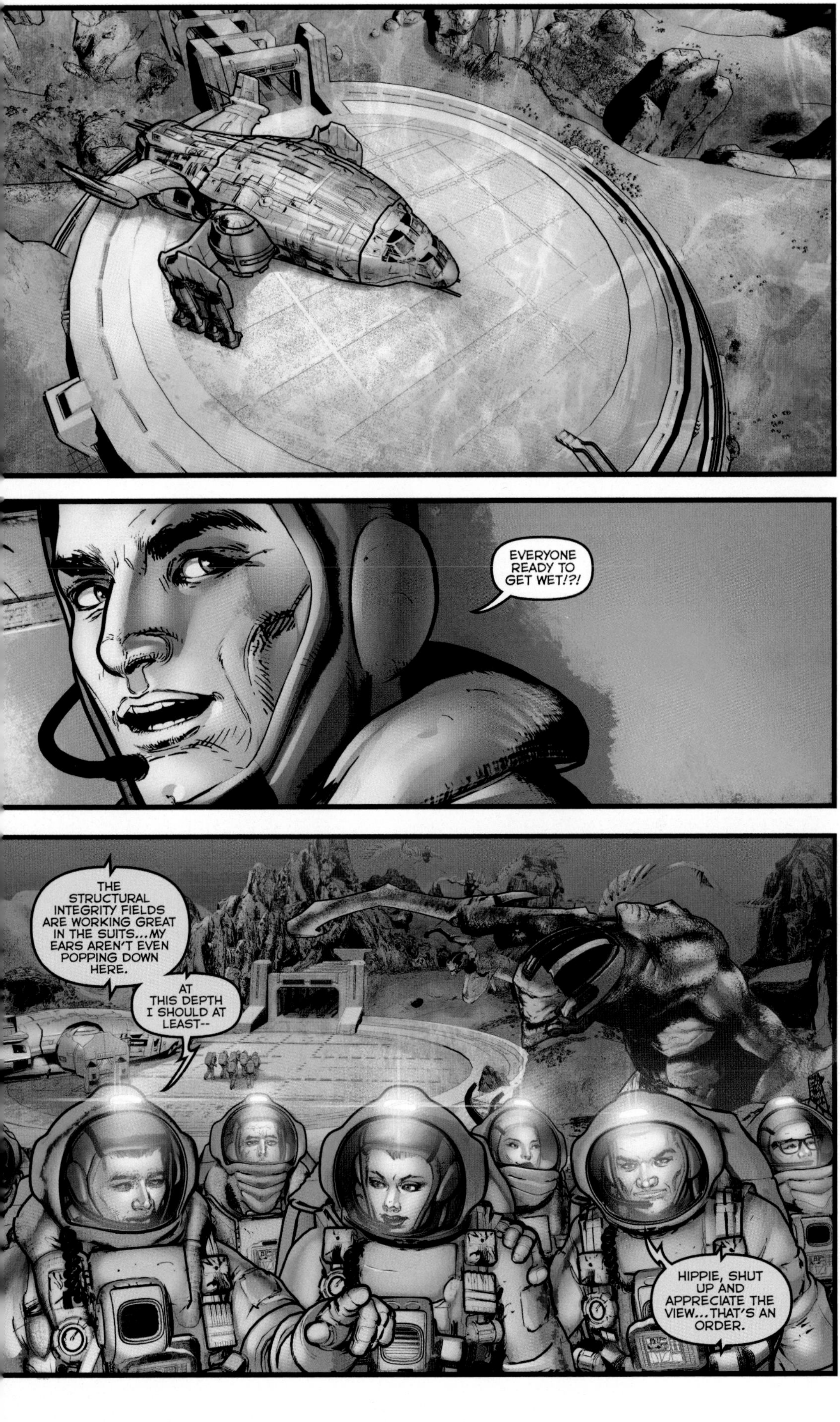
EVERYONE READY TO GET WET!?!
THE STRUCTURAL INTEGRITY FIELDS ARE WORKING GREAT IN THE SUITS...MY EARS AREN'T EVEN POPPING DOWN HERE.
AT THIS DEPTH I SHOULD AT LEAST--
HIPPIE, SHUT UP AND APPRECIATE THE VIEW...THAT'S AN ORDER.

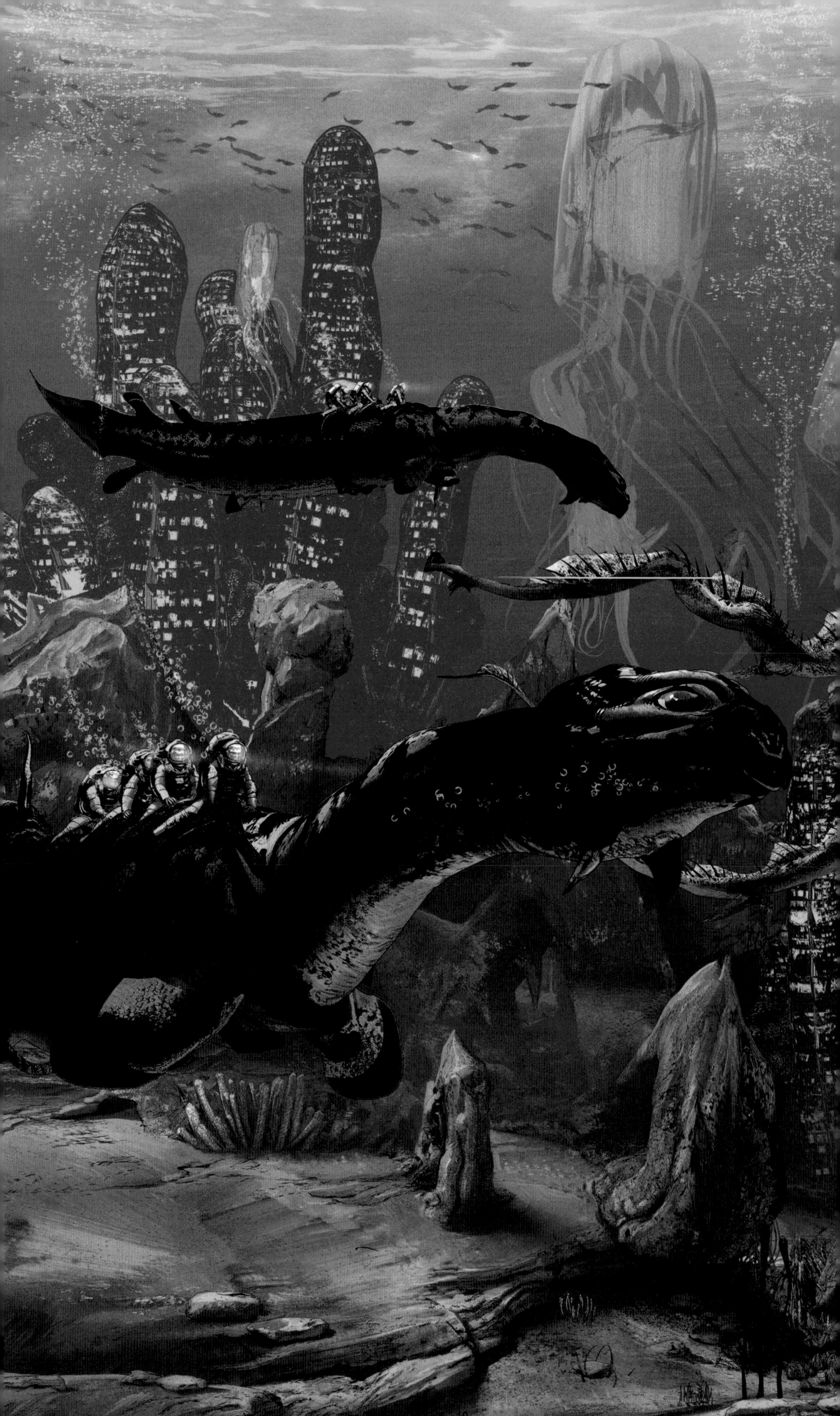

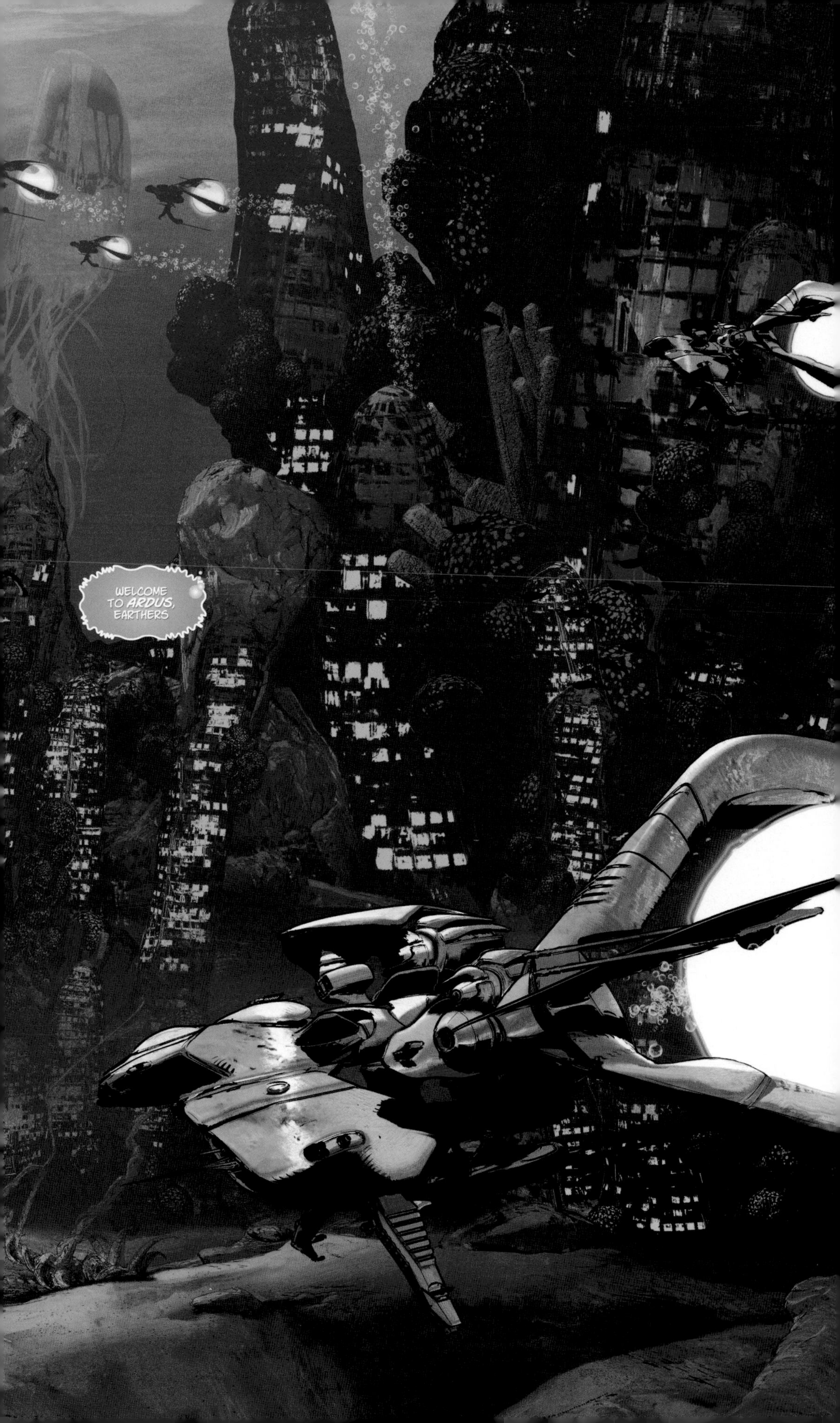
WELCOME TO ARDUS, EARTHERS

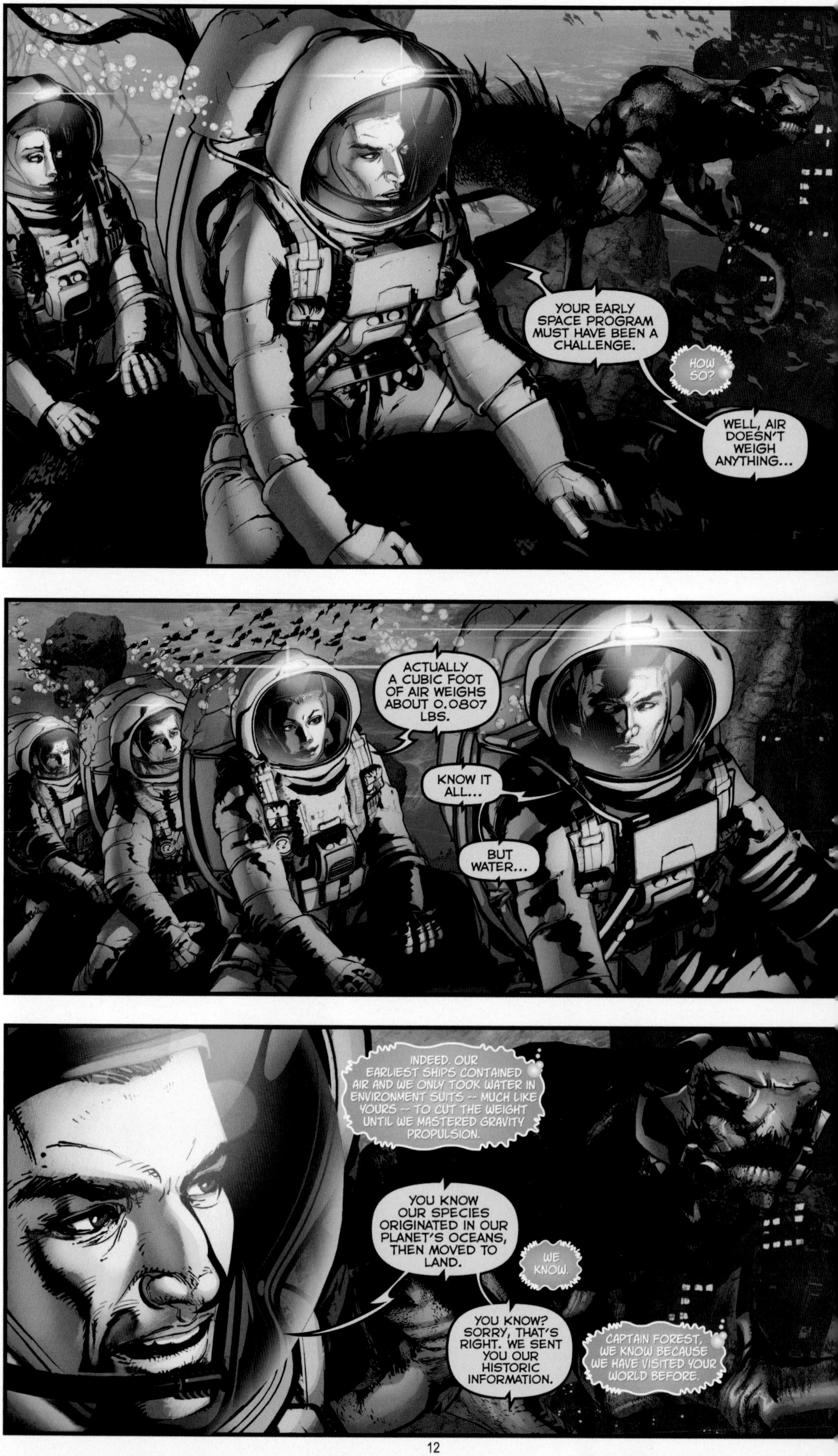
YOUR EARLY SPACE PROGRAM MUST HAVE BEEN A CHALLENGE.
HOW SO?
WELL, AIR DOESN'T WEIGH ANYTHING...
ACTUALLY A CUBIC FOOT OF AIR WEIGHS ABOUT 0.0807 LBS.
KNOW IT ALL...
BUT WATER...
INDEED. OUR EARLIEST SHIPS CONTAINED AIR AND WE ONLY TOOK WATER IN ENVIRONMENT SUITS -- MUCH LIKE YOURS -- TO CUT THE WEIGHT UNTIL WE MASTERED GRAVITY PROPULSION.
YOU KNOW OUR SPECIES ORIGINATED IN OUR PLANET'S OCEANS, THEN MOVED TO LAND.
WE KNOW.
YOU KNOW? SORRY, THAT'S RIGHT. WE SENT YOU OUR HISTORIC INFORMATION.
CAPTAIN FOREST, WE KNOW BECAUSE WE HAVE VISITED YOUR WORLD BEFORE.

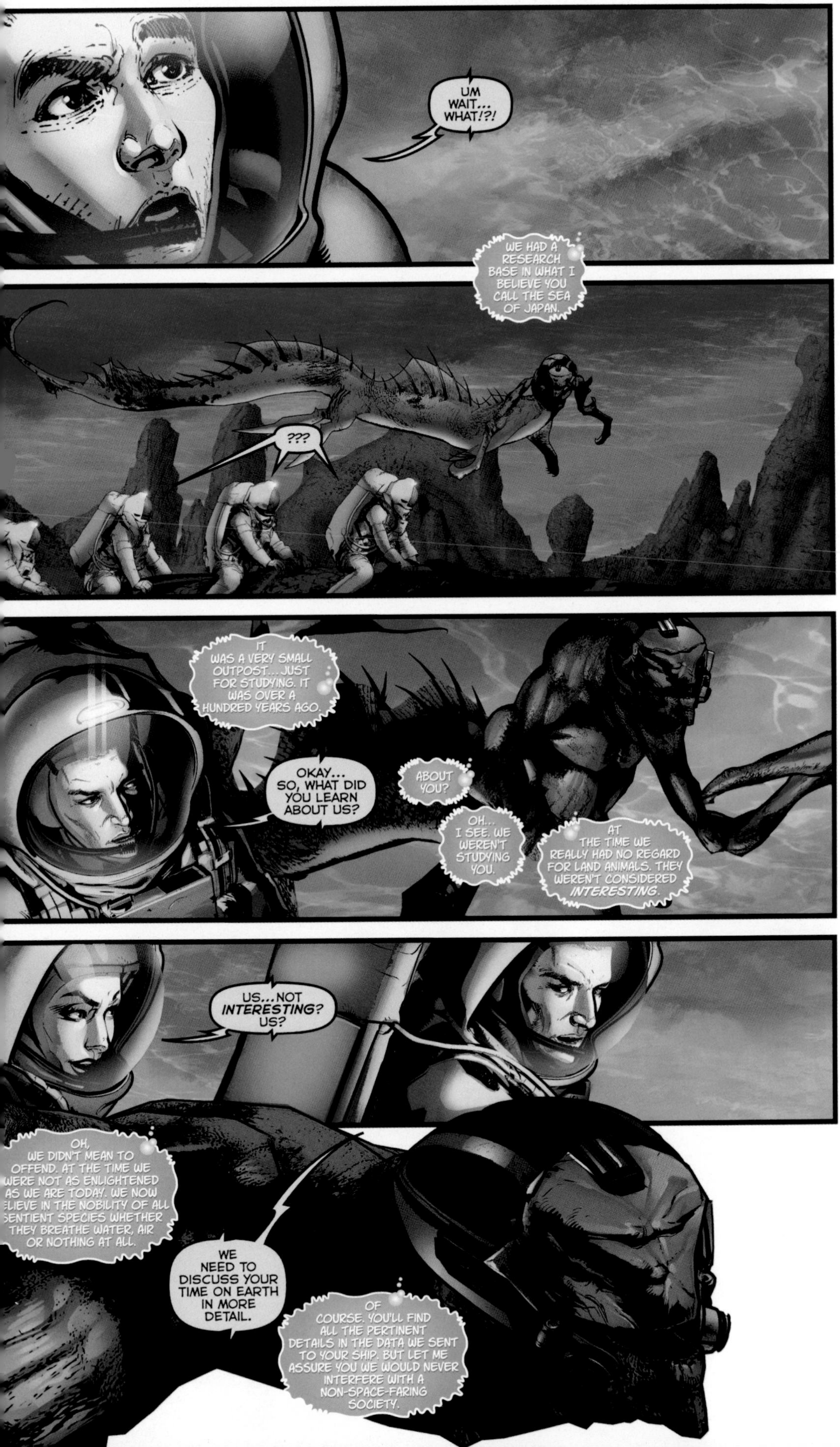
UM WAIT... WHAT!?!
WE HAD A RESEARCH BASE IN WHAT I BELIEVE YOU CALL THE SEA OF JAPAN.
???
IT WAS A VERY SMALL OUTPOST... JUST FOR STUDYING. IT WAS OVER A HUNDRED YEARS AGO.
OKAY... SO, WHAT DID YOU LEARN ABOUT US?
ABOUT YOU?
OH... I SEE. WE WEREN'T STUDYING YOU.
AT THE TIME WE REALLY HAD NO REGARD FOR LAND ANIMALS. THEY WEREN'T CONSIDERED INTERESTING.
US... NOT INTERESTING? US?
OH, WE DIDN'T MEAN TO OFFEND. AT THE TIME WE WERE NOT AS ENLIGHTENED AS WE ARE TODAY. WE NOW BELIEVE IN THE NOBILITY OF ALL SENTIENT SPECIES WHETHER THEY BREATHE WATER, AIR OR NOTHING AT ALL.
WE NEED TO DISCUSS YOUR TIME ON EARTH IN MORE DETAIL.
OF COURSE. YOU'LL FIND ALL THE PERTINENT DETAILS IN THE DATA WE SENT TO YOUR SHIP. BUT LET ME ASSURE YOU WE WOULD NEVER INTERFERE WITH A NON-SPACE-FARING SOCIETY.

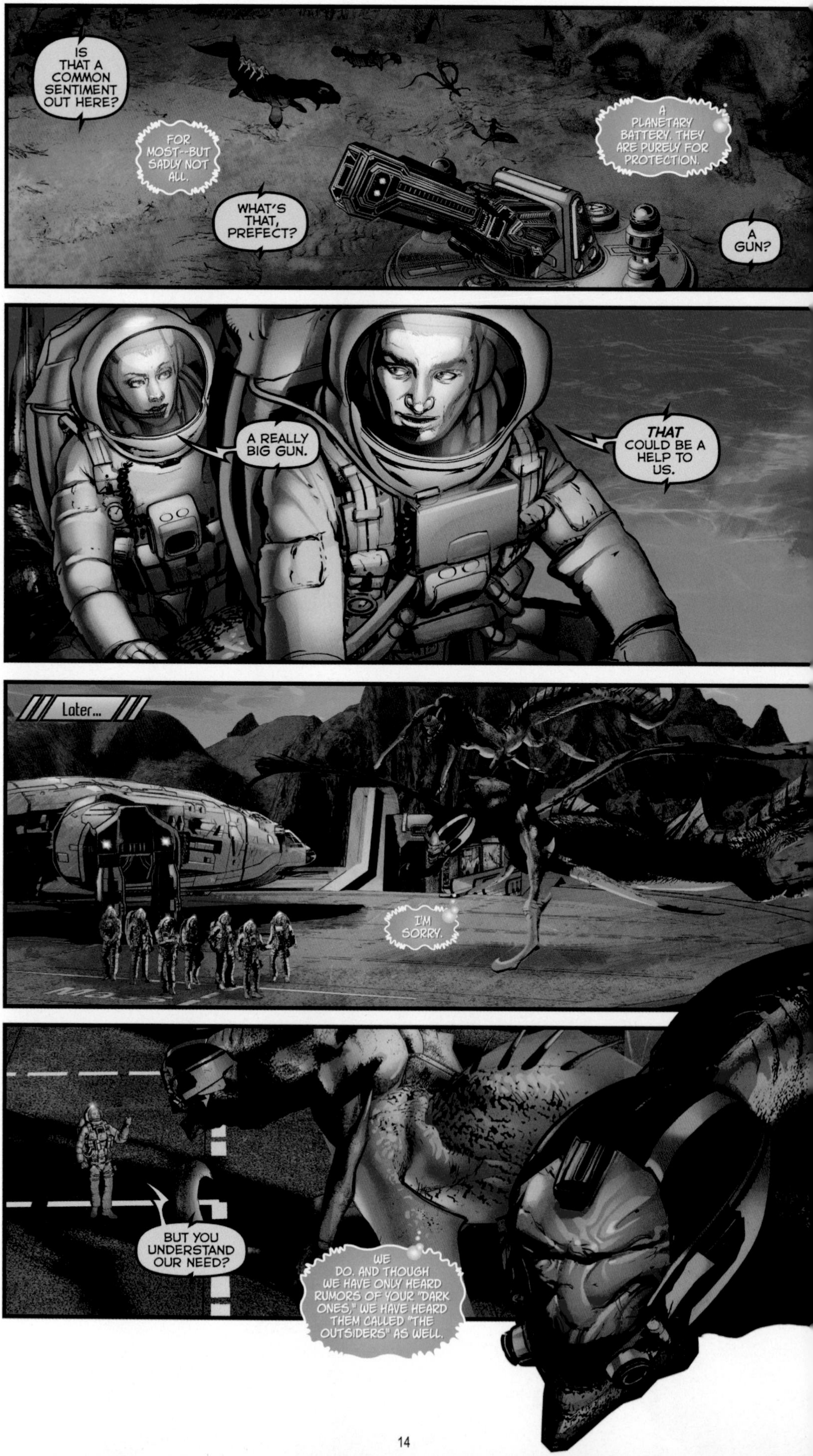
IS THAT A COMMON SENTIMENT OUT HERE?
FOR MOST--BUT SADLY NOT ALL.
WHAT'S THAT, PREFECT?
A PLANETARY BATTERY. THEY ARE PURELY FOR PROTECTION.
A GUN?
A REALLY BIG GUN.
THAT COULD BE A HELP TO US.
Later...
I'M SORRY.
BUT YOU UNDERSTAND OUR NEED?
WE DO. AND THOUGH WE HAVE ONLY HEARD RUMORS OF YOUR "DARK ONES," WE HAVE HEARD THEM CALLED "THE OUTSIDERS" AS WELL.

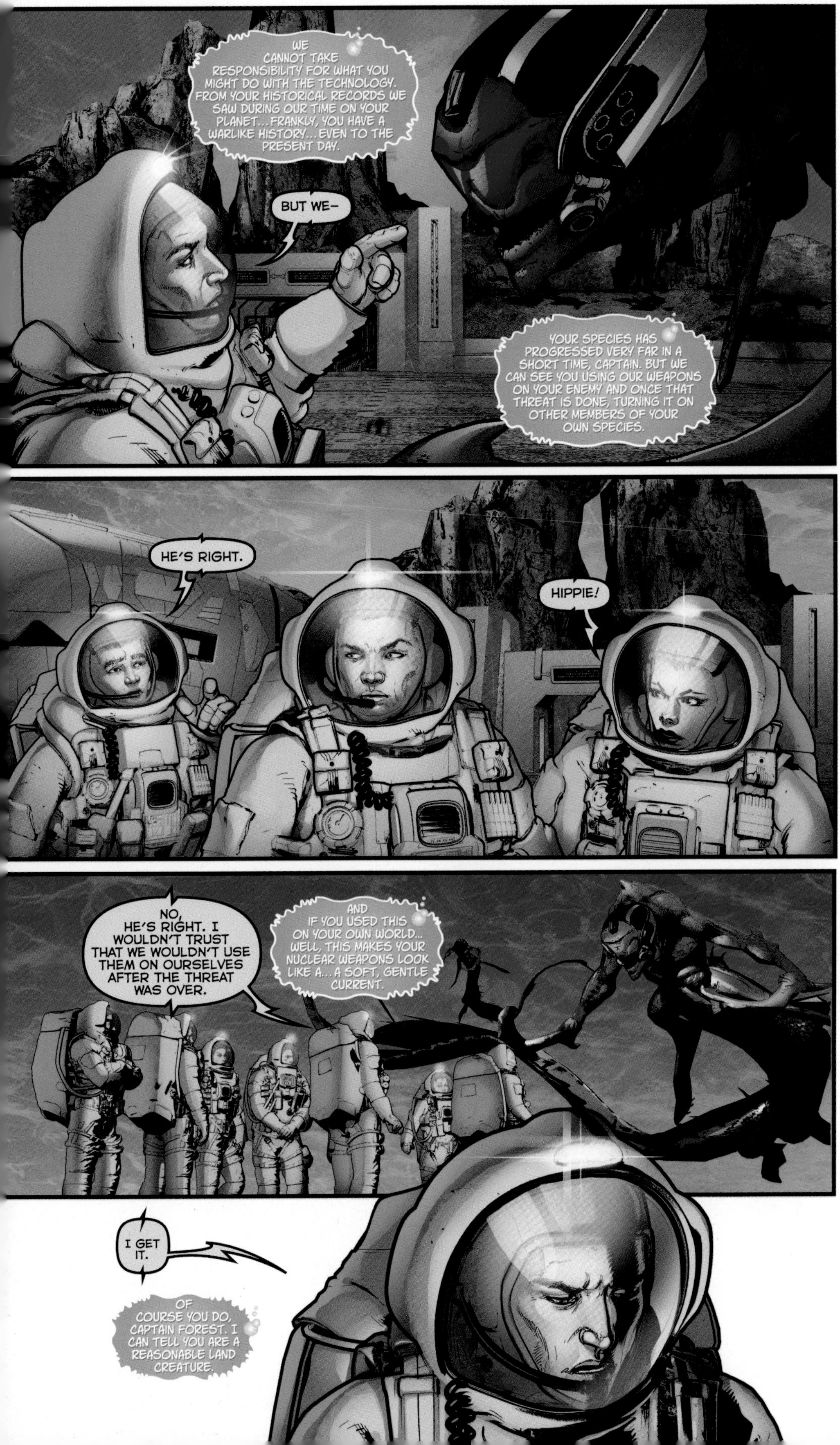
WE CANNOT TAKE RESPONSIBILITY FOR WHAT YOU MIGHT DO WITH THE TECHNOLOGY. FROM YOUR HISTORICAL RECORDS WE SAW DURING OUR TIME ON YOUR PLANET... FRANKLY, YOU HAVE A WARLIKE HISTORY... EVEN TO THE PRESENT DAY.
BUT WE–
YOUR SPECIES HAS PROGRESSED VERY FAR IN A SHORT TIME, CAPTAIN. BUT WE CAN SEE YOU USING OUR WEAPONS ON YOUR ENEMY AND ONCE THAT THREAT IS DONE, TURNING IT ON OTHER MEMBERS OF YOUR OWN SPECIES.
HE'S RIGHT.
HIPPIE!
NO, HE'S RIGHT. I WOULDN'T TRUST THAT WE WOULDN'T USE THEM ON OURSELVES AFTER THE THREAT WAS OVER.
AND IF YOU USED THIS ON YOUR OWN WORLD... WELL, THIS MAKES YOUR NUCLEAR WEAPONS LOOK LIKE A... A SOFT, GENTLE CURRENT.
I GET IT.
OF COURSE YOU DO, CAPTAIN FOREST. I CAN TELL YOU ARE A REASONABLE LAND CREATURE.

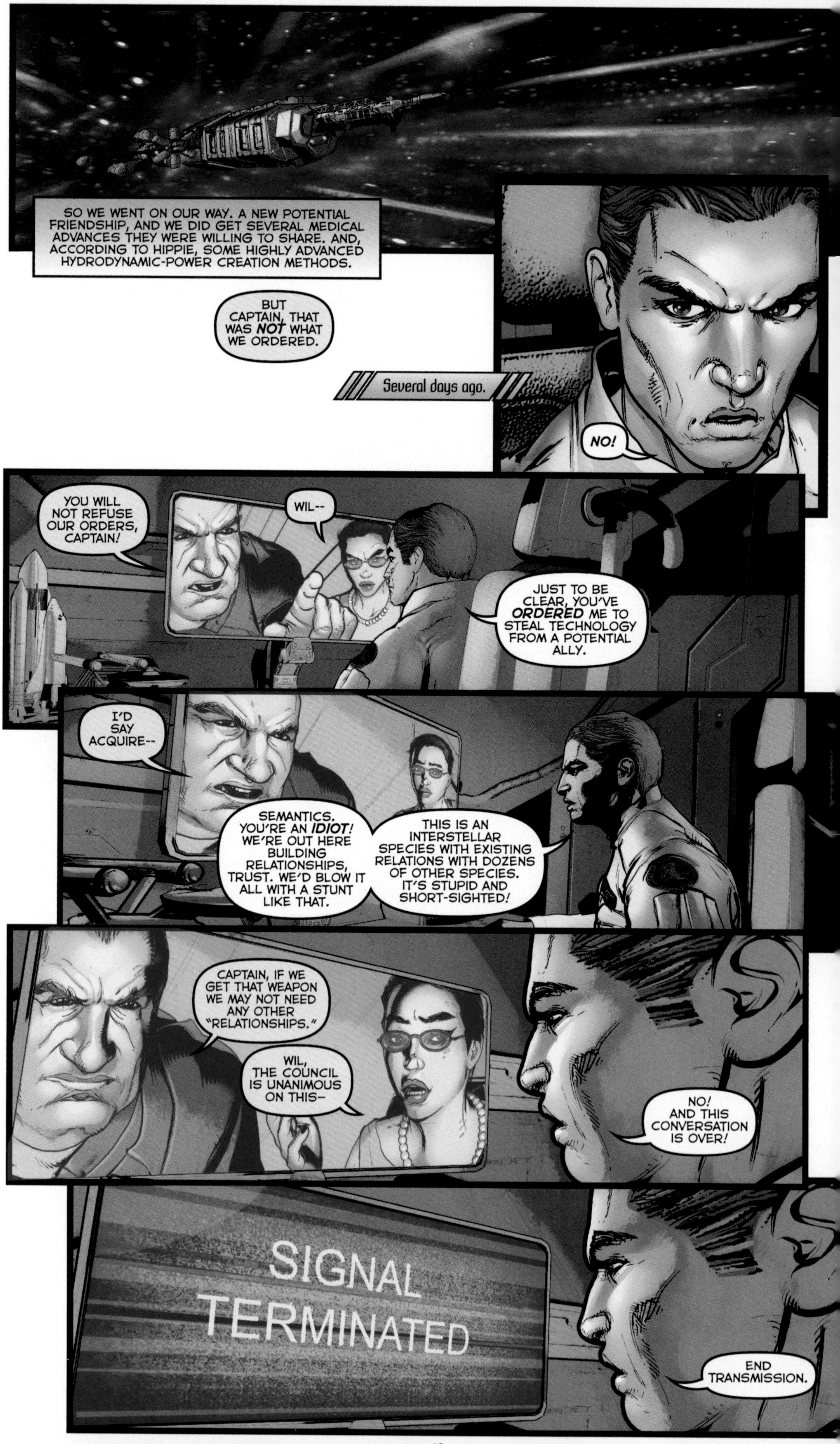
SO WE WENT ON OUR WAY. A NEW POTENTIAL FRIENDSHIP, AND WE DID GET SEVERAL MEDICAL ADVANCES THEY WERE WILLING TO SHARE. AND, ACCORDING TO HIPPIE, SOME HIGHLY ADVANCED HYDRODYNAMIC-POWER CREATION METHODS.
BUT CAPTAIN, THAT WAS NOT WHAT WE ORDERED.
Several days ago.
NO!
YOU WILL NOT REFUSE OUR ORDERS, CAPTAIN!
WIL--
JUST TO BE CLEAR, YOU'VE ORDERED ME TO STEAL TECHNOLOGY FROM A POTENTIAL ALLY.
I'D SAY ACQUIRE--
SEMANTICS. YOU'RE AN IDIOT! WE'RE OUT HERE BUILDING RELATIONSHIPS, TRUST. WE'D BLOW IT ALL WITH A STUNT LIKE THAT.
THIS IS AN INTERSTELLAR SPECIES WITH EXISTING RELATIONS WITH DOZENS OF OTHER SPECIES. IT'S STUPID AND SHORT-SIGHTED!
CAPTAIN, IF WE GET THAT WEAPON WE MAY NOT NEED ANY OTHER "RELATIONSHIPS."
WIL, THE COUNCIL IS UNANIMOUS ON THIS–
NO! AND THIS CONVERSATION IS OVER!
SIGNAL TERMINATED
END TRANSMISSION.

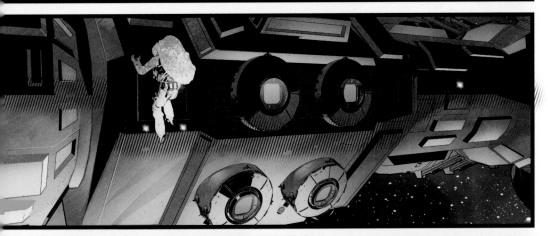

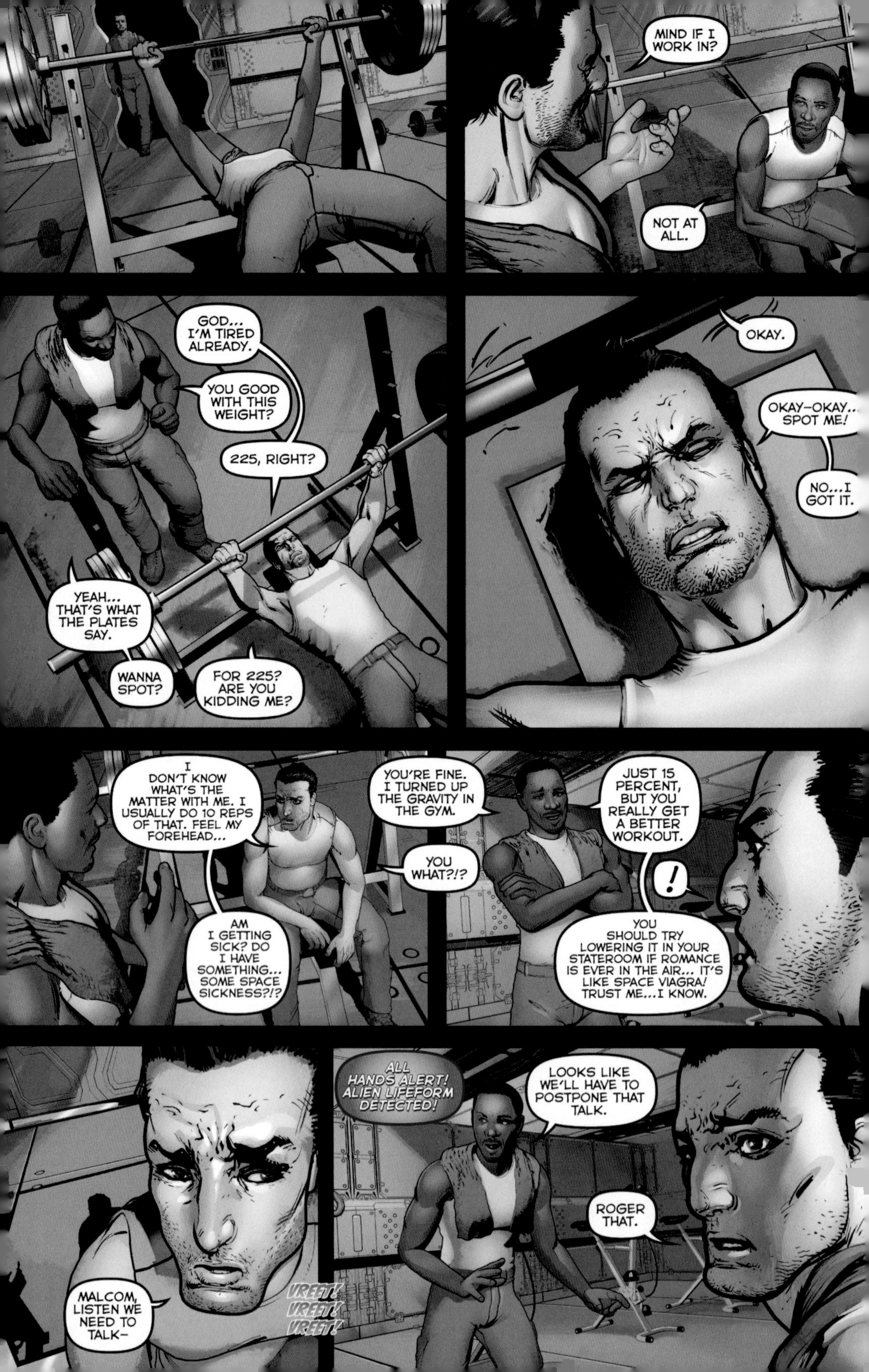
MIND IF I WORK IN?
NOT AT ALL.
GOD... I'M TIRED ALREADY.
YOU GOOD WITH THIS WEIGHT?
225, RIGHT?
YEAH... THAT'S WHAT THE PLATES SAY.
WANNA SPOT?
FOR 225? ARE YOU KIDDING ME?
OKAY.
OKAY-OKAY... SPOT ME!
NO...I GOT IT.
I DON'T KNOW WHAT'S THE MATTER WITH ME. I USUALLY DO 10 REPS OF THAT. FEEL MY FOREHEAD...
AM I GETTING SICK? DO I HAVE SOMETHING... SOME SPACE SICKNESS?!?
YOU'RE FINE. I TURNED UP THE GRAVITY IN THE GYM.
YOU WHAT?!?
JUST 15 PERCENT, BUT YOU REALLY GET A BETTER WORKOUT.
!
YOU SHOULD TRY LOWERING IT IN YOUR STATEROOM IF ROMANCE IS EVER IN THE AIR... IT'S LIKE SPACE VIAGRA! TRUST ME...I KNOW.
MALCOM, LISTEN WE NEED TO TALK-
VREET! VREET! VREET!
ALL HANDS ALERT! ALIEN LIFEFORM DETECTED!
LOOKS LIKE WE'LL HAVE TO POSTPONE THAT TALK.
ROGER THAT.

Later...

DO YOU HAVE A FIX ON THE INTRUDERS' LOCATION YET?

DO WE NEED TO RECALIBRATE INTERNAL SENSORS?

NO, THEY'RE FINE...IT'S LIKE IT HAS SOMETHING THAT SCRAMBLES OUR SCANS.

I THINK WHATEVER THEY'RE USING IS FAILING...

THERE. STORAGE BAY 6...I THINK IT'S A BOERBOE.

RYAN, SEAL OFF THE SURROUNDING DECKS.

YES, SIR.

STORAGE BAY 6

STAY SHARP. THESE BOERBOES ARE NOT TO BE TRUSTED.

AYE TO THAT, SIR.

WARNING
Acid
High toxicity!
Protection level 6

Fs-St-SSsTt!

GRRRR.... STUPID PIECE OF SPACE JUNK!

WE KNOW YOU'RE HERE. COME OUT WITH YOU HANDS RAISED.

!?!

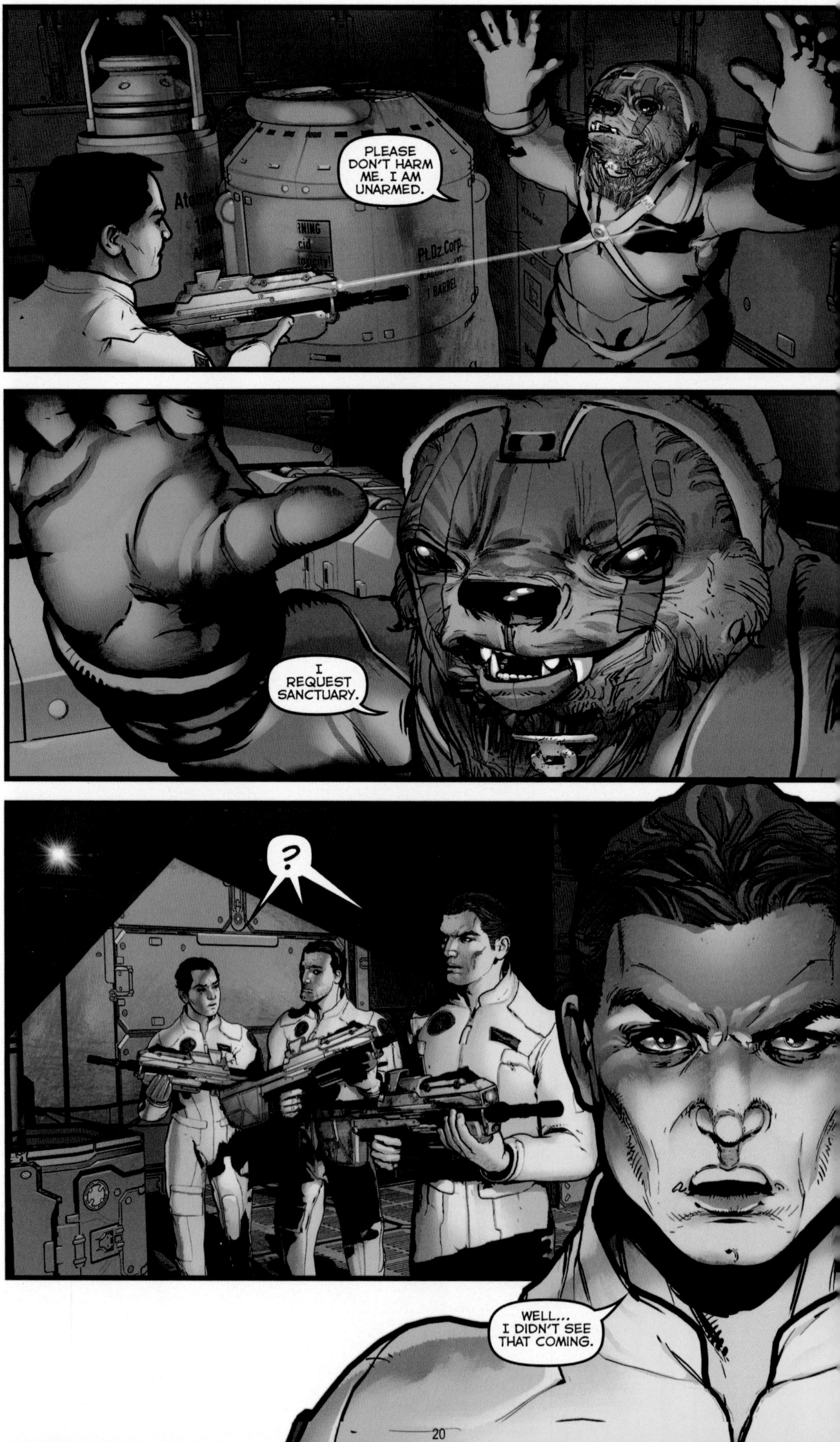
PLEASE DON'T HARM ME. I AM UNARMED.
I REQUEST SANCTUARY.
?
WELL... I DIDN'T SEE THAT COMING.

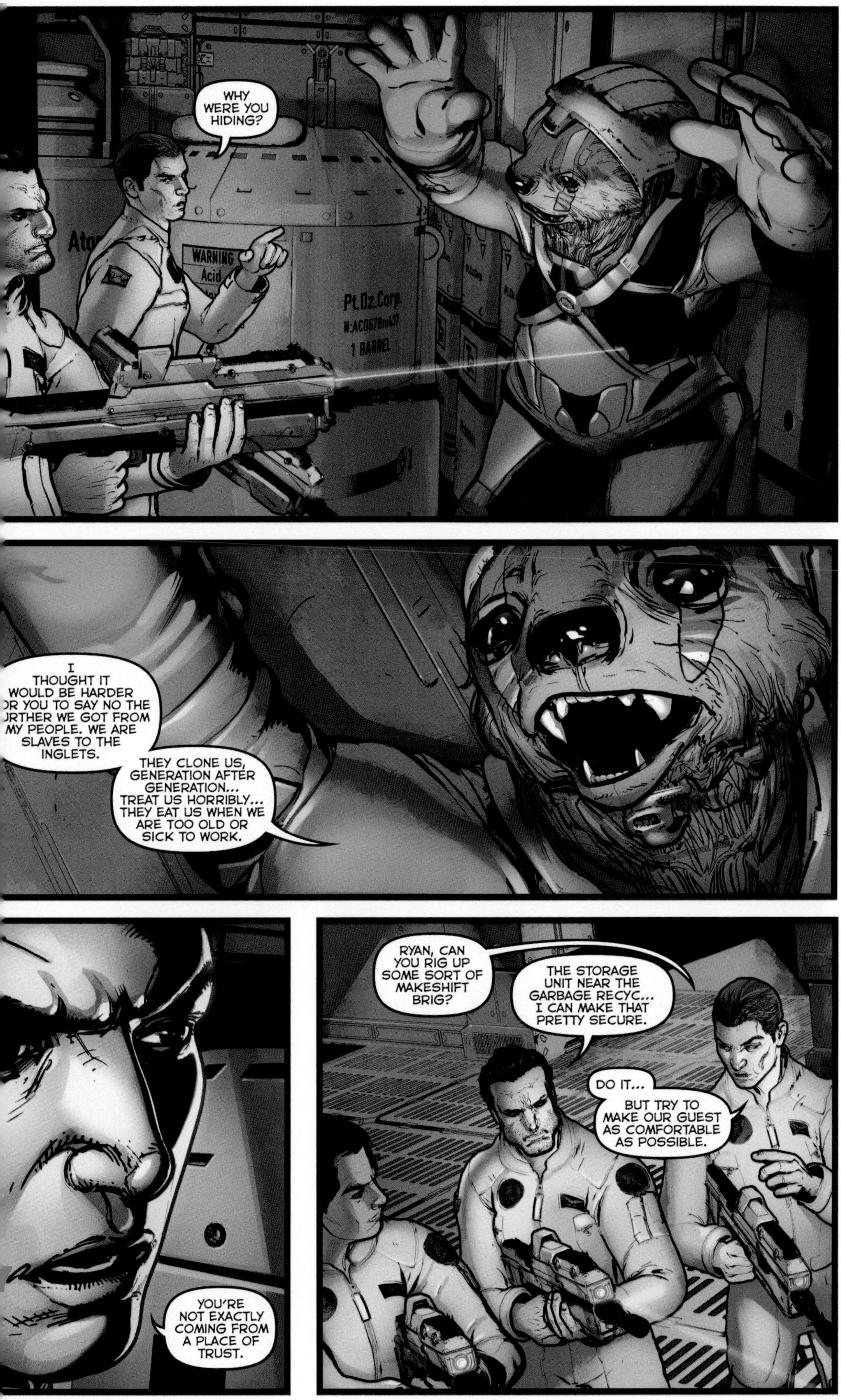
WHY WERE YOU HIDING?
WARNING Acid
Pt.Dz.Corp. N:AC0678m437 1 BARREL
I THOUGHT IT WOULD BE HARDER OR YOU TO SAY NO THE URTHER WE GOT FROM MY PEOPLE. WE ARE SLAVES TO THE INGLETS.
THEY CLONE US, GENERATION AFTER GENERATION... TREAT US HORRIBLY... THEY EAT US WHEN WE ARE TOO OLD OR SICK TO WORK.
YOU'RE NOT EXACTLY COMING FROM A PLACE OF TRUST.
RYAN, CAN YOU RIG UP SOME SORT OF MAKESHIFT BRIG?
THE STORAGE UNIT NEAR THE GARBAGE RECYC... I CAN MAKE THAT PRETTY SECURE.
DO IT...
BUT TRY TO MAKE OUR GUEST AS COMFORTABLE AS POSSIBLE.

THANK YOU, CAPTAIN! THANK YOU!!!
PLD/ Corp.
N:98241
EASY THERE.
!
IT'S OKAY, RYAN. NO HARM DONE.
Atomi
WARNING
Acid
High toxicity!
THE COUNCIL IS GOING TO *LOVE* THIS...OH, BOY.

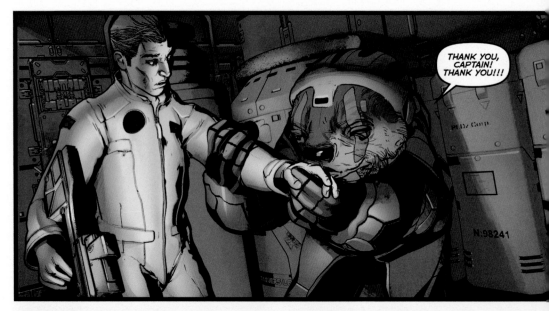

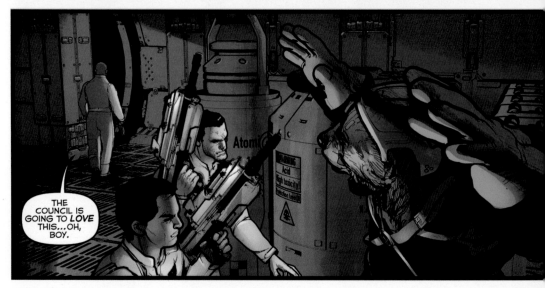

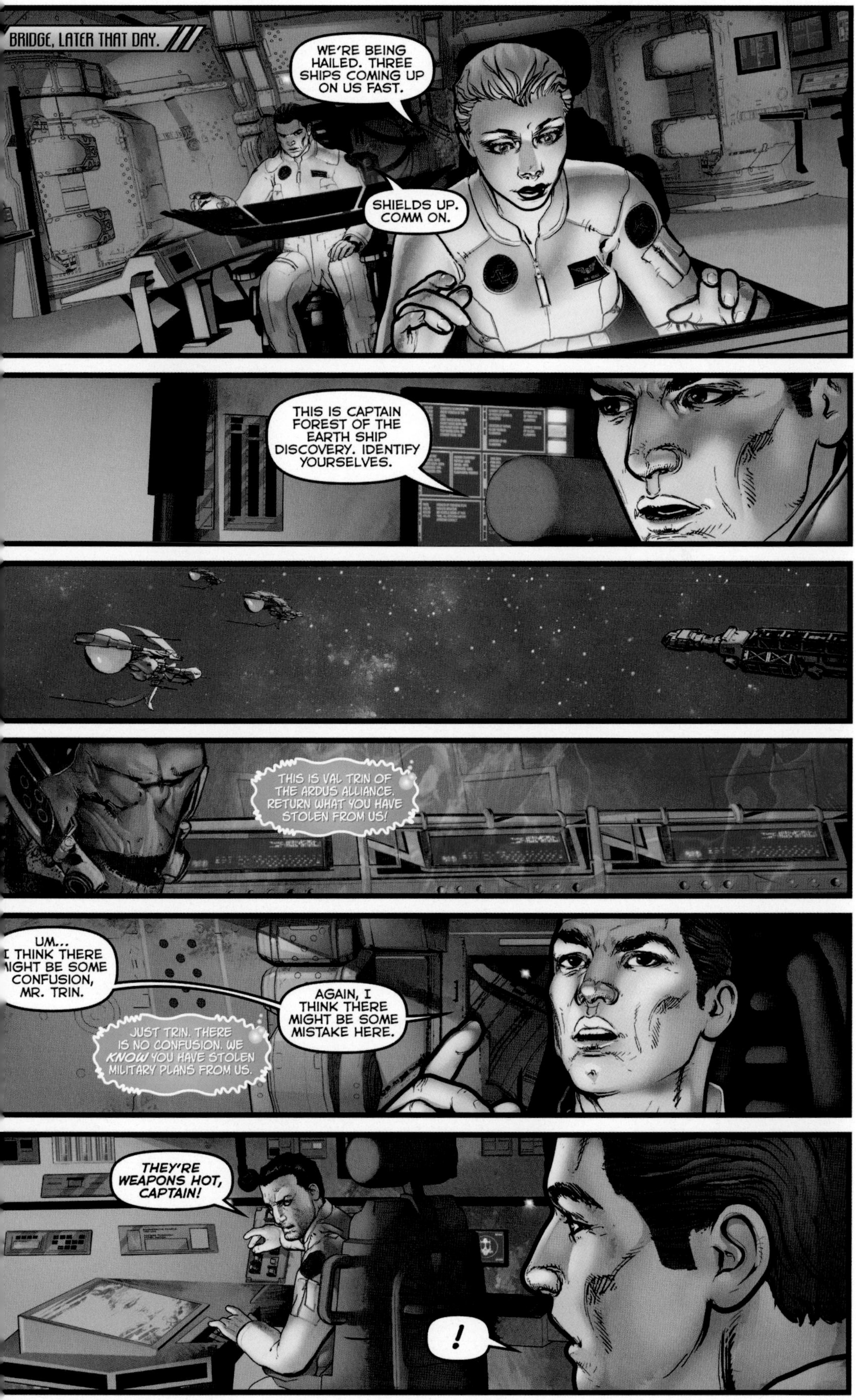
BRIDGE, LATER THAT DAY.
WE'RE BEING HAILED. THREE SHIPS COMING UP ON US FAST.
SHIELDS UP. COMM ON.
THIS IS CAPTAIN FOREST OF THE EARTH SHIP DISCOVERY. IDENTIFY YOURSELVES.
THIS IS VAL TRIN OF THE ARDUS ALLIANCE. RETURN WHAT YOU HAVE STOLEN FROM US!
UM... I THINK THERE MIGHT BE SOME CONFUSION, MR. TRIN.
JUST TRIN. THERE IS NO CONFUSION. WE KNOW YOU HAVE STOLEN MILITARY PLANS FROM US.
AGAIN, I THINK THERE MIGHT BE SOME MISTAKE HERE.
THEY'RE WEAPONS HOT, CAPTAIN!
!

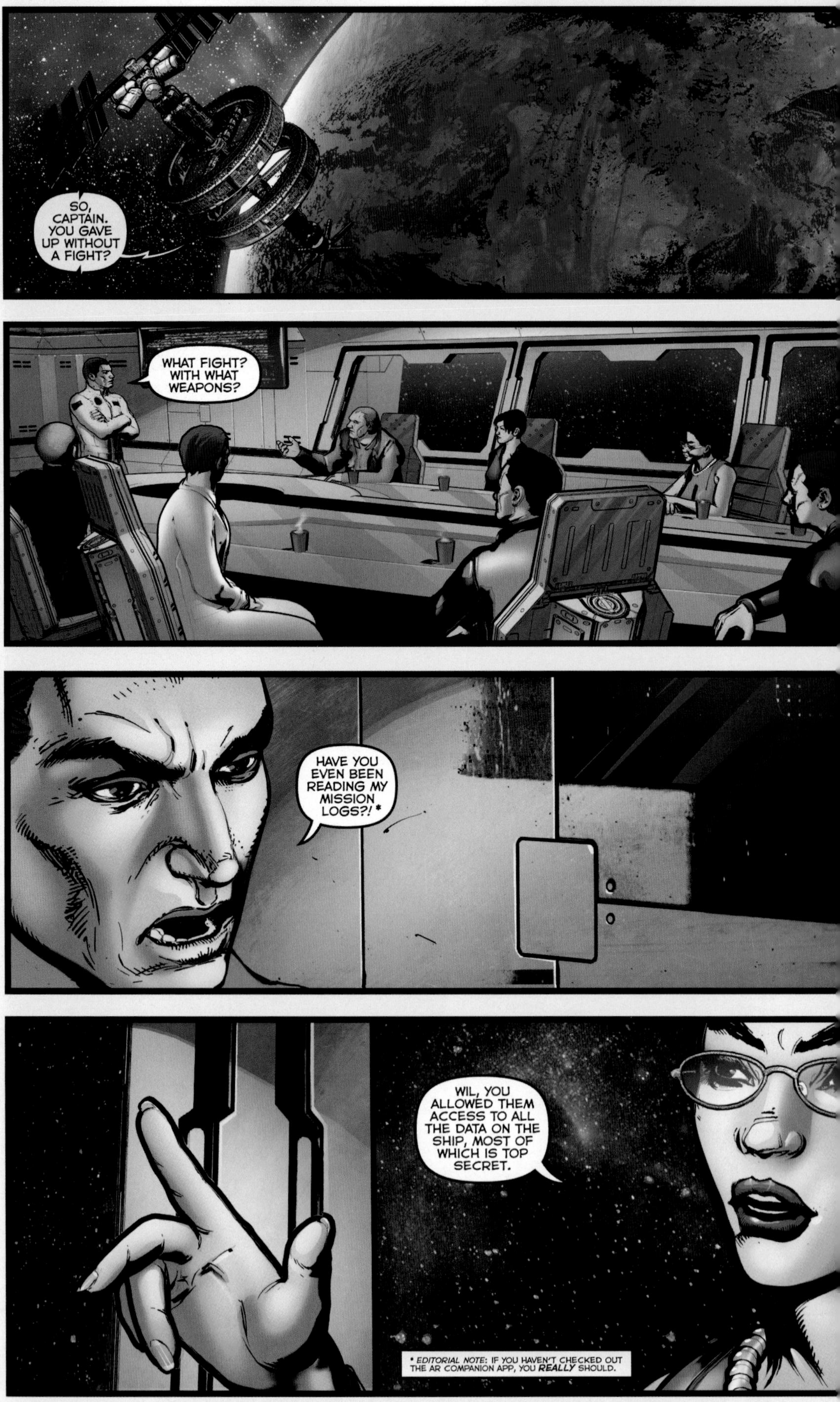
SO, CAPTAIN. YOU GAVE UP WITHOUT A FIGHT?
WHAT FIGHT? WITH WHAT WEAPONS?
HAVE YOU EVEN BEEN READING MY MISSION LOGS?! *
WIL, YOU ALLOWED THEM ACCESS TO ALL THE DATA ON THE SHIP, MOST OF WHICH IS TOP SECRET.
* EDITORIAL NOTE: IF YOU HAVEN'T CHECKED OUT THE AR COMPANION APP, YOU REALLY SHOULD.

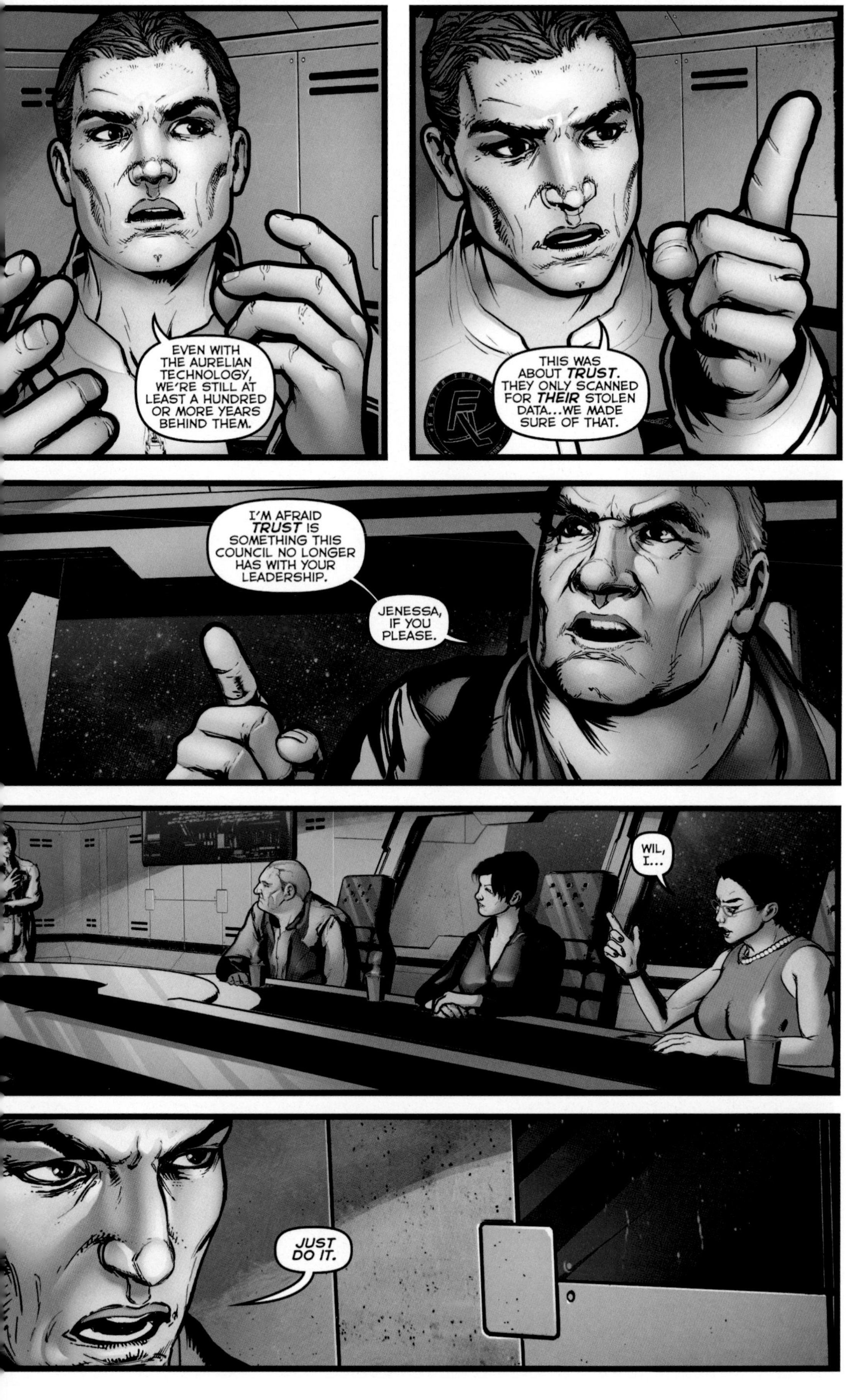
EVEN WITH THE AURELIAN TECHNOLOGY, WE'RE STILL AT LEAST A HUNDRED OR MORE YEARS BEHIND THEM.
THIS WAS ABOUT TRUST. THEY ONLY SCANNED FOR THEIR STOLEN DATA...WE MADE SURE OF THAT.
I'M AFRAID TRUST IS SOMETHING THIS COUNCIL NO LONGER HAS WITH YOUR LEADERSHIP.
JENESSA, IF YOU PLEASE.
WIL, I...
JUST DO IT.

I'M SORRY, WIL. REALLY, I AM.

BY MAJORITY VOTE OF THE COUNCIL, WILLIAM M. FOREST IS STRIPPED OF COMMAND OF THE IGS DISCOVERY.

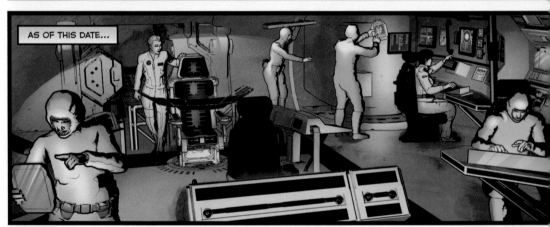

AS OF THIS DATE...

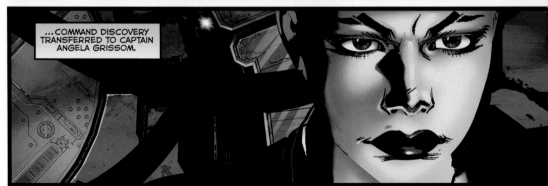

...COMMAND DISCOVERY TRANSFERRED TO CAPTAIN ANGELA GRISSOM.

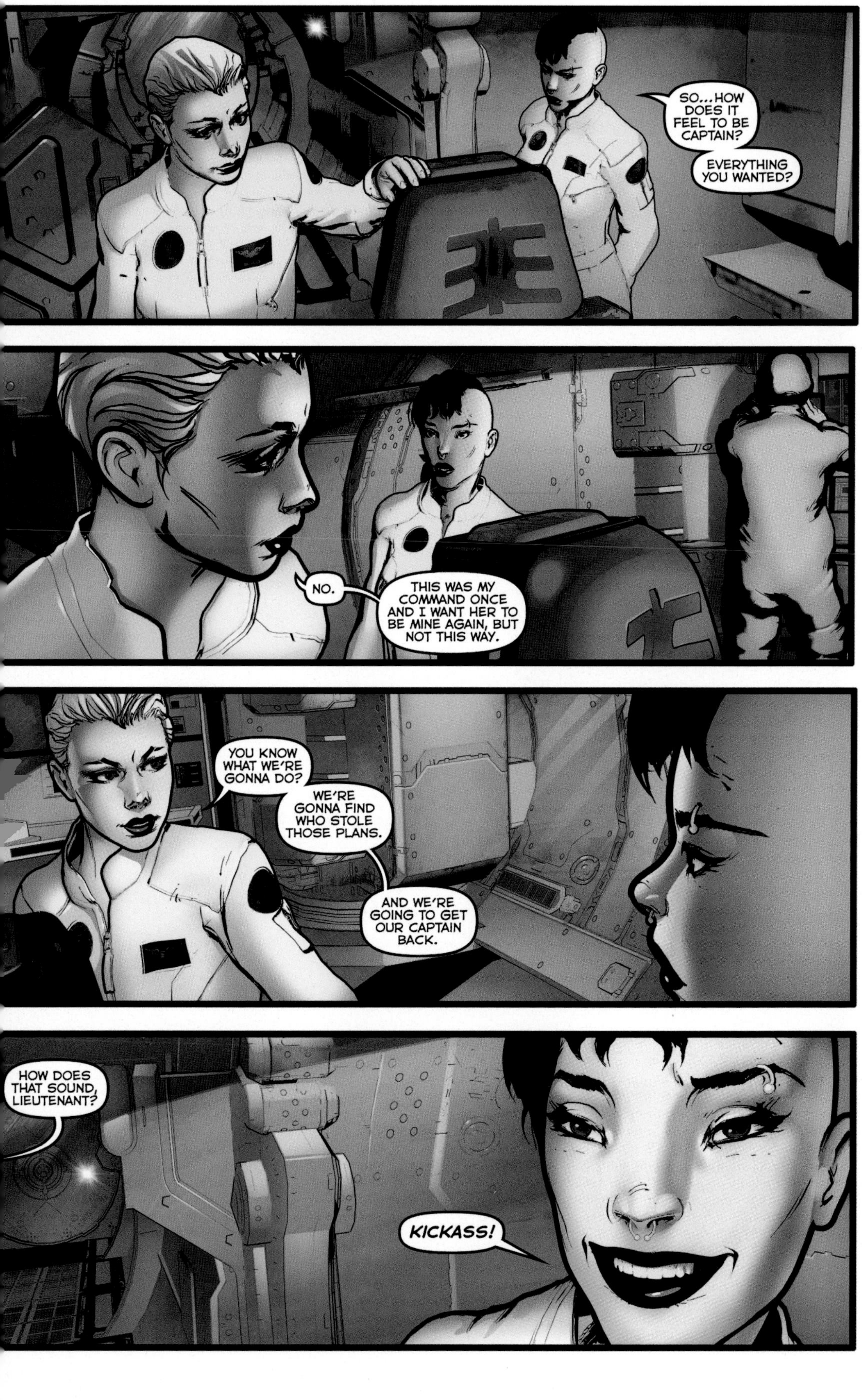
SO...HOW DOES IT FEEL TO BE CAPTAIN?
EVERYTHING YOU WANTED?
NO.
THIS WAS MY COMMAND ONCE AND I WANT HER TO BE MINE AGAIN, BUT NOT THIS WAY.
YOU KNOW WHAT WE'RE GONNA DO?
WE'RE GONNA FIND WHO STOLE THOSE PLANS.
AND WE'RE GOING TO GET OUR CAPTAIN BACK.
HOW DOES THAT SOUND, LIEUTENANT?
KICKASS!

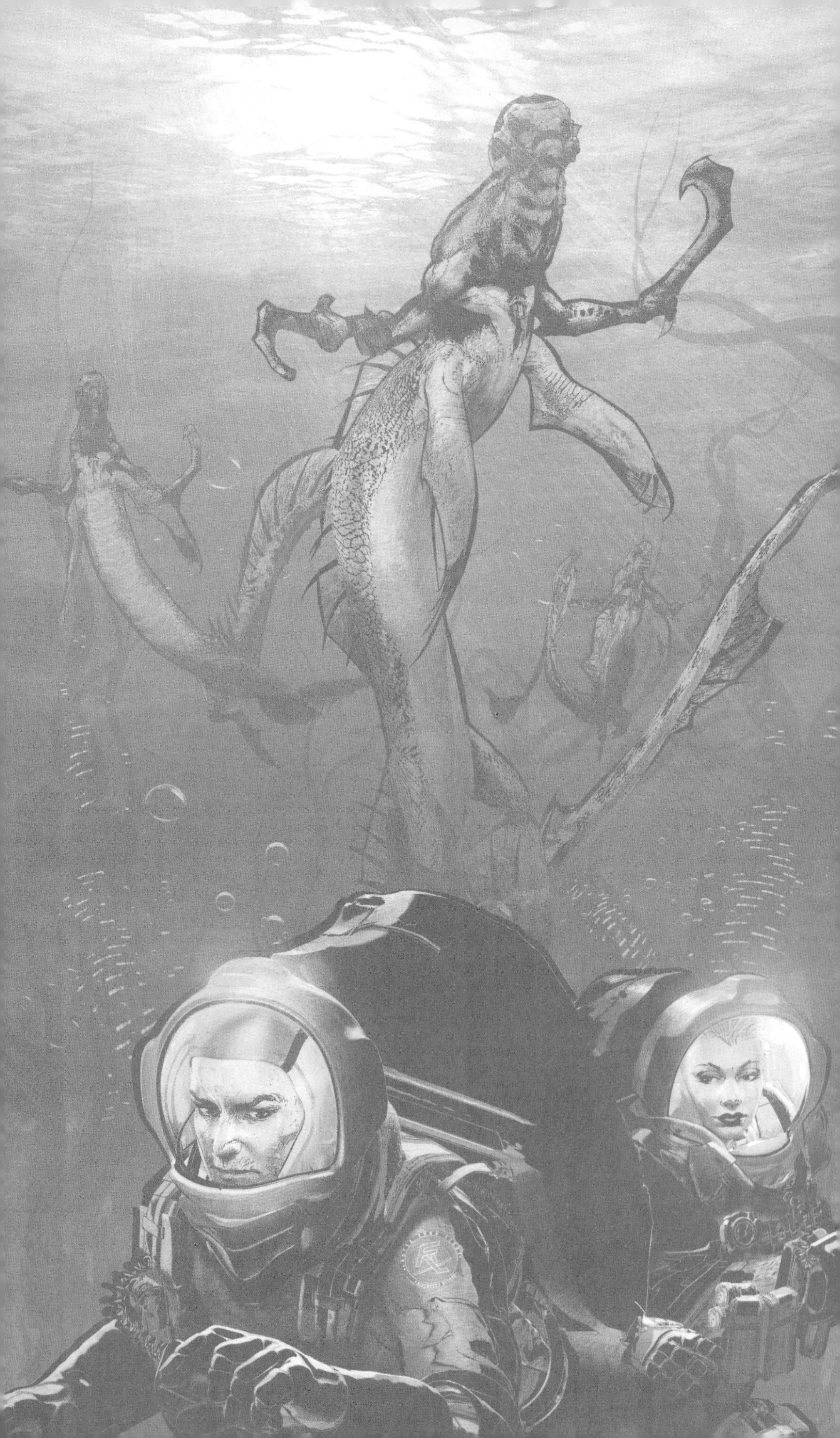

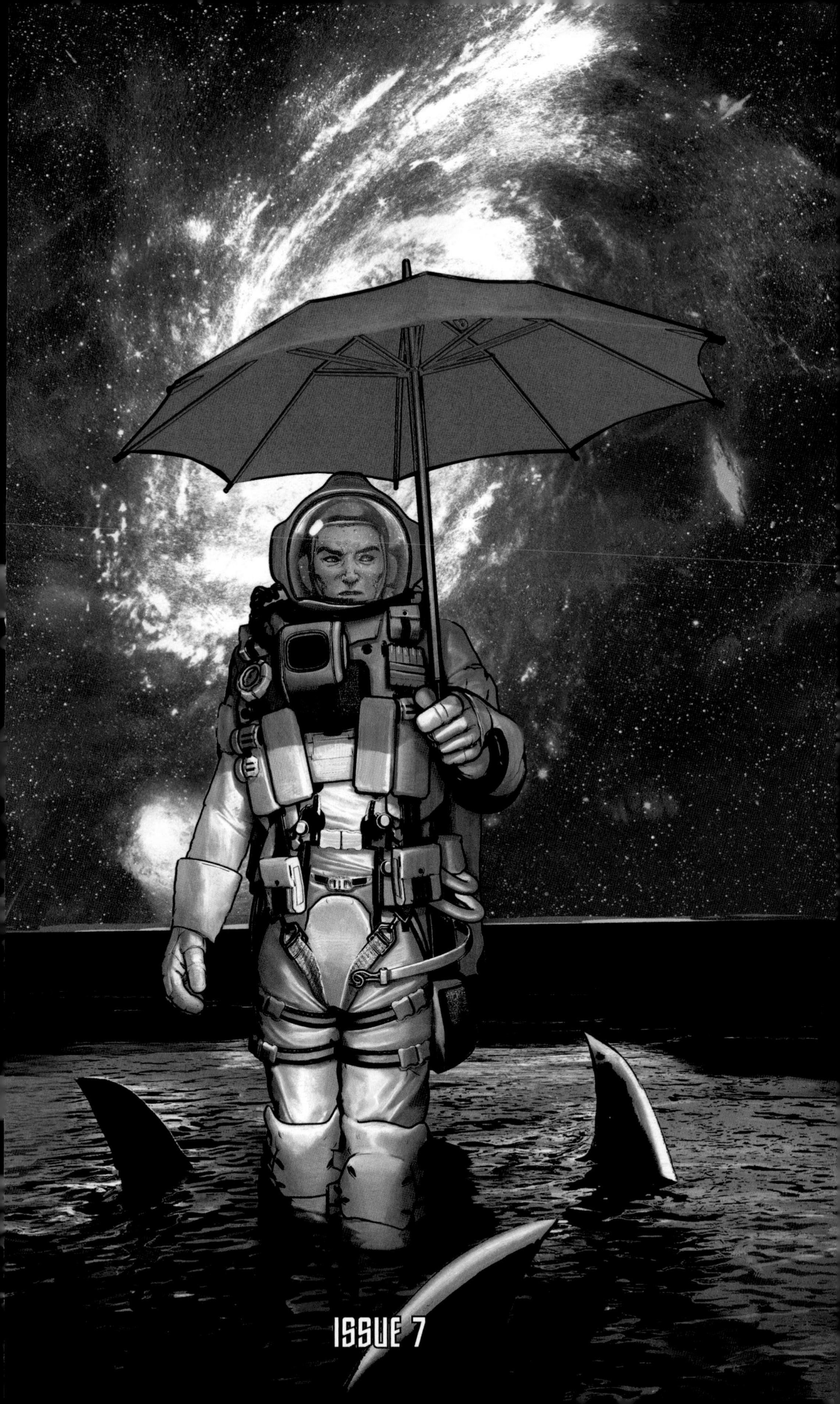
ISSUE 7

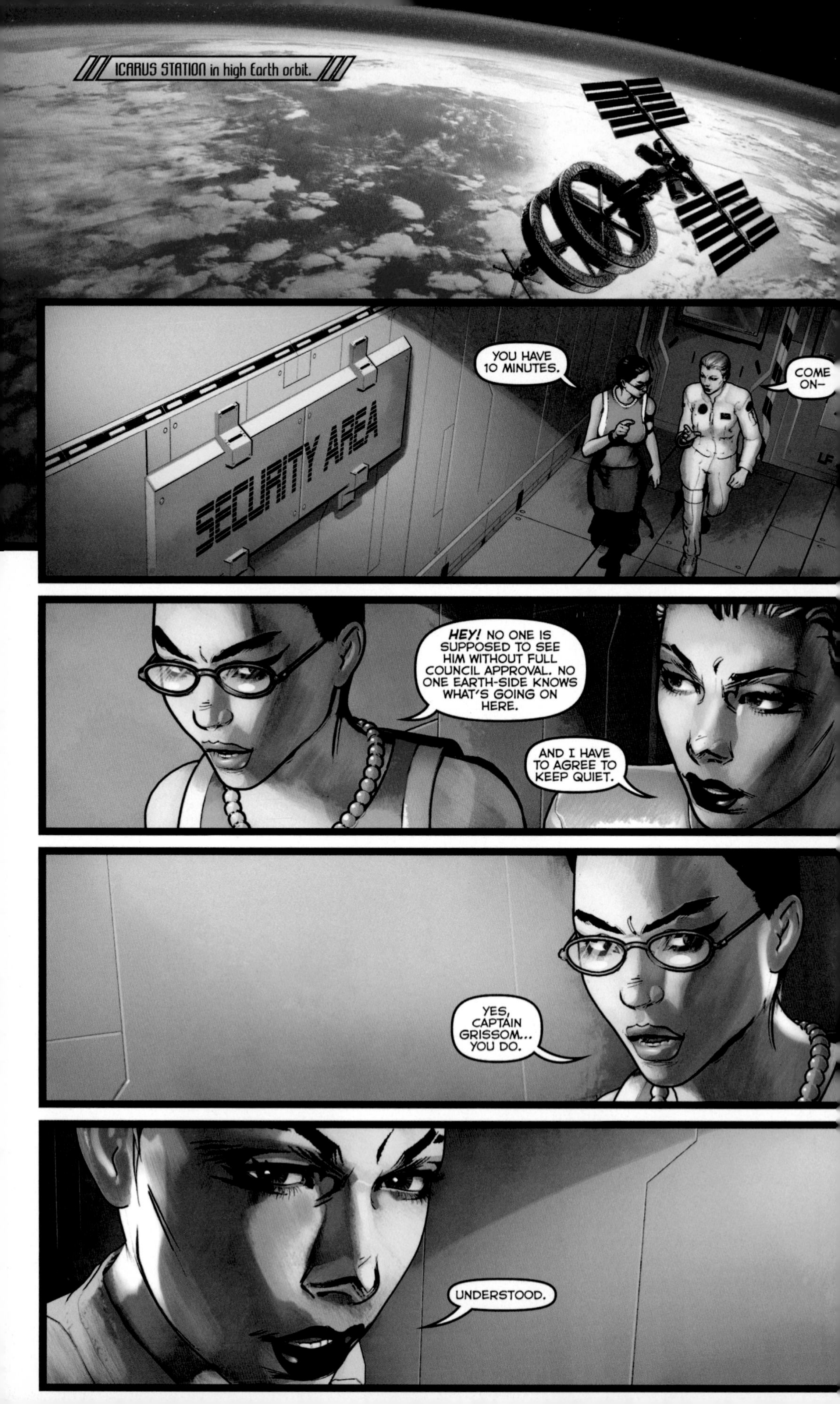
ICARUS STATION in high Earth orbit.
SECURITY AREA
YOU HAVE 10 MINUTES.
COME ON—
HEY! NO ONE IS SUPPOSED TO SEE HIM WITHOUT FULL COUNCIL APPROVAL. NO ONE EARTH-SIDE KNOWS WHAT'S GOING ON HERE.
AND I HAVE TO AGREE TO KEEP QUIET.
YES, CAPTAIN GRISSOM... YOU DO.
UNDERSTOOD.

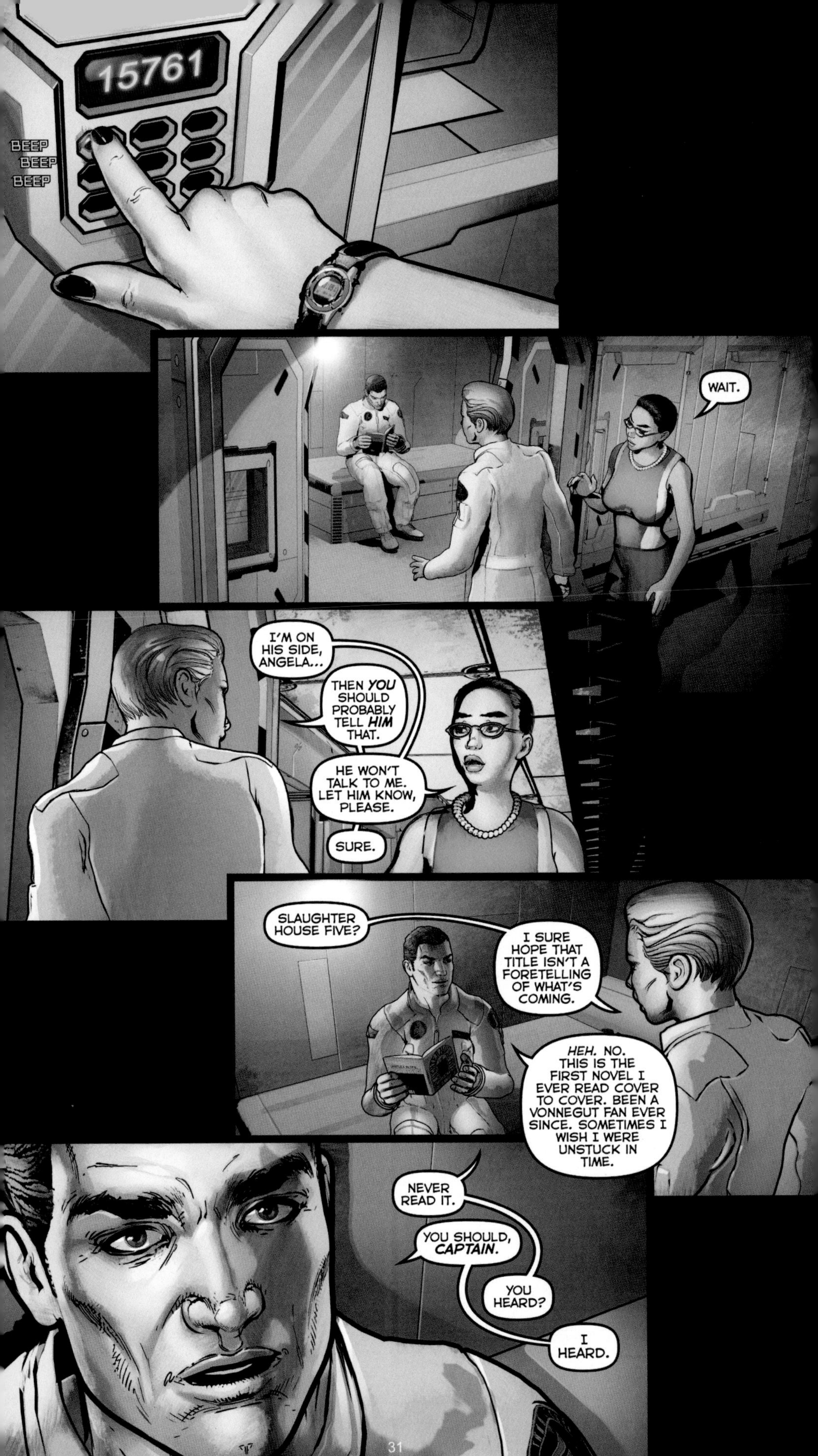
15761
BEEP
BEEP
BEEP
WAIT.
I'M ON HIS SIDE, ANGELA...
THEN *YOU* SHOULD PROBABLY TELL *HIM* THAT.
HE WON'T TALK TO ME. LET HIM KNOW, PLEASE.
SURE.
SLAUGHTER HOUSE FIVE?
I SURE HOPE THAT TITLE ISN'T A FORETELLING OF WHAT'S COMING.
HEH. NO. THIS IS THE FIRST NOVEL I EVER READ COVER TO COVER. BEEN A VONNEGUT FAN EVER SINCE. SOMETIMES I WISH I WERE UNSTUCK IN TIME.
NEVER READ IT.
YOU SHOULD, ***CAPTAIN.***
YOU HEARD?
I HEARD.

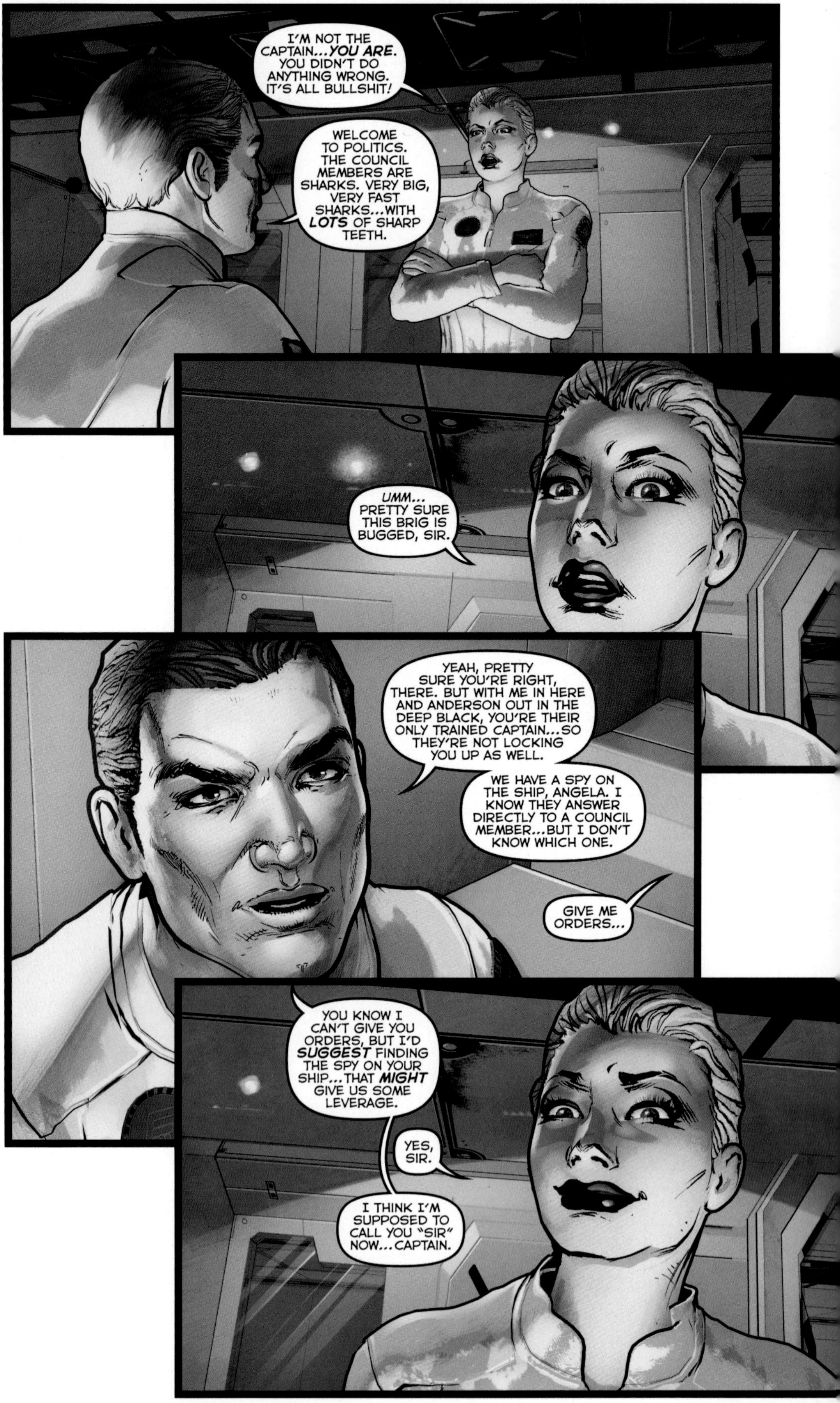
I'M NOT THE CAPTAIN...YOU ARE. YOU DIDN'T DO ANYTHING WRONG. IT'S ALL BULLSHIT!
WELCOME TO POLITICS. THE COUNCIL MEMBERS ARE SHARKS. VERY BIG, VERY FAST SHARKS...WITH LOTS OF SHARP TEETH.
UMM... PRETTY SURE THIS BRIG IS BUGGED, SIR.
YEAH, PRETTY SURE YOU'RE RIGHT, THERE. BUT WITH ME IN HERE AND ANDERSON OUT IN THE DEEP BLACK, YOU'RE THEIR ONLY TRAINED CAPTAIN...SO THEY'RE NOT LOCKING YOU UP AS WELL.
WE HAVE A SPY ON THE SHIP, ANGELA. I KNOW THEY ANSWER DIRECTLY TO A COUNCIL MEMBER...BUT I DON'T KNOW WHICH ONE.
GIVE ME ORDERS...
YOU KNOW I CAN'T GIVE YOU ORDERS, BUT I'D SUGGEST FINDING THE SPY ON YOUR SHIP...THAT MIGHT GIVE US SOME LEVERAGE.
YES, SIR.
I THINK I'M SUPPOSED TO CALL YOU "SIR" NOW...CAPTAIN.

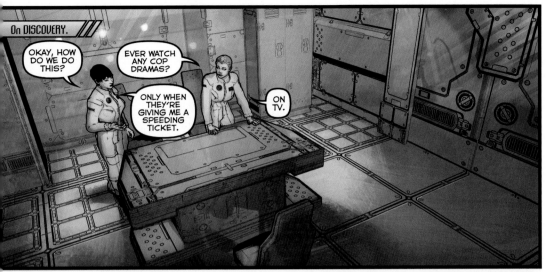

OKAY, HOW DO WE DO THIS?

EVER WATCH ANY COP DRAMAS?

ONLY WHEN THEY'RE GIVING ME A SPEEDING TICKET.

ON TV.

DON'T WATCH IT. TV, I MEAN.

OKAY...WELL, WE'LL JUST START WITH QUESTIONING THE LANDING PARTY.

JUST FOLLOW MY LEAD.

GOTCHA.

YOU WANTED TO SEE ME?

WHAT'S THIS ALL ABOUT?

...

SO...

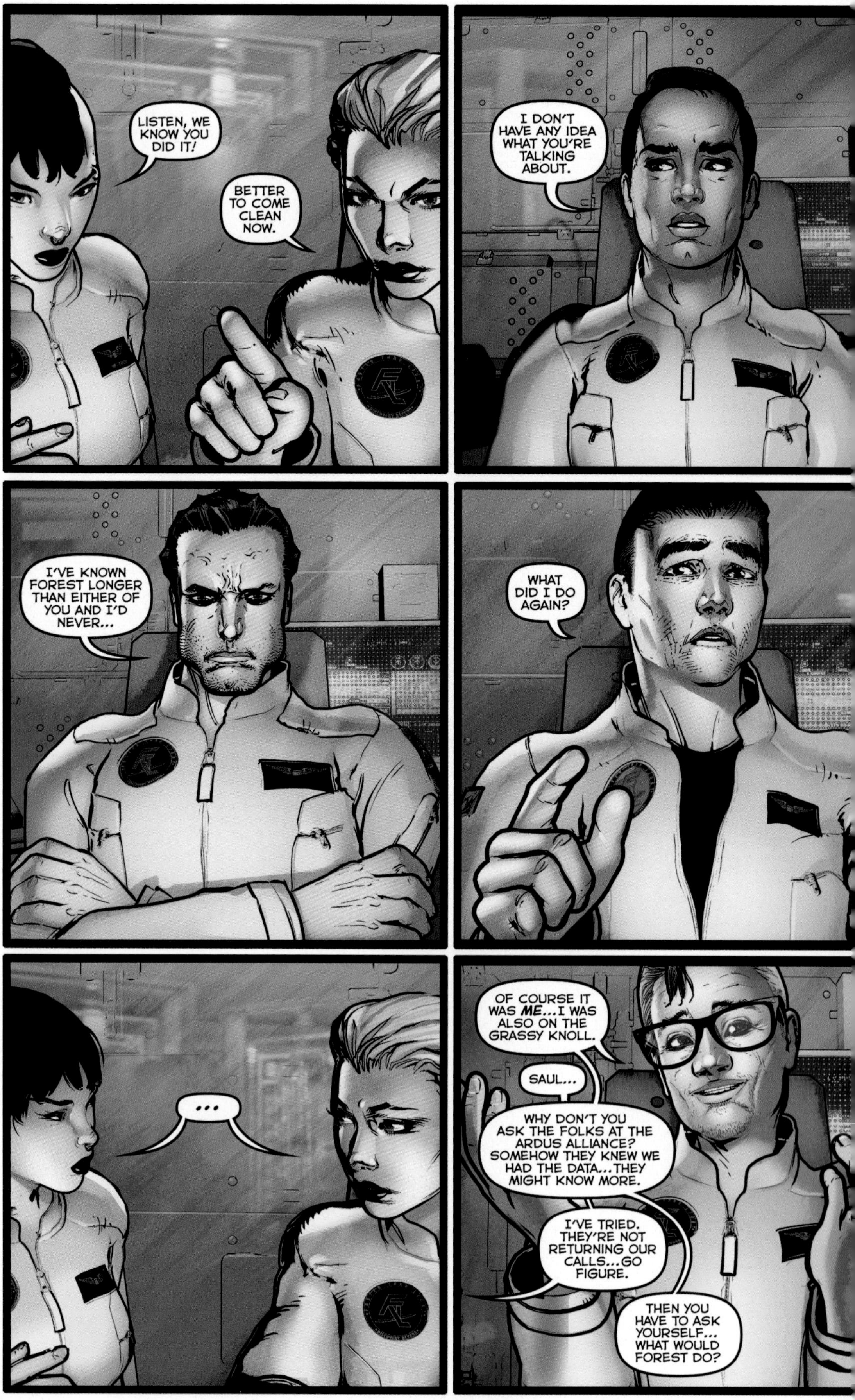
LISTEN, WE KNOW YOU DID IT!
BETTER TO COME CLEAN NOW.
I DON'T HAVE ANY IDEA WHAT YOU'RE TALKING ABOUT.
I'VE KNOWN FOREST LONGER THAN EITHER OF YOU AND I'D NEVER...
WHAT DID I DO AGAIN?
...
OF COURSE IT WAS ME...I WAS ALSO ON THE GRASSY KNOLL.
SAUL...
WHY DON'T YOU ASK THE FOLKS AT THE ARDUS ALLIANCE? SOMEHOW THEY KNEW WE HAD THE DATA...THEY MIGHT KNOW MORE.
I'VE TRIED. THEY'RE NOT RETURNING OUR CALLS...GO FIGURE.
THEN YOU HAVE TO ASK YOURSELF... WHAT WOULD FOREST DO?

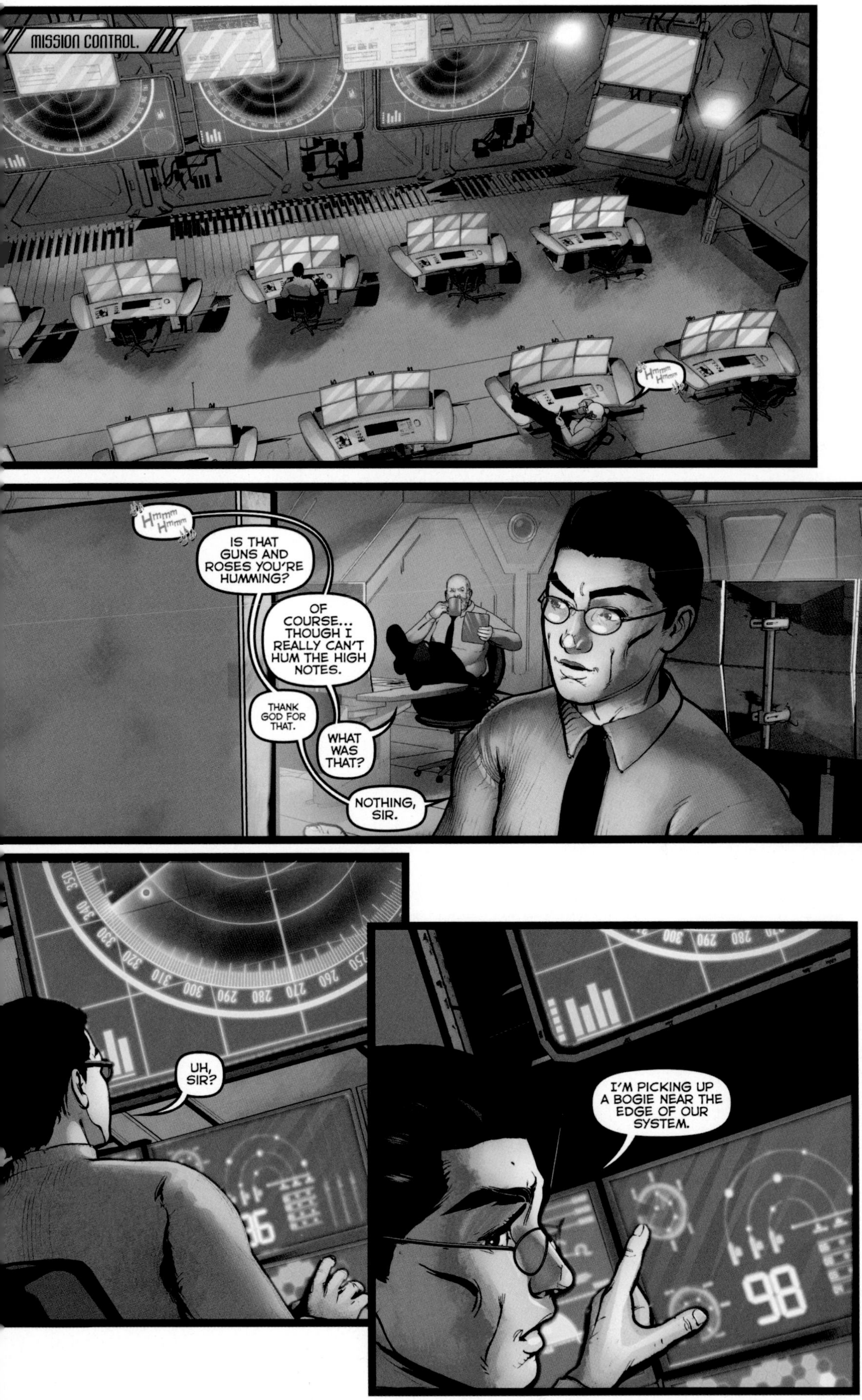
MISSION CONTROL.
Hmmm Hmmm
Hmmm Hmmm
IS THAT GUNS AND ROSES YOU'RE HUMMING?
OF COURSE... THOUGH I REALLY CAN'T HUM THE HIGH NOTES.
THANK GOD FOR THAT.
WHAT WAS THAT?
NOTHING, SIR.
UH, SIR?
I'M PICKING UP A BOGIE NEAR THE EDGE OF OUR SYSTEM.

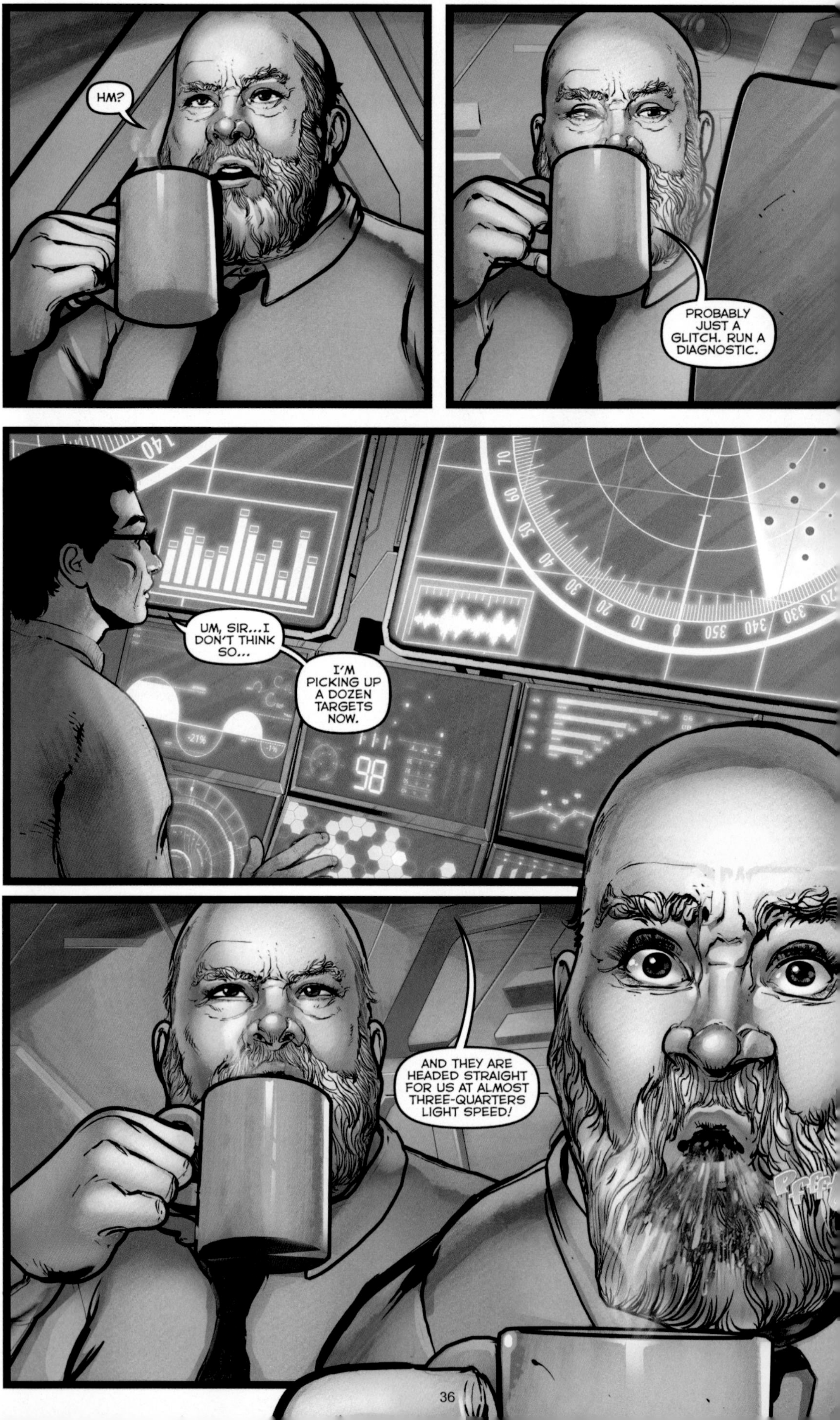
HM?
PROBABLY JUST A GLITCH. RUN A DIAGNOSTIC.
UM, SIR...I DON'T THINK SO...
I'M PICKING UP A DOZEN TARGETS NOW.
AND THEY ARE HEADED STRAIGHT FOR US AT ALMOST THREE-QUARTERS LIGHT SPEED!

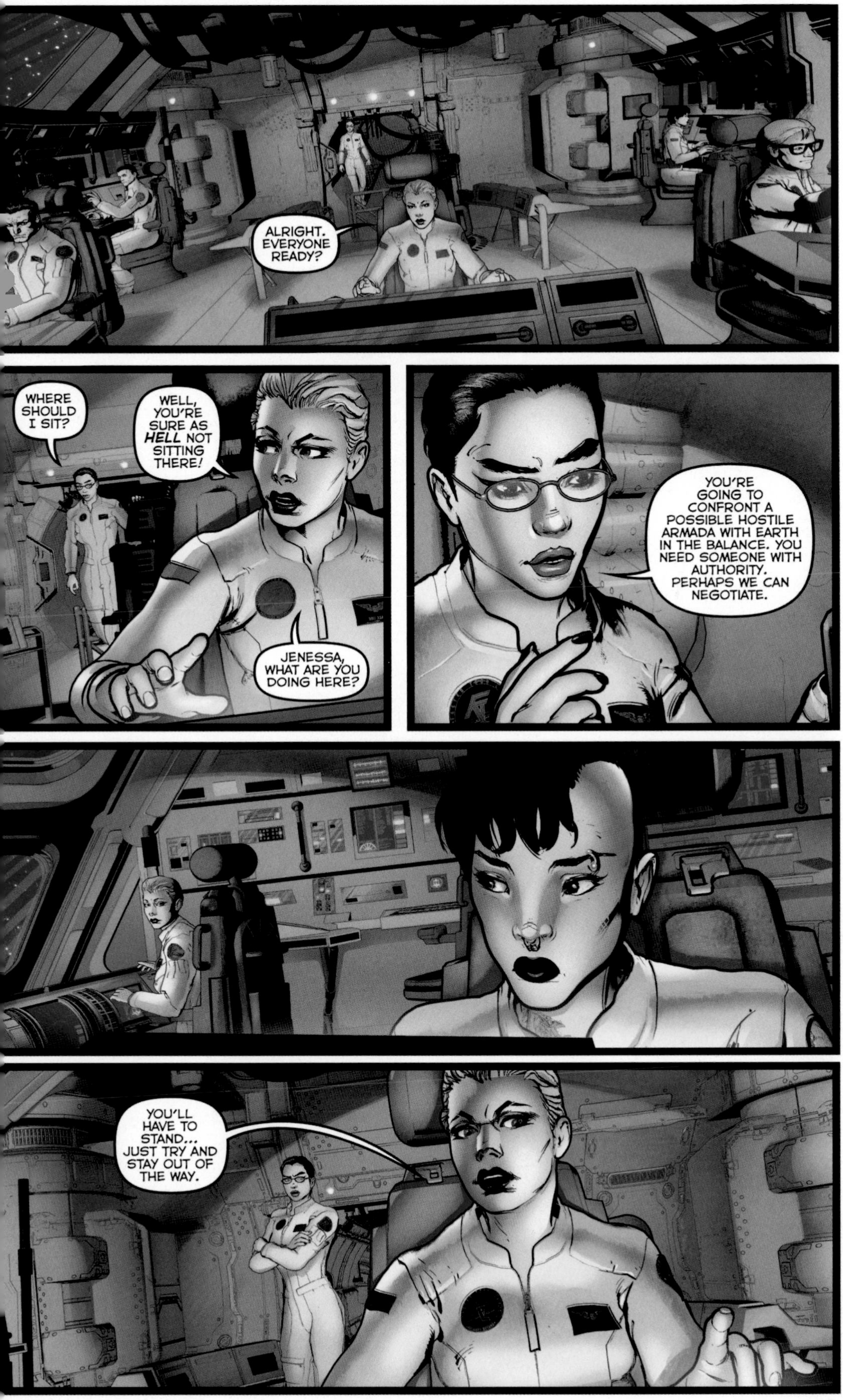
ALRIGHT. EVERYONE READY?
WHERE SHOULD I SIT?
WELL, YOU'RE SURE AS HELL NOT SITTING THERE!
JENESSA, WHAT ARE YOU DOING HERE?
YOU'RE GOING TO CONFRONT A POSSIBLE HOSTILE ARMADA WITH EARTH IN THE BALANCE. YOU NEED SOMEONE WITH AUTHORITY. PERHAPS WE CAN NEGOTIATE.
YOU'LL HAVE TO STAND... JUST TRY AND STAY OUT OF THE WAY.

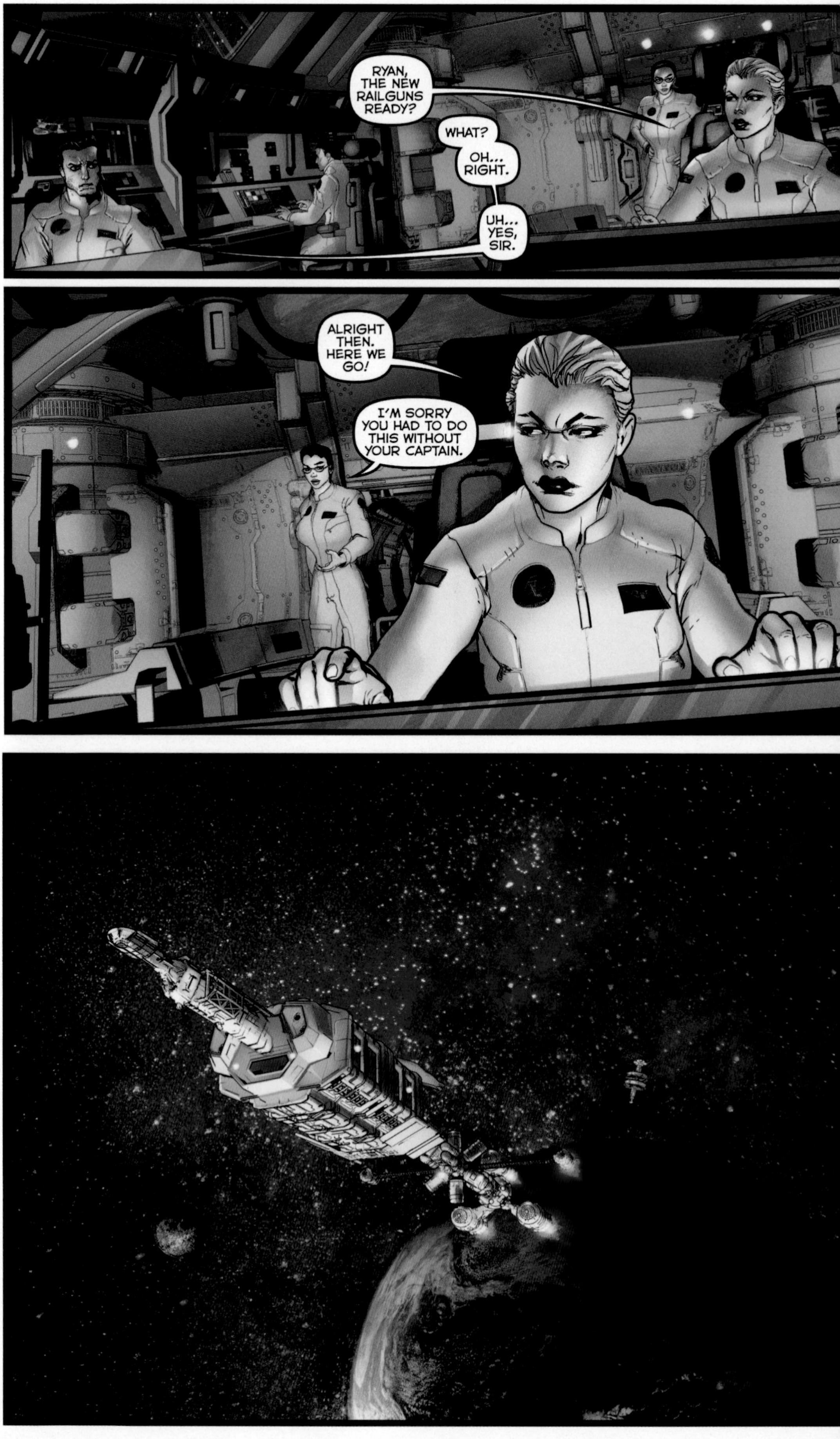
RYAN, THE NEW RAILGUNS READY?
WHAT?
OH... RIGHT.
UH... YES, SIR.
ALRIGHT THEN. HERE WE GO!
I'M SORRY YOU HAD TO DO THIS WITHOUT YOUR CAPTAIN.

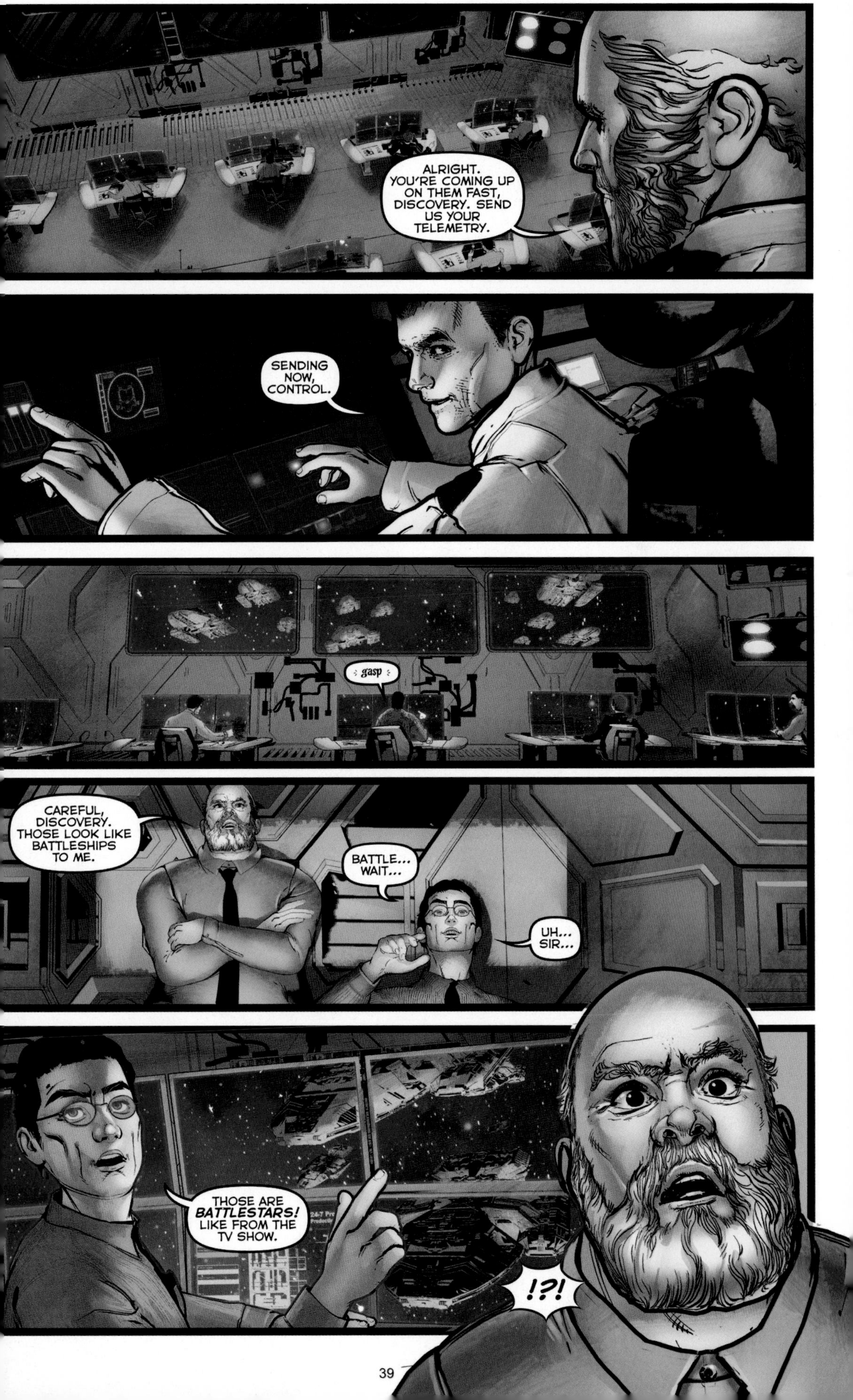
ALRIGHT. YOU'RE COMING UP ON THEM FAST, DISCOVERY. SEND US YOUR TELEMETRY.
SENDING NOW, CONTROL.
gasp
CAREFUL, DISCOVERY. THOSE LOOK LIKE BATTLESHIPS TO ME.
BATTLE... WAIT...
UH... SIR...
THOSE ARE *BATTLESTARS!* LIKE FROM THE TV SHOW.
!?!

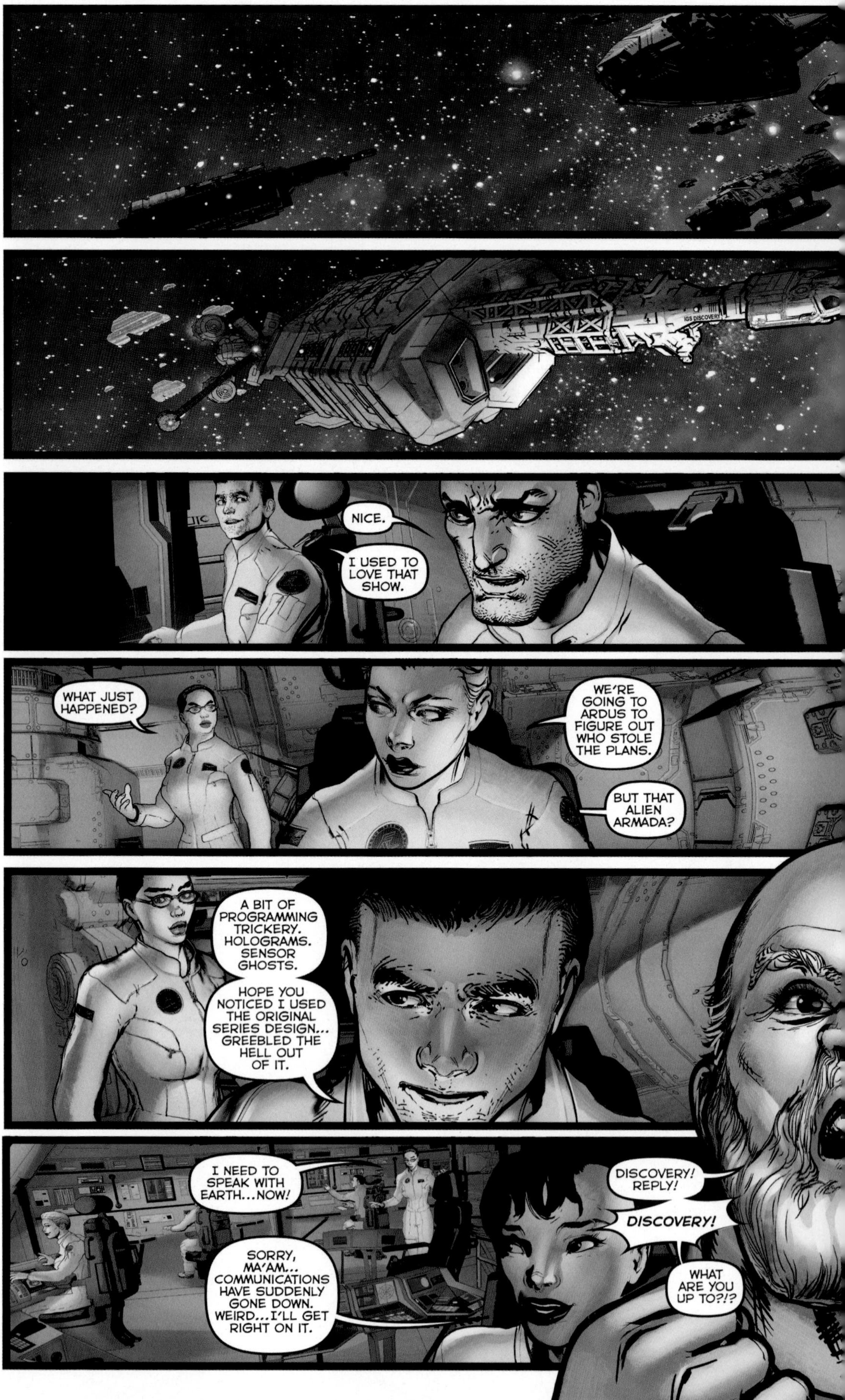
IGS DISCOVERY
NICE.
I USED TO LOVE THAT SHOW.
WHAT JUST HAPPENED?
WE'RE GOING TO ARDUS TO FIGURE OUT WHO STOLE THE PLANS.
BUT THAT ALIEN ARMADA?
A BIT OF PROGRAMMING TRICKERY. HOLOGRAMS. SENSOR GHOSTS.
HOPE YOU NOTICED I USED THE ORIGINAL SERIES DESIGN... GREEBLED THE HELL OUT OF IT.
I NEED TO SPEAK WITH EARTH...NOW!
SORRY, MA'AM... COMMUNICATIONS HAVE SUDDENLY GONE DOWN. WEIRD...I'LL GET RIGHT ON IT.
DISCOVERY! REPLY!
DISCOVERY!
WHAT ARE YOU UP TO?!?

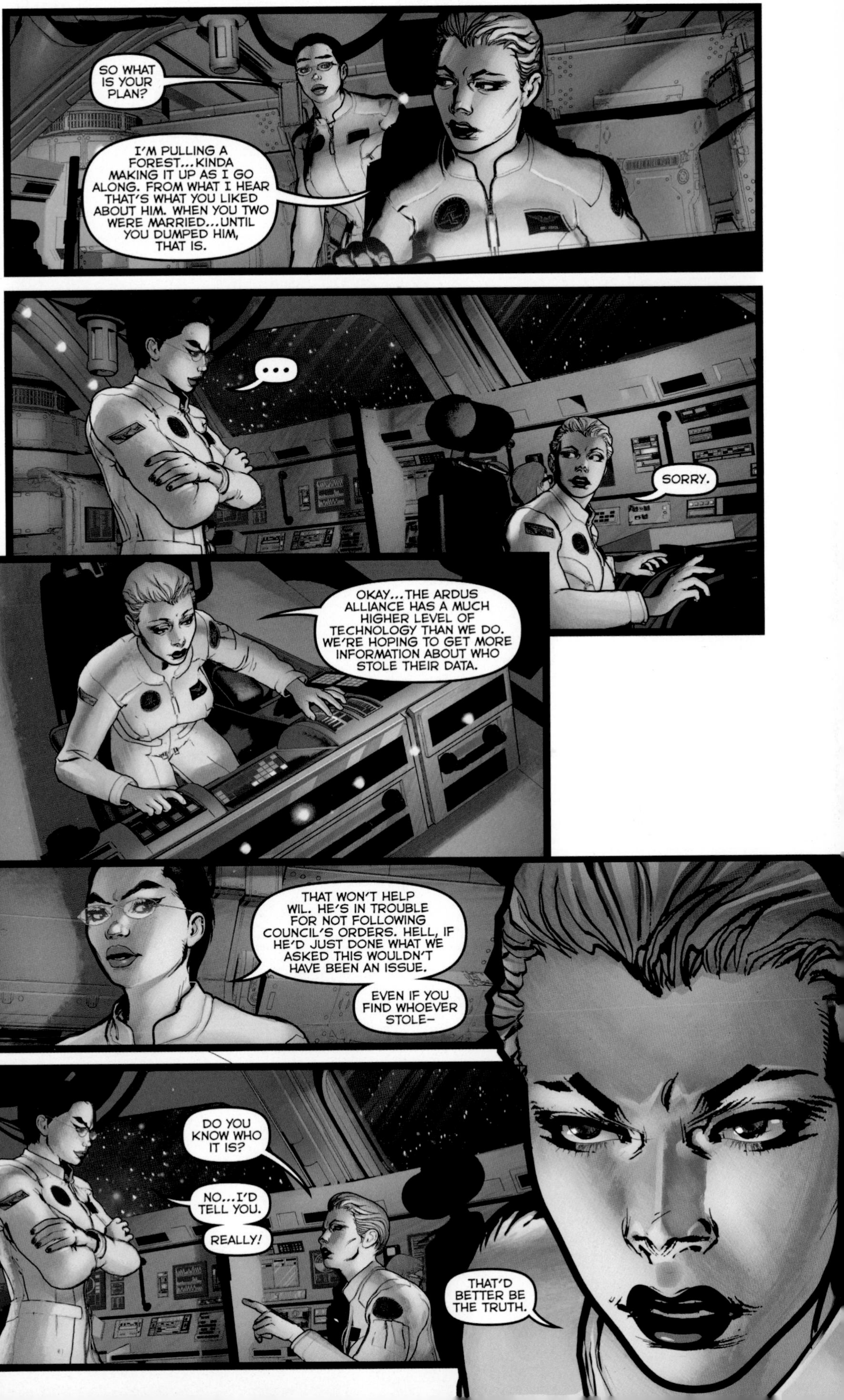
SO WHAT IS YOUR PLAN?
I'M PULLING A FOREST...KINDA MAKING IT UP AS I GO ALONG. FROM WHAT I HEAR THAT'S WHAT YOU LIKED ABOUT HIM. WHEN YOU TWO WERE MARRIED...UNTIL YOU DUMPED HIM, THAT IS.
...
SORRY.
OKAY...THE ARDUS ALLIANCE HAS A MUCH HIGHER LEVEL OF TECHNOLOGY THAN WE DO. WE'RE HOPING TO GET MORE INFORMATION ABOUT WHO STOLE THEIR DATA.
THAT WON'T HELP WIL. HE'S IN TROUBLE FOR NOT FOLLOWING COUNCIL'S ORDERS. HELL, IF HE'D JUST DONE WHAT WE ASKED THIS WOULDN'T HAVE BEEN AN ISSUE.
EVEN IF YOU FIND WHOEVER STOLE-
DO YOU KNOW WHO IT IS?
NO...I'D TELL YOU.
REALLY!
THAT'D BETTER BE THE TRUTH.

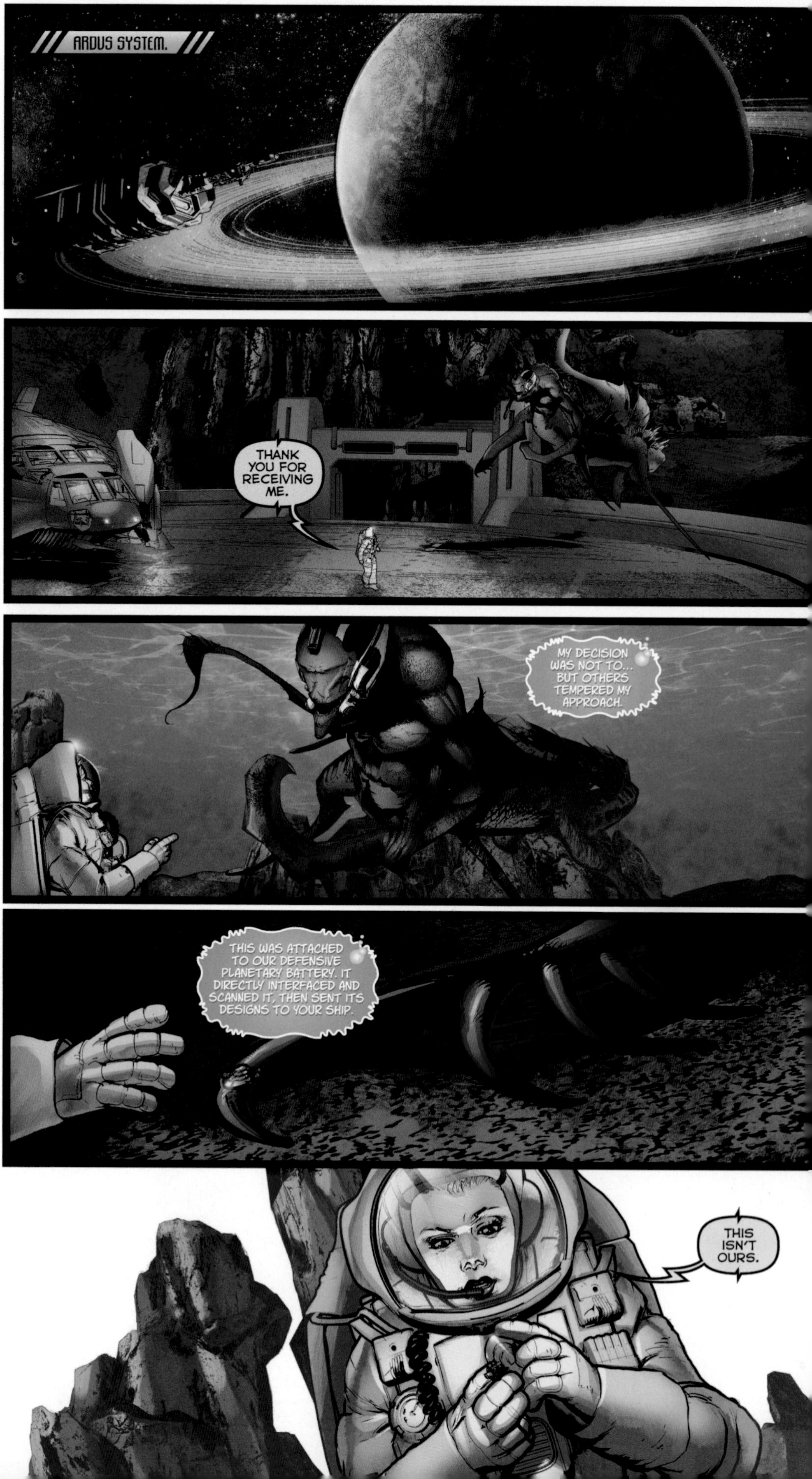
ARDUS SYSTEM.
THANK YOU FOR RECEIVING ME.
MY DECISION WAS NOT TO... BUT OTHERS TEMPERED MY APPROACH.
THIS WAS ATTACHED TO OUR DEFENSIVE PLANETARY BATTERY. IT DIRECTLY INTERFACED AND SCANNED IT, THEN SENT ITS DESIGNS TO YOUR SHIP.
THIS ISN'T OURS.

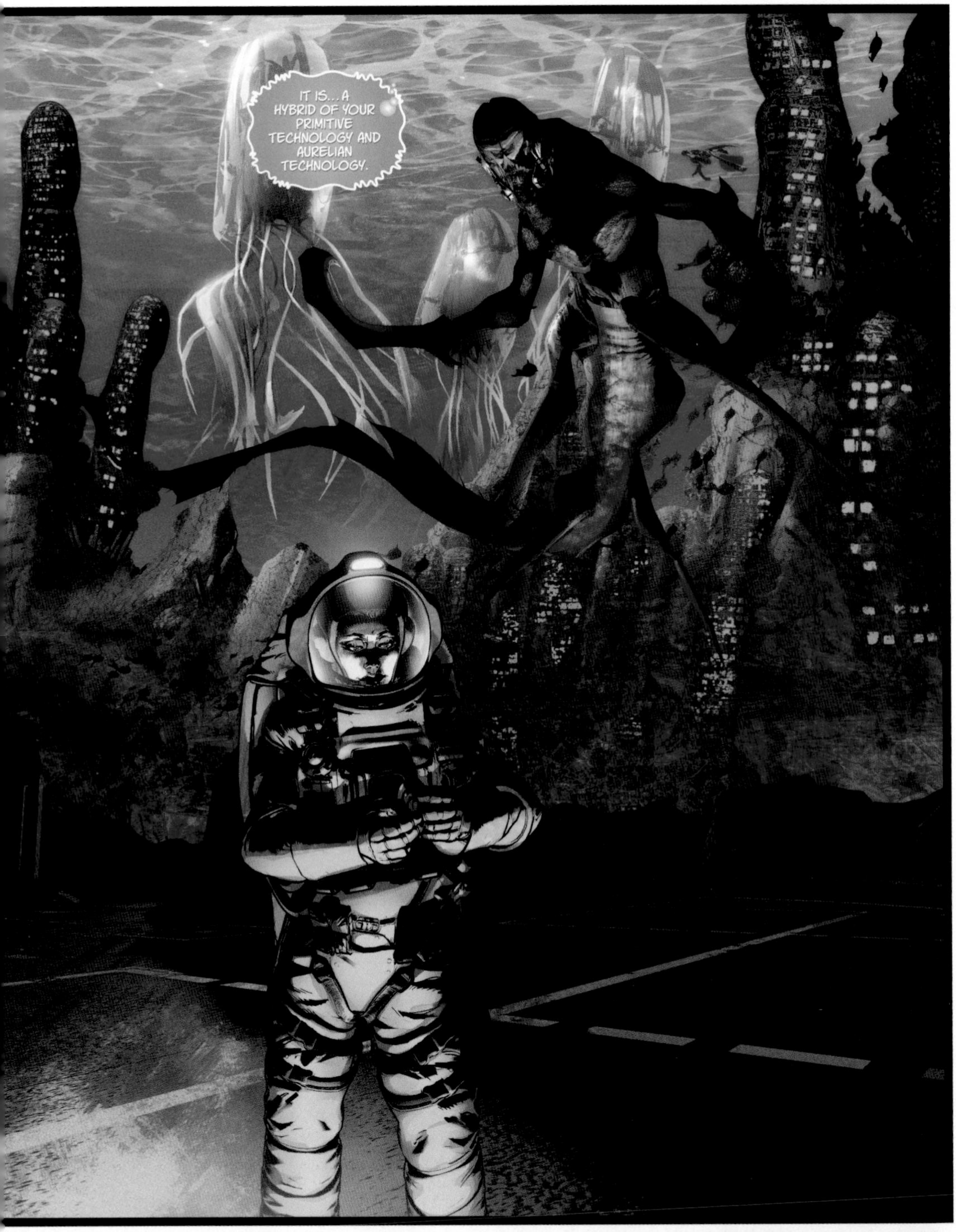
IT IS... A HYBRID OF YOUR PRIMITIVE TECHNOLOGY AND AURELIAN TECHNOLOGY.

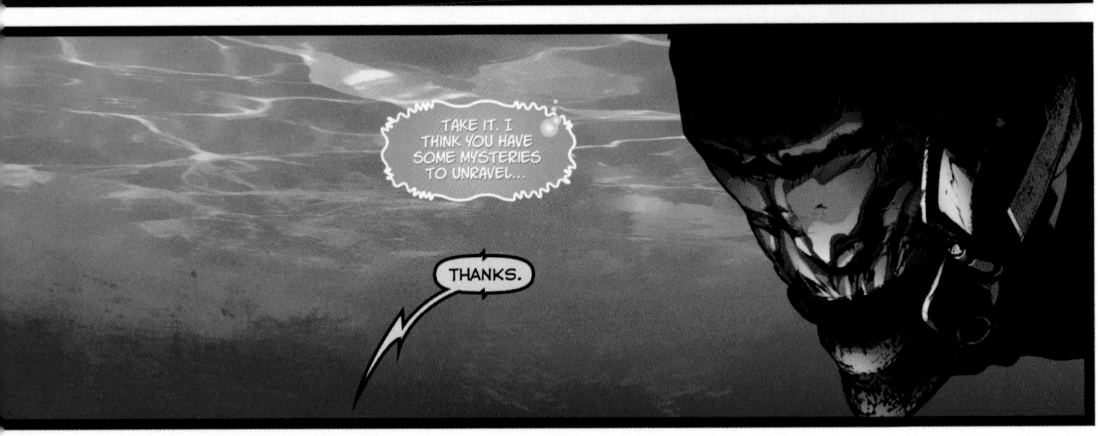
TAKE IT. I THINK YOU HAVE SOME MYSTERIES TO UNRAVEL...
THANKS.

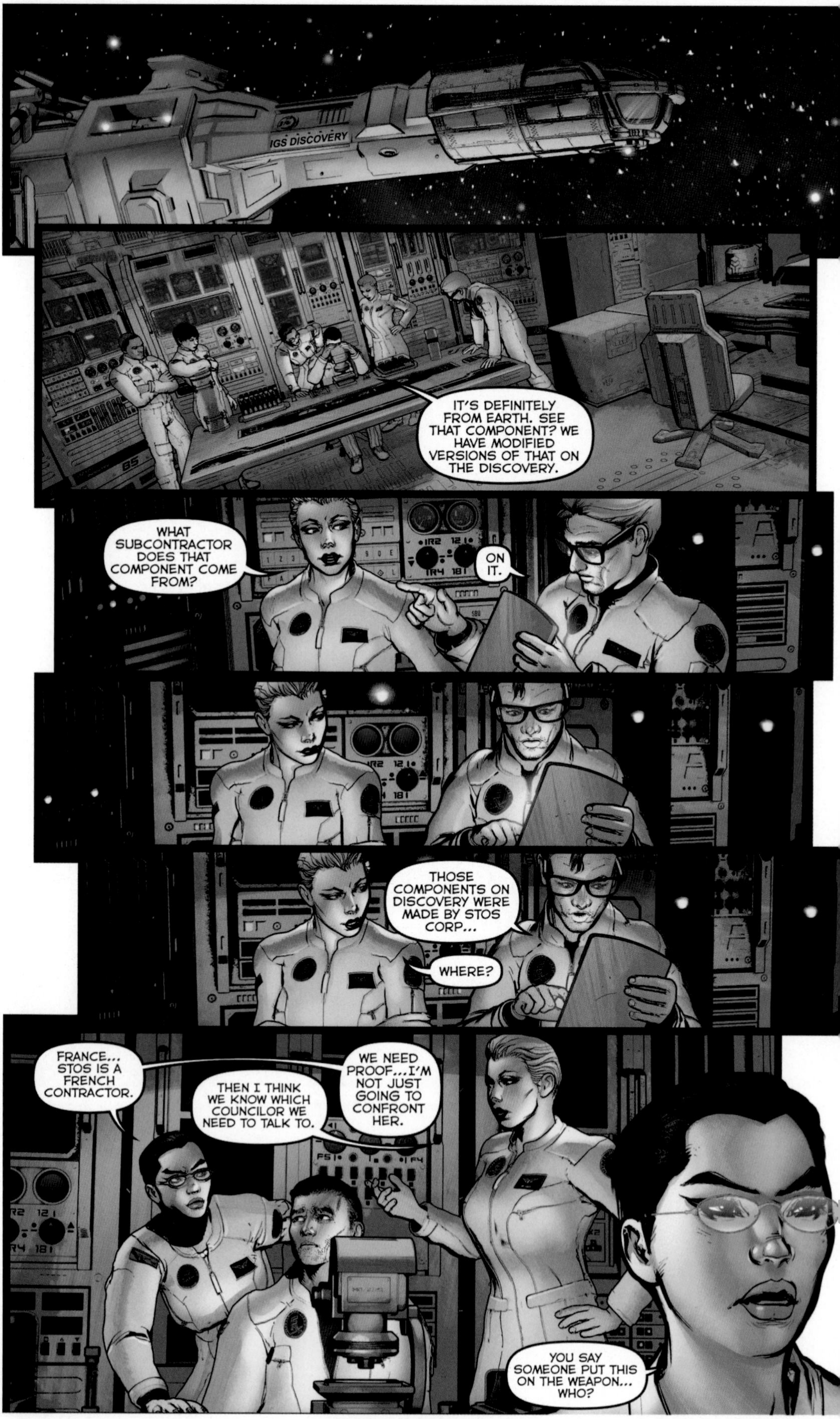
IGS DISCOVERY
IT'S DEFINITELY FROM EARTH. SEE THAT COMPONENT? WE HAVE MODIFIED VERSIONS OF THAT ON THE DISCOVERY.
WHAT SUBCONTRACTOR DOES THAT COMPONENT COME FROM?
ON IT.
THOSE COMPONENTS ON DISCOVERY WERE MADE BY STOS CORP...
WHERE?
FRANCE... STOS IS A FRENCH CONTRACTOR.
THEN I THINK WE KNOW WHICH COUNCILOR WE NEED TO TALK TO.
WE NEED PROOF...I'M NOT JUST GOING TO CONFRONT HER.
YOU SAY SOMEONE PUT THIS ON THE WEAPON... WHO?

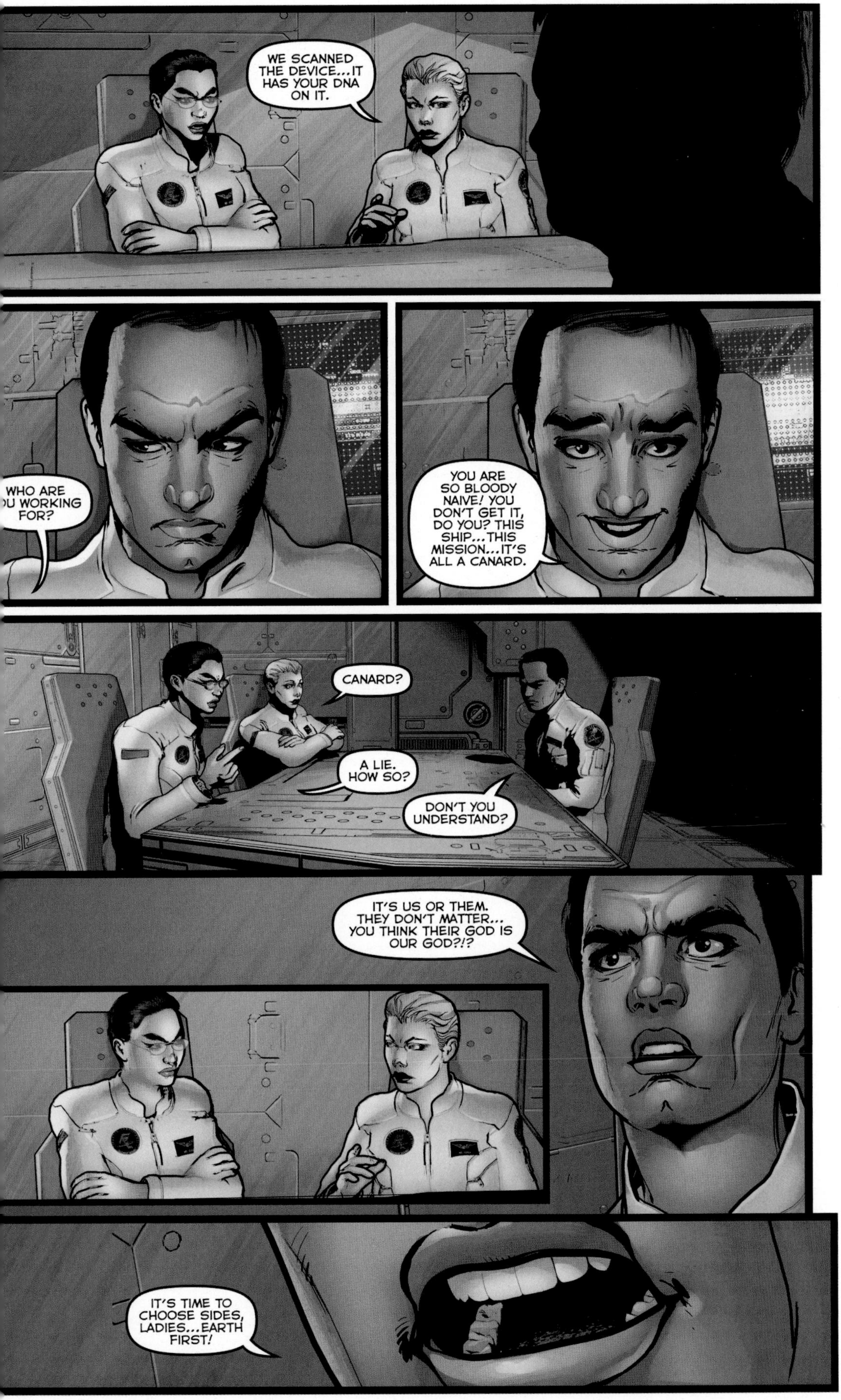

WE SCANNED THE DEVICE...IT HAS YOUR DNA ON IT.
WHO ARE YOU WORKING FOR?
YOU ARE SO BLOODY NAIVE! YOU DON'T GET IT, DO YOU? THIS SHIP...THIS MISSION...IT'S ALL A CANARD.
CANARD?
A LIE. HOW SO?
DON'T YOU UNDERSTAND?
IT'S US OR THEM. THEY DON'T MATTER... YOU THINK THEIR GOD IS OUR GOD?!?
IT'S TIME TO CHOOSE SIDES, LADIES...EARTH FIRST!

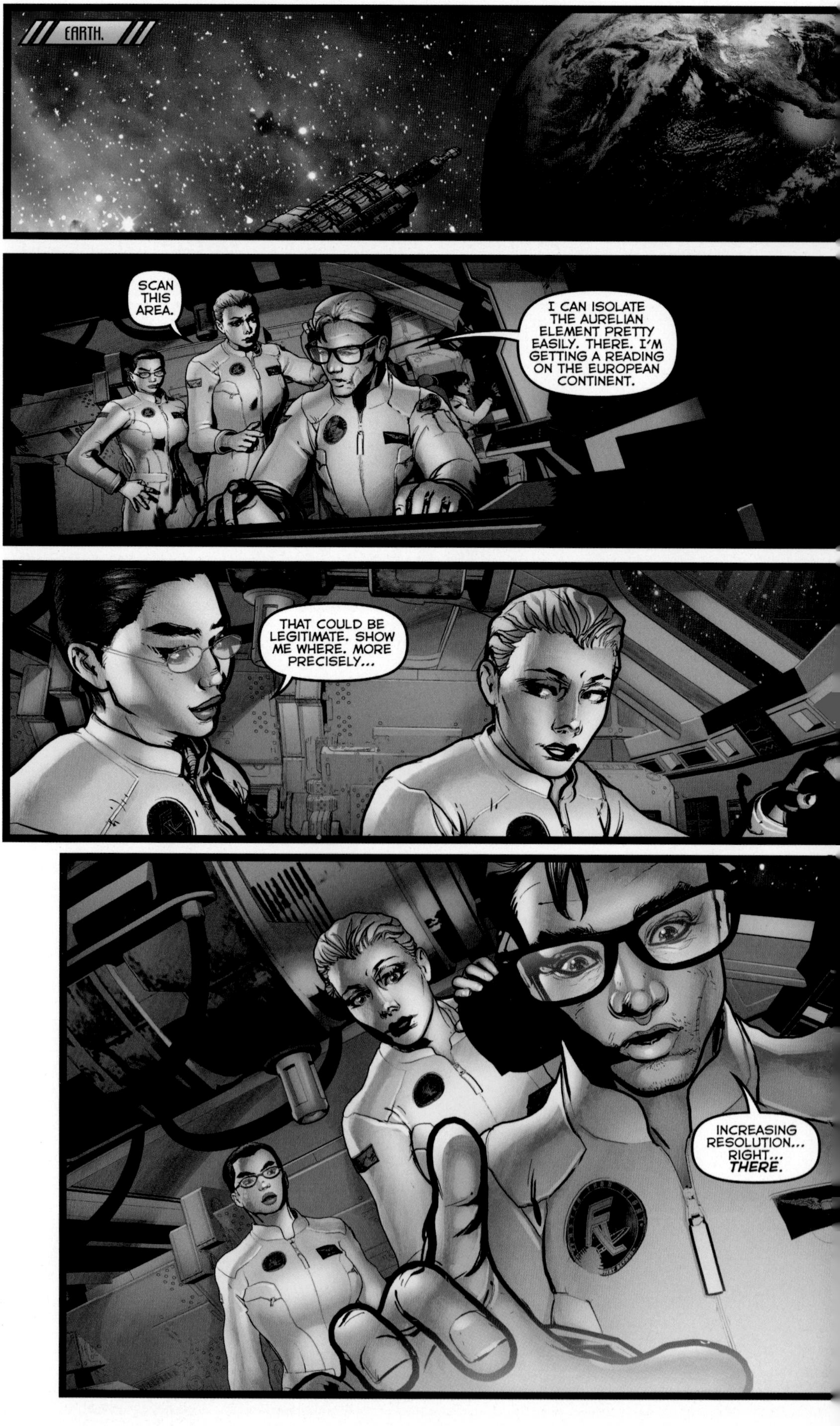
EARTH.
SCAN THIS AREA.
I CAN ISOLATE THE AURELIAN ELEMENT PRETTY EASILY. THERE. I'M GETTING A READING ON THE EUROPEAN CONTINENT.
THAT COULD BE LEGITIMATE. SHOW ME WHERE. MORE PRECISELY...
INCREASING RESOLUTION... RIGHT... *THERE*.

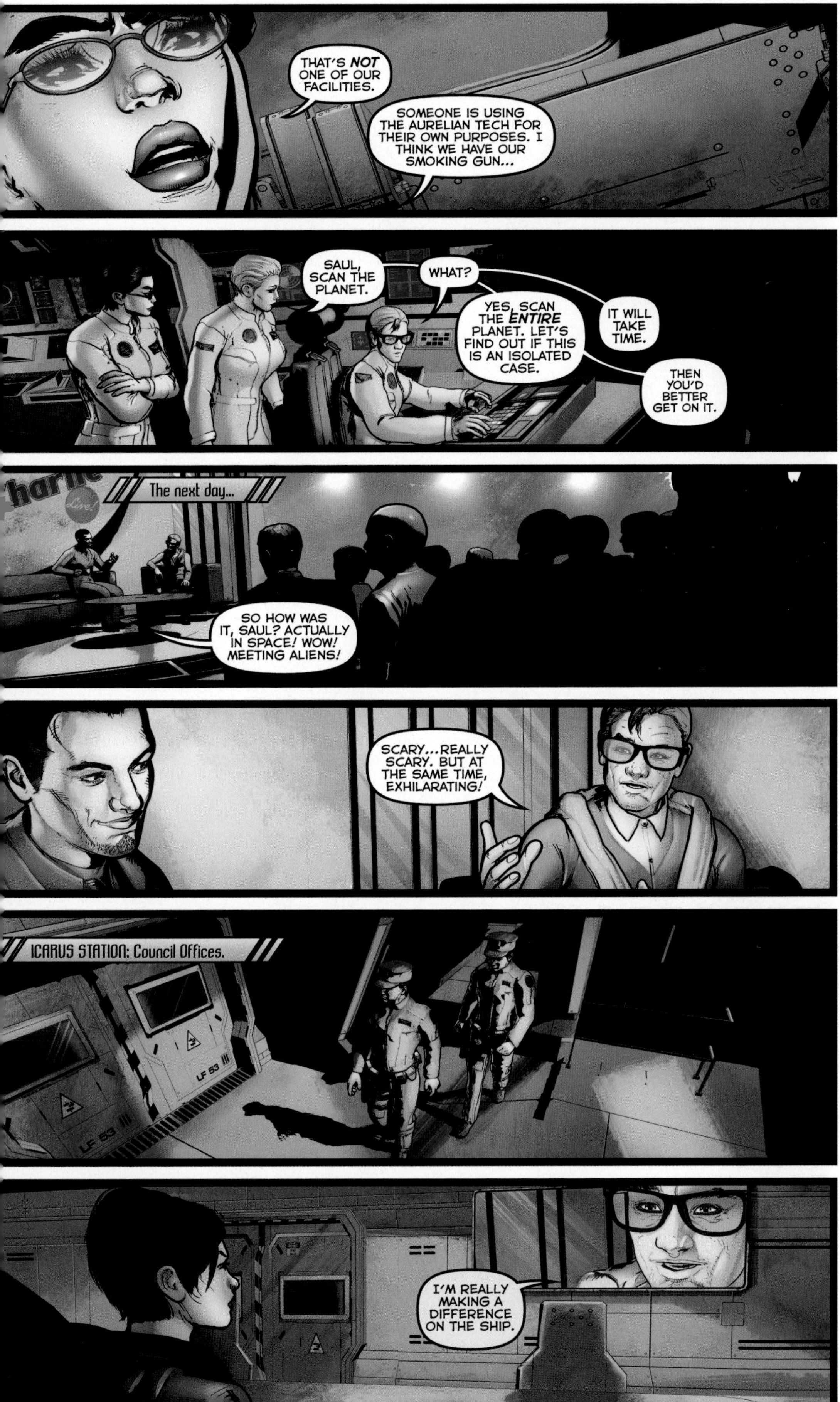
THAT'S NOT ONE OF OUR FACILITIES.
SOMEONE IS USING THE AURELIAN TECH FOR THEIR OWN PURPOSES. I THINK WE HAVE OUR SMOKING GUN...
SAUL, SCAN THE PLANET.
WHAT?
YES, SCAN THE ENTIRE PLANET. LET'S FIND OUT IF THIS IS AN ISOLATED CASE.
IT WILL TAKE TIME.
THEN YOU'D BETTER GET ON IT.
The next day...
SO HOW WAS IT, SAUL? ACTUALLY IN SPACE! WOW! MEETING ALIENS!
SCARY...REALLY SCARY. BUT AT THE SAME TIME, EXHILARATING!
ICARUS STATION: Council Offices.
LF 53
I'M REALLY MAKING A DIFFERENCE ON THE SHIP.

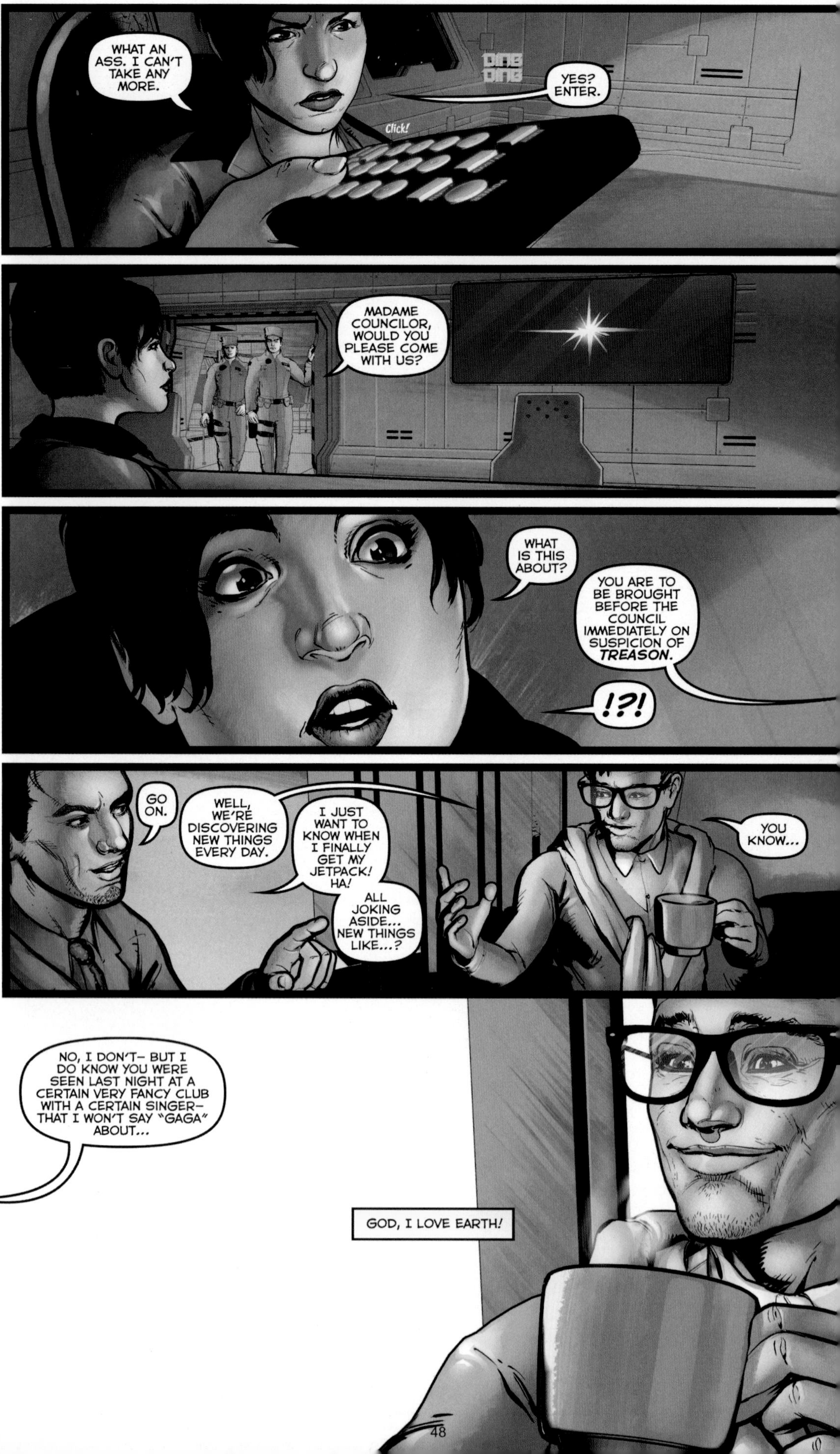

WHAT AN ASS. I CAN'T TAKE ANY MORE.
DING DING
YES? ENTER.
Click!
MADAME COUNCILOR, WOULD YOU PLEASE COME WITH US?
WHAT IS THIS ABOUT?
YOU ARE TO BE BROUGHT BEFORE THE COUNCIL IMMEDIATELY ON SUSPICION OF *TREASON*.
!?!
GO ON.
WELL, WE'RE DISCOVERING NEW THINGS EVERY DAY.
I JUST WANT TO KNOW WHEN I FINALLY GET MY JETPACK! HA!
ALL JOKING ASIDE... NEW THINGS LIKE...?
YOU KNOW...
NO, I DON'T– BUT I DO KNOW YOU WERE SEEN LAST NIGHT AT A CERTAIN VERY FANCY CLUB WITH A CERTAIN SINGER– THAT I WON'T SAY "GAGA" ABOUT...
GOD, I LOVE EARTH!

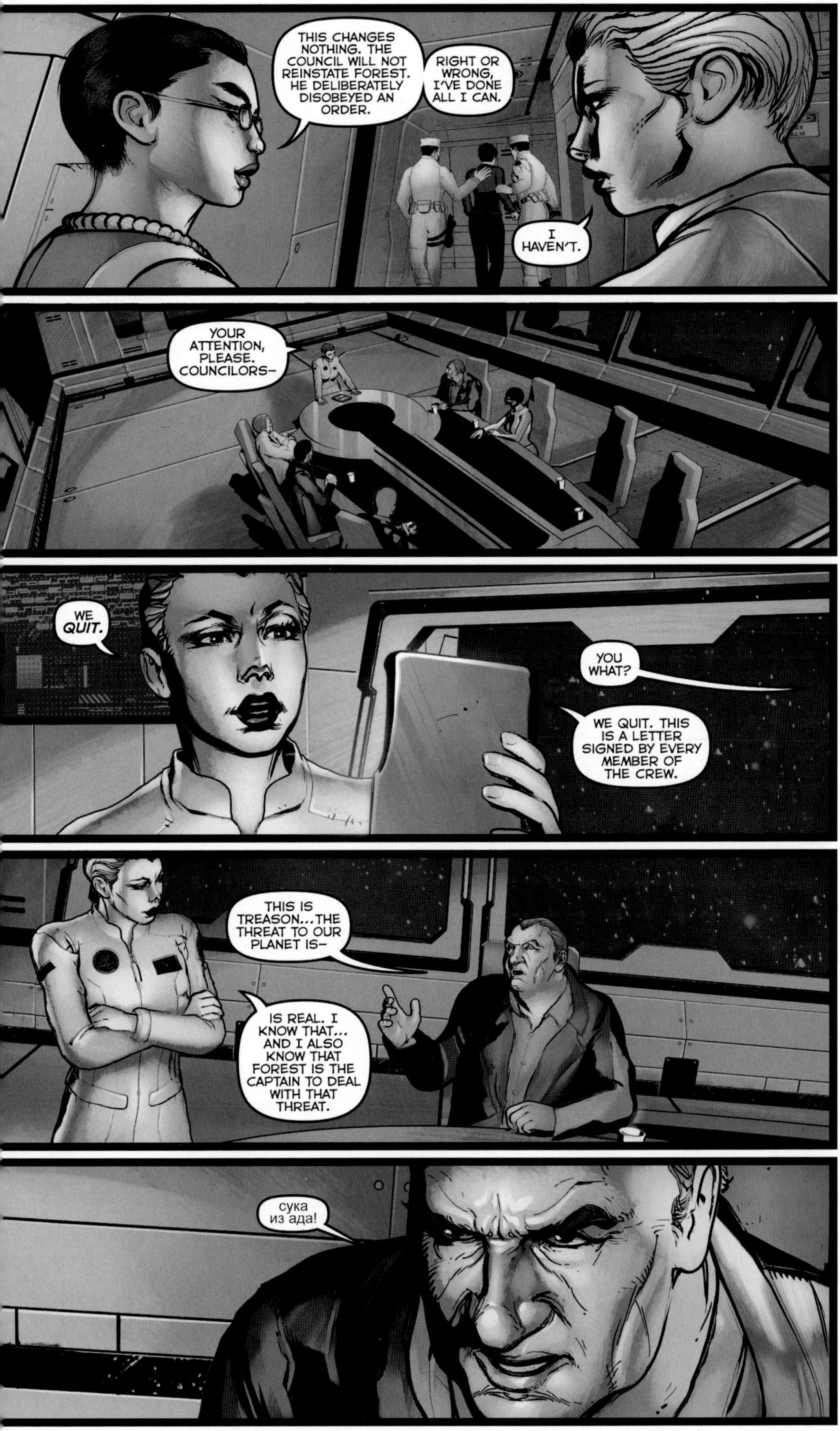
THIS CHANGES NOTHING. THE COUNCIL WILL NOT REINSTATE FOREST. HE DELIBERATELY DISOBEYED AN ORDER.
RIGHT OR WRONG, I'VE DONE ALL I CAN.
I HAVEN'T.
YOUR ATTENTION, PLEASE. COUNCILORS–
WE QUIT.
YOU WHAT?
WE QUIT. THIS IS A LETTER SIGNED BY EVERY MEMBER OF THE CREW.
THIS IS TREASON...THE THREAT TO OUR PLANET IS–
IS REAL. I KNOW THAT... AND I ALSO KNOW THAT FOREST IS THE CAPTAIN TO DEAL WITH THAT THREAT.
сука из ада!

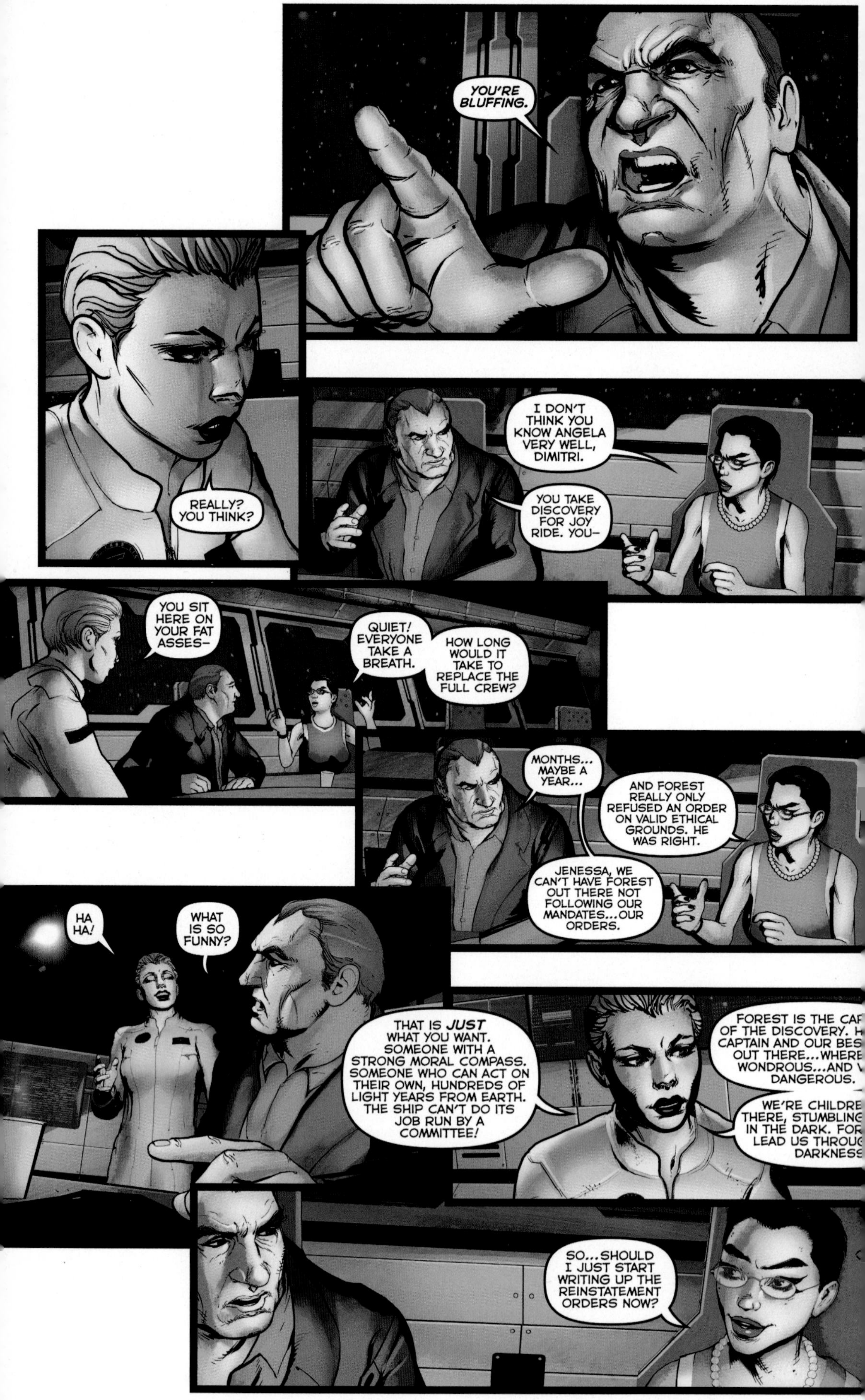
YOU'RE BLUFFING.
REALLY? YOU THINK?
I DON'T THINK YOU KNOW ANGELA VERY WELL, DIMITRI.
YOU TAKE DISCOVERY FOR JOY RIDE. YOU–
YOU SIT HERE ON YOUR FAT ASSES–
QUIET! EVERYONE TAKE A BREATH.
HOW LONG WOULD IT TAKE TO REPLACE THE FULL CREW?
MONTHS... MAYBE A YEAR...
AND FOREST REALLY ONLY REFUSED AN ORDER ON VALID ETHICAL GROUNDS. HE WAS RIGHT.
JENESSA, WE CAN'T HAVE FOREST OUT THERE NOT FOLLOWING OUR MANDATES...OUR ORDERS.
HA HA!
WHAT IS SO FUNNY?
THAT IS JUST WHAT YOU WANT. SOMEONE WITH A STRONG MORAL COMPASS. SOMEONE WHO CAN ACT ON THEIR OWN, HUNDREDS OF LIGHT YEARS FROM EARTH. THE SHIP CAN'T DO ITS JOB RUN BY A COMMITTEE!
SO...SHOULD I JUST START WRITING UP THE REINSTATEMENT ORDERS NOW?

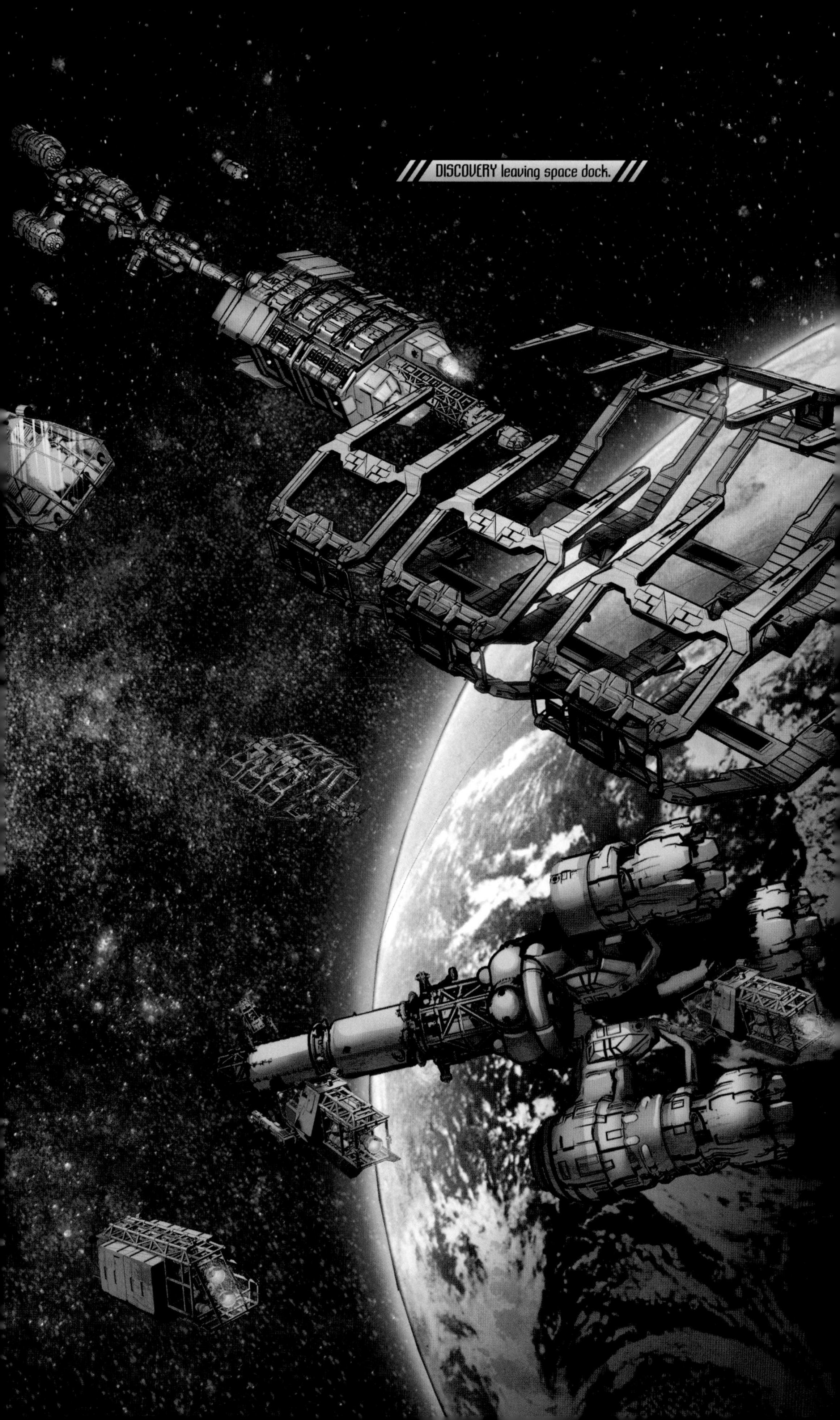
DISCOVERY leaving space dock.

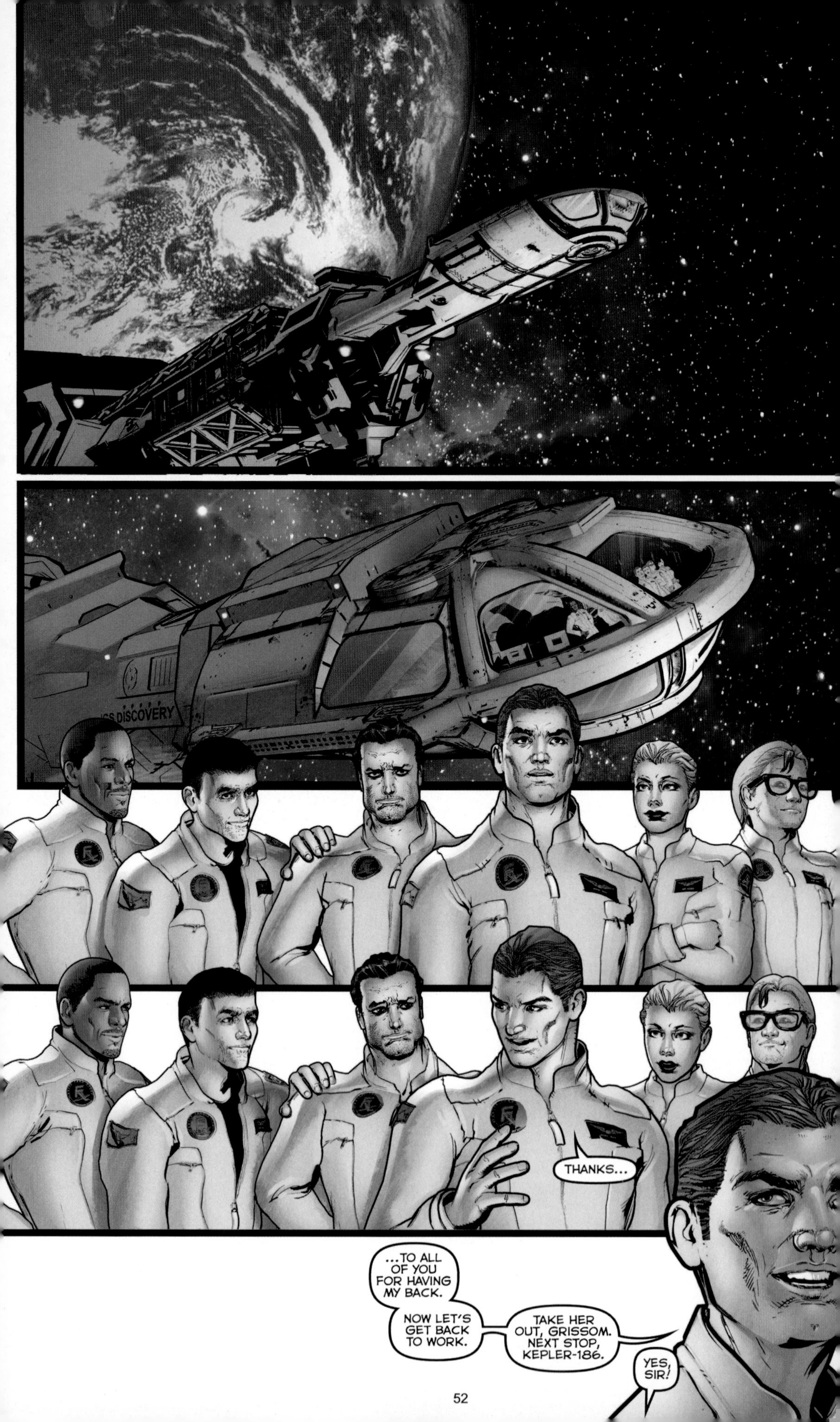

US DISCOVERY
THANKS...
...TO ALL OF YOU FOR HAVING MY BACK.
NOW LET'S GET BACK TO WORK.
TAKE HER OUT, GRISSOM. NEXT STOP, KEPLER-186.
YES, SIR!

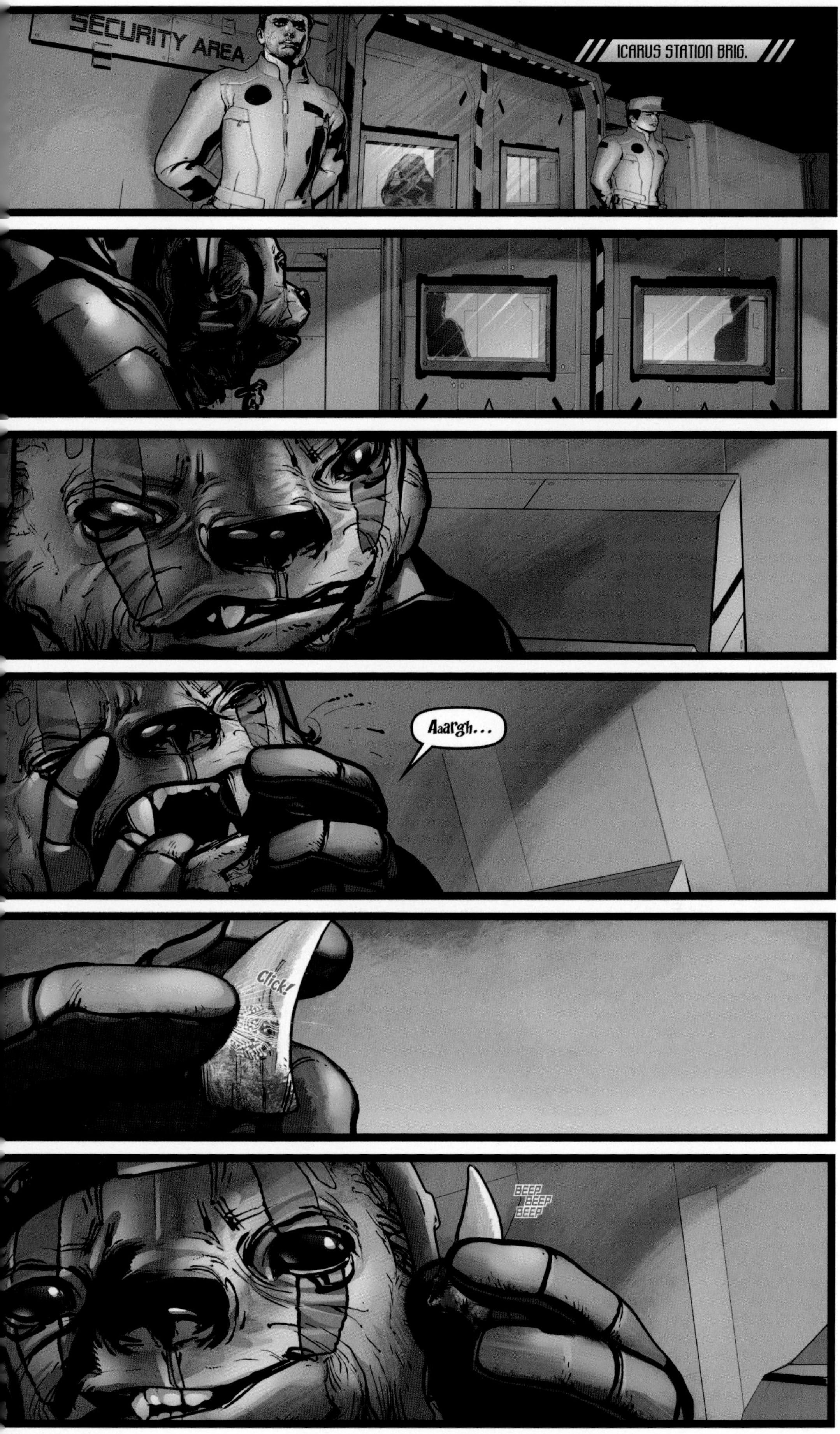
SECURITY AREA
ICARUS STATION BRIG.
Aaargh...
Click!
BEEP
BEEP
BEEP

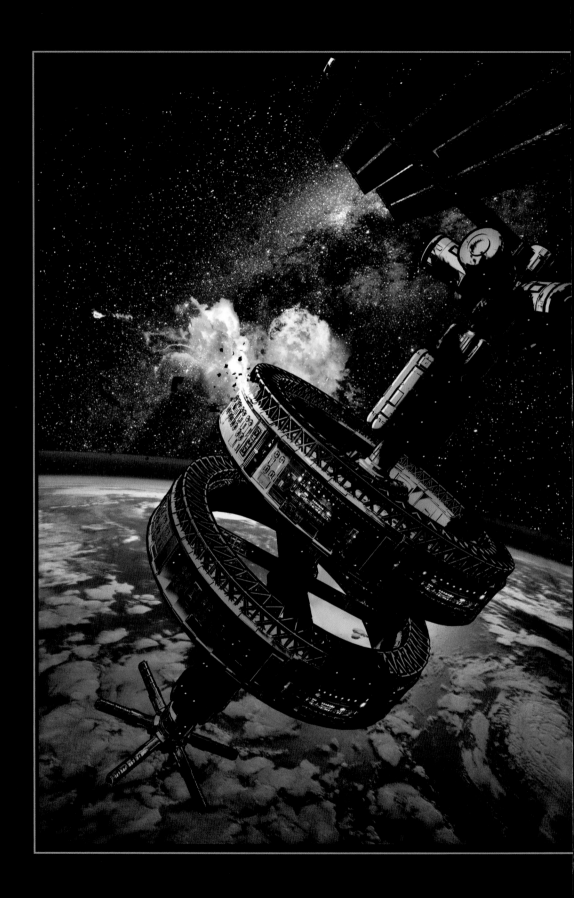

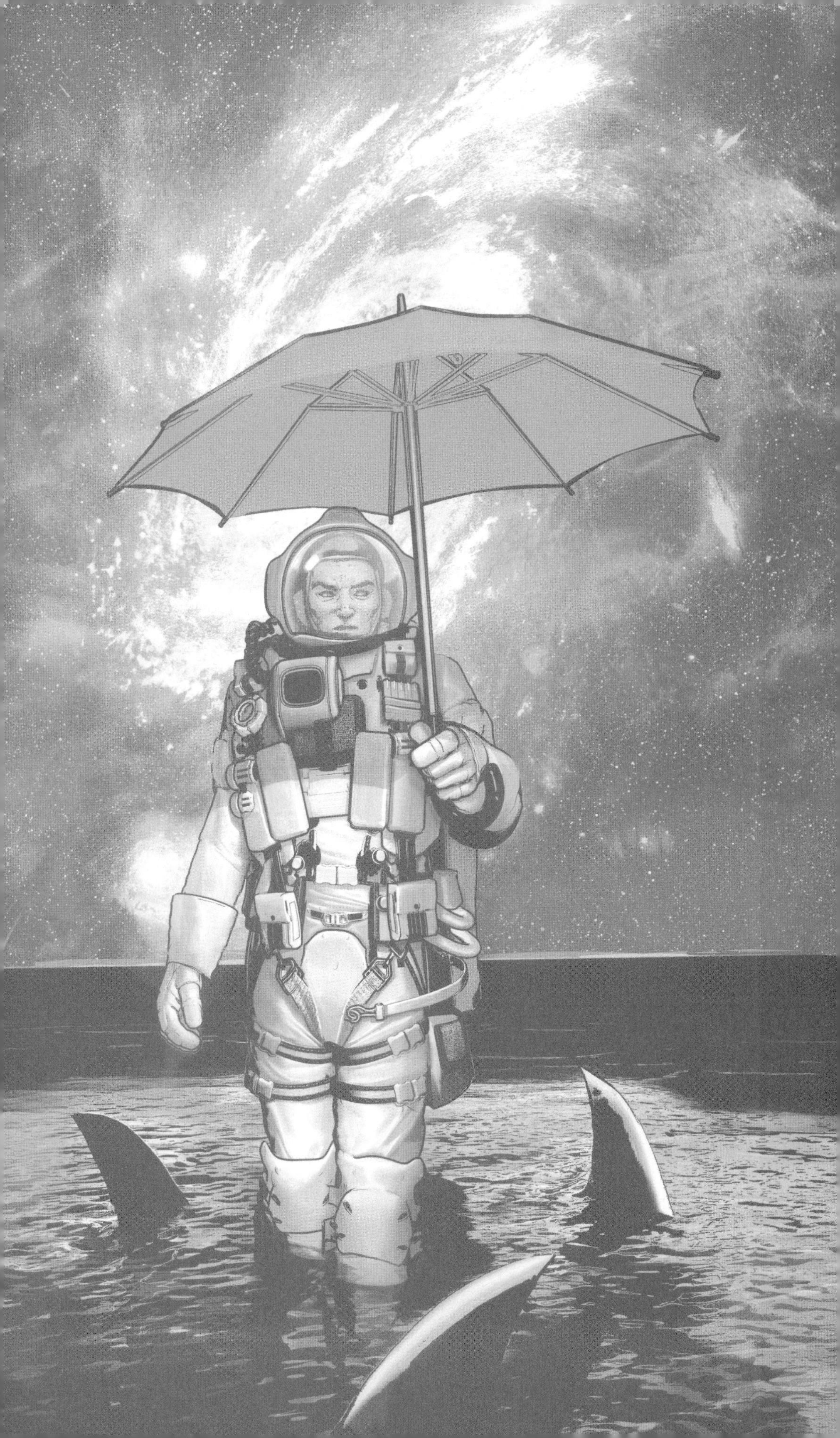

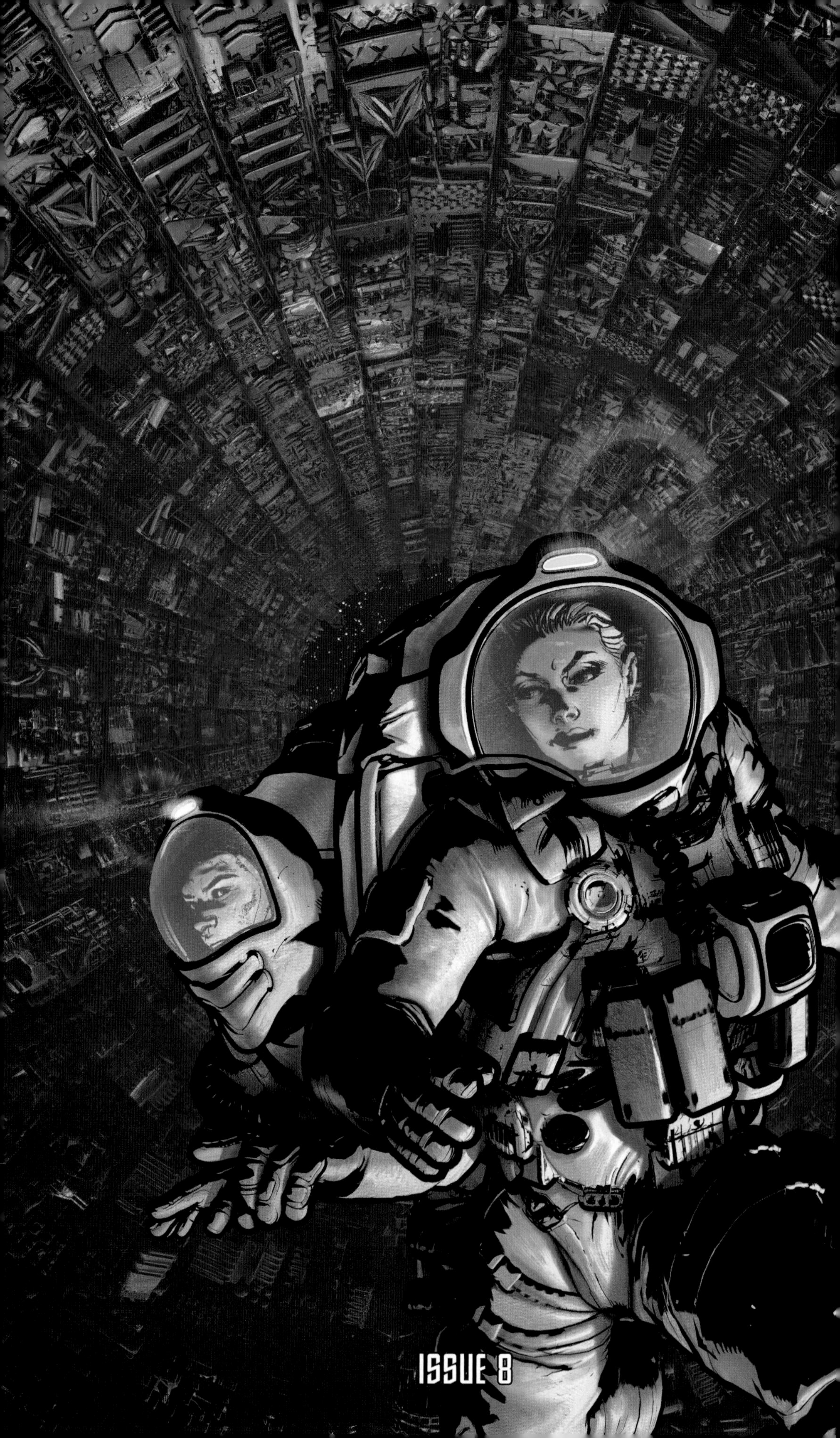
ISSUE 8

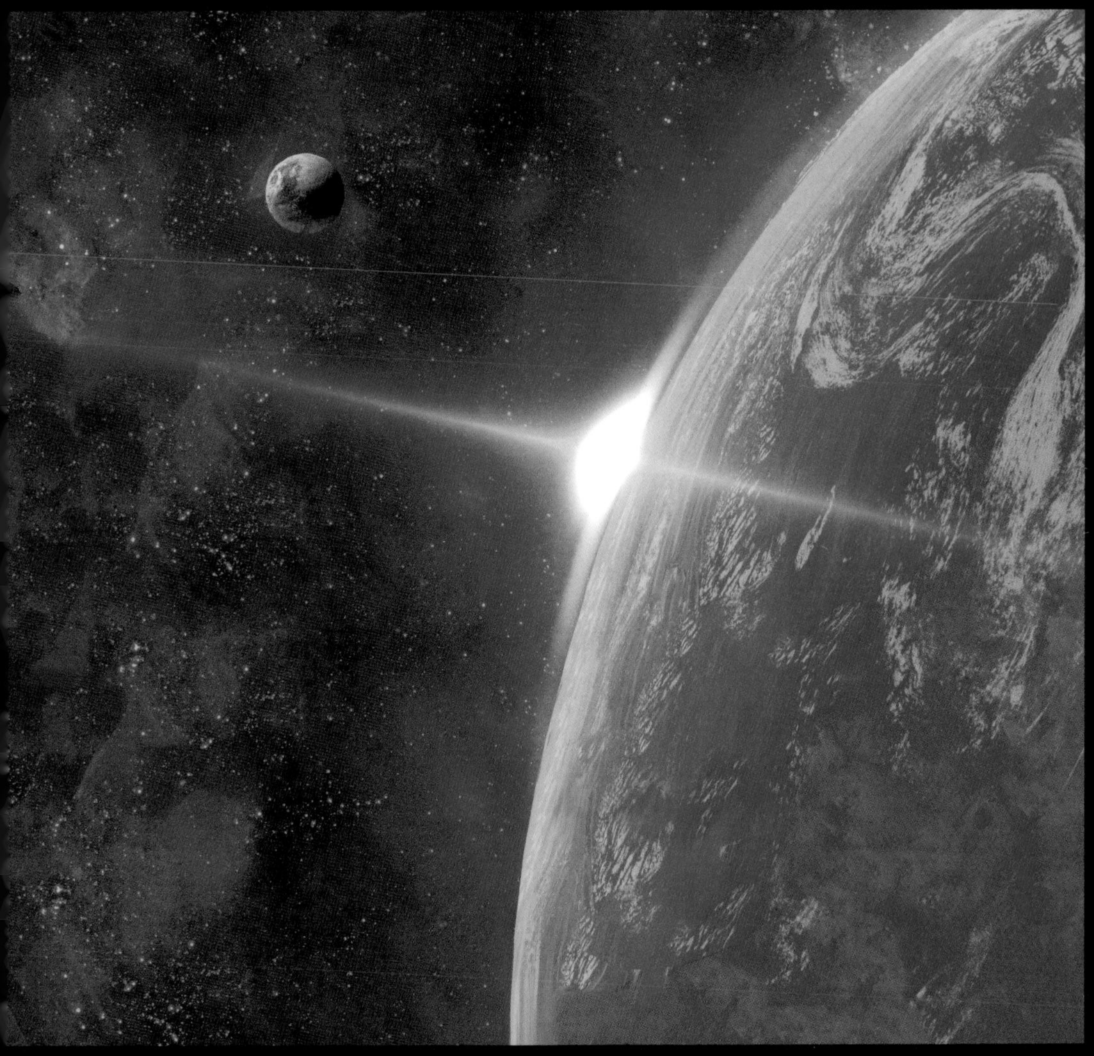

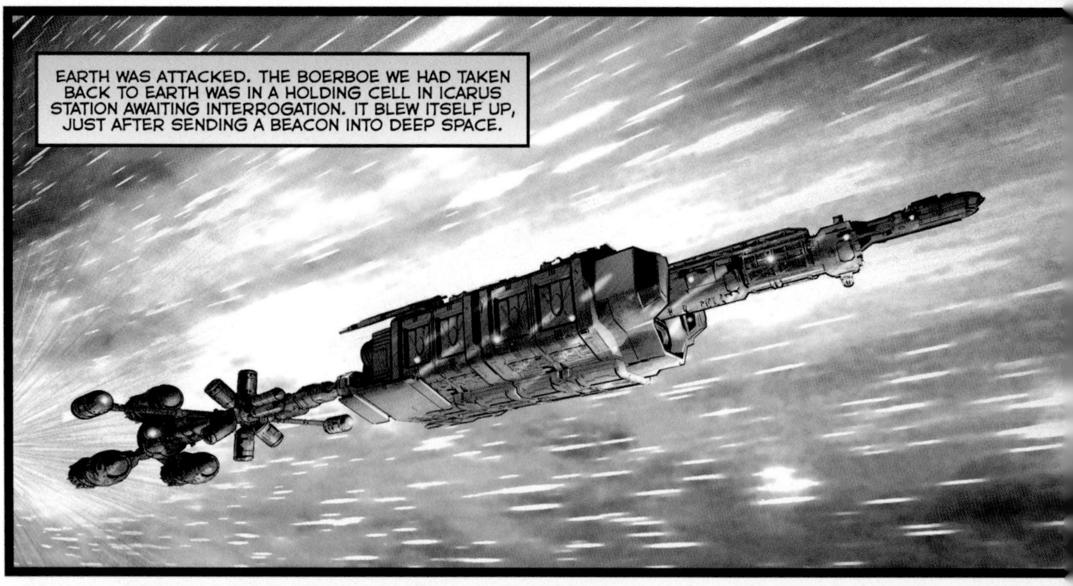
EARTH WAS ATTACKED. THE BOERBOE WE HAD TAKEN BACK TO EARTH WAS IN A HOLDING CELL IN ICARUS STATION AWAITING INTERROGATION. IT BLEW ITSELF UP, JUST AFTER SENDING A BEACON INTO DEEP SPACE.

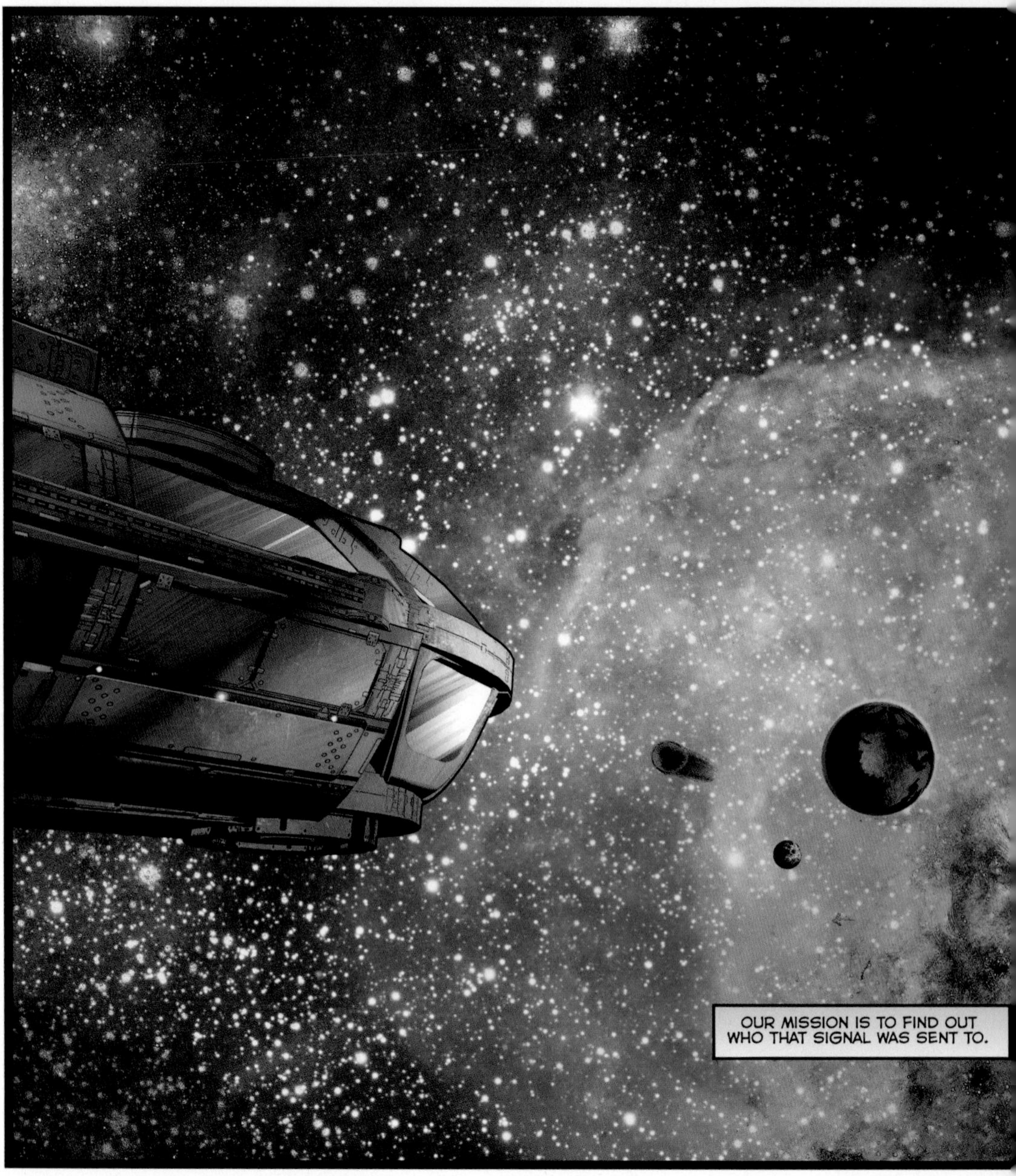
OUR MISSION IS TO FIND OUT WHO THAT SIGNAL WAS SENT TO.

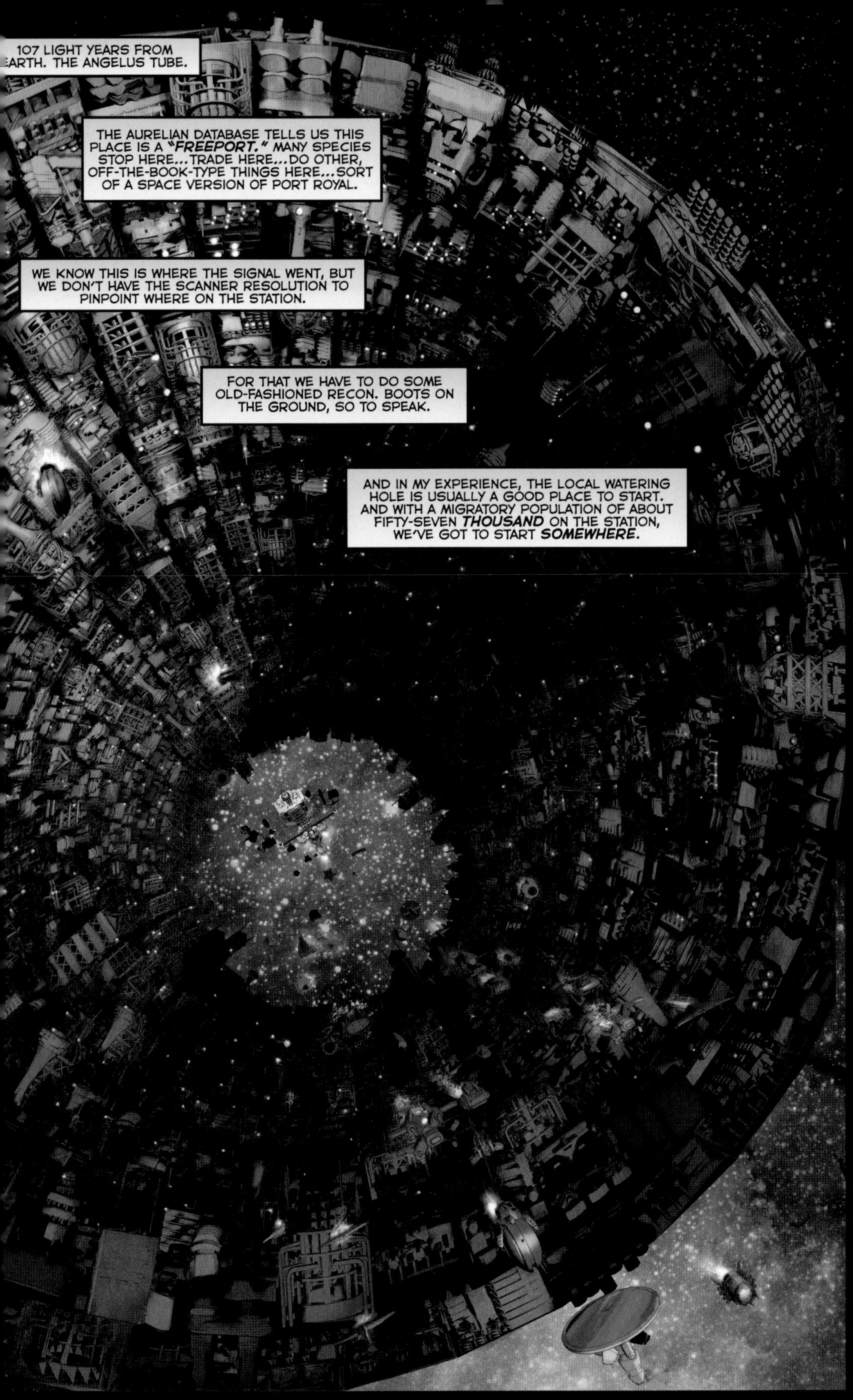
107 LIGHT YEARS FROM ARTH. THE ANGELUS TUBE.
THE AURELIAN DATABASE TELLS US THIS PLACE IS A "FREEPORT." MANY SPECIES STOP HERE...TRADE HERE...DO OTHER, OFF-THE-BOOK-TYPE THINGS HERE...SORT OF A SPACE VERSION OF PORT ROYAL.
WE KNOW THIS IS WHERE THE SIGNAL WENT, BUT WE DON'T HAVE THE SCANNER RESOLUTION TO PINPOINT WHERE ON THE STATION.
FOR THAT WE HAVE TO DO SOME OLD-FASHIONED RECON. BOOTS ON THE GROUND, SO TO SPEAK.
AND IN MY EXPERIENCE, THE LOCAL WATERING HOLE IS USUALLY A GOOD PLACE TO START. AND WITH A MIGRATORY POPULATION OF ABOUT FIFTY-SEVEN THOUSAND ON THE STATION, WE'VE GOT TO START SOMEWHERE.

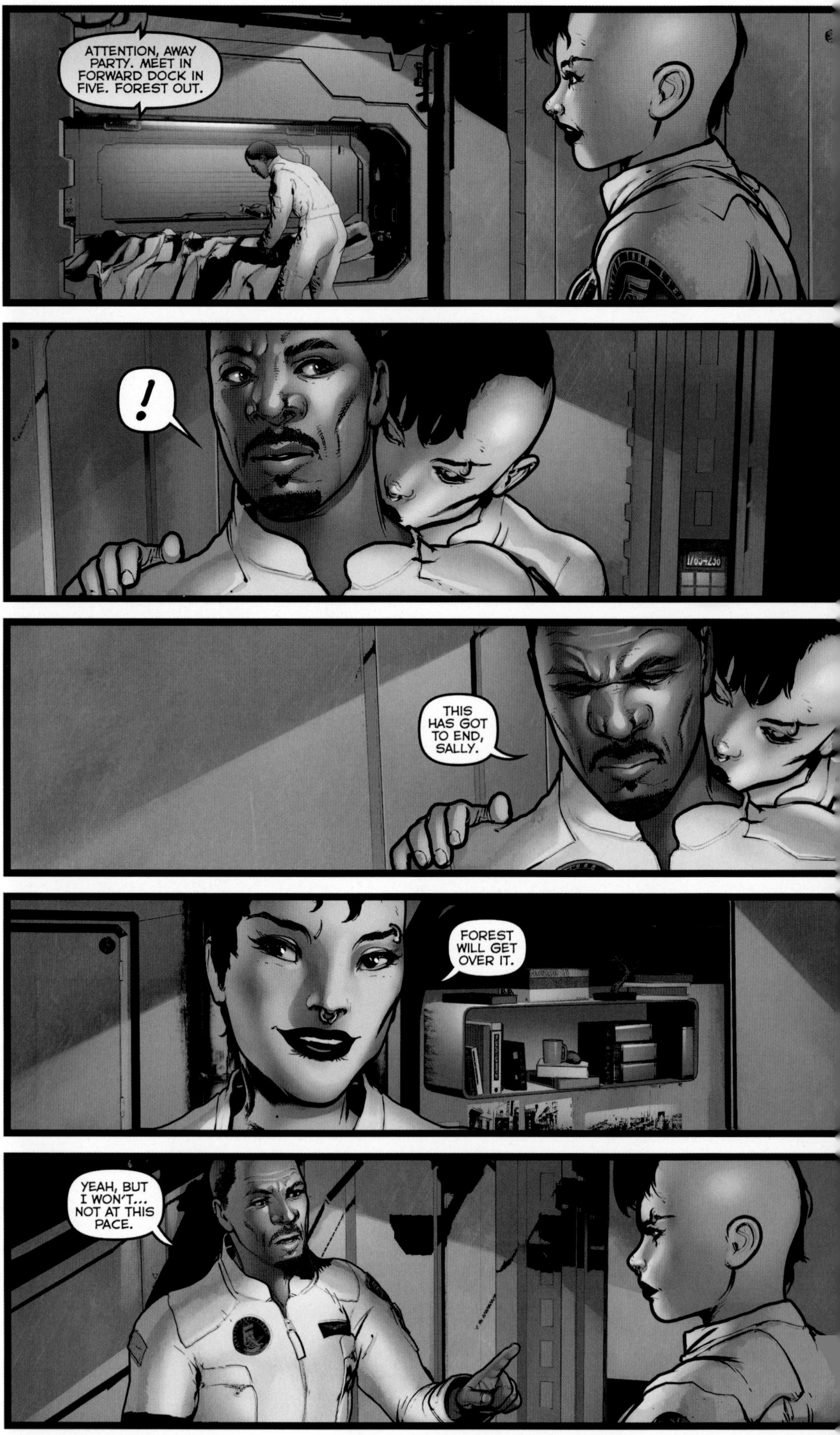
ATTENTION, AWAY PARTY. MEET IN FORWARD DOCK IN FIVE. FOREST OUT.
!
THIS HAS GOT TO END, SALLY.
FOREST WILL GET OVER IT.
YEAH, BUT I WON'T... NOT AT THIS PACE.

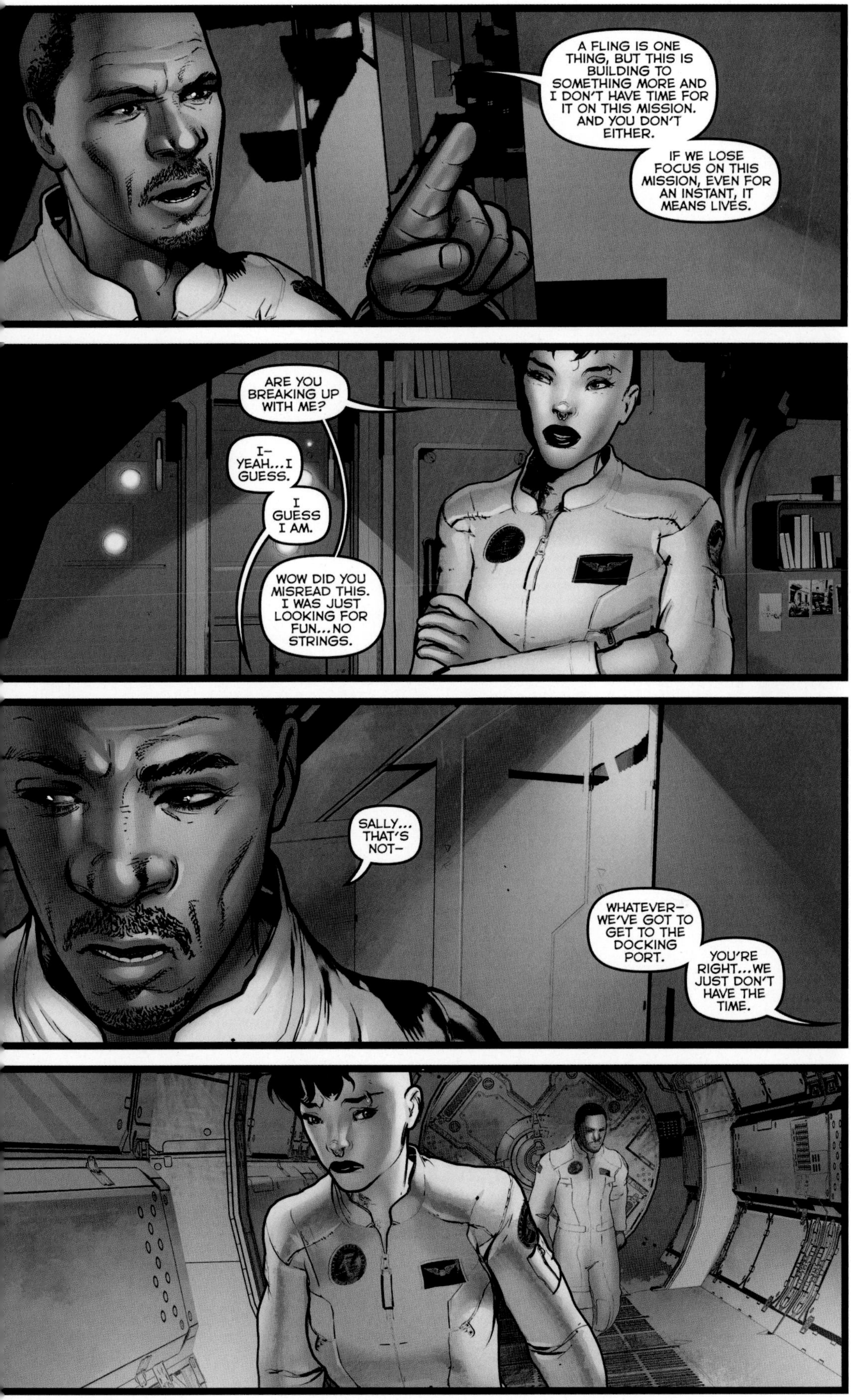
A FLING IS ONE THING, BUT THIS IS BUILDING TO SOMETHING MORE AND I DON'T HAVE TIME FOR IT ON THIS MISSION. AND YOU DON'T EITHER.
IF WE LOSE FOCUS ON THIS MISSION, EVEN FOR AN INSTANT, IT MEANS LIVES.
ARE YOU BREAKING UP WITH ME?
I– YEAH...I GUESS.
I GUESS I AM.
WOW DID YOU MISREAD THIS. I WAS JUST LOOKING FOR FUN...NO STRINGS.
SALLY... THAT'S NOT–
WHATEVER– WE'VE GOT TO GET TO THE DOCKING PORT.
YOU'RE RIGHT...WE JUST DON'T HAVE THE TIME.

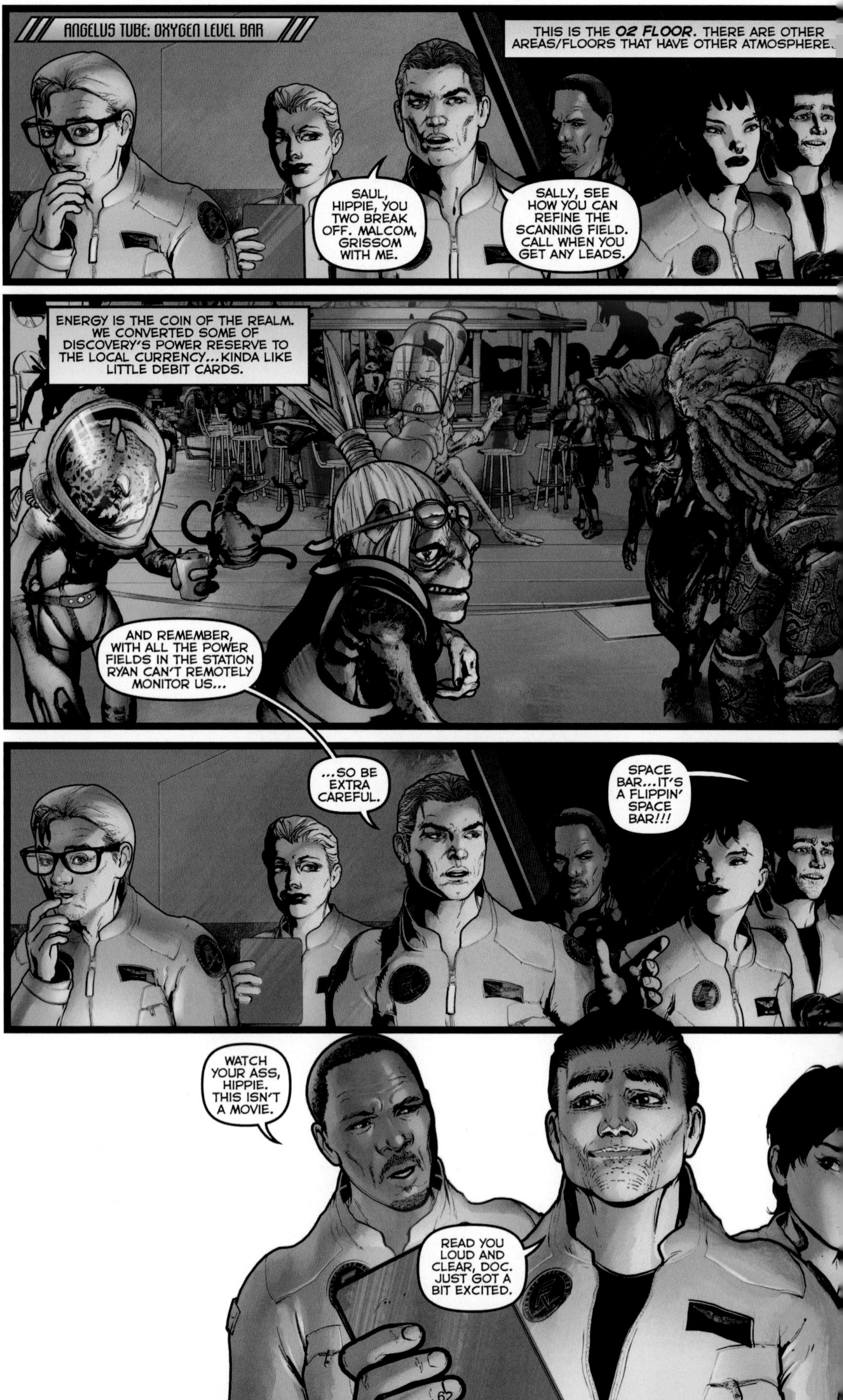
ANGELUS TUBE: OXYGEN LEVEL BAR
THIS IS THE O2 FLOOR. THERE ARE OTHER AREAS/FLOORS THAT HAVE OTHER ATMOSPHERES.
SAUL, HIPPIE, YOU TWO BREAK OFF. MALCOM, GRISSOM WITH ME.
SALLY, SEE HOW YOU CAN REFINE THE SCANNING FIELD. CALL WHEN YOU GET ANY LEADS.
ENERGY IS THE COIN OF THE REALM. WE CONVERTED SOME OF DISCOVERY'S POWER RESERVE TO THE LOCAL CURRENCY...KINDA LIKE LITTLE DEBIT CARDS.
AND REMEMBER, WITH ALL THE POWER FIELDS IN THE STATION RYAN CAN'T REMOTELY MONITOR US...
...SO BE EXTRA CAREFUL.
SPACE BAR...IT'S A FLIPPIN' SPACE BAR!!!
WATCH YOUR ASS, HIPPIE. THIS ISN'T A MOVIE.
READ YOU LOUD AND CLEAR, DOC. JUST GOT A BIT EXCITED.

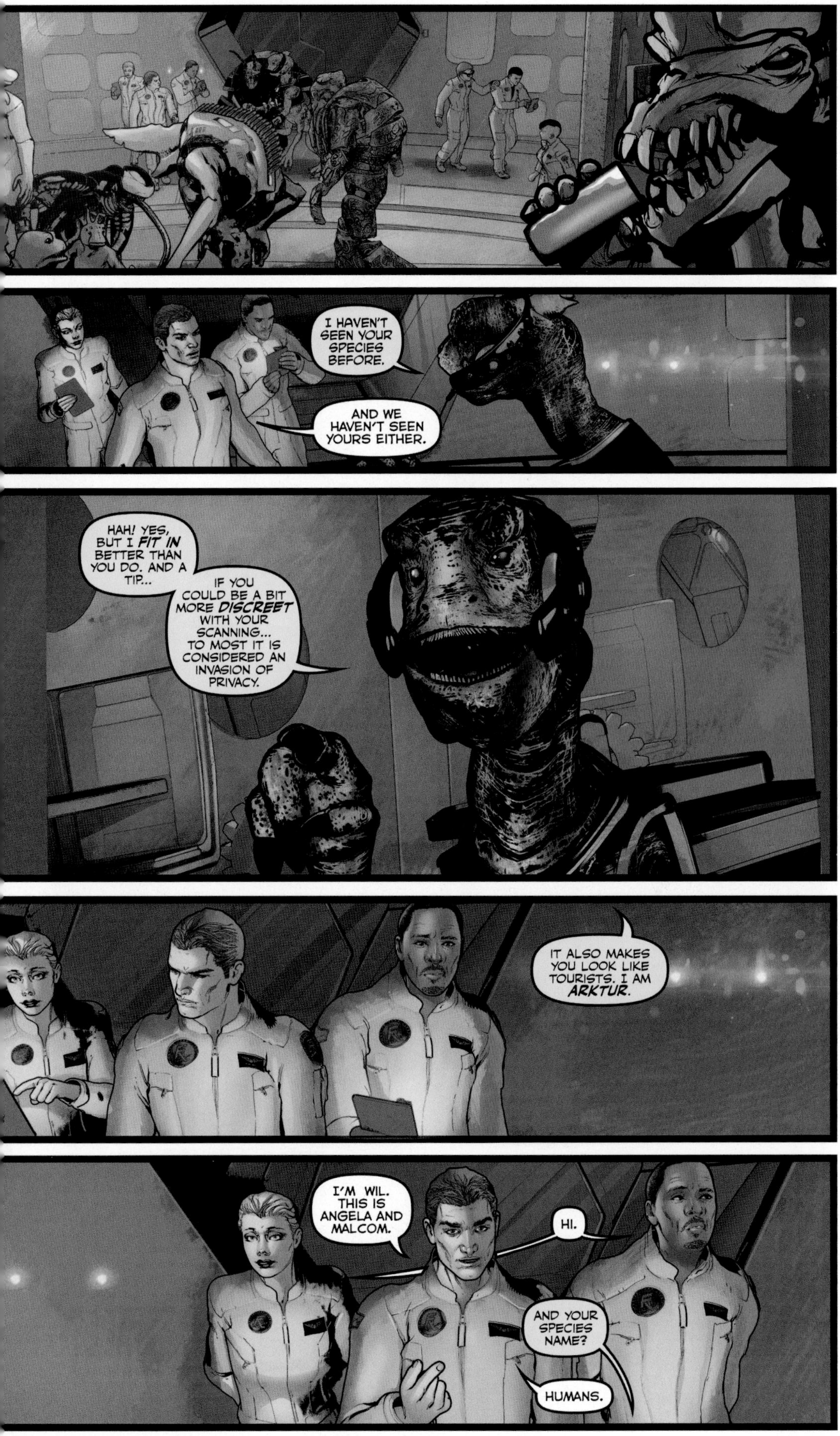

I HAVEN'T SEEN YOUR SPECIES BEFORE.
AND WE HAVEN'T SEEN YOURS EITHER.
HAH! YES, BUT I *FIT IN* BETTER THAN YOU DO. AND A TIP...
IF YOU COULD BE A BIT MORE *DISCREET* WITH YOUR SCANNING... TO MOST IT IS CONSIDERED AN INVASION OF PRIVACY.
IT ALSO MAKES YOU LOOK LIKE TOURISTS. I AM *ARKTUR*.
I'M WIL. THIS IS ANGELA AND MALCOM.
HI.
AND YOUR SPECIES NAME?
HUMANS.

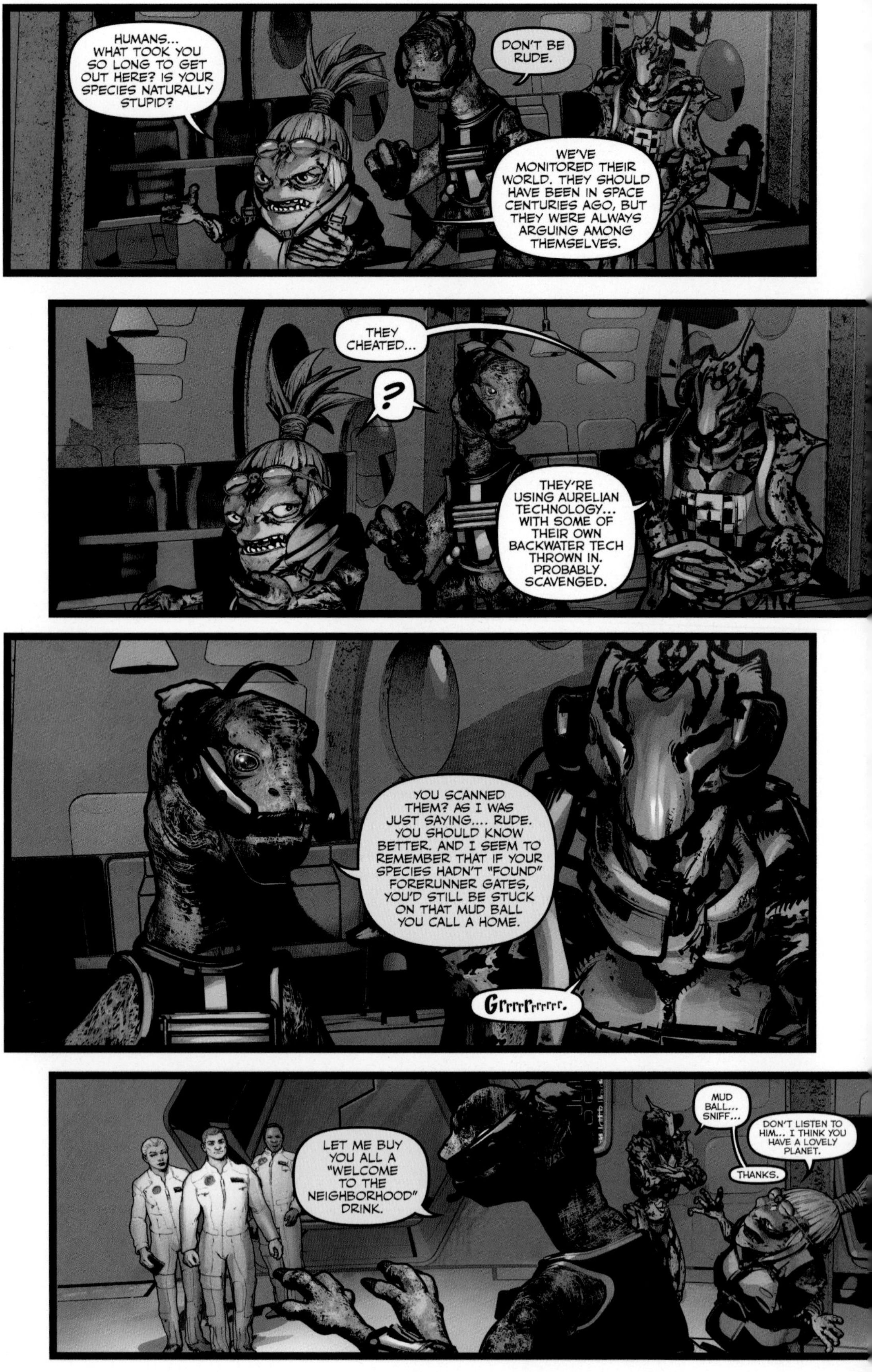
HUMANS... WHAT TOOK YOU SO LONG TO GET OUT HERE? IS YOUR SPECIES NATURALLY STUPID?
DON'T BE RUDE.
WE'VE MONITORED THEIR WORLD. THEY SHOULD HAVE BEEN IN SPACE CENTURIES AGO, BUT THEY WERE ALWAYS ARGUING AMONG THEMSELVES.
THEY CHEATED...
?
THEY'RE USING AURELIAN TECHNOLOGY... WITH SOME OF THEIR OWN BACKWATER TECH THROWN IN. PROBABLY SCAVENGED.
YOU SCANNED THEM? AS I WAS JUST SAYING.... RUDE. YOU SHOULD KNOW BETTER. AND I SEEM TO REMEMBER THAT IF YOUR SPECIES HADN'T "FOUND" FORERUNNER GATES, YOU'D STILL BE STUCK ON THAT MUD BALL YOU CALL A HOME.
Grrrrrrrrrr.
LET ME BUY YOU ALL A "WELCOME TO THE NEIGHBORHOOD" DRINK.
MUD BALL... SNIFF...
DON'T LISTEN TO HIM... I THINK YOU HAVE A LOVELY PLANET.
THANKS.

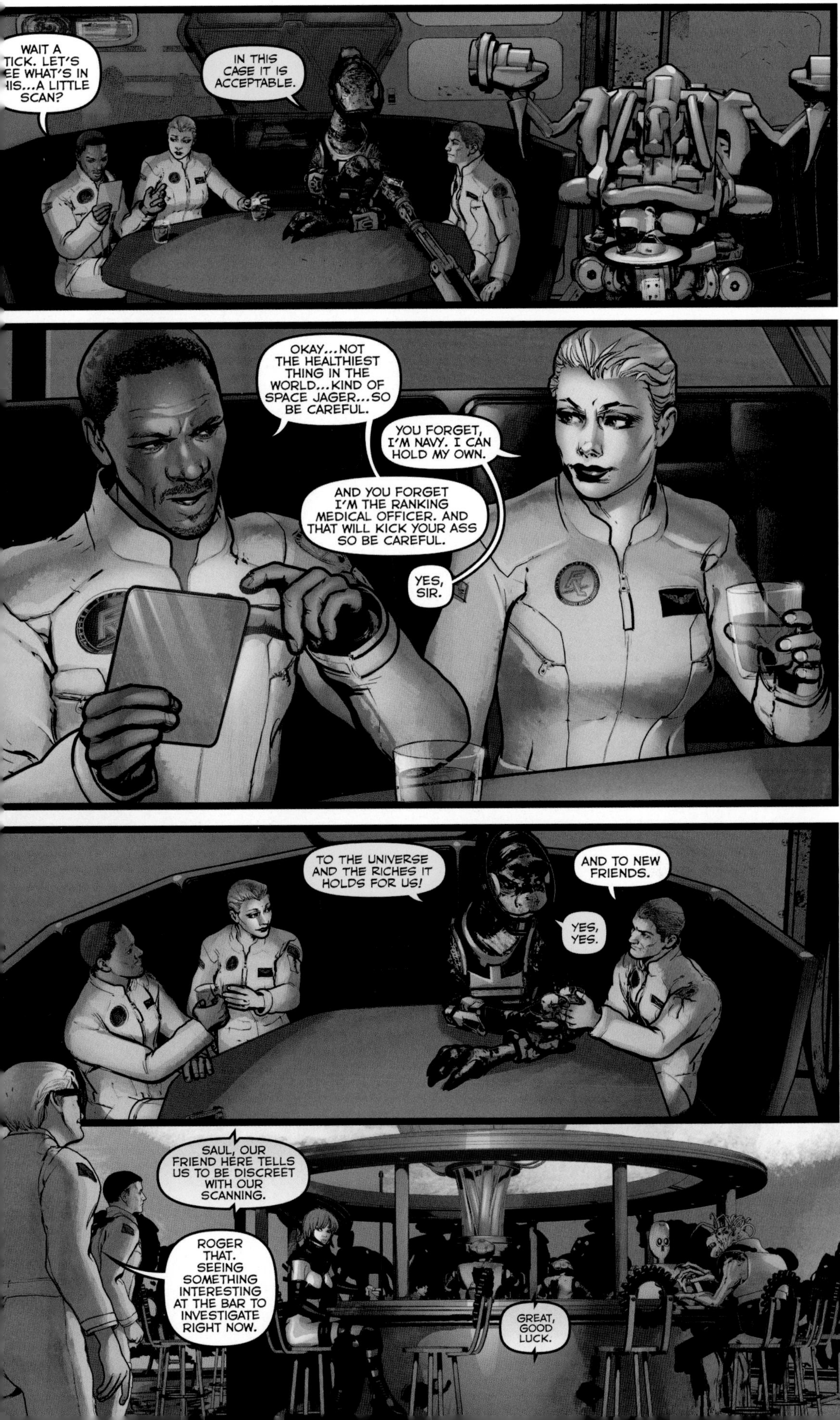
WAIT A
TICK. LET'S
EE WHAT'S IN
IIS...A LITTLE
SCAN?
IN THIS
CASE IT IS
ACCEPTABLE.
OKAY...NOT THE HEALTHIEST THING IN THE WORLD...KIND OF SPACE JAGER...SO BE CAREFUL.
YOU FORGET, I'M NAVY. I CAN HOLD MY OWN.
AND YOU FORGET I'M THE RANKING MEDICAL OFFICER. AND THAT WILL KICK YOUR ASS SO BE CAREFUL.
YES, SIR.
TO THE UNIVERSE AND THE RICHES IT HOLDS FOR US!
AND TO NEW FRIENDS.
YES, YES.
SAUL, OUR FRIEND HERE TELLS US TO BE DISCREET WITH OUR SCANNING.
ROGER THAT. SEEING SOMETHING INTERESTING AT THE BAR TO INVESTIGATE RIGHT NOW.
GREAT, GOOD LUCK.

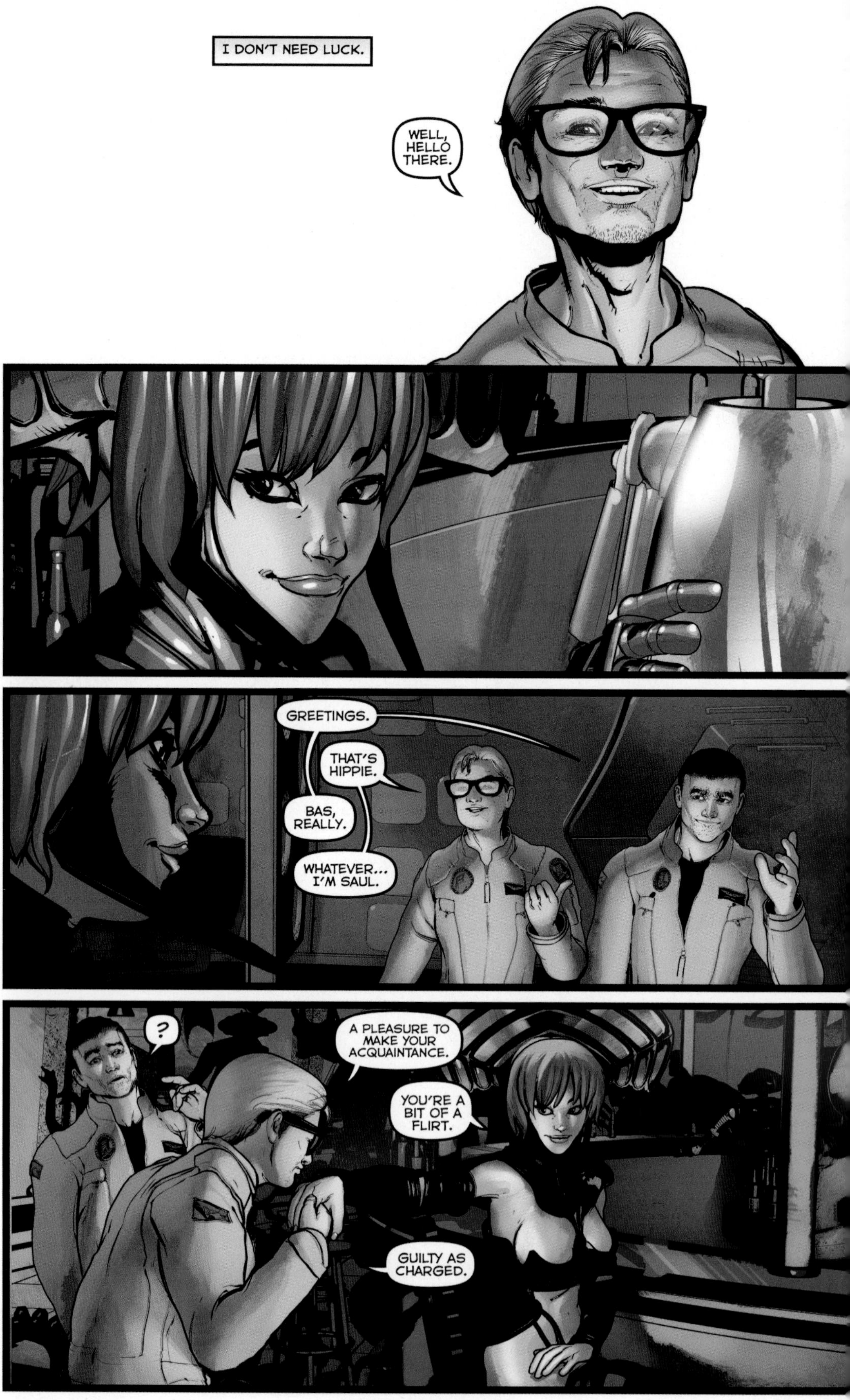

I DON'T NEED LUCK.
WELL, HELLO THERE.
GREETINGS.
THAT'S HIPPIE.
BAS, REALLY.
WHATEVER... I'M SAUL.
?
A PLEASURE TO MAKE YOUR ACQUAINTANCE.
YOU'RE A BIT OF A FLIRT.
GUILTY AS CHARGED.

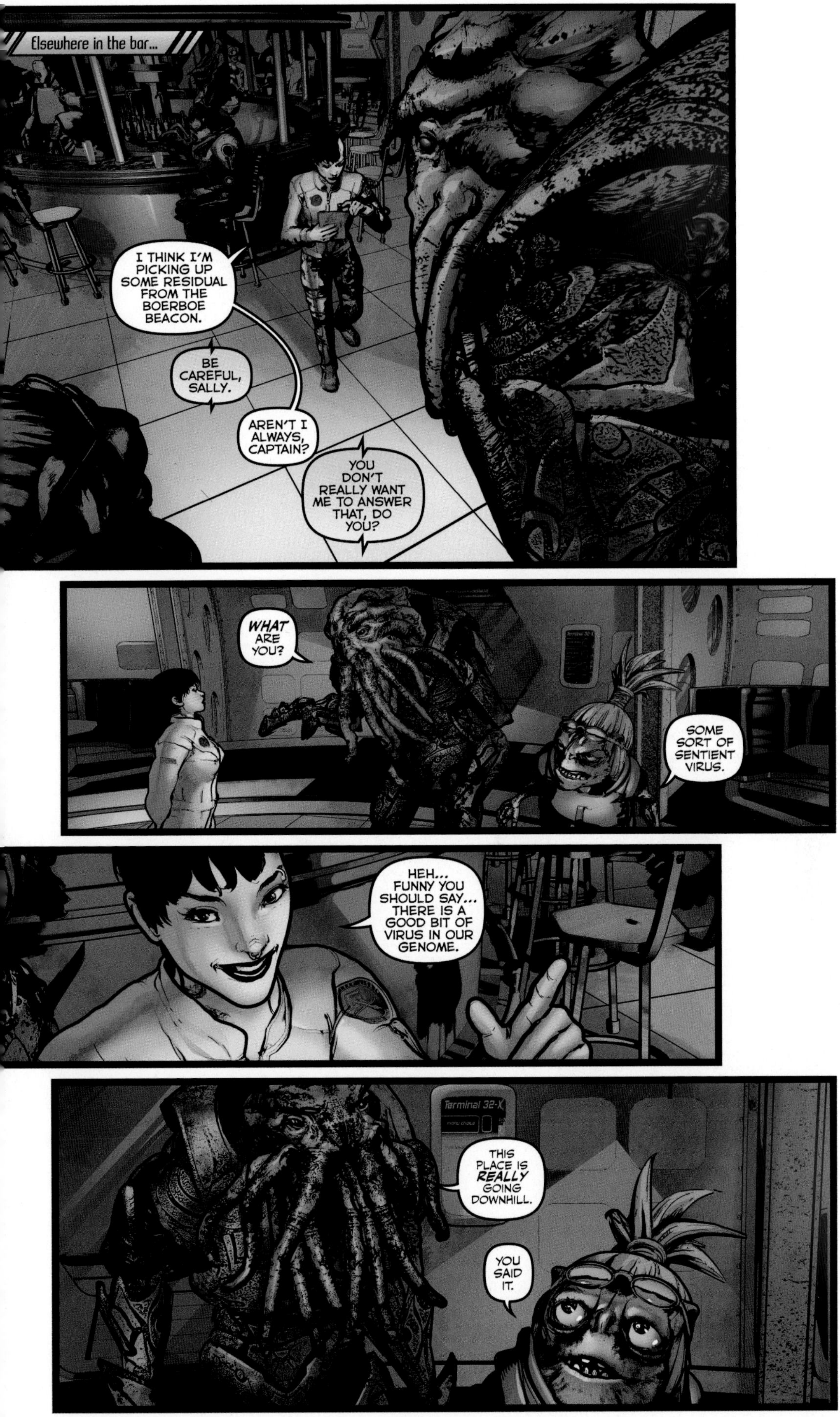
Elsewhere in the bar...
I THINK I'M PICKING UP SOME RESIDUAL FROM THE BOERBOE BEACON.
BE CAREFUL, SALLY.
AREN'T I ALWAYS, CAPTAIN?
YOU DON'T REALLY WANT ME TO ANSWER THAT, DO YOU?
WHAT ARE YOU?
SOME SORT OF SENTIENT VIRUS.
HEH... FUNNY YOU SHOULD SAY... THERE IS A GOOD BIT OF VIRUS IN OUR GENOME.
Terminal 32-X
THIS PLACE IS REALLY GOING DOWNHILL.
YOU SAID IT.

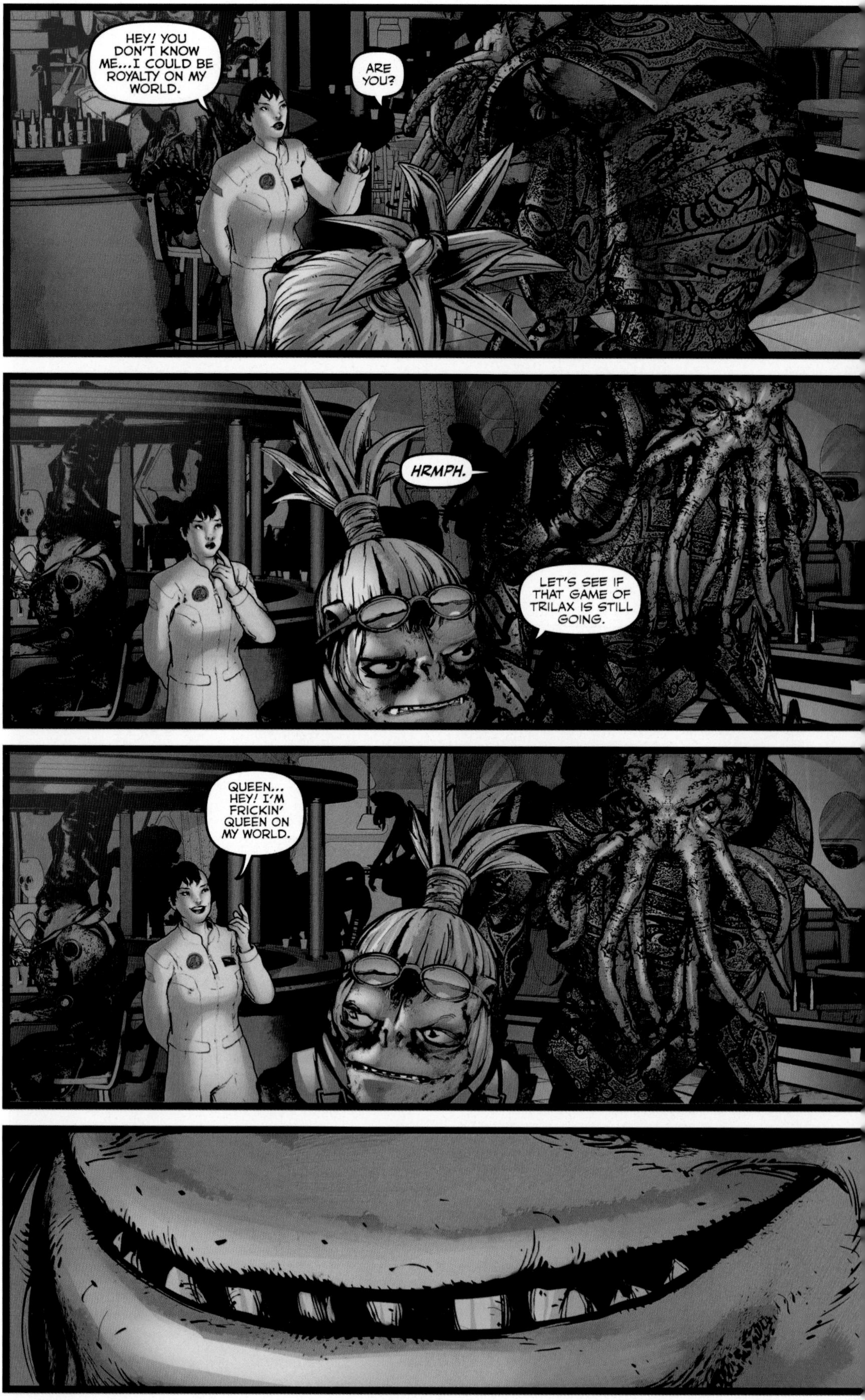
HEY! YOU DON'T KNOW ME...I COULD BE ROYALTY ON MY WORLD.
ARE YOU?
HRMPH.
LET'S SEE IF THAT GAME OF TRILAX IS STILL GOING.
QUEEN... HEY! I'M FRICKIN' QUEEN ON MY WORLD.

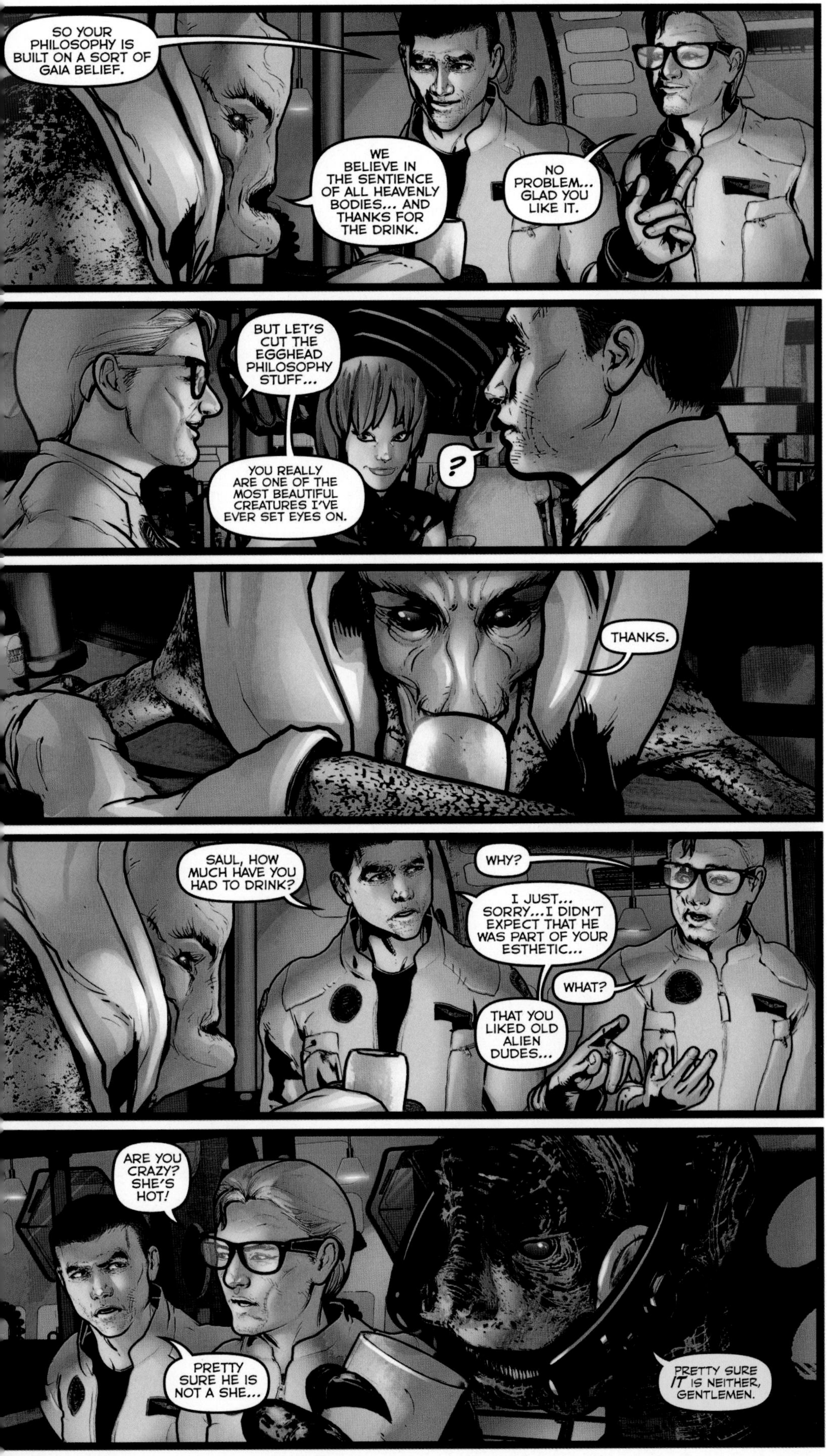
SO YOUR PHILOSOPHY IS BUILT ON A SORT OF GAIA BELIEF.
WE BELIEVE IN THE SENTIENCE OF ALL HEAVENLY BODIES... AND THANKS FOR THE DRINK.
NO PROBLEM... GLAD YOU LIKE IT.
BUT LET'S CUT THE EGGHEAD PHILOSOPHY STUFF...
YOU REALLY ARE ONE OF THE MOST BEAUTIFUL CREATURES I'VE EVER SET EYES ON.
?
THANKS.
SAUL, HOW MUCH HAVE YOU HAD TO DRINK?
WHY?
I JUST... SORRY...I DIDN'T EXPECT THAT HE WAS PART OF YOUR ESTHETIC...
WHAT?
THAT YOU LIKED OLD ALIEN DUDES...
ARE YOU CRAZY? SHE'S HOT!
PRETTY SURE HE IS NOT A SHE...
PRETTY SURE *IT* IS NEITHER, GENTLEMEN.

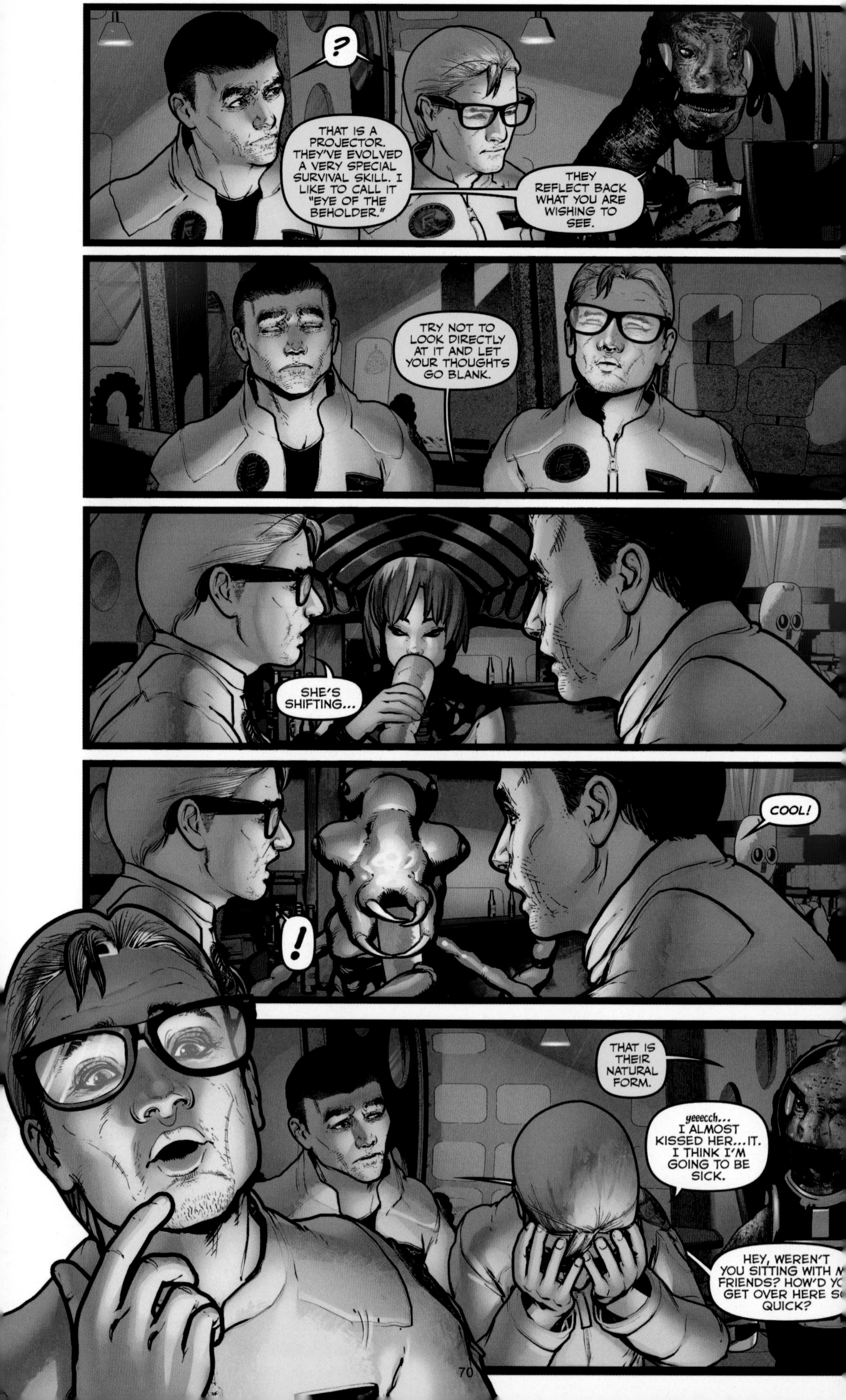
?
THAT IS A PROJECTOR. THEY'VE EVOLVED A VERY SPECIAL SURVIVAL SKILL. I LIKE TO CALL IT "EYE OF THE BEHOLDER."
THEY REFLECT BACK WHAT YOU ARE WISHING TO SEE.
TRY NOT TO LOOK DIRECTLY AT IT AND LET YOUR THOUGHTS GO BLANK.
SHE'S SHIFTING...
COOL!
!
THAT IS THEIR NATURAL FORM.
yeeecch... I ALMOST KISSED HER...IT. I THINK I'M GOING TO BE SICK.
HEY, WEREN'T YOU SITTING WITH M FRIENDS? HOW'D YO GET OVER HERE S QUICK?

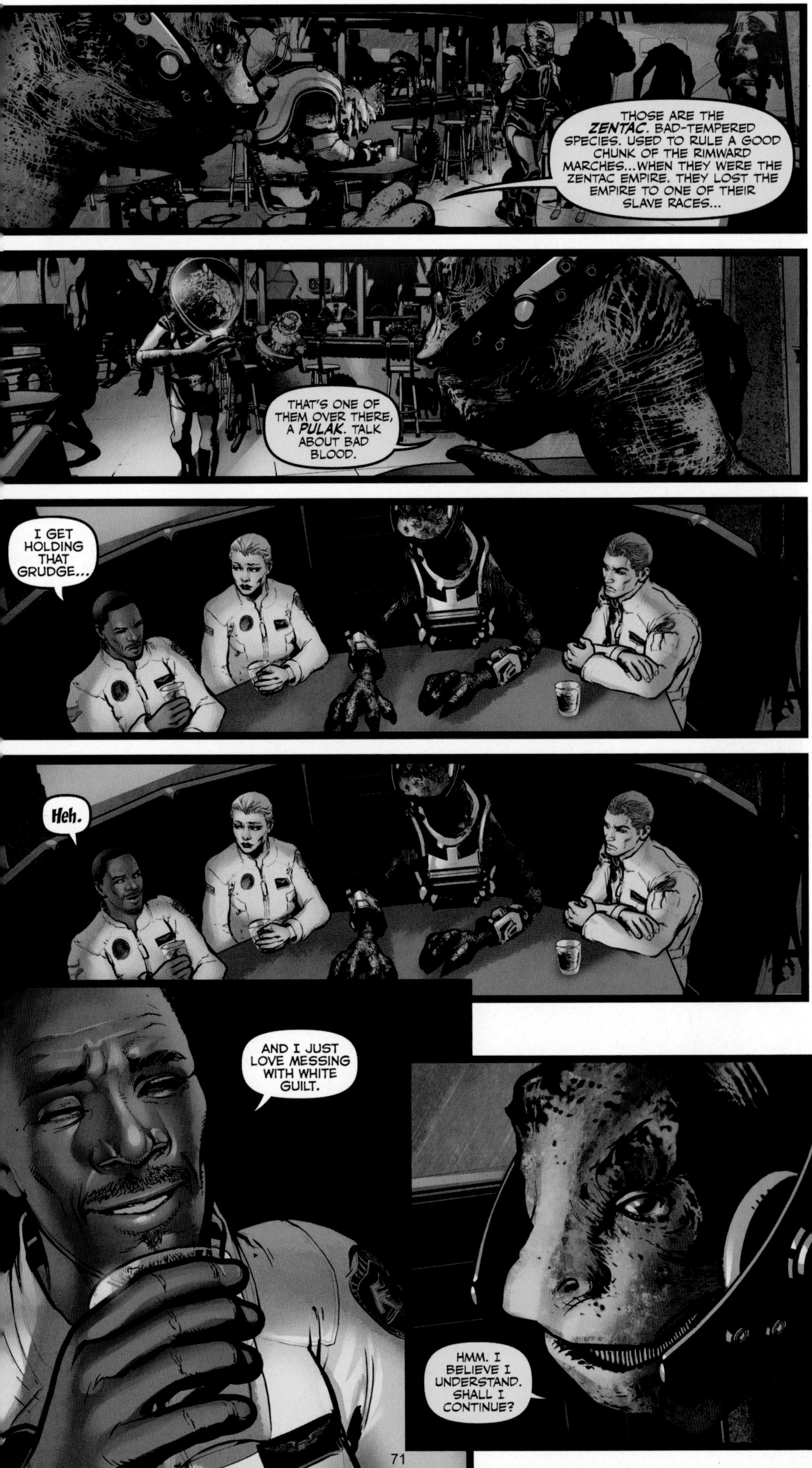
THOSE ARE THE ZENTAC. BAD-TEMPERED SPECIES. USED TO RULE A GOOD CHUNK OF THE RIMWARD MARCHES...WHEN THEY WERE THE ZENTAC EMPIRE. THEY LOST THE EMPIRE TO ONE OF THEIR SLAVE RACES...
THAT'S ONE OF THEM OVER THERE, A PULAK. TALK ABOUT BAD BLOOD.
I GET HOLDING THAT GRUDGE...
Heh.
AND I JUST LOVE MESSING WITH WHITE GUILT.
HMM. I BELIEVE I UNDERSTAND. SHALL I CONTINUE?

WELL, THOSE ARE *EFREETI*. BE CAREFUL, THEY ARE FROM A HIGH G WORLD...VERY STRONG AND THEY TEND TO BE MOSTLY INEBRIATED.

AND IT'S RARE TO SEE A *BULBOUS*...THEY ARE ALMOST FORERUNNER AGE.

FORERUNNER?

THOSE WHO WERE HERE WHEN OUR SPECIES WERE ALL STILL SINGLE CELLS, OR EVEN LONG BEFORE THAT. YOU CAN FIND EVIDENCE ALL AROUND.

SOME HAD TECHNOLOGY THAT MADE THEM SEEM LIKE GODS...SOME EVEN PRETENDED TO BE GODS. OR MAYBE THEY REALLY BELIEVED IT...

THE EFREETI TRAVEL USING ONE OF THE FORERUNNERS' GATE SYSTEMS.... HUNDREDS OF THOUSANDS OF YEARS OLD.

IF I MAY ASK, WHAT METHOD DO YOU USE FOR SPACE TRAVEL?

WE'VE BEEN CALLING IT A SLIPSTREAM DRIVE. BASICALLY, THE SHIP SHIFTS INTO SUBSPACE THEN COMES OUT WHEN WE REACH OUR DESTINATION. YOU SEE IN SUBSPACE--

NO NEED FOR AN EXPLANATION. I AM FAMILIAR WITH THAT METHOD.

HOW MANY WAYS ARE THERE?

DOZENS. BUT THE MOST COMMON ARE ARTIFICIAL WORM HOLES...

LIKE THE GATES, OR WARP OR YOUR METHOD. HAVE YOU RUN INTO ANYTHING YET IN SUBSPACE?

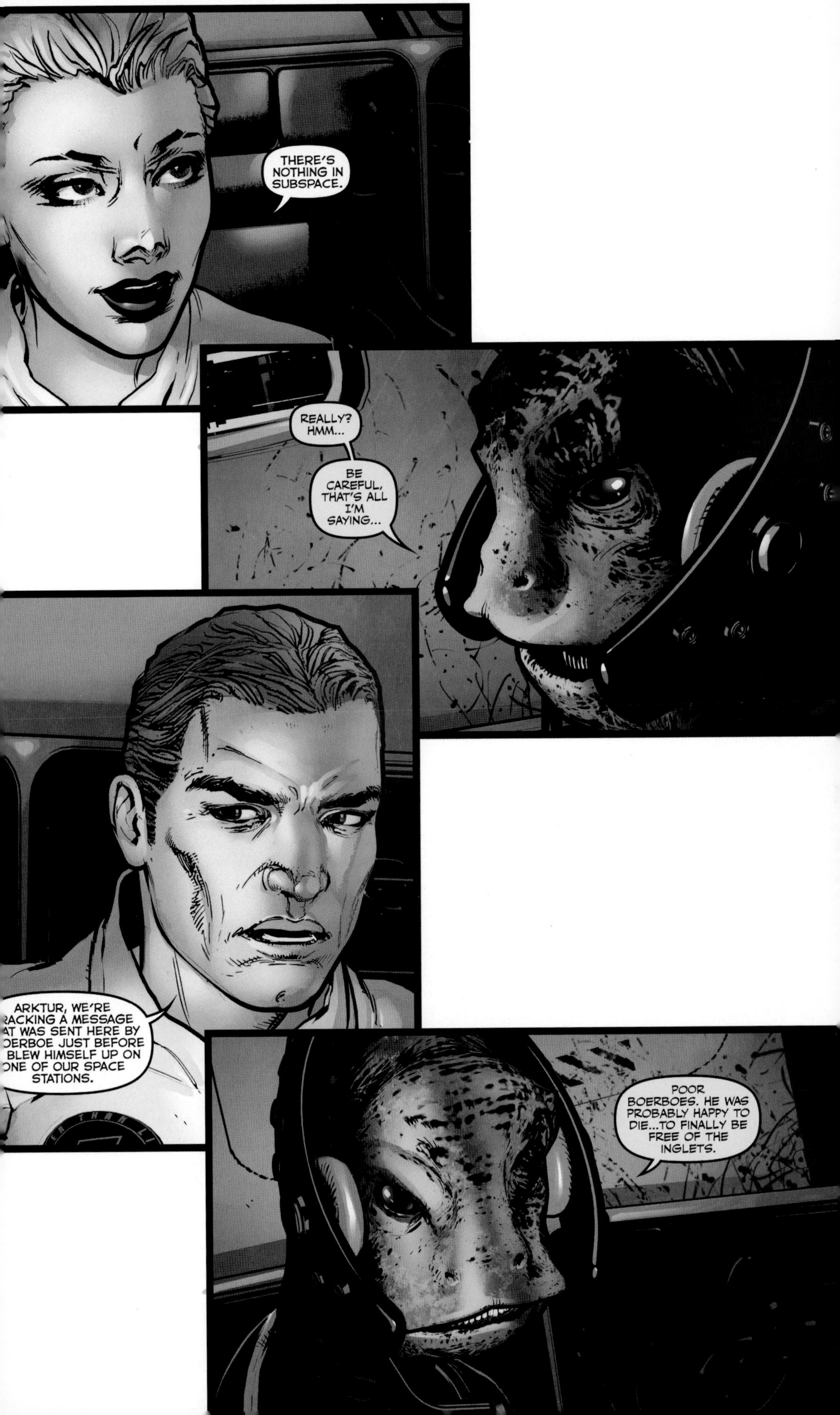
THERE'S NOTHING IN SUBSPACE.
REALLY? HMM...
BE CAREFUL, THAT'S ALL I'M SAYING...
ARKTUR, WE'RE RACKING A MESSAGE AT WAS SENT HERE BY OERBOE JUST BEFORE BLEW HIMSELF UP ON ONE OF OUR SPACE STATIONS.
POOR BOERBOES. HE WAS PROBABLY HAPPY TO DIE...TO FINALLY BE FREE OF THE INGLETS.

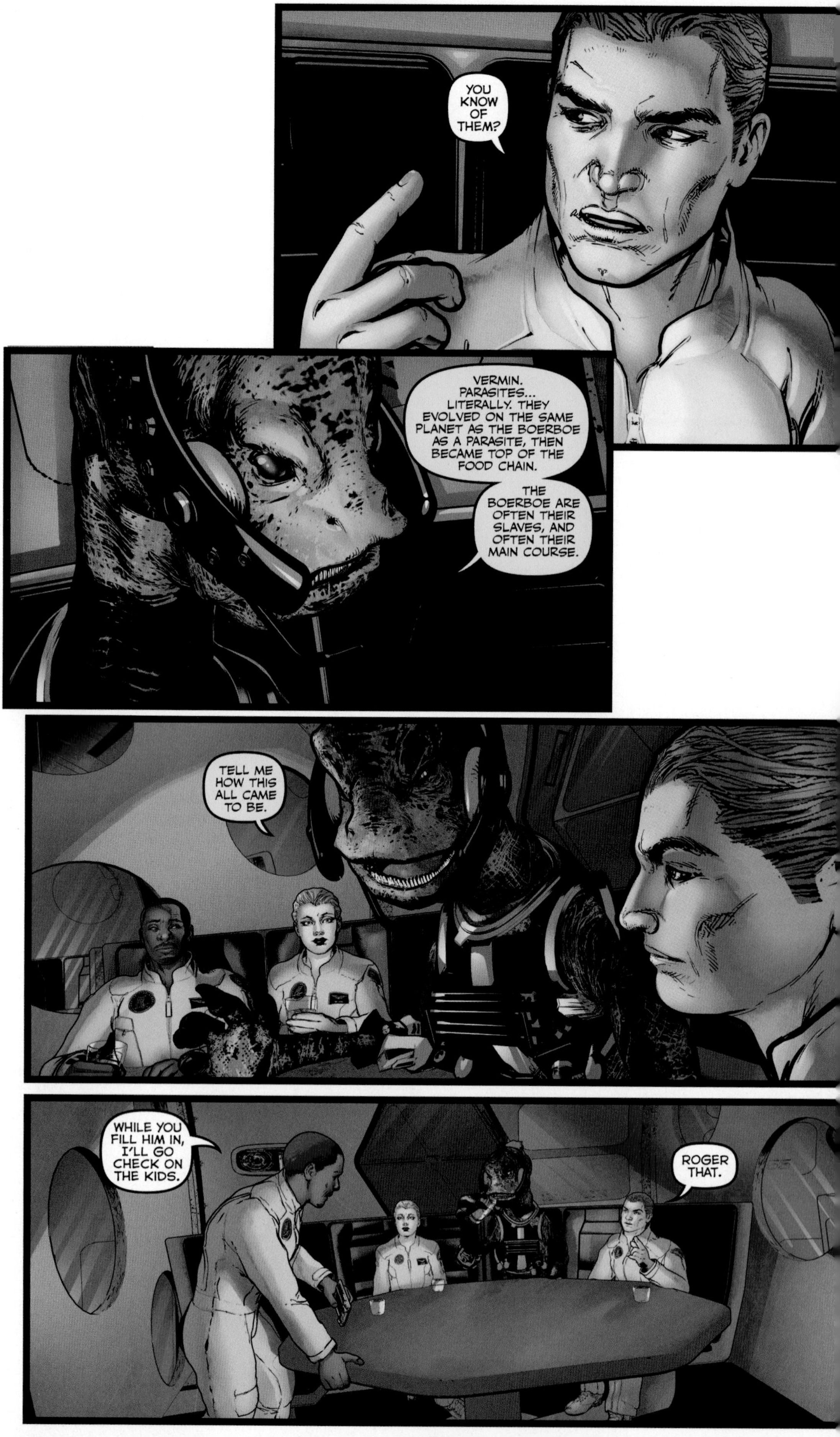
YOU KNOW OF THEM?
VERMIN. PARASITES... LITERALLY. THEY EVOLVED ON THE SAME PLANET AS THE BOERBOE AS A PARASITE, THEN BECAME TOP OF THE FOOD CHAIN.
THE BOERBOE ARE OFTEN THEIR SLAVES, AND OFTEN THEIR MAIN COURSE.
TELL ME HOW THIS ALL CAME TO BE.
WHILE YOU FILL HIM IN, I'LL GO CHECK ON THE KIDS.
ROGER THAT.

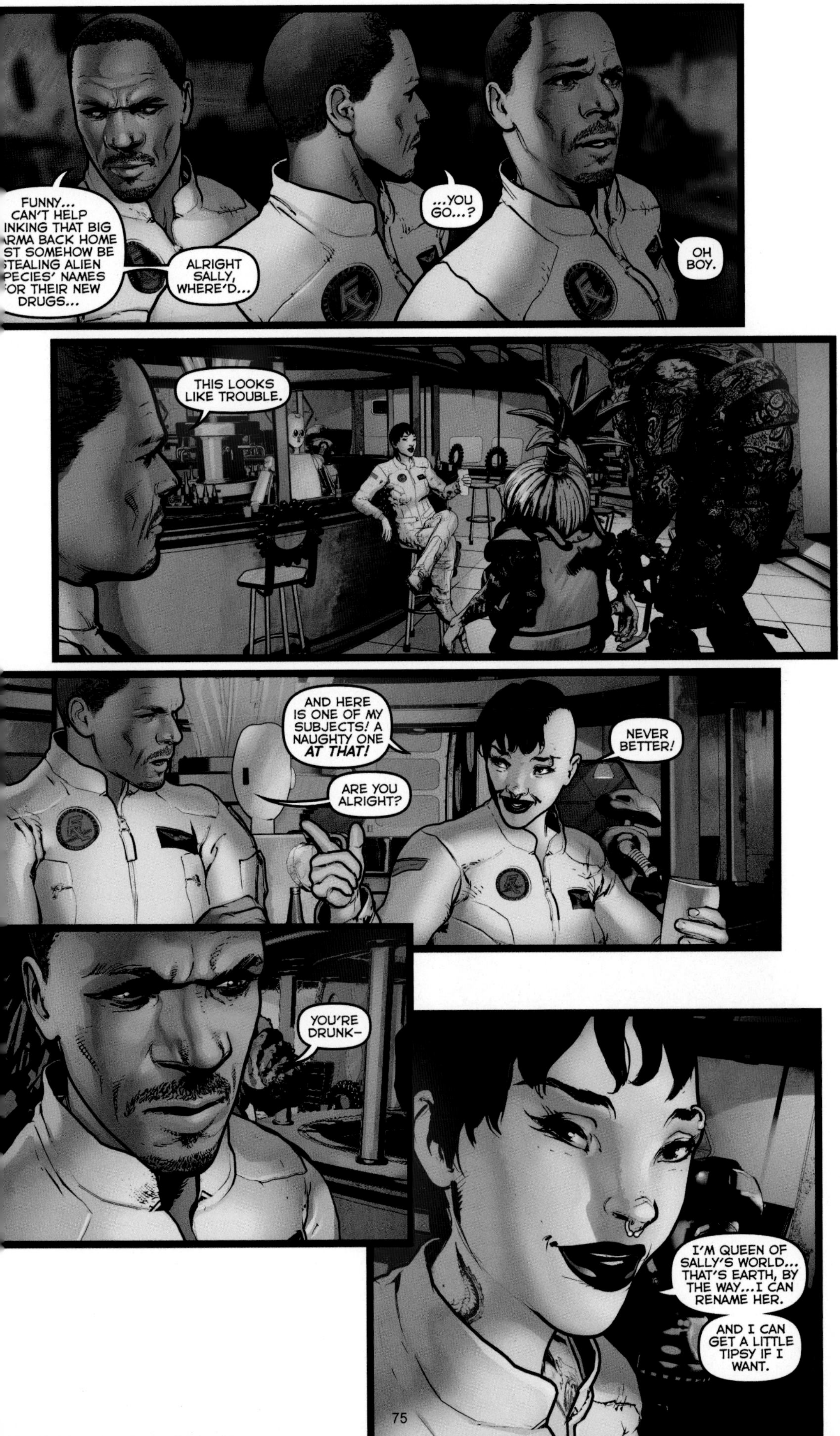
FUNNY... CAN'T HELP INKING THAT BIG ARMA BACK HOME ST SOMEHOW BE STEALING ALIEN PECIES' NAMES FOR THEIR NEW DRUGS...
ALRIGHT SALLY, WHERE'D...
...YOU GO...?
OH BOY.
THIS LOOKS LIKE TROUBLE.
AND HERE IS ONE OF MY SUBJECTS! A NAUGHTY ONE *AT THAT!*
ARE YOU ALRIGHT?
NEVER BETTER!
YOU'RE DRUNK–
I'M QUEEN OF SALLY'S WORLD... THAT'S EARTH, BY THE WAY...I CAN RENAME HER.
AND I CAN GET A LITTLE TIPSY IF I WANT.

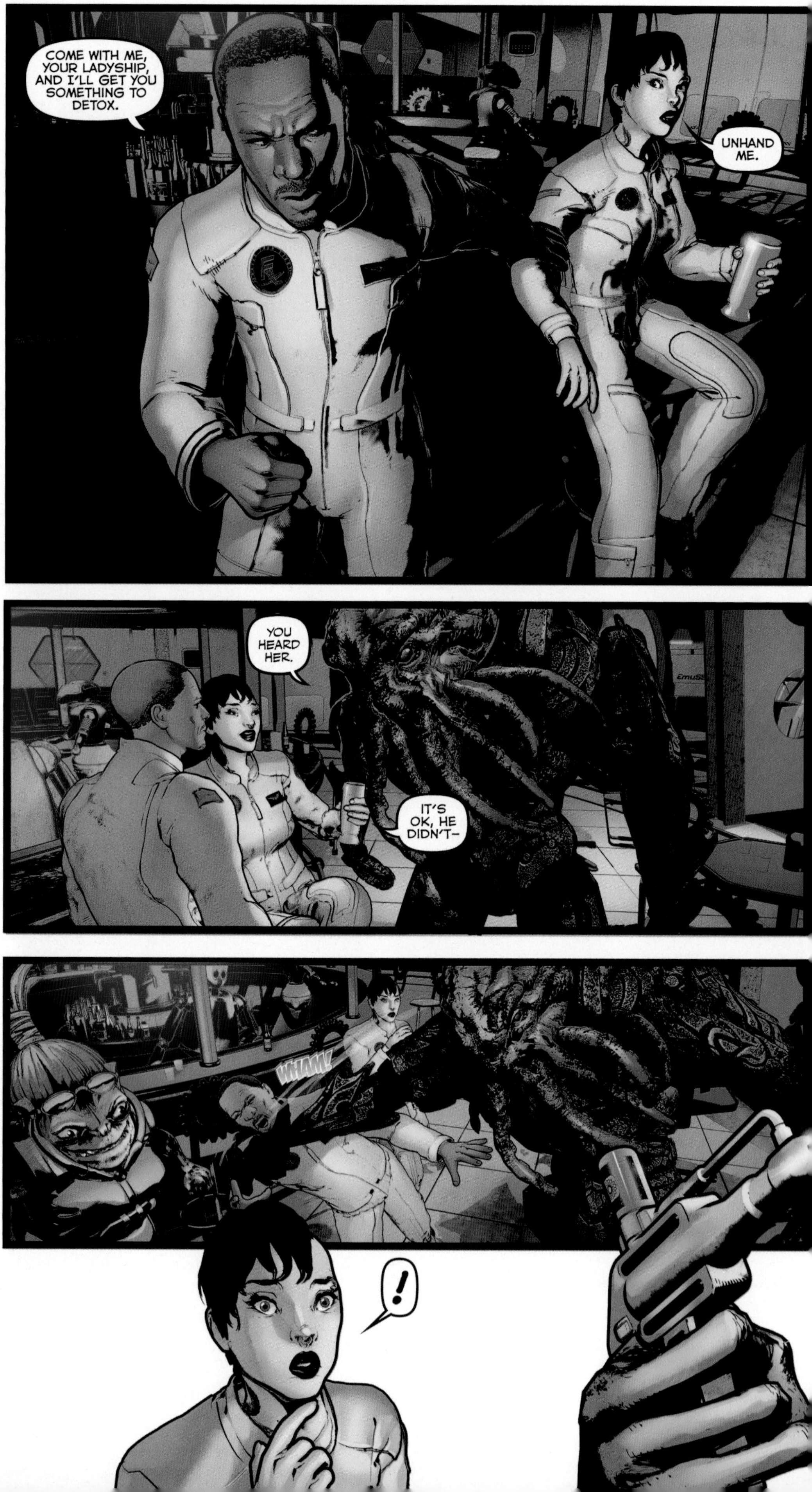
COME WITH ME, YOUR LADYSHIP, AND I'LL GET YOU SOMETHING TO DETOX.
UNHAND ME.
YOU HEARD HER.
IT'S OK, HE DIDN'T–
WHAM!
!

NO, WAIT....FOR-- UGGGGGH....

SLEEP TIGHT, YOUR MAJESTY.

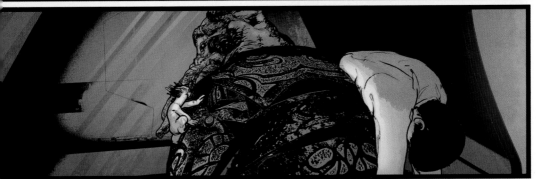

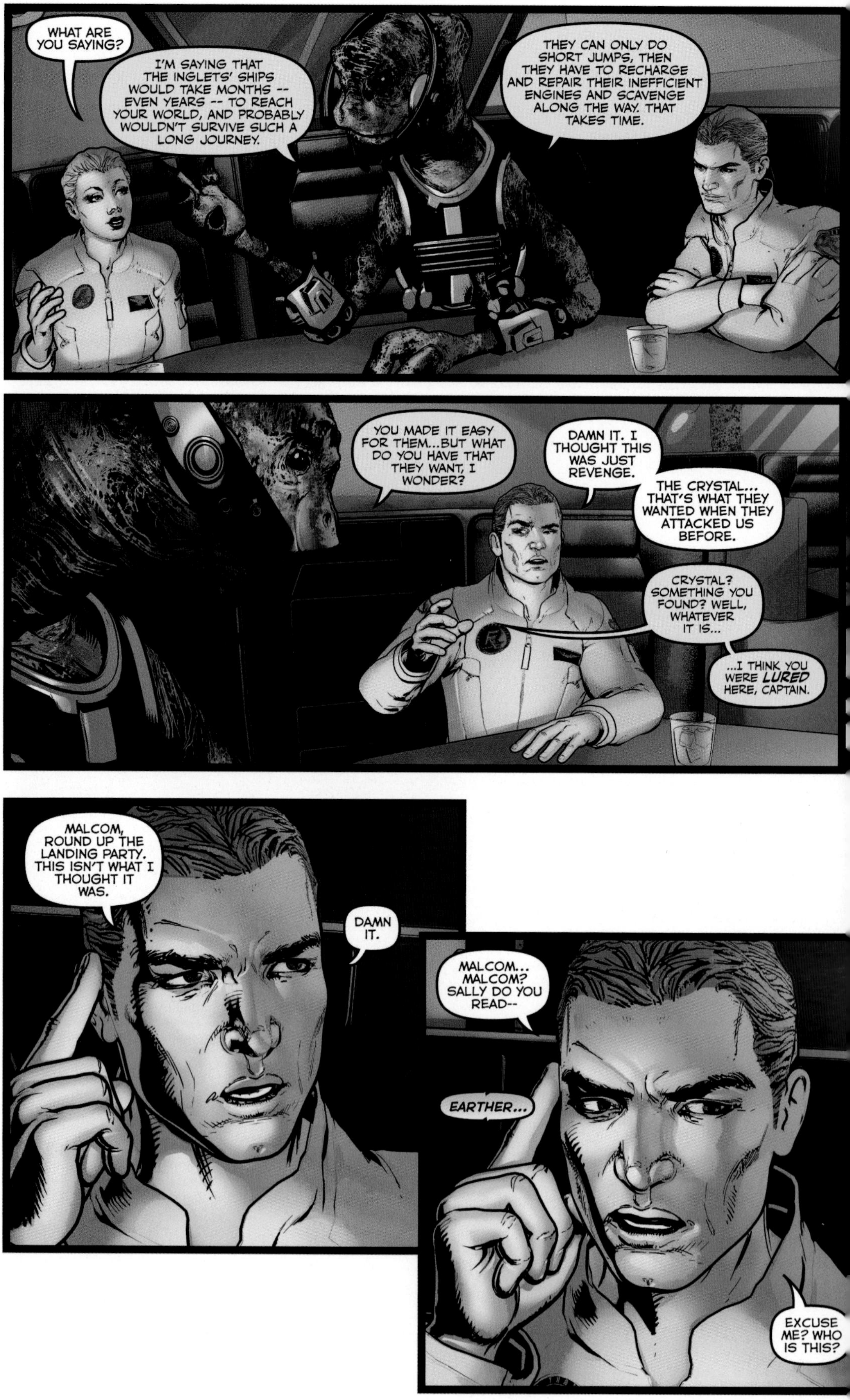
WHAT ARE YOU SAYING?
I'M SAYING THAT THE INGLETS' SHIPS WOULD TAKE MONTHS -- EVEN YEARS -- TO REACH YOUR WORLD, AND PROBABLY WOULDN'T SURVIVE SUCH A LONG JOURNEY.
THEY CAN ONLY DO SHORT JUMPS, THEN THEY HAVE TO RECHARGE AND REPAIR THEIR INEFFICIENT ENGINES AND SCAVENGE ALONG THE WAY. THAT TAKES TIME.
YOU MADE IT EASY FOR THEM...BUT WHAT DO YOU HAVE THAT THEY WANT, I WONDER?
DAMN IT. I THOUGHT THIS WAS JUST REVENGE.
THE CRYSTAL... THAT'S WHAT THEY WANTED WHEN THEY ATTACKED US BEFORE.
CRYSTAL? SOMETHING YOU FOUND? WELL, WHATEVER IT IS...
...I THINK YOU WERE *LURED* HERE, CAPTAIN.
MALCOM, ROUND UP THE LANDING PARTY. THIS ISN'T WHAT I THOUGHT IT WAS.
DAMN IT.
MALCOM... MALCOM? SALLY DO YOU READ--
EARTHER...
EXCUSE ME? WHO IS THIS?

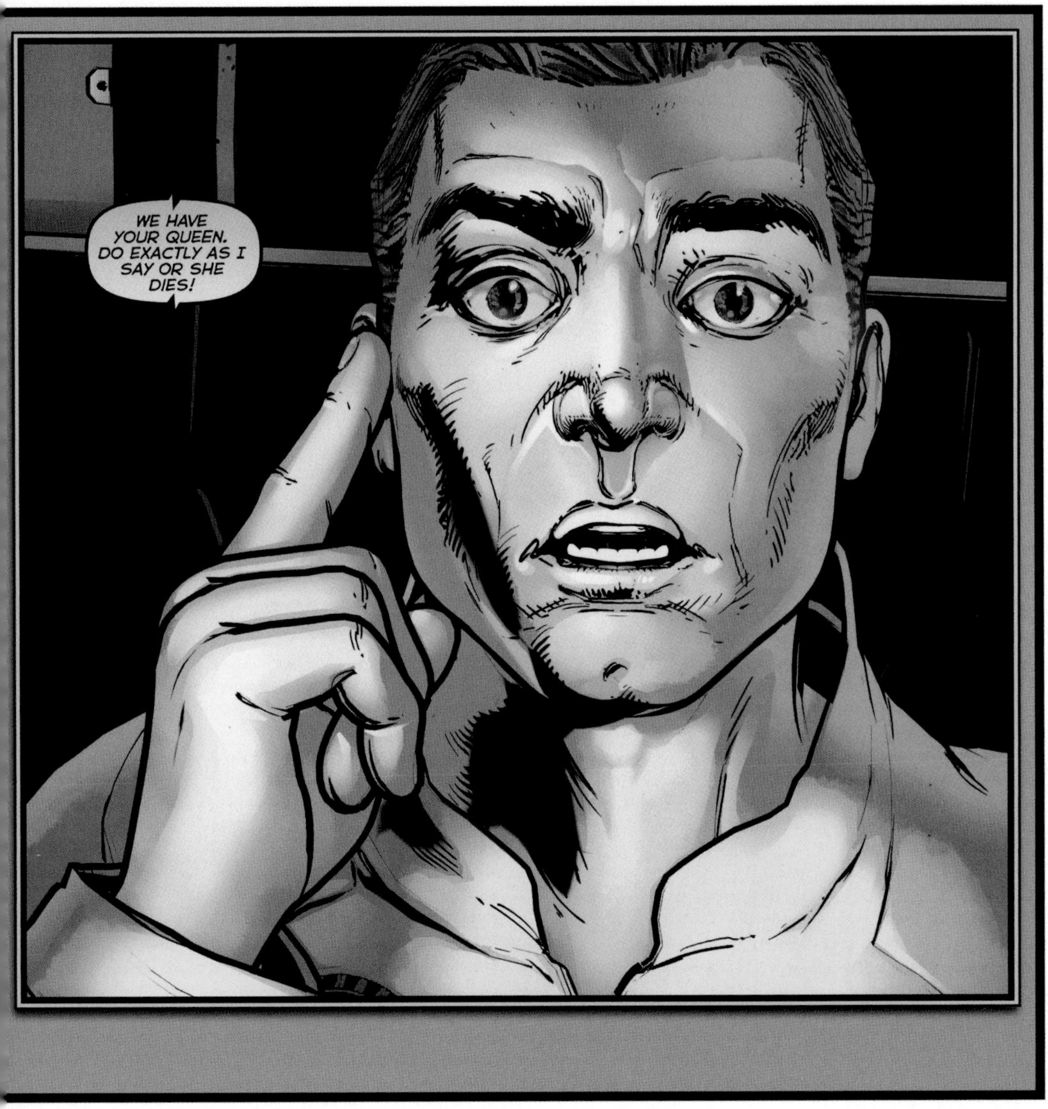
WE HAVE YOUR QUEEN. DO EXACTLY AS I SAY OR SHE DIES!

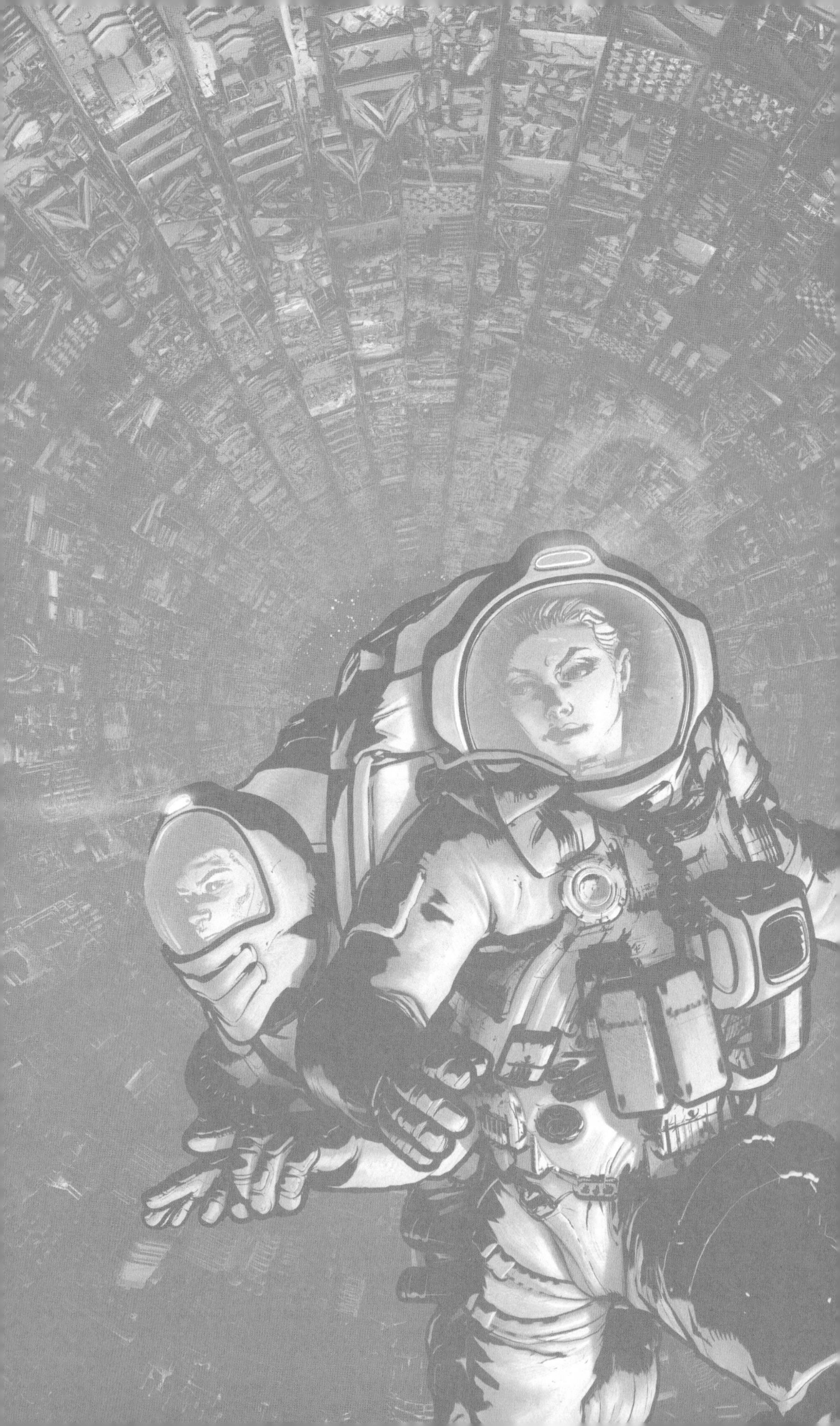

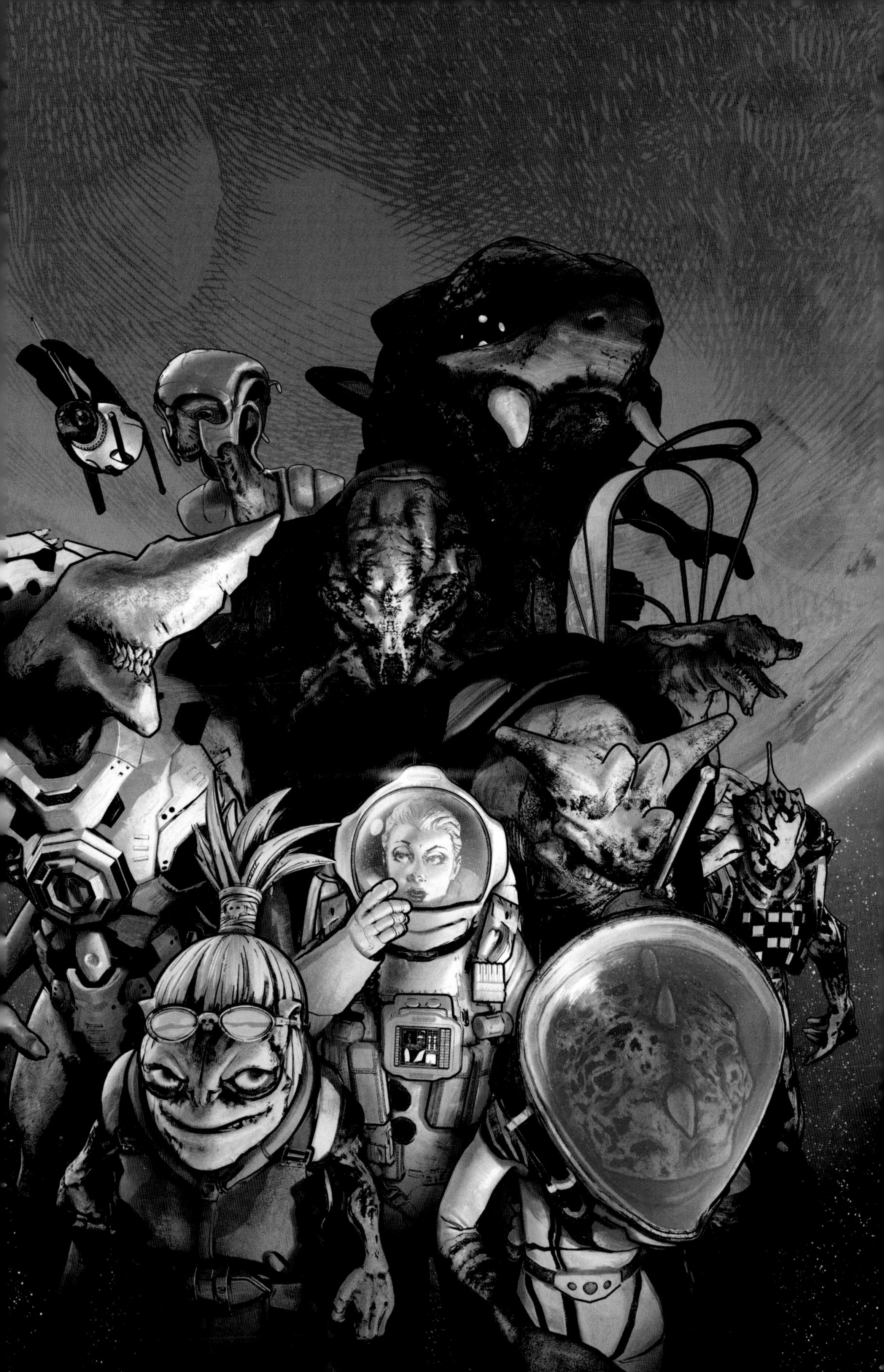

ISSUE 9

ugggh... SALLY...

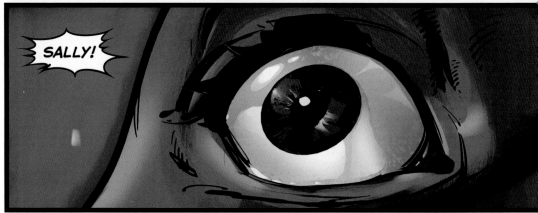

SALLY!

GLAD TO SEE YOU'RE BACK WITH US.

YOU HAVE A CONCUSSION AND FRACTURE. TAKE IT EASY, DOC.

YEAH...I CAN FEEL THAT. OwwW.

WHERE'S SALLY?

WE'RE SCANNING. NOTHING YET.

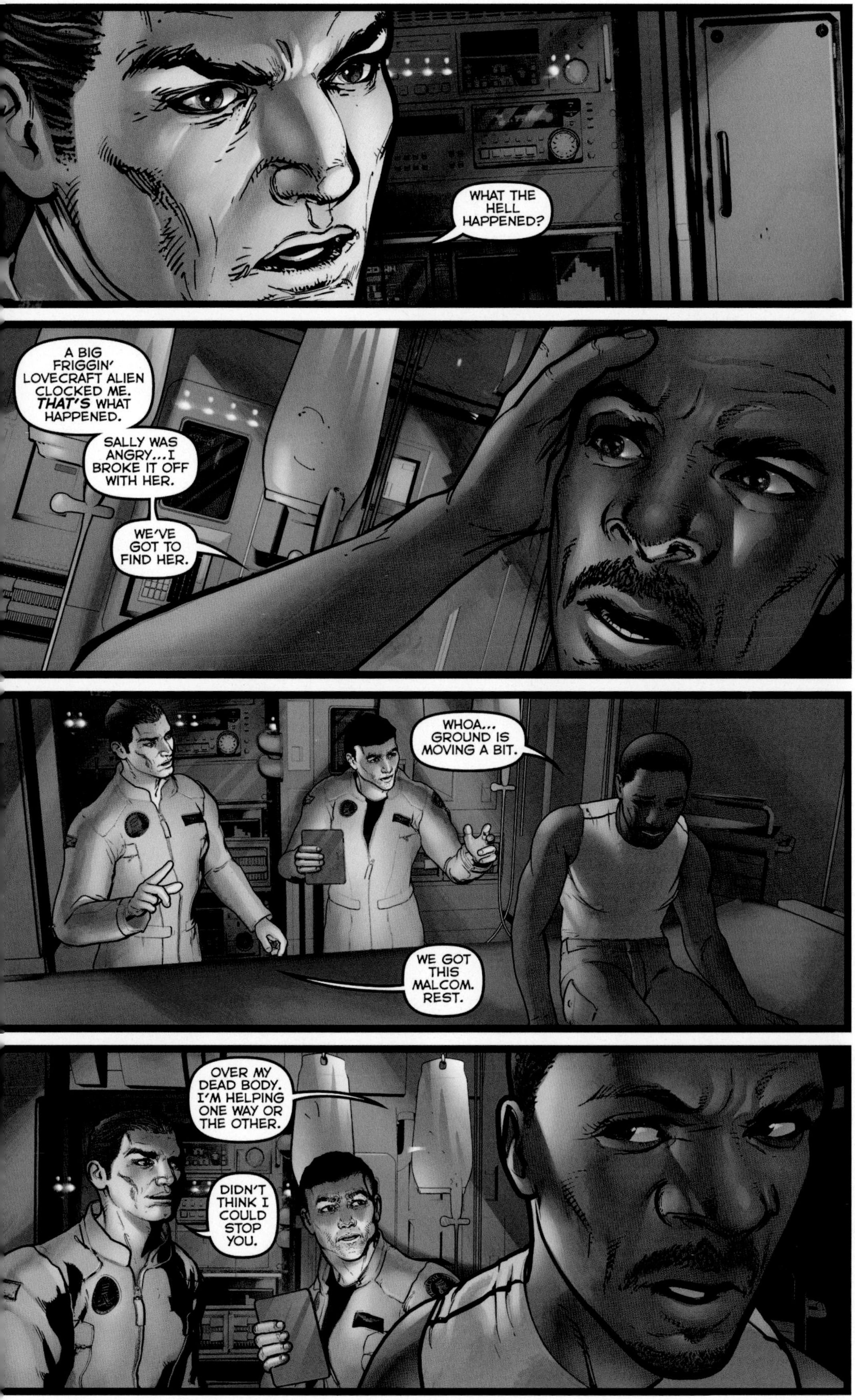

WHAT THE HELL HAPPENED?
A BIG FRIGGIN' LOVECRAFT ALIEN CLOCKED ME. *THAT'S* WHAT HAPPENED.
SALLY WAS ANGRY...I BROKE IT OFF WITH HER.
WE'VE GOT TO FIND HER.
WHOA... GROUND IS MOVING A BIT.
WE GOT THIS MALCOM. REST.
OVER MY DEAD BODY. I'M HELPING ONE WAY OR THE OTHER.
DIDN'T THINK I COULD STOP YOU.

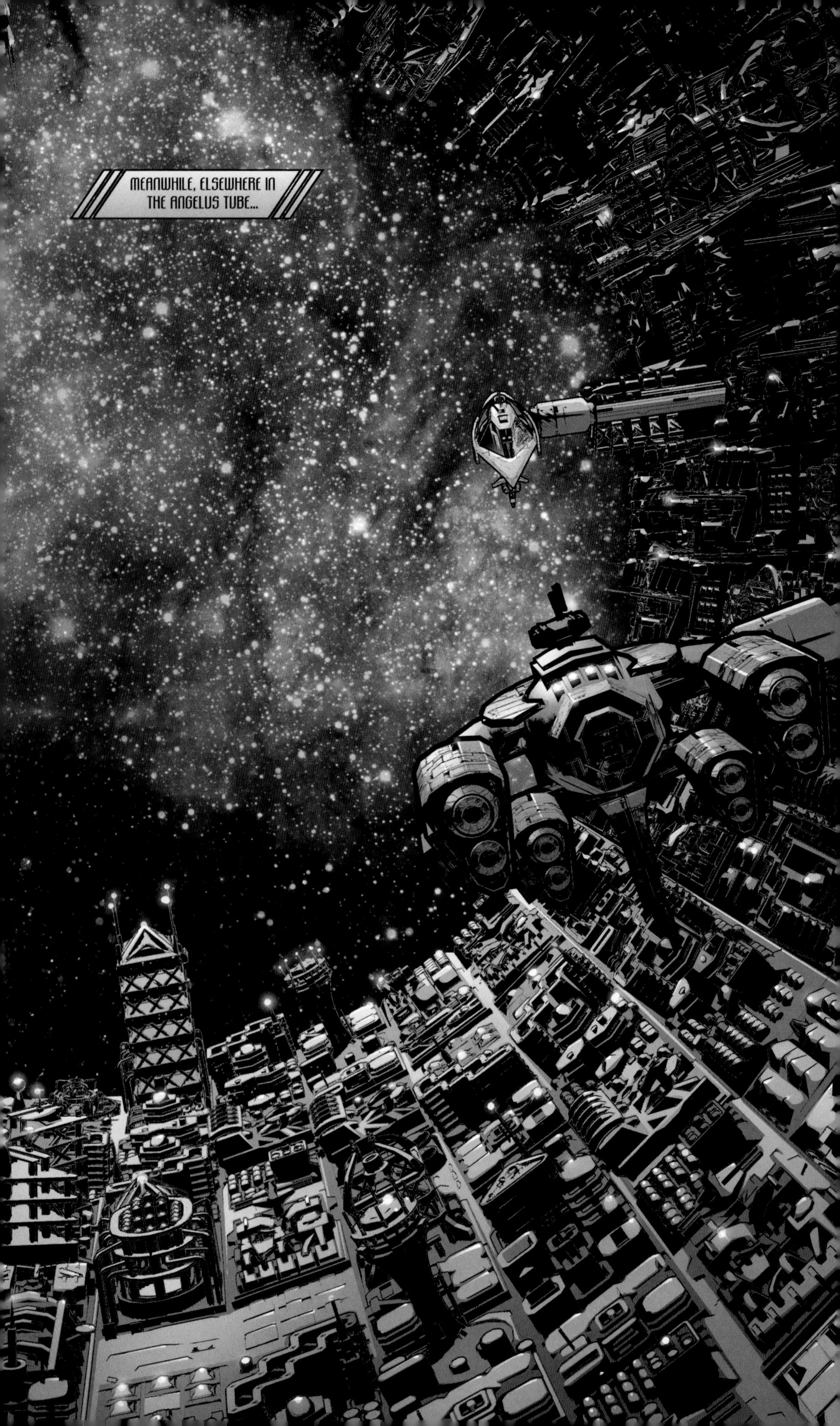
MEANWHILE, ELSEWHERE IN THE ANGELUS TUBE...

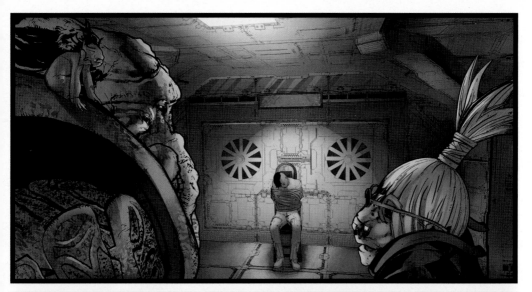

SO WHAT'S OUR STAKE?

YOU SAID YOU WANTED *SOMETHING* STOLEN...THEN WE'D GET OUR FEE.

YEAH, BUT THIS IS AN ALIEN QUEEN. OUR CUT SHOULD BE BIGGER...MUCH, *MUCH* BIGGER!

AGREED.

WHAT COULD BE BIGGER THAN THE RANSOM ON AN ALIEN QUEEN?

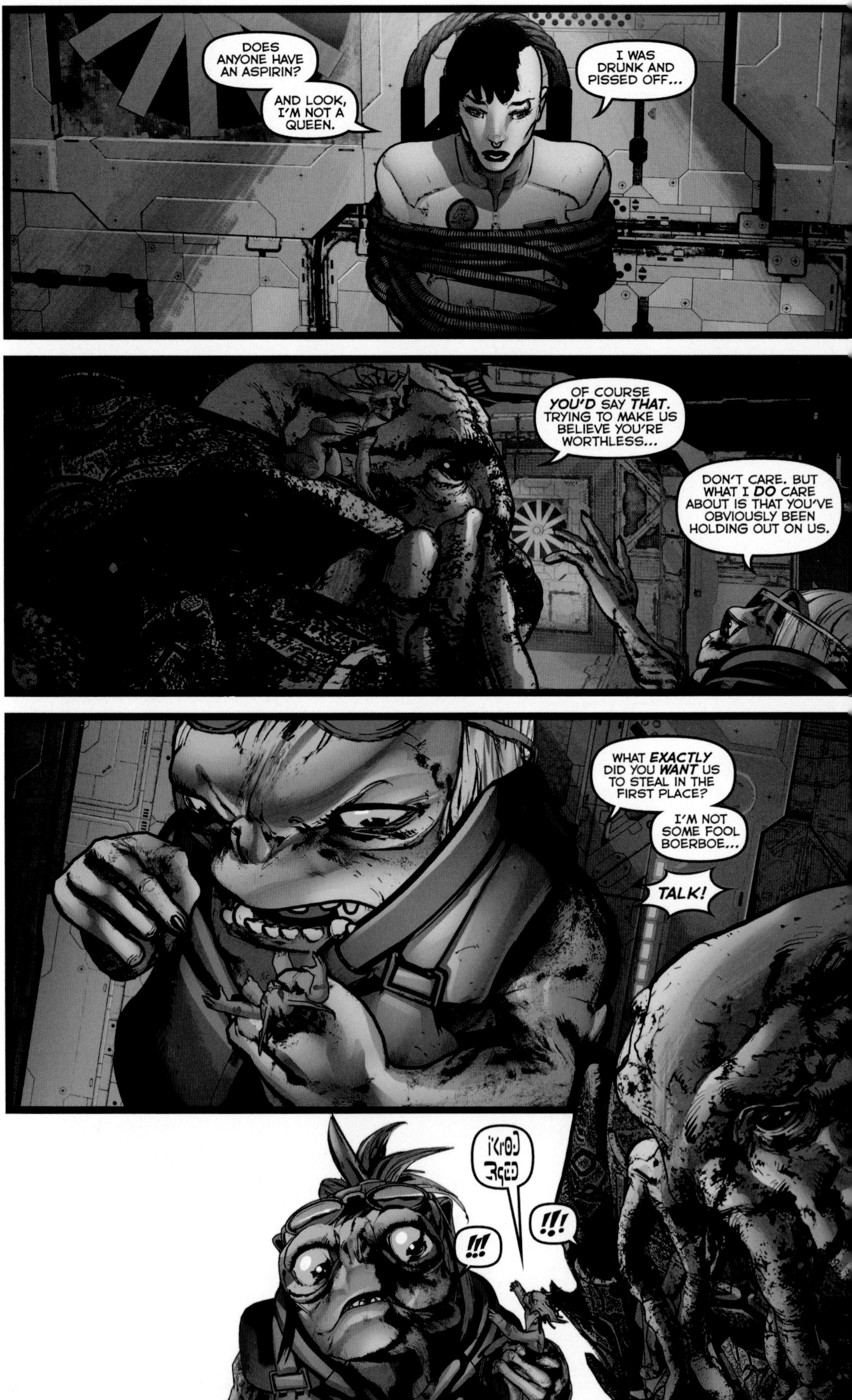
DOES ANYONE HAVE AN ASPIRIN?
AND LOOK, I'M NOT A QUEEN.
I WAS DRUNK AND PISSED OFF...
OF COURSE YOU'D SAY THAT. TRYING TO MAKE US BELIEVE YOU'RE WORTHLESS...
DON'T CARE. BUT WHAT I DO CARE ABOUT IS THAT YOU'VE OBVIOUSLY BEEN HOLDING OUT ON US.
WHAT EXACTLY DID YOU WANT US TO STEAL IN THE FIRST PLACE?
I'M NOT SOME FOOL BOERBOE...
TALK!
!!!
!!!

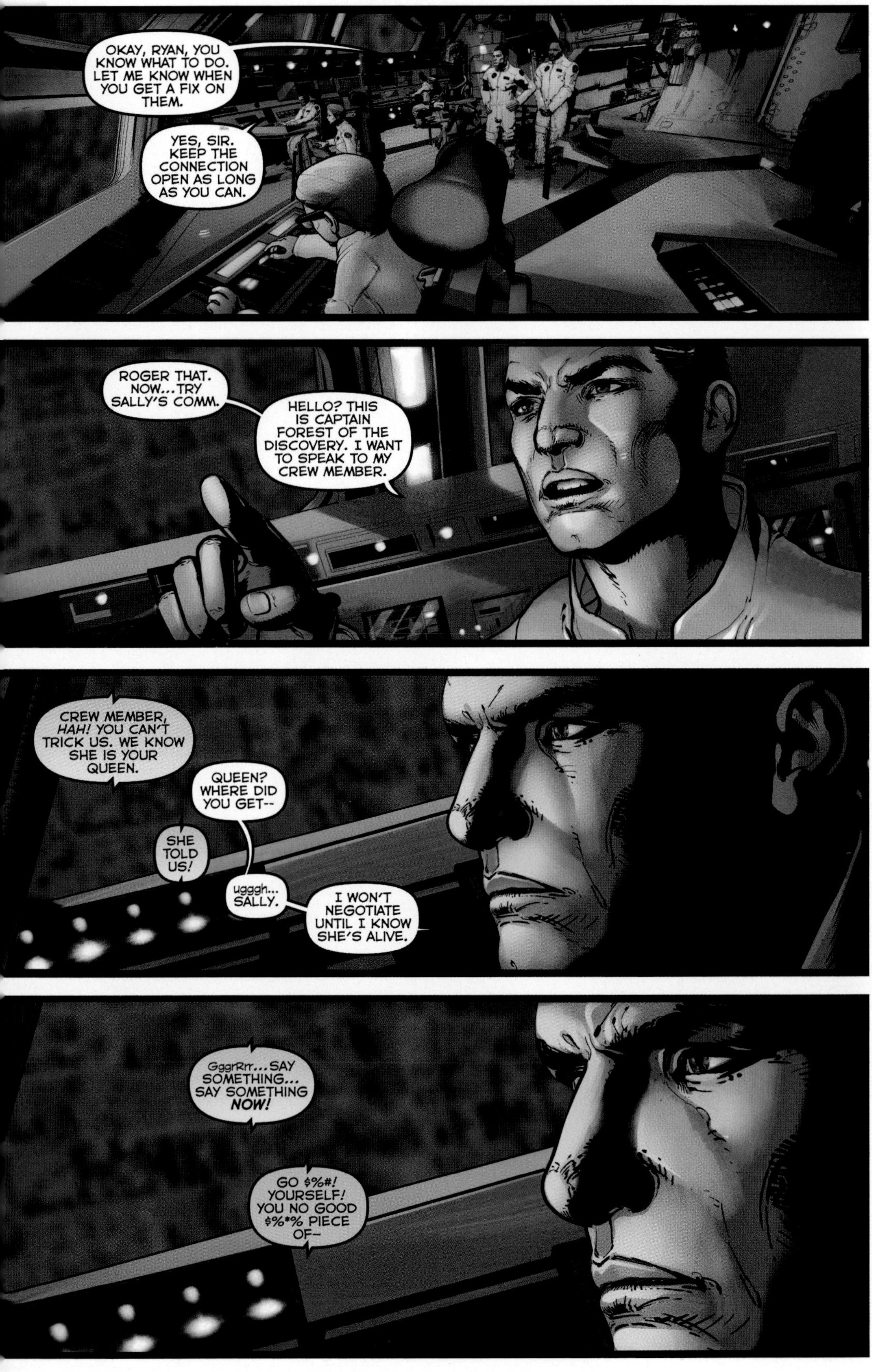
OKAY, RYAN, YOU KNOW WHAT TO DO. LET ME KNOW WHEN YOU GET A FIX ON THEM.
YES, SIR. KEEP THE CONNECTION OPEN AS LONG AS YOU CAN.
ROGER THAT. NOW...TRY SALLY'S COMM.
HELLO? THIS IS CAPTAIN FOREST OF THE DISCOVERY. I WANT TO SPEAK TO MY CREW MEMBER.
CREW MEMBER, *HAH!* YOU CAN'T TRICK US. WE KNOW SHE IS YOUR QUEEN.
QUEEN? WHERE DID YOU GET--
SHE TOLD US!
uggh... SALLY.
I WON'T NEGOTIATE UNTIL I KNOW SHE'S ALIVE.
GggrRrr...SAY SOMETHING... SAY SOMETHING **NOW!**
GO $%#! YOURSELF! YOU NO GOOD $%*% PIECE OF–

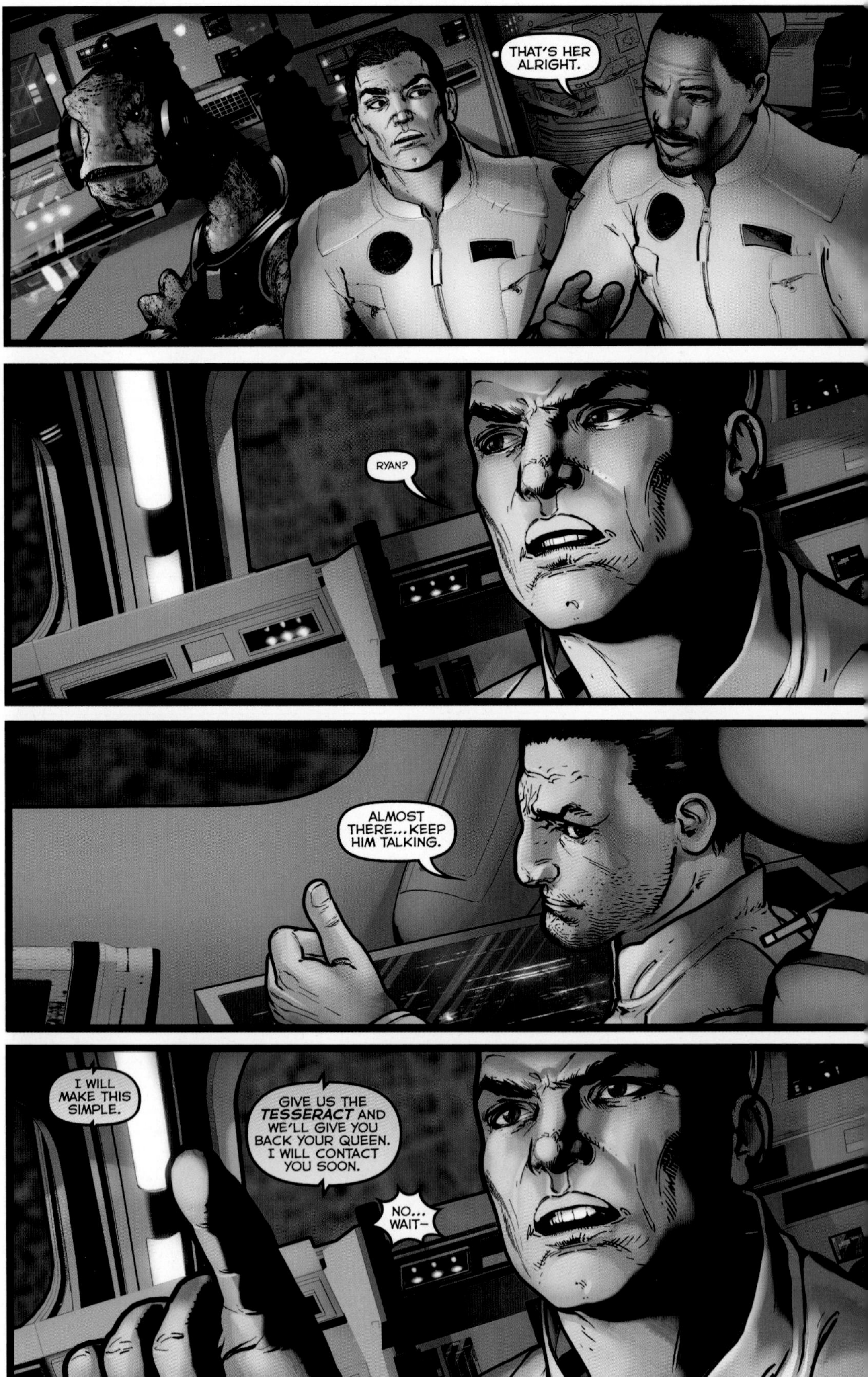

THAT'S HER ALRIGHT.
RYAN?
ALMOST THERE...KEEP HIM TALKING.
I WILL MAKE THIS SIMPLE.
GIVE US THE *TESSERACT* AND WE'LL GIVE YOU BACK YOUR QUEEN. I WILL CONTACT YOU SOON.
NO... WAIT—

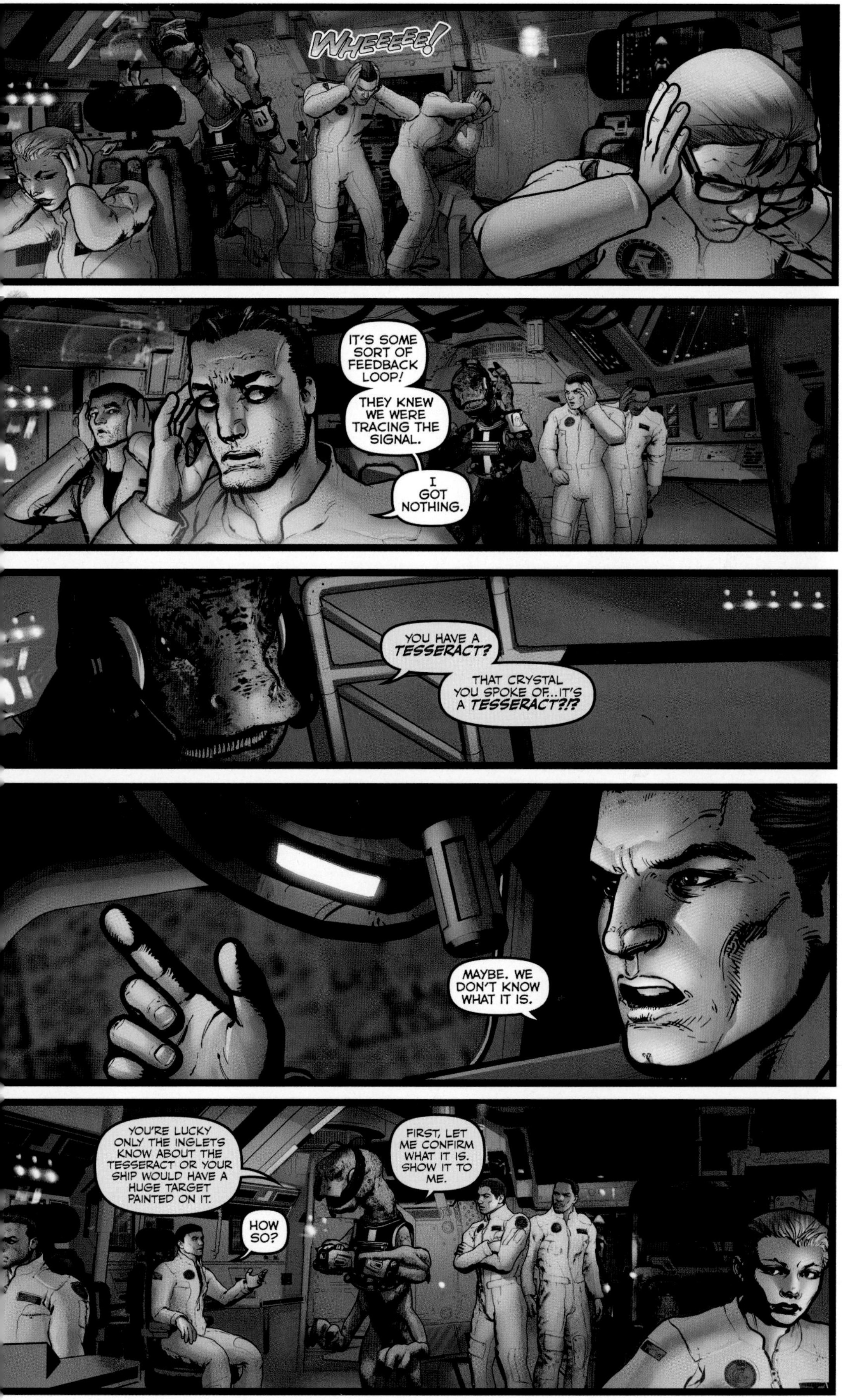
WHEEEEE!
IT'S SOME SORT OF FEEDBACK LOOP!
THEY KNEW WE WERE TRACING THE SIGNAL.
I GOT NOTHING.
YOU HAVE A TESSERACT?
THAT CRYSTAL YOU SPOKE OF...IT'S A TESSERACT?!?
MAYBE. WE DON'T KNOW WHAT IT IS.
YOU'RE LUCKY ONLY THE INGLETS KNOW ABOUT THE TESSERACT OR YOUR SHIP WOULD HAVE A HUGE TARGET PAINTED ON IT.
HOW SO?
FIRST, LET ME CONFIRM WHAT IT IS. SHOW IT TO ME.

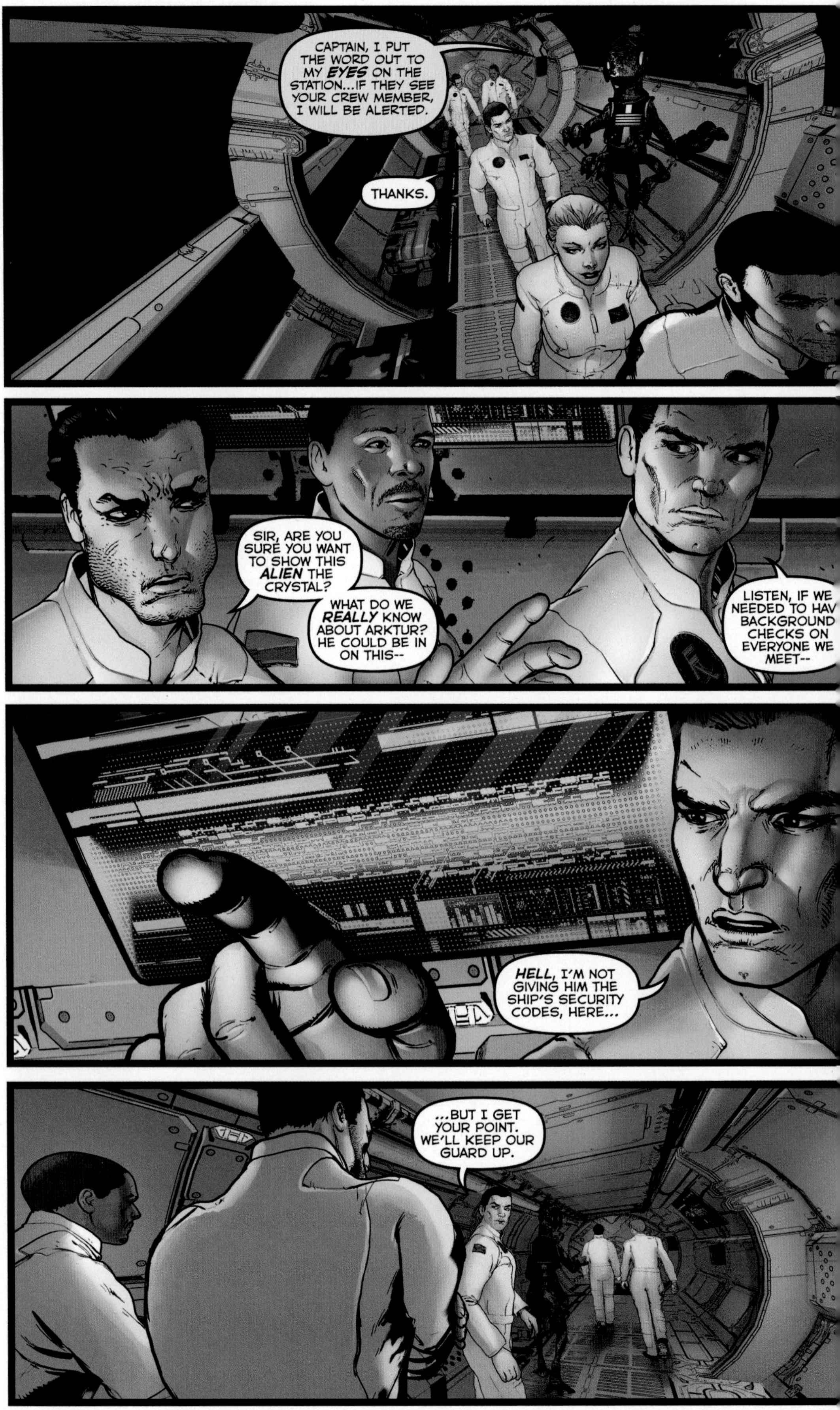
CAPTAIN, I PUT THE WORD OUT TO MY *EYES* ON THE STATION...IF THEY SEE YOUR CREW MEMBER, I WILL BE ALERTED.
THANKS.
SIR, ARE YOU SURE YOU WANT TO SHOW THIS *ALIEN* THE CRYSTAL?
WHAT DO WE *REALLY* KNOW ABOUT ARKTUR? HE COULD BE IN ON THIS--
LISTEN, IF WE NEEDED TO HAV BACKGROUND CHECKS ON EVERYONE WE MEET--
HELL, I'M NOT GIVING HIM THE SHIP'S SECURITY CODES, HERE...
...BUT I GET YOUR POINT. WE'LL KEEP OUR GUARD UP.

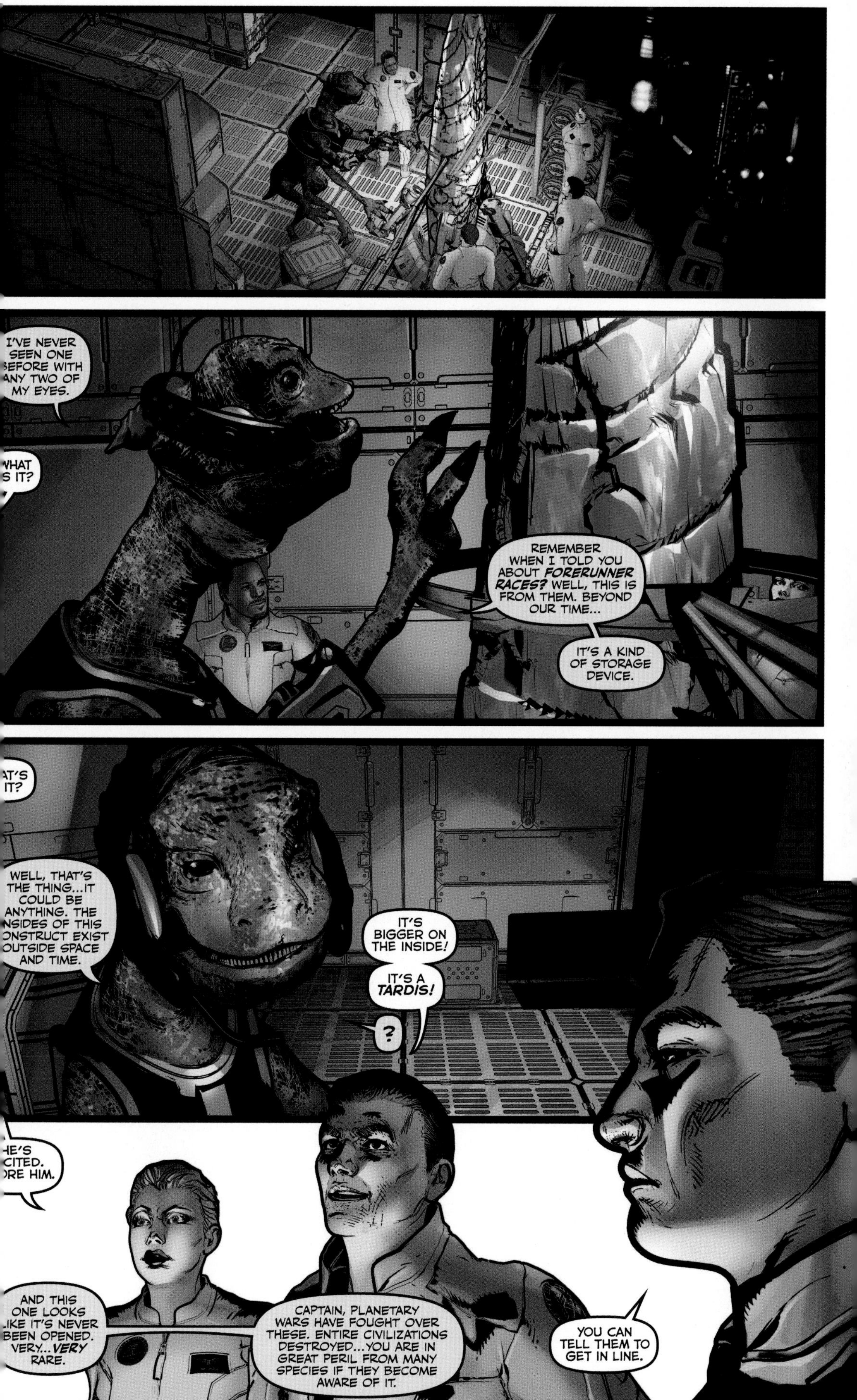

I'VE NEVER SEEN ONE BEFORE WITH ANY TWO OF MY EYES.
WHAT S IT?
REMEMBER WHEN I TOLD YOU ABOUT FORERUNNER RACES? WELL, THIS IS FROM THEM. BEYOND OUR TIME...
IT'S A KIND OF STORAGE DEVICE.
AT'S IT?
WELL, THAT'S THE THING...IT COULD BE ANYTHING. THE NSIDES OF THIS ONSTRUCT EXIST OUTSIDE SPACE AND TIME.
IT'S BIGGER ON THE INSIDE!
IT'S A TARDIS!
?
HE'S CITED. ORE HIM.
AND THIS ONE LOOKS LIKE IT'S NEVER BEEN OPENED. VERY...VERY RARE.
CAPTAIN, PLANETARY WARS HAVE FOUGHT OVER THESE. ENTIRE CIVILIZATIONS DESTROYED...YOU ARE IN GREAT PERIL FROM MANY SPECIES IF THEY BECOME AWARE OF IT.
YOU CAN TELL THEM TO GET IN LINE.

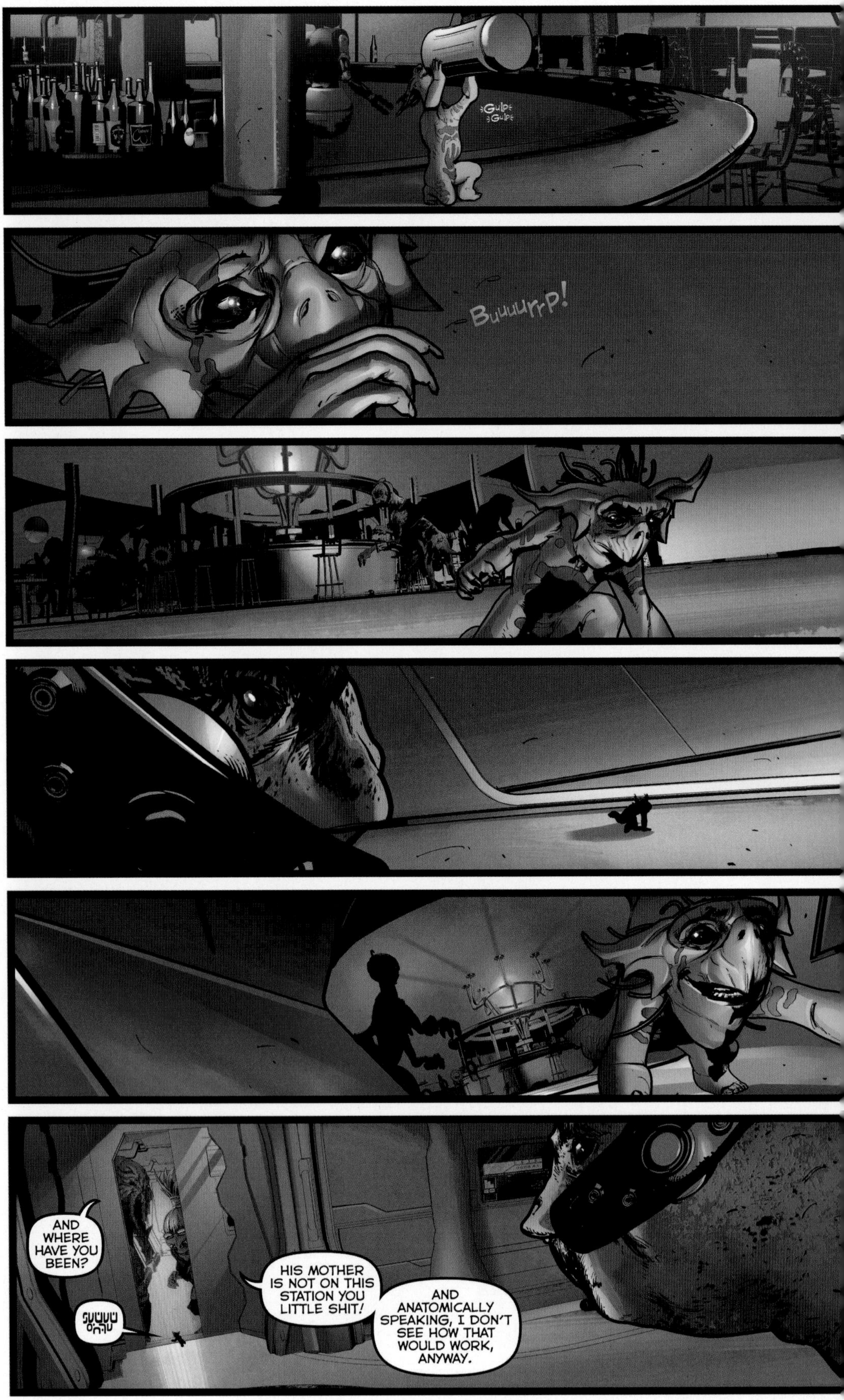

Gulp
Gulp
BuuuurrP!
AND WHERE HAVE YOU BEEN?
HIS MOTHER IS NOT ON THIS STATION YOU LITTLE SHIT!
AND ANATOMICALLY SPEAKING, I DON'T SEE HOW THAT WOULD WORK, ANYWAY.

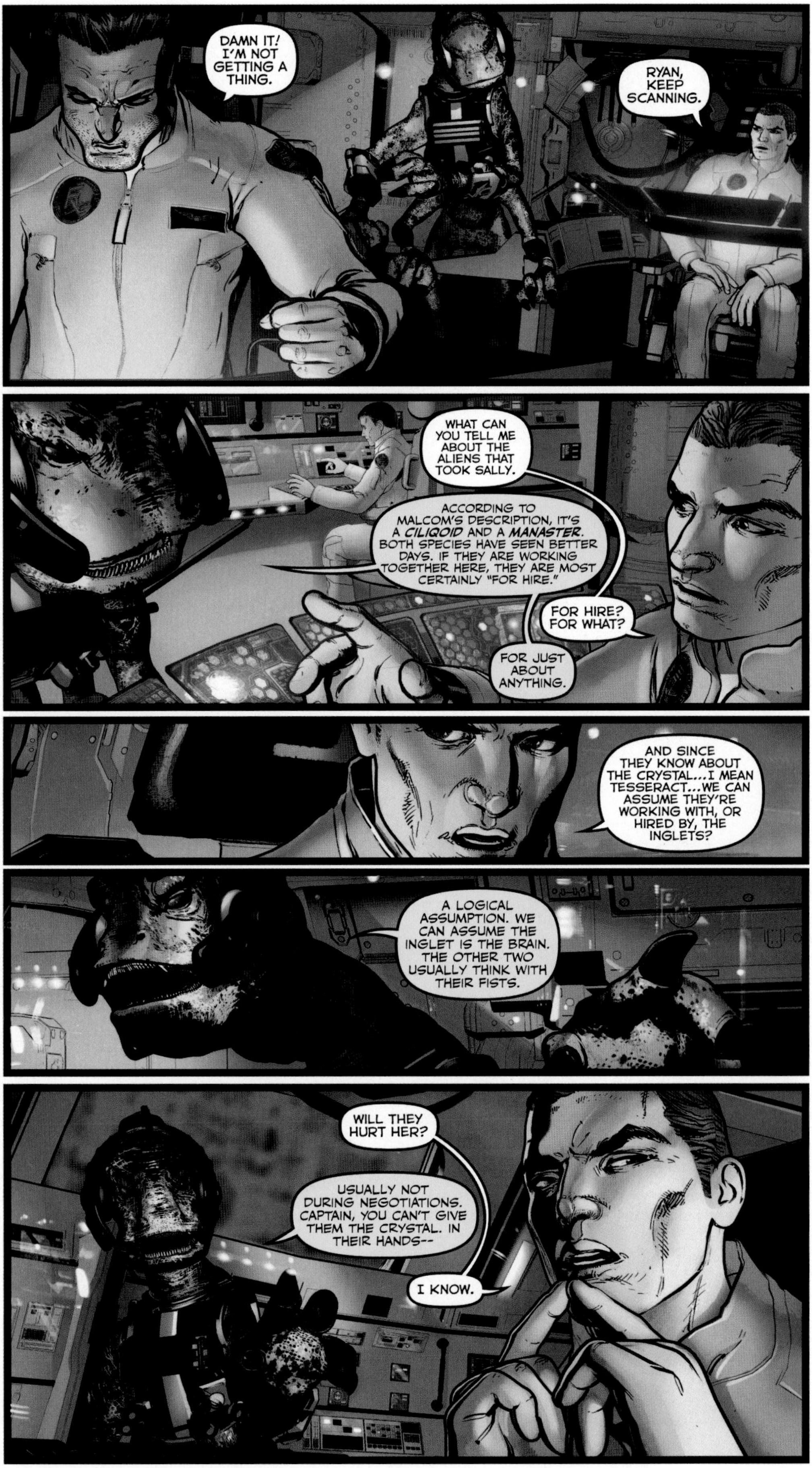
DAMN IT! I'M NOT GETTING A THING.
RYAN, KEEP SCANNING.
WHAT CAN YOU TELL ME ABOUT THE ALIENS THAT TOOK SALLY.
ACCORDING TO MALCOM'S DESCRIPTION, IT'S A *CILIQOID* AND A *MANASTER*. BOTH SPECIES HAVE SEEN BETTER DAYS. IF THEY ARE WORKING TOGETHER HERE, THEY ARE MOST CERTAINLY "FOR HIRE."
FOR HIRE? FOR WHAT?
FOR JUST ABOUT ANYTHING.
AND SINCE THEY KNOW ABOUT THE CRYSTAL...I MEAN TESSERACT...WE CAN ASSUME THEY'RE WORKING WITH, OR HIRED BY, THE INGLETS?
A LOGICAL ASSUMPTION. WE CAN ASSUME THE INGLET IS THE BRAIN. THE OTHER TWO USUALLY THINK WITH THEIR FISTS.
WILL THEY HURT HER?
USUALLY NOT DURING NEGOTIATIONS. CAPTAIN, YOU CAN'T GIVE THEM THE CRYSTAL. IN THEIR HANDS--
I KNOW.

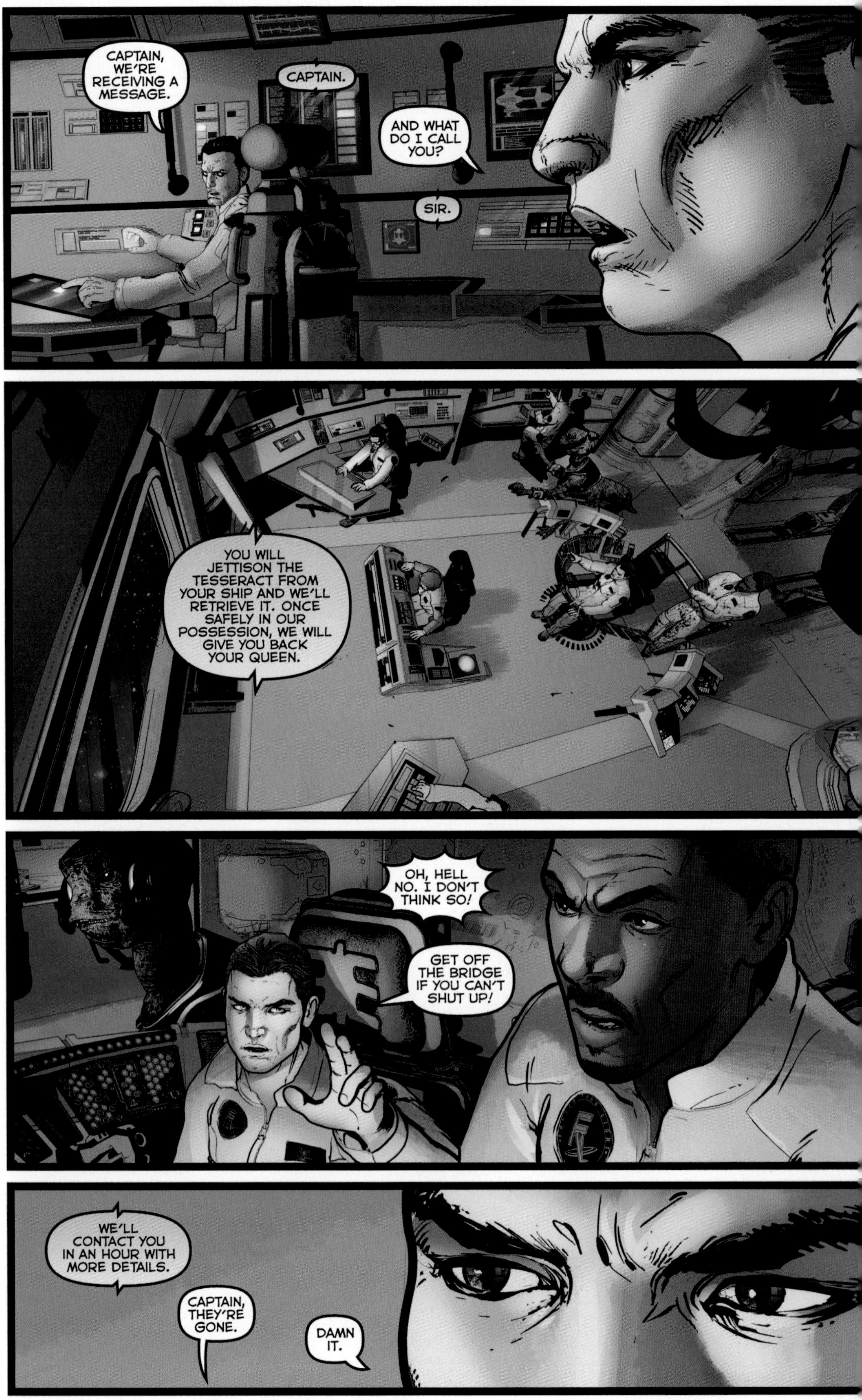
CAPTAIN, WE'RE RECEIVING A MESSAGE.
CAPTAIN.
AND WHAT DO I CALL YOU?
SIR.
YOU WILL JETTISON THE TESSERACT FROM YOUR SHIP AND WE'LL RETRIEVE IT. ONCE SAFELY IN OUR POSSESSION, WE WILL GIVE YOU BACK YOUR QUEEN.
OH, HELL NO. I DON'T THINK SO!
GET OFF THE BRIDGE IF YOU CAN'T SHUT UP!
WE'LL CONTACT YOU IN AN HOUR WITH MORE DETAILS.
CAPTAIN, THEY'RE GONE.
DAMN IT.

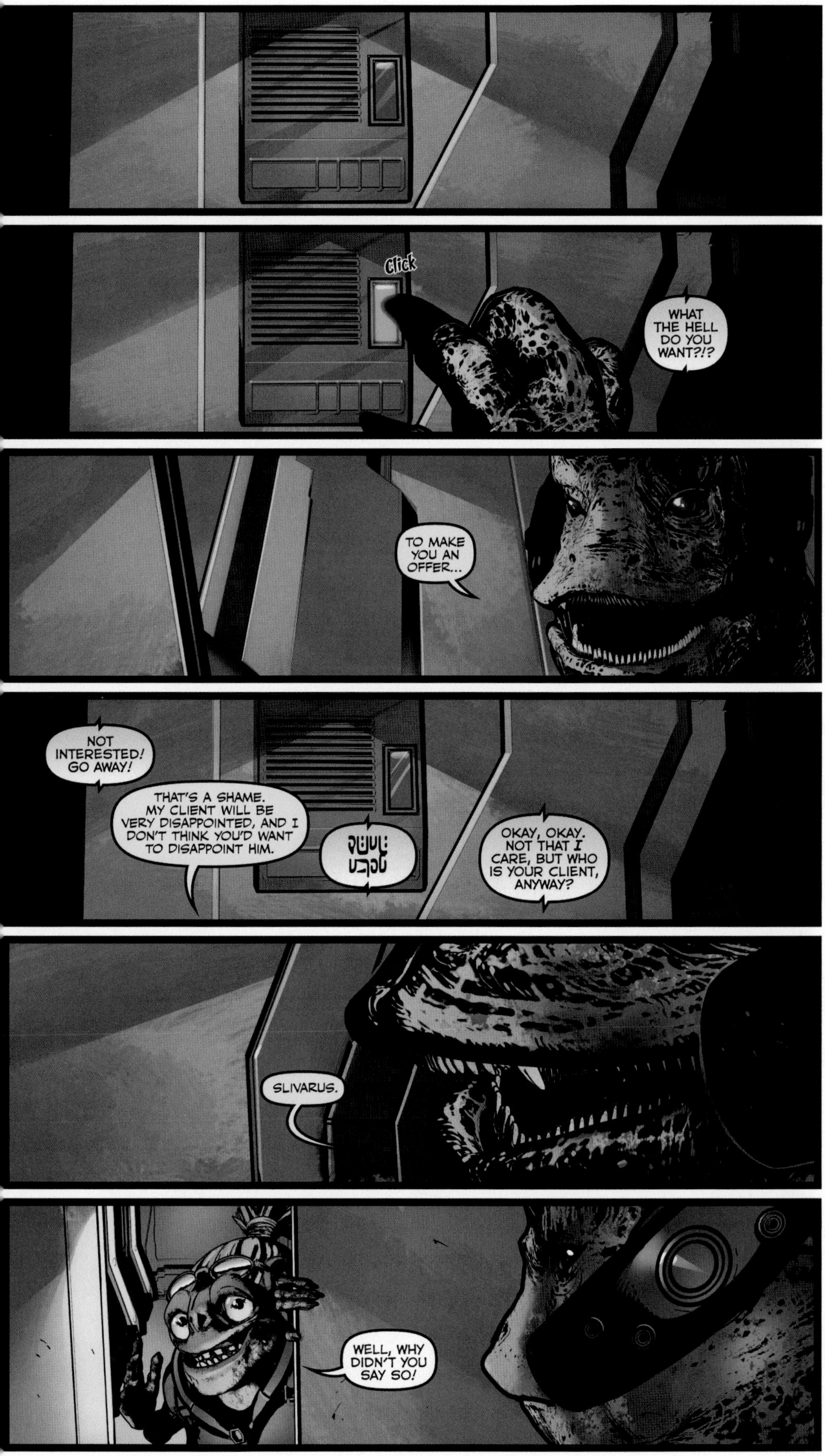
CLICK
WHAT THE HELL DO YOU WANT?!?
TO MAKE YOU AN OFFER...
NOT INTERESTED! GO AWAY!
THAT'S A SHAME. MY CLIENT WILL BE VERY DISAPPOINTED, AND I DON'T THINK YOU'D WANT TO DISAPPOINT HIM.
OKAY, OKAY. NOT THAT I CARE, BUT WHO IS YOUR CLIENT, ANYWAY?
SLIVARUS.
WELL, WHY DIDN'T YOU SAY SO!

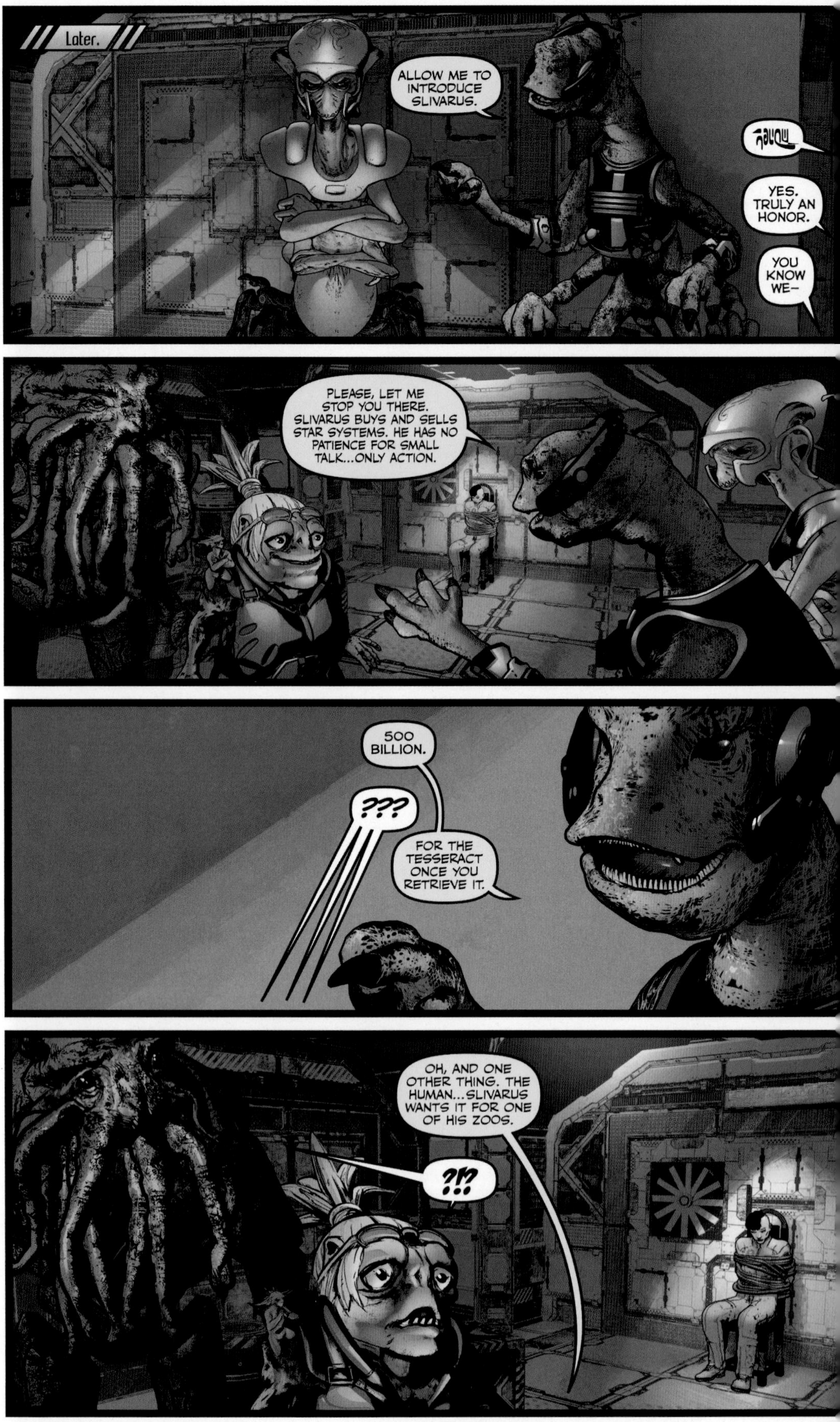
Later.
ALLOW ME TO INTRODUCE SLIVARUS.
YES. TRULY AN HONOR.
YOU KNOW WE-
PLEASE, LET ME STOP YOU THERE. SLIVARUS BUYS AND SELLS STAR SYSTEMS. HE HAS NO PATIENCE FOR SMALL TALK...ONLY ACTION.
500 BILLION.
???
FOR THE TESSERACT ONCE YOU RETRIEVE IT.
OH, AND ONE OTHER THING. THE HUMAN...SLIVARUS WANTS IT FOR ONE OF HIS ZOOS.
?!?

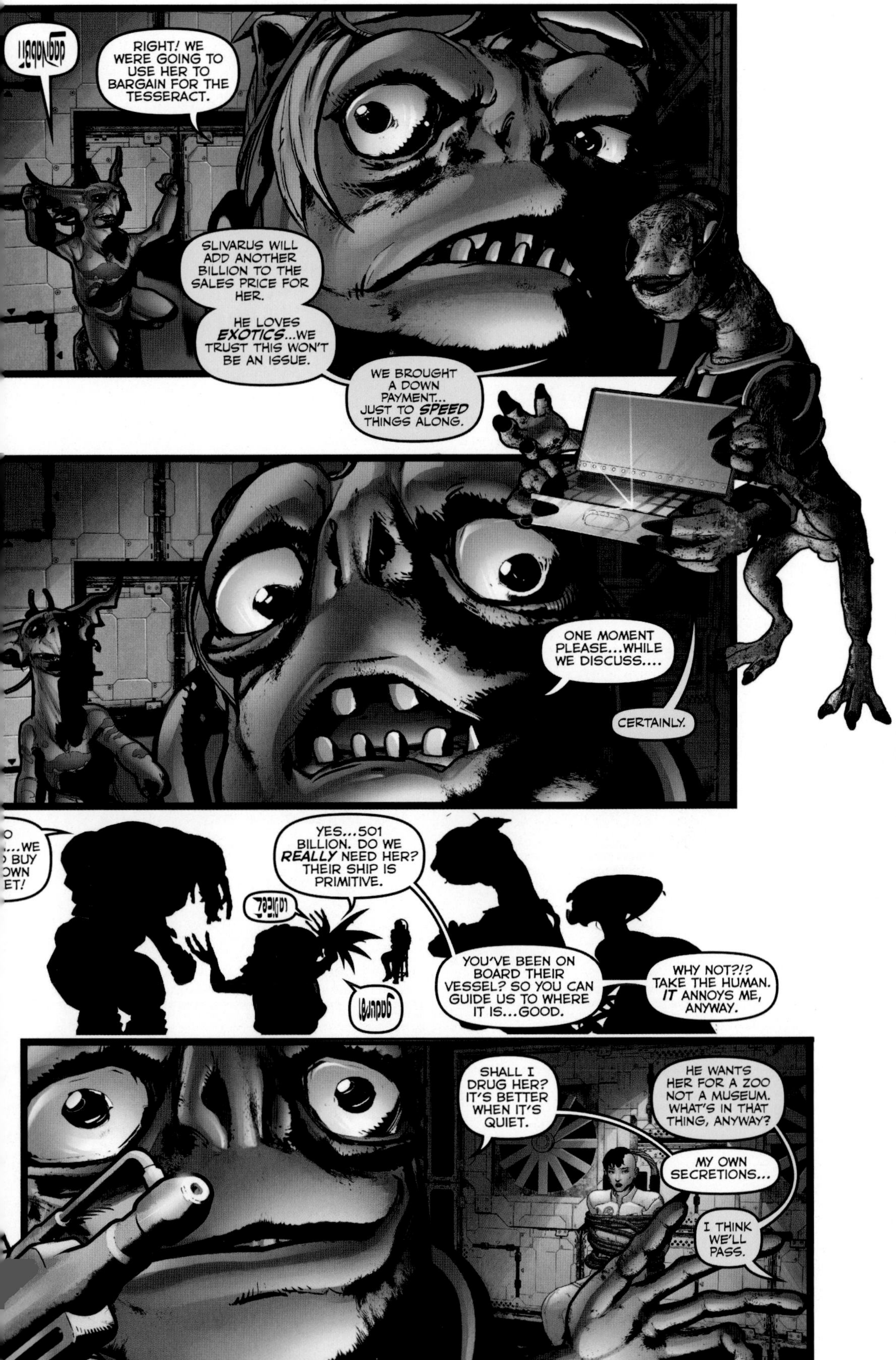
RIGHT! WE WERE GOING TO USE HER TO BARGAIN FOR THE TESSERACT.
SLIVARUS WILL ADD ANOTHER BILLION TO THE SALES PRICE FOR HER.
HE LOVES EXOTICS...WE TRUST THIS WON'T BE AN ISSUE.
WE BROUGHT A DOWN PAYMENT... JUST TO SPEED THINGS ALONG.
ONE MOMENT PLEASE...WHILE WE DISCUSS....
CERTAINLY.
YES...501 BILLION. DO WE REALLY NEED HER? THEIR SHIP IS PRIMITIVE.
YOU'VE BEEN ON BOARD THEIR VESSEL? SO YOU CAN GUIDE US TO WHERE IT IS...GOOD.
WHY NOT?!? TAKE THE HUMAN. IT ANNOYS ME, ANYWAY.
SHALL I DRUG HER? IT'S BETTER WHEN IT'S QUIET.
HE WANTS HER FOR A ZOO NOT A MUSEUM. WHAT'S IN THAT THING, ANYWAY?
MY OWN SECRETIONS...
I THINK WE'LL PASS.

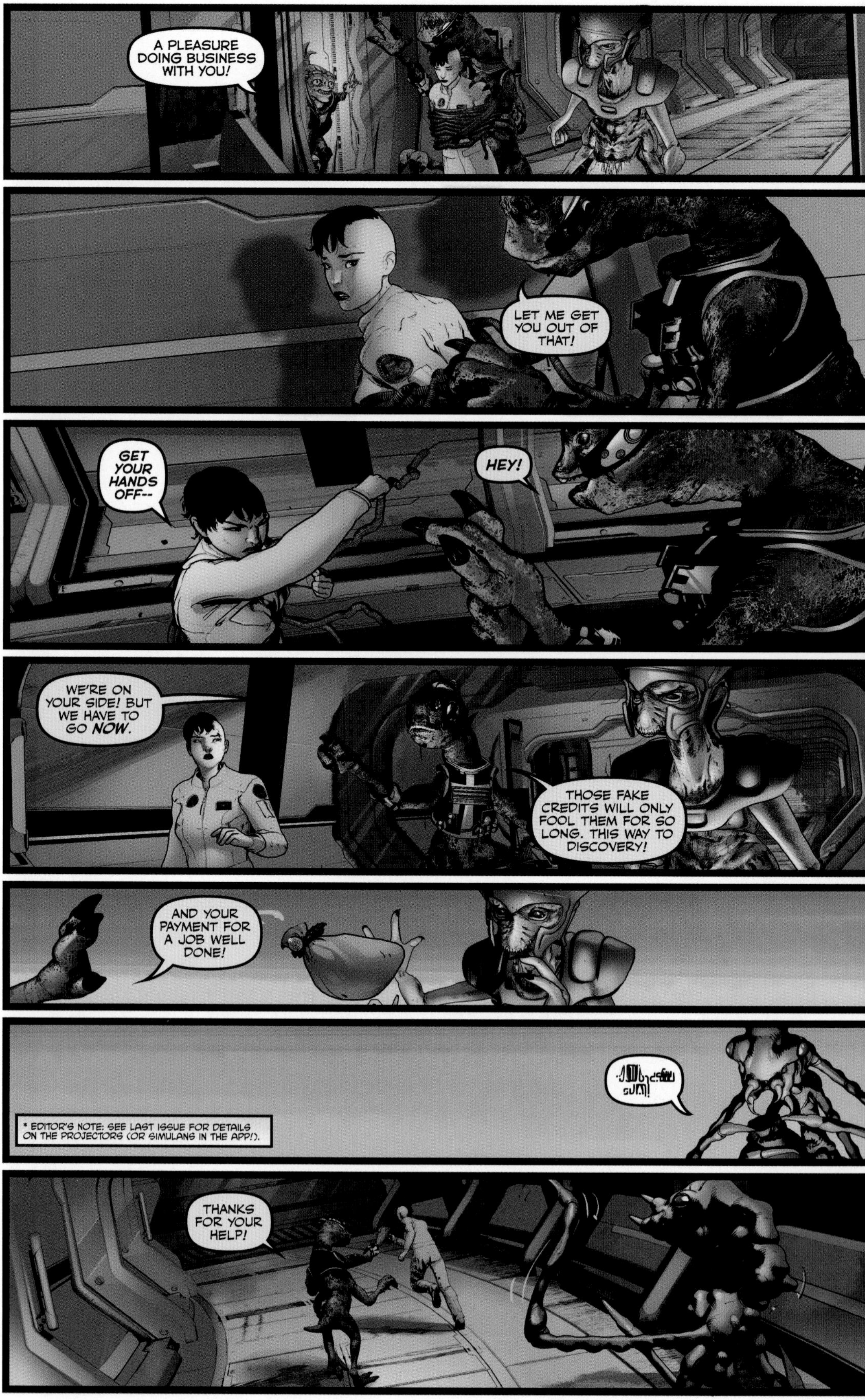
A PLEASURE DOING BUSINESS WITH YOU!
LET ME GET YOU OUT OF THAT!
GET YOUR HANDS OFF--
HEY!
WE'RE ON YOUR SIDE! BUT WE HAVE TO GO NOW.
THOSE FAKE CREDITS WILL ONLY FOOL THEM FOR SO LONG. THIS WAY TO DISCOVERY!
AND YOUR PAYMENT FOR A JOB WELL DONE!
* EDITOR'S NOTE: SEE LAST ISSUE FOR DETAILS ON THE PROJECTORS (OR SIMULANS IN THE APP!).
THANKS FOR YOUR HELP!

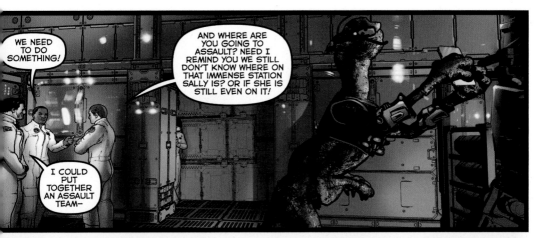

WE NEED TO DO SOMETHING!

AND WHERE ARE YOU GOING TO ASSAULT? NEED I REMIND YOU WE STILL DON'T KNOW WHERE ON THAT IMMENSE STATION SALLY IS? OR IF SHE IS STILL EVEN ON IT!

I COULD PUT TOGETHER AN ASSAULT TEAM—

I'M RIGHT HERE. DID YA MISS ME?

I GUESS THAT'S A YES.

SOMEHOW, I KNEW YOU'D GET YOURSELF FREE.

NOT ON MY OWN.

HOW, THEN?

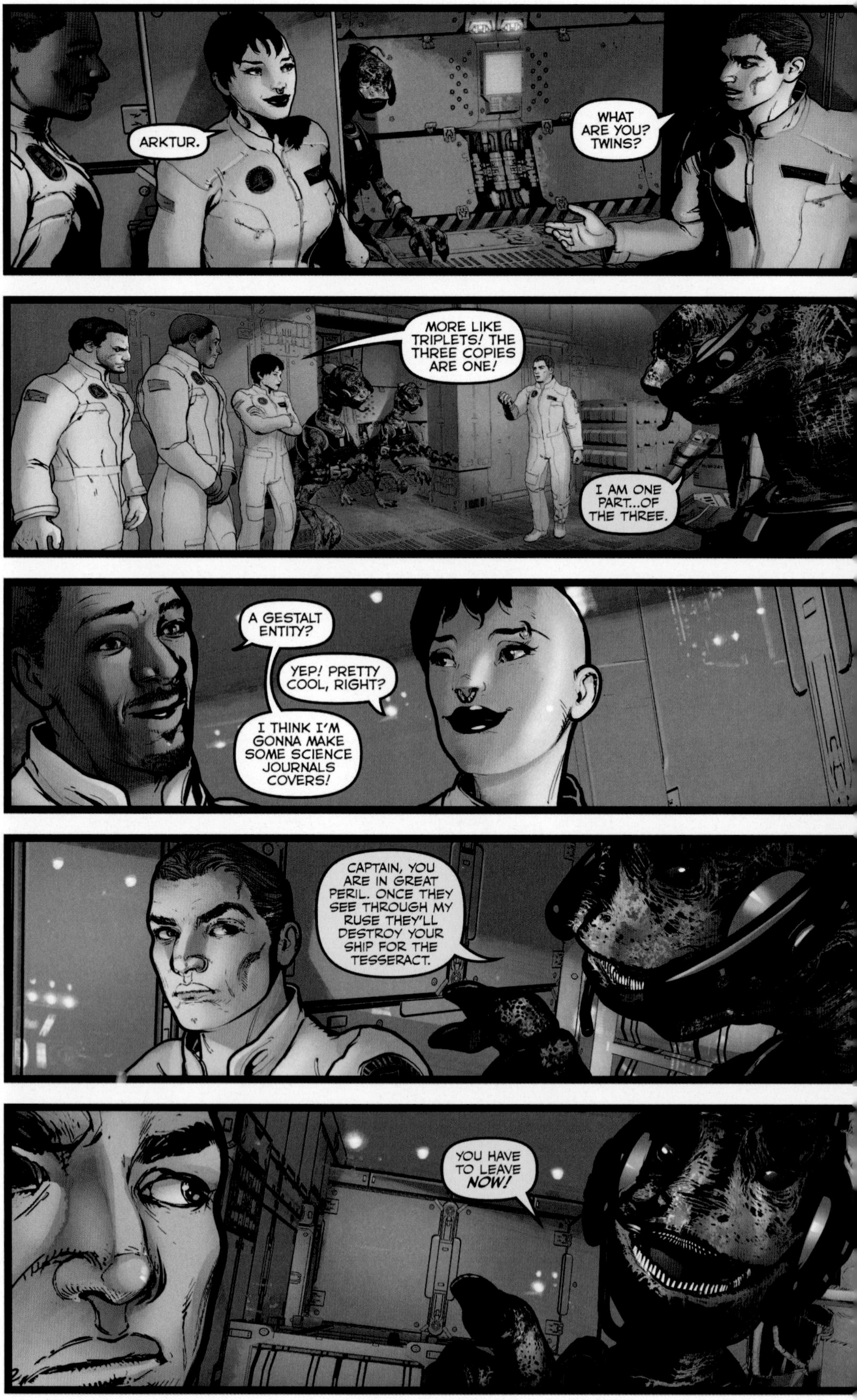
ARKTUR.
WHAT ARE YOU? TWINS?
MORE LIKE TRIPLETS! THE THREE COPIES ARE ONE!
I AM ONE PART...OF THE THREE.
A GESTALT ENTITY?
YEP! PRETTY COOL, RIGHT?
I THINK I'M GONNA MAKE SOME SCIENCE JOURNALS COVERS!
CAPTAIN, YOU ARE IN GREAT PERIL. ONCE THEY SEE THROUGH MY RUSE THEY'LL DESTROY YOUR SHIP FOR THE TESSERACT.
YOU HAVE TO LEAVE *NOW!*

GRISSOM, DETACH FROM DOCK AND PREPARE THE FTL ENGINES.

WE GOT HER.

BUT SALLY--

YES, SIR.

...KTUR, ...CAN'T ...NK YOU ...OUGH ...R YOUR ...ELP.

THE UNIVERSE IS NOT A DARK PLACE AS LONG AS WE LIGHT IT WITH OUR GOOD DEEDS.

WELL SAID.

MY OTHER SELVES HAVE BEEN LOOKING INTO YOUR OTHER PROBLEM...THE OUTSIDERS.

TOGETHER OUR INSIGHTS CAN BE QUITE REMARKABLE. THE WHOLE GREATER THAN THE SUM OF ITS PARTS.

YOU HAVE INFORMATION ON THEM? THE OUTSIDERS?

I BELIEVE WE DO. IT'S VERY INTERESTING...THEY ARE NOT WHAT YOU THINK--

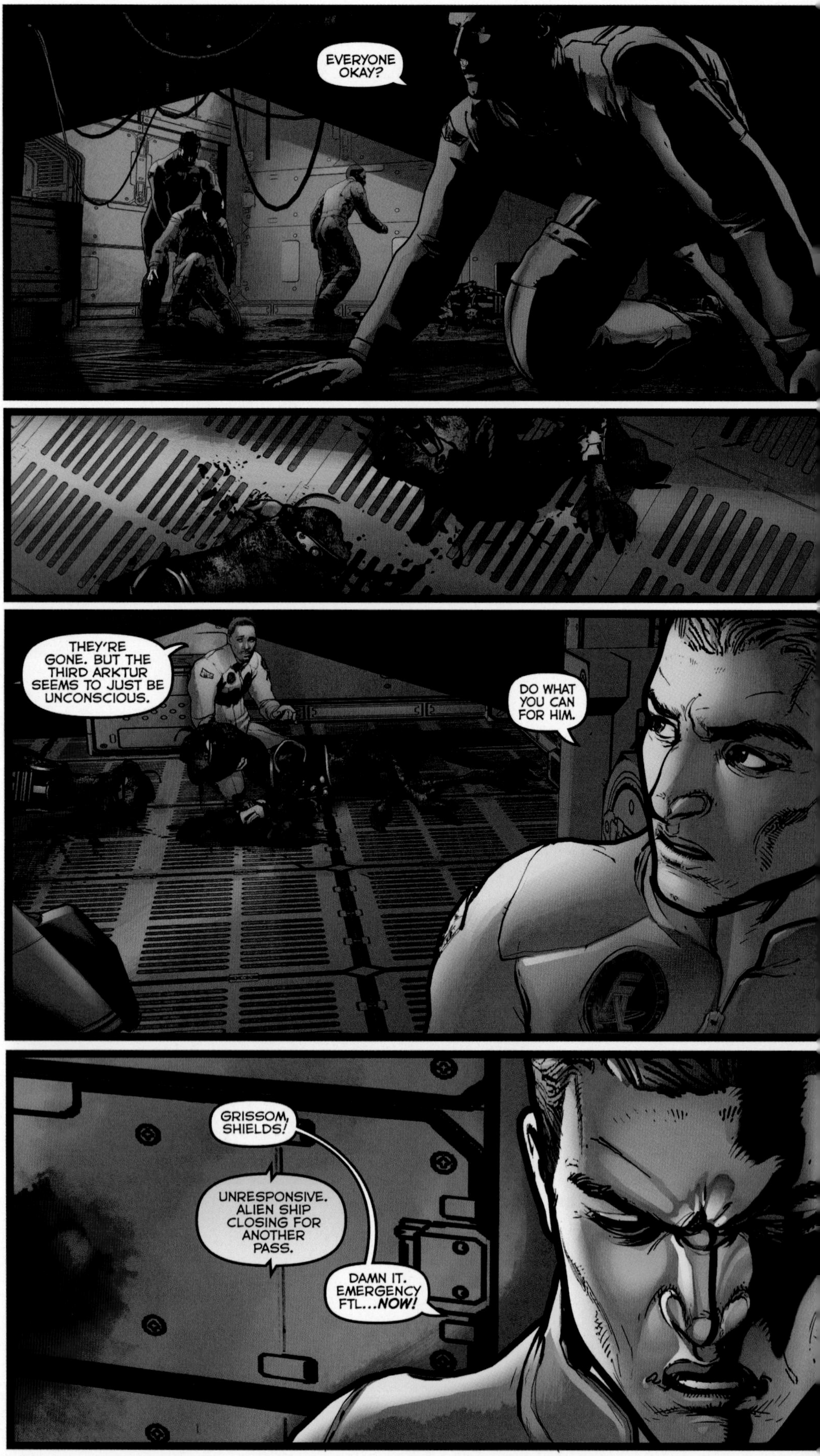
EVERYONE OKAY?
THEY'RE GONE. BUT THE THIRD ARKTUR SEEMS TO JUST BE UNCONSCIOUS.
DO WHAT YOU CAN FOR HIM.
GRISSOM, SHIELDS!
UNRESPONSIVE. ALIEN SHIP CLOSING FOR ANOTHER PASS.
DAMN IT. EMERGENCY FTL...NOW!

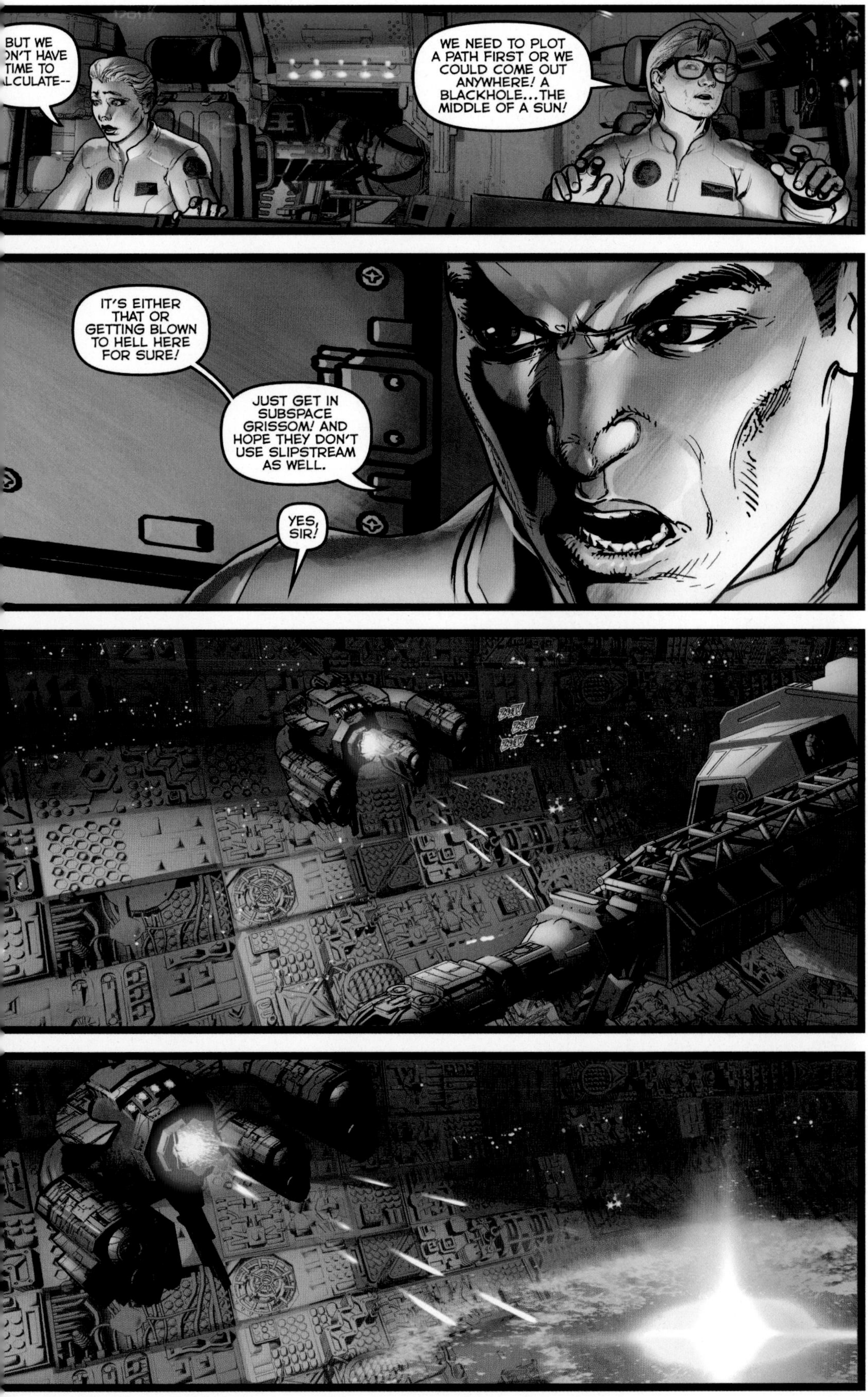

BUT WE N'T HAVE TIME TO LCULATE--
WE NEED TO PLOT A PATH FIRST OR WE COULD COME OUT ANYWHERE! A BLACKHOLE...THE MIDDLE OF A SUN!
IT'S EITHER THAT OR GETTING BLOWN TO HELL HERE FOR SURE!
JUST GET IN SUBSPACE GRISSOM! AND HOPE THEY DON'T USE SLIPSTREAM AS WELL.
YES, SIR!

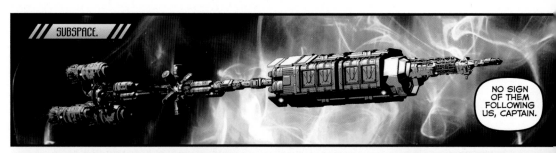

NO SIGN OF THEM FOLLOWING US, CAPTAIN.

HOW IS SHIP INTEGRITY WITH THAT HOLE IN OUR SIDE?

I GOT SHIELDS BACK. WITH THEM IN PLACE, WE SHOULD BE GOOD.

ALRIGHT, FINGERS CROSSED EVERYONE. CREW, SECURE YOURSELVES... THIS IS GOING TO BE A BIT ROUGH.

DISENGAGE SLIPSTREAM.

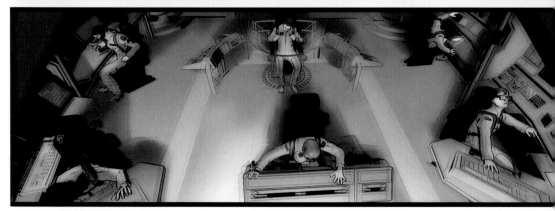

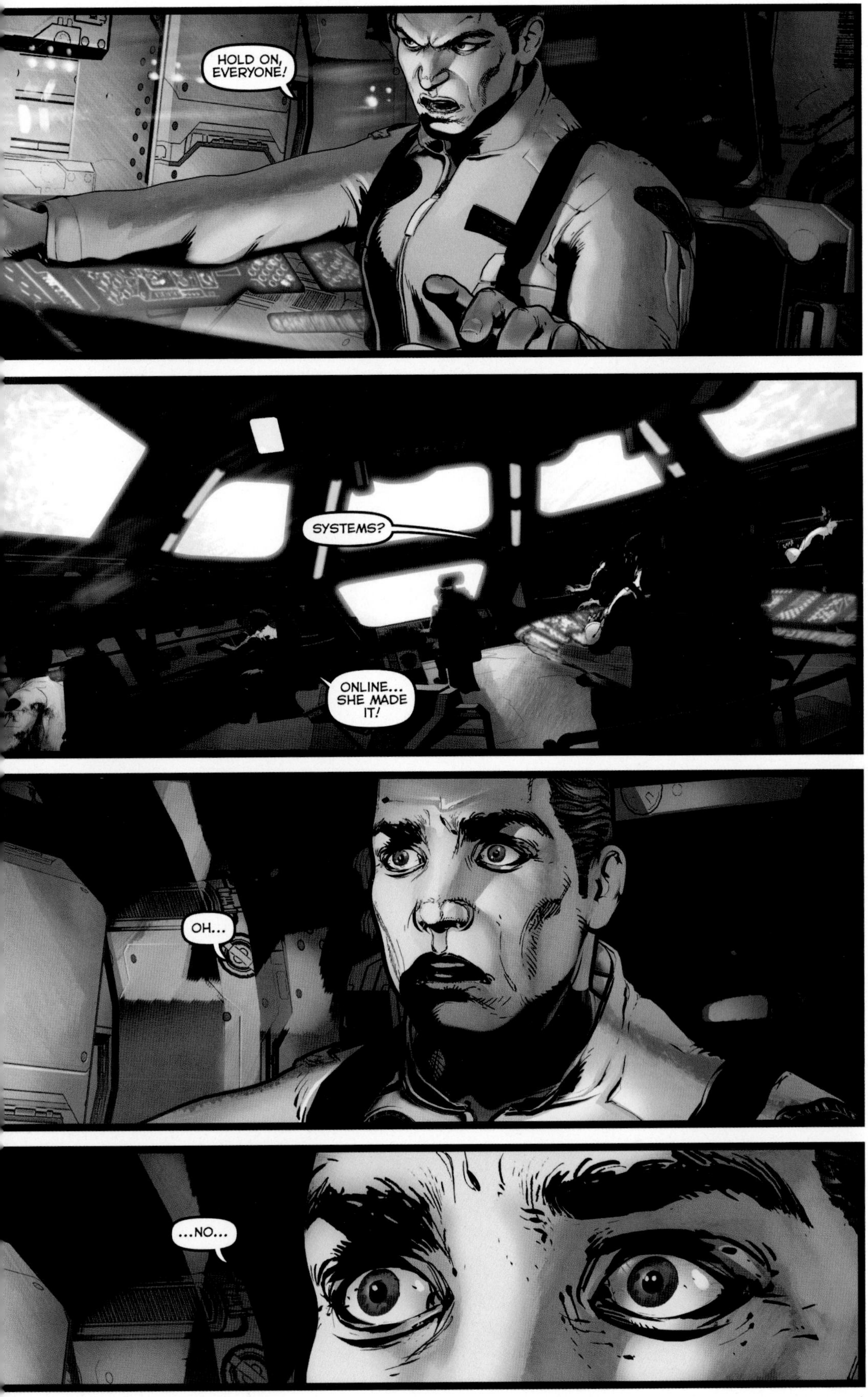
HOLD ON, EVERYONE!
SYSTEMS?
ONLINE... SHE MADE IT!
OH...
...NO...

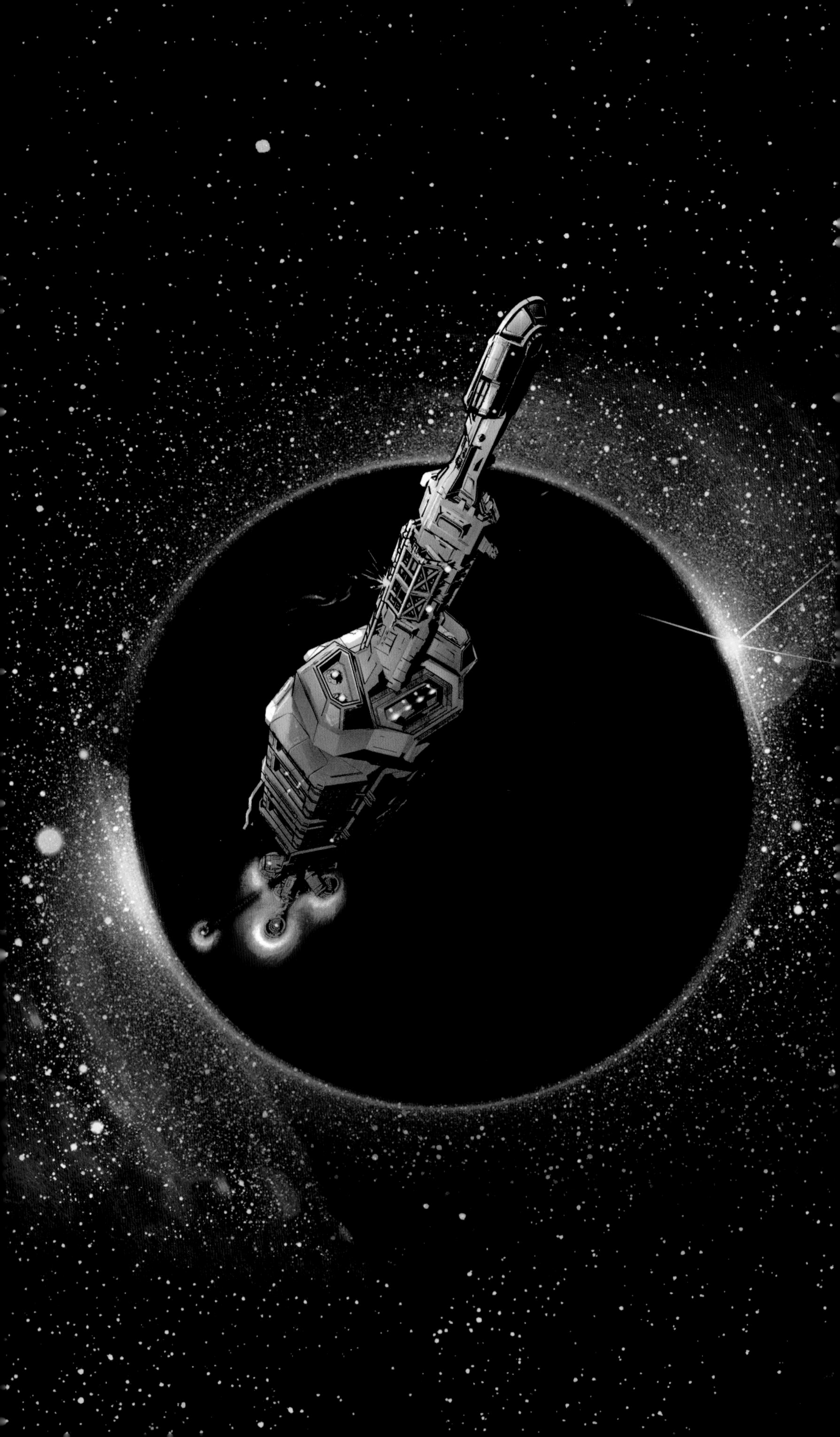

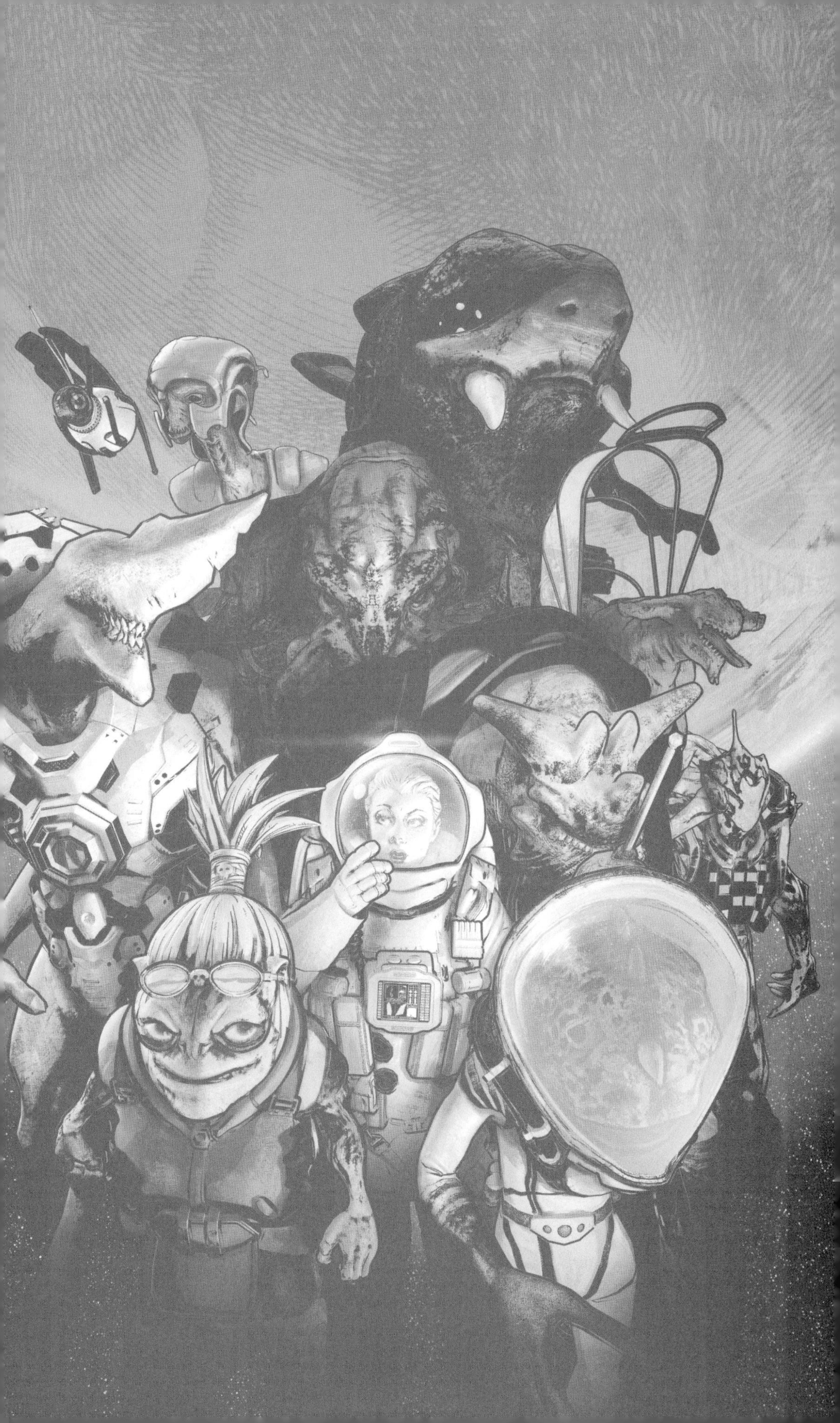

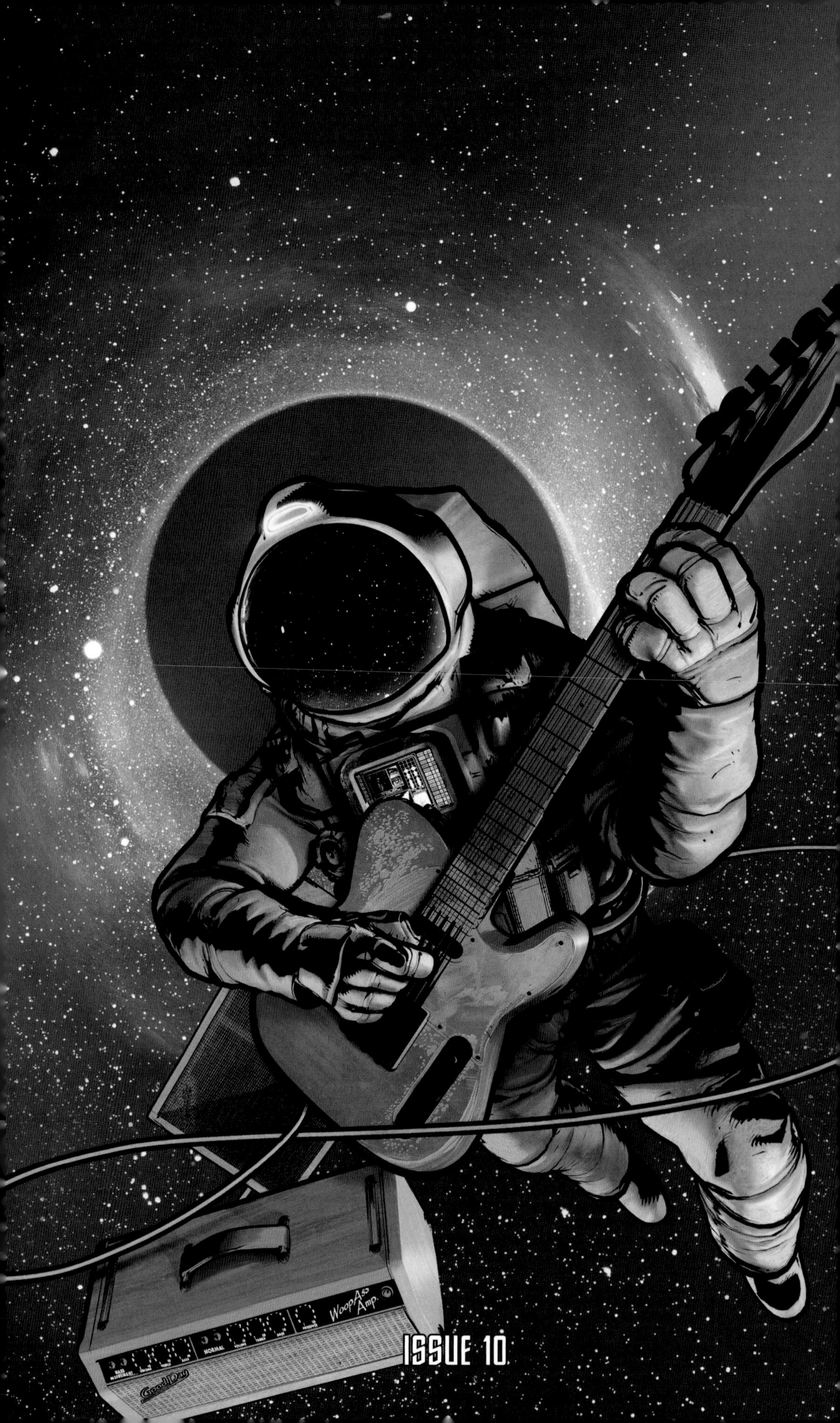
WoopAss Amp.
NORMAL
Good Day
ISSUE 10

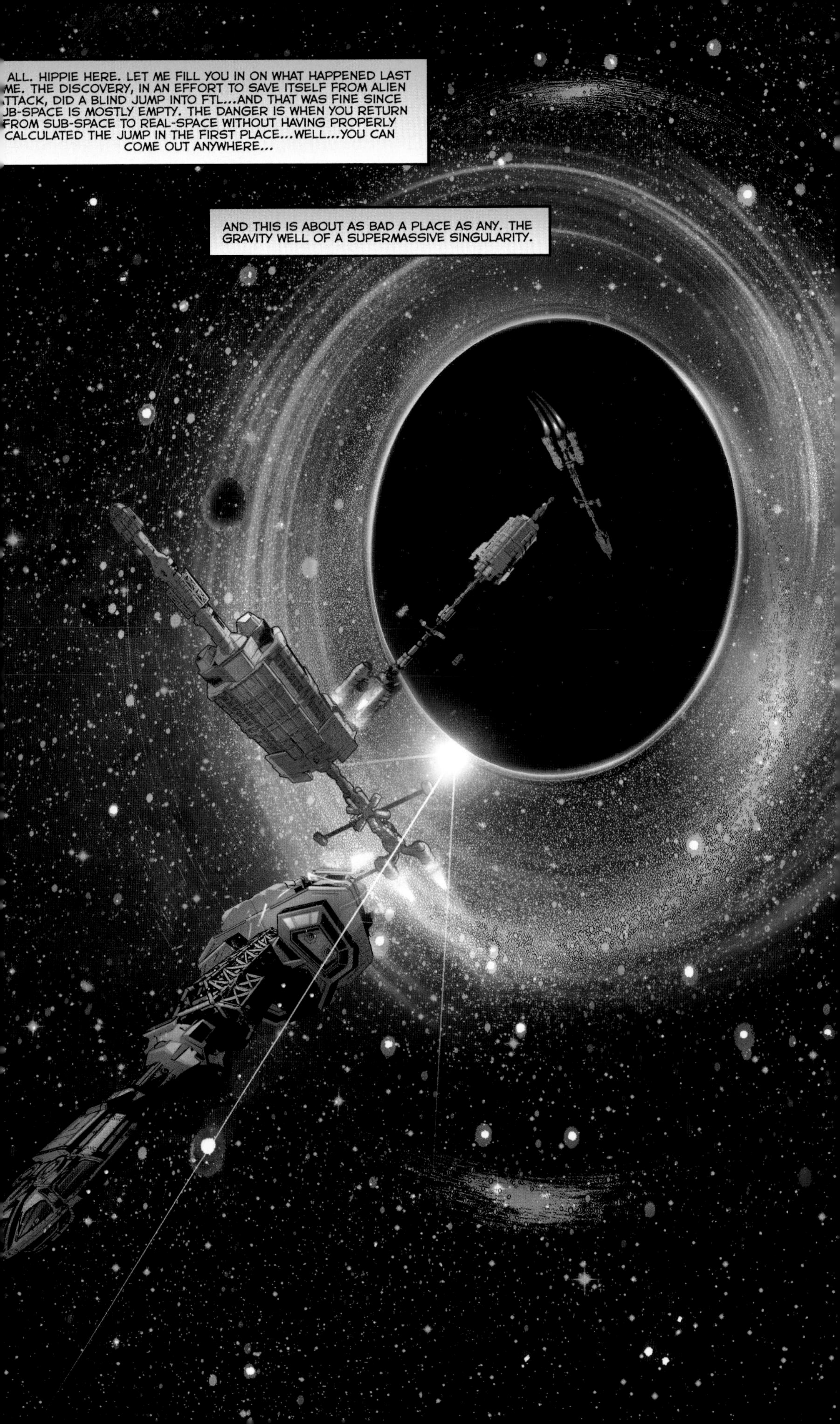
ALL. HIPPIE HERE. LET ME FILL YOU IN ON WHAT HAPPENED LAST ME. THE DISCOVERY, IN AN EFFORT TO SAVE ITSELF FROM ALIEN TTACK, DID A BLIND JUMP INTO FTL...AND THAT WAS FINE SINCE JB-SPACE IS MOSTLY EMPTY. THE DANGER IS WHEN YOU RETURN FROM SUB-SPACE TO REAL-SPACE WITHOUT HAVING PROPERLY CALCULATED THE JUMP IN THE FIRST PLACE...WELL...YOU CAN COME OUT ANYWHERE...
AND THIS IS ABOUT AS BAD A PLACE AS ANY. THE GRAVITY WELL OF A SUPERMASSIVE SINGULARITY.

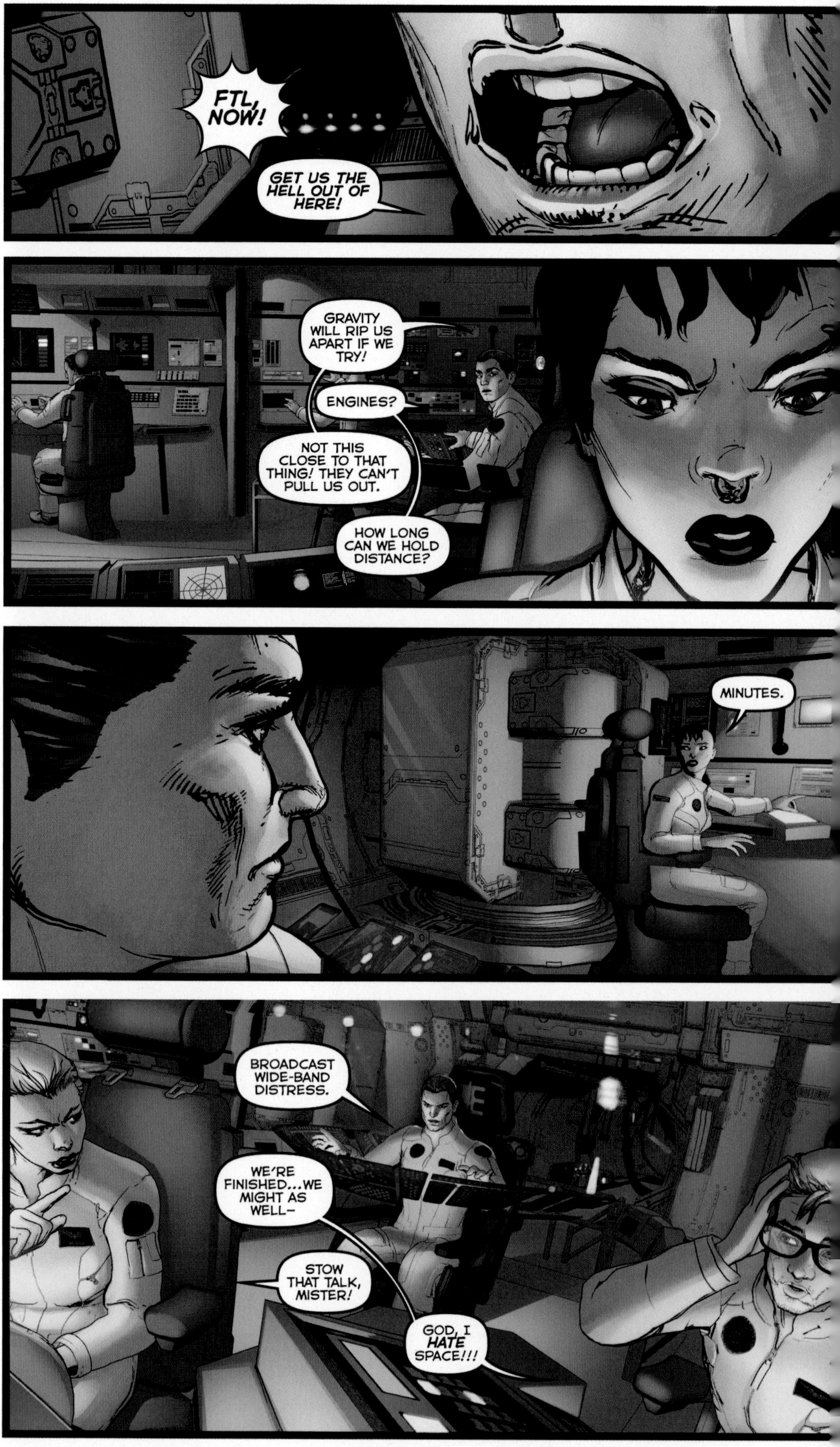
FTL, NOW!
GET US THE HELL OUT OF HERE!
GRAVITY WILL RIP US APART IF WE TRY!
ENGINES?
NOT THIS CLOSE TO THAT THING! THEY CAN'T PULL US OUT.
HOW LONG CAN WE HOLD DISTANCE?
MINUTES.
BROADCAST WIDE-BAND DISTRESS.
WE'RE FINISHED...WE MIGHT AS WELL-
STOW THAT TALK, MISTER!
GOD, I HATE SPACE!!!

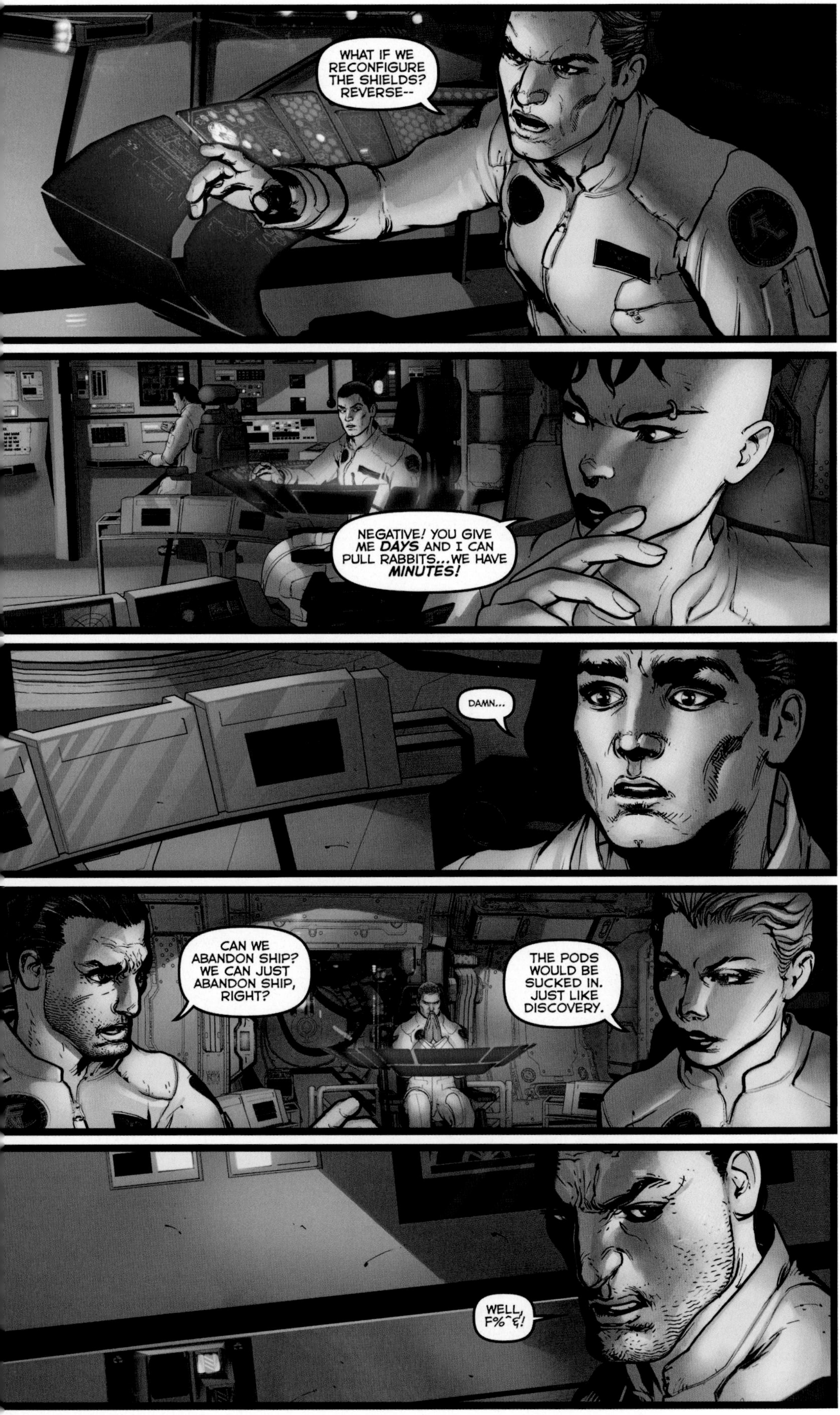
WHAT IF WE RECONFIGURE THE SHIELDS? REVERSE--
NEGATIVE! YOU GIVE ME DAYS AND I CAN PULL RABBITS...WE HAVE MINUTES!
DAMN...
CAN WE ABANDON SHIP? WE CAN JUST ABANDON SHIP, RIGHT?
THE PODS WOULD BE SUCKED IN. JUST LIKE DISCOVERY.
WELL, F%^&!

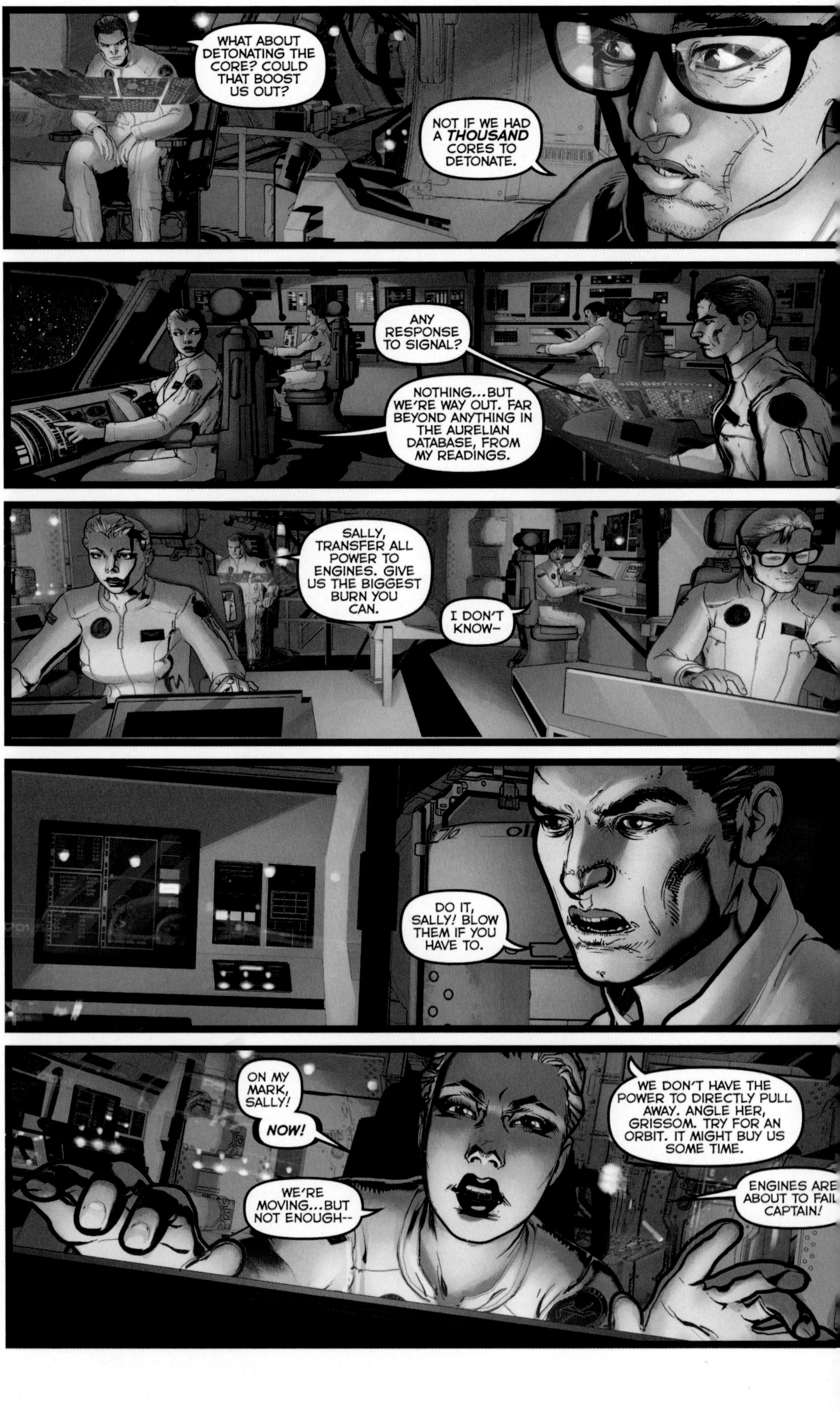

WHAT ABOUT DETONATING THE CORE? COULD THAT BOOST US OUT?
NOT IF WE HAD A *THOUSAND* CORES TO DETONATE.
ANY RESPONSE TO SIGNAL?
NOTHING...BUT WE'RE WAY OUT. FAR BEYOND ANYTHING IN THE AURELIAN DATABASE, FROM MY READINGS.
SALLY, TRANSFER ALL POWER TO ENGINES. GIVE US THE BIGGEST BURN YOU CAN.
I DON'T KNOW-
DO IT, SALLY! BLOW THEM IF YOU HAVE TO.
ON MY MARK, SALLY!
NOW!
WE DON'T HAVE THE POWER TO DIRECTLY PULL AWAY. ANGLE HER, GRISSOM. TRY FOR AN ORBIT. IT MIGHT BUY US SOME TIME.
WE'RE MOVING...BUT NOT ENOUGH--
ENGINES ARE ABOUT TO FAIL CAPTAIN!

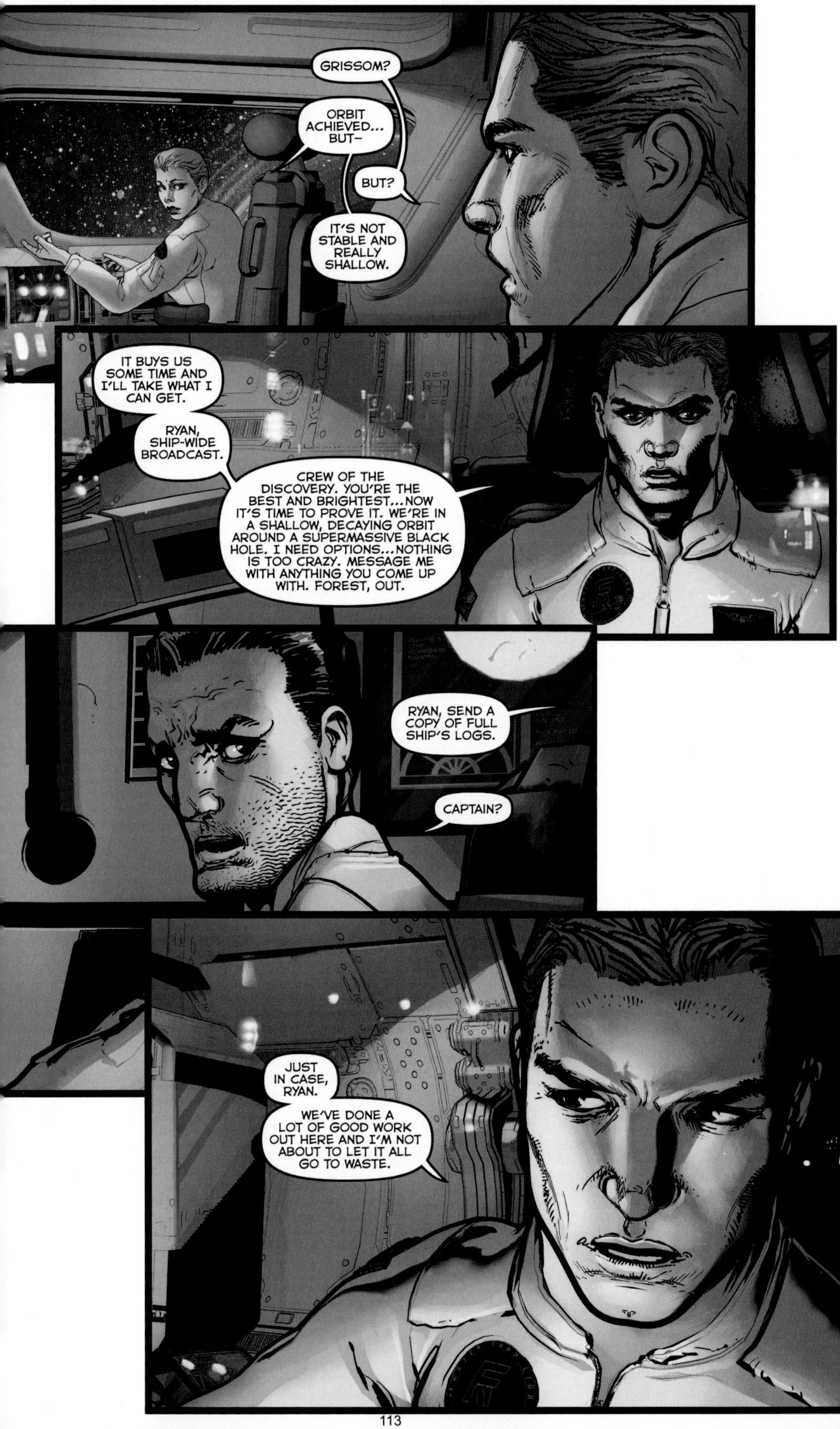
GRISSOM?
ORBIT ACHIEVED... BUT–
BUT?
IT'S NOT STABLE AND REALLY SHALLOW.
IT BUYS US SOME TIME AND I'LL TAKE WHAT I CAN GET.
RYAN, SHIP-WIDE BROADCAST.
CREW OF THE DISCOVERY. YOU'RE THE BEST AND BRIGHTEST...NOW IT'S TIME TO PROVE IT. WE'RE IN A SHALLOW, DECAYING ORBIT AROUND A SUPERMASSIVE BLACK HOLE. I NEED OPTIONS...NOTHING IS TOO CRAZY. MESSAGE ME WITH ANYTHING YOU COME UP WITH. FOREST, OUT.
RYAN, SEND A COPY OF FULL SHIP'S LOGS.
CAPTAIN?
JUST IN CASE, RYAN.
WE'VE DONE A LOT OF GOOD WORK OUT HERE AND I'M NOT ABOUT TO LET IT ALL GO TO WASTE.

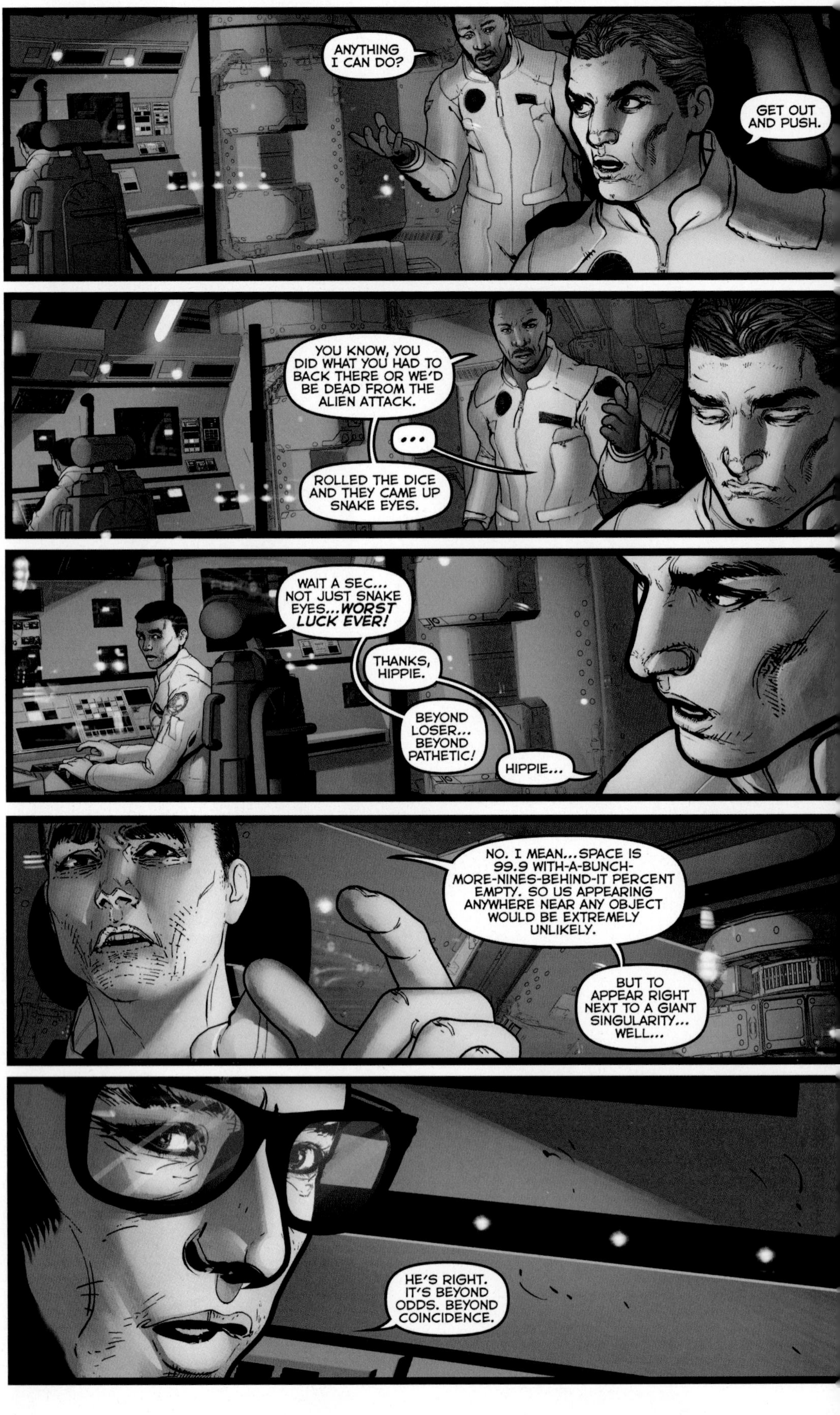

ANYTHING I CAN DO?
GET OUT AND PUSH.
YOU KNOW, YOU DID WHAT YOU HAD TO BACK THERE OR WE'D BE DEAD FROM THE ALIEN ATTACK.
...
ROLLED THE DICE AND THEY CAME UP SNAKE EYES.
WAIT A SEC... NOT JUST SNAKE EYES...*WORST LUCK EVER!*
THANKS, HIPPIE.
BEYOND LOSER... BEYOND PATHETIC!
HIPPIE...
NO. I MEAN...SPACE IS 99.9 WITH-A-BUNCH-MORE-NINES-BEHIND-IT PERCENT EMPTY. SO US APPEARING ANYWHERE NEAR ANY OBJECT WOULD BE EXTREMELY UNLIKELY.
BUT TO APPEAR RIGHT NEXT TO A GIANT SINGULARITY... WELL...
HE'S RIGHT. IT'S BEYOND ODDS. BEYOND COINCIDENCE.

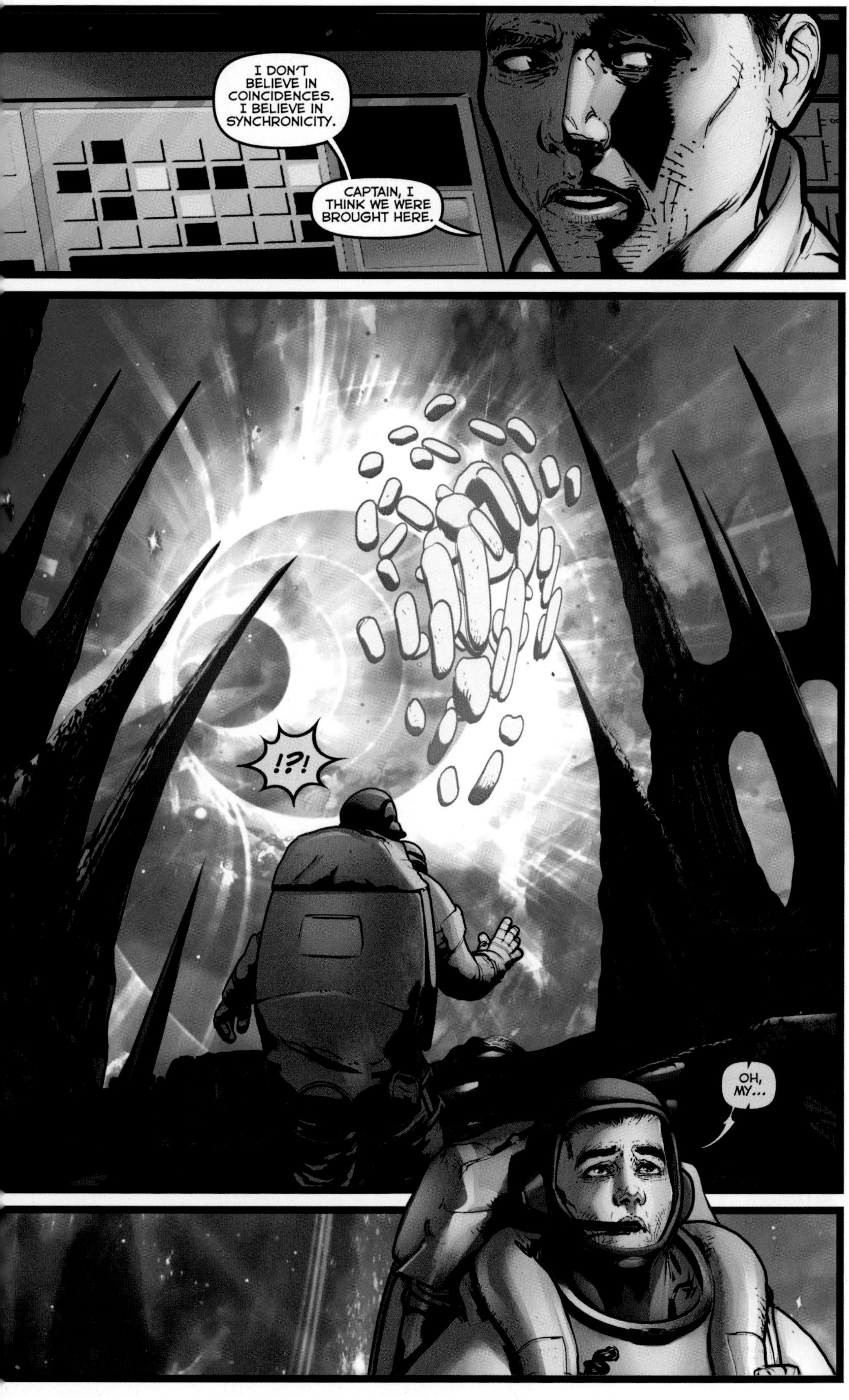
I DON'T BELIEVE IN COINCIDENCES. I BELIEVE IN SYNCHRONICITY.
CAPTAIN, I THINK WE WERE BROUGHT HERE.
!?!
OH, MY...

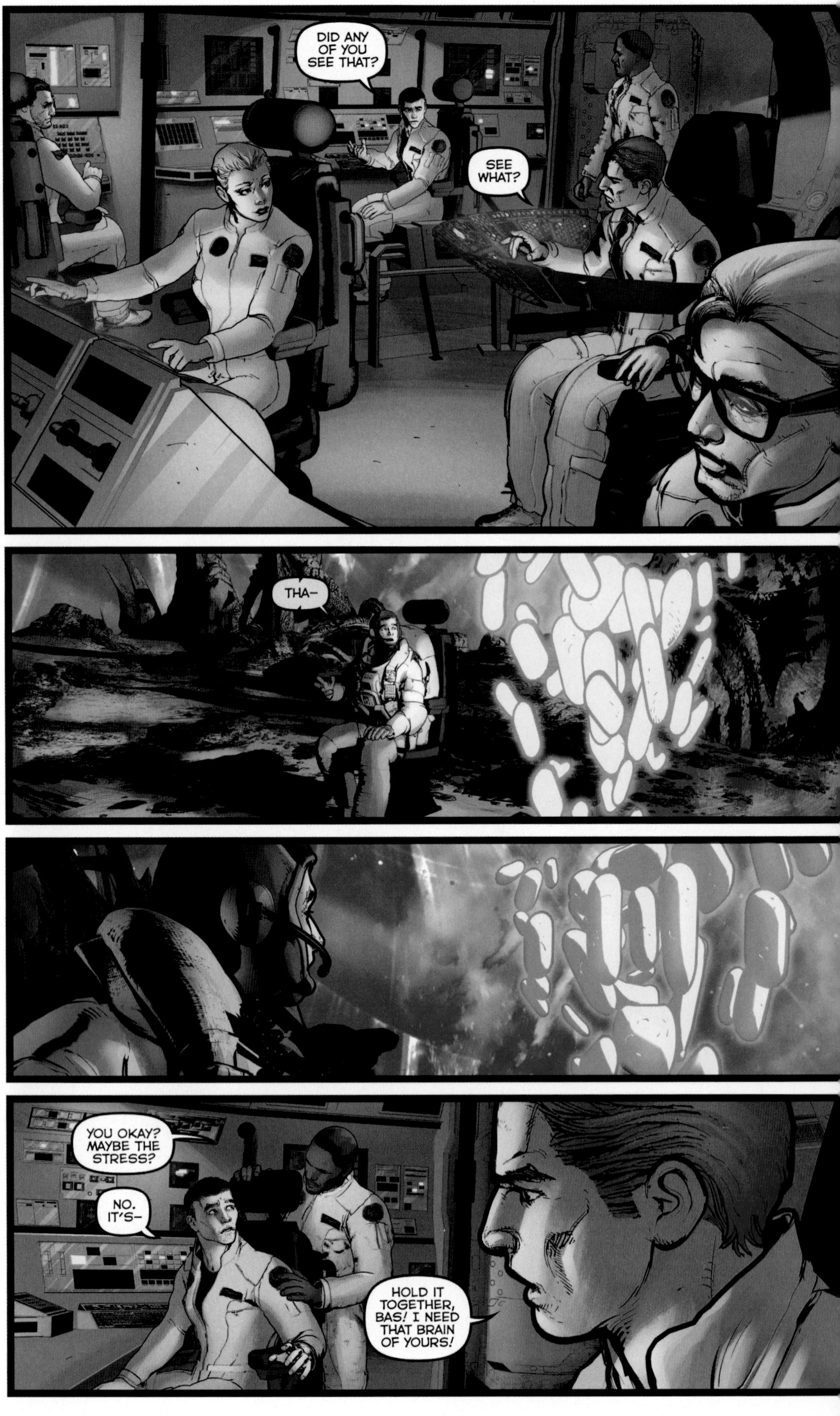
DID ANY OF YOU SEE THAT?
SEE WHAT?
THA-
YOU OKAY? MAYBE THE STRESS?
NO. IT'S-
HOLD IT TOGETHER, BAS! I NEED THAT BRAIN OF YOURS!

YES, SIR.

BUT...I THINK WHATEVER BROUGHT US HERE IS TRYING TO COMMUNICATE.

THAT'S A *BIG LEAP!* YOUR AURELIAN ASTROLOGY TELL YOU THAT?!?!

HATEVER...

CAPTAIN... I THINK IT'S THE CRYSTAL TRYING TO COMMUNICATE.

WHAT DOES IT SAY?

YOU'RE ACTUALLY BUYING THIS?

THAT'S THE THING... I'M SEEING THINGS... IT'S NON-VERBAL...

YOU'RE HIGH!

NO MORE THAN USUAL...I'M TELLING YOU SOMETHING'S GOING ON.

CAPTAIN, WE CAN'T—

IT'S REACHED OUT BEFORE... I FELT IT, TOO, BUT IT WAS JUST FEELINGS BEFORE.

IT'S TAKING IT UP A NOTCH. I'M SEEING THINGS...OUROBOROS... AND SHAPES...I THINK IT'S TRYING TO FIND OUR—

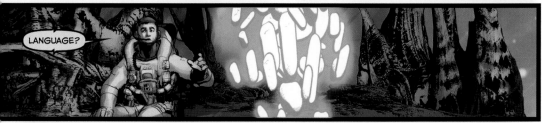

LANGUAGE?

IT'S LIKE A SEIZURE. HIPPIE, YOU'RE OKAY. YOU'RE OKAY NOW. IT'S OVER.

TAKE HIM TO MEDICAL. STAY WITH HIM. MONITOR HIM. SOMETHING *IS* HAPPENING, BUT I NEED TO SEE WHAT MORE *PRACTICAL* OPTIONS WE HAVE.

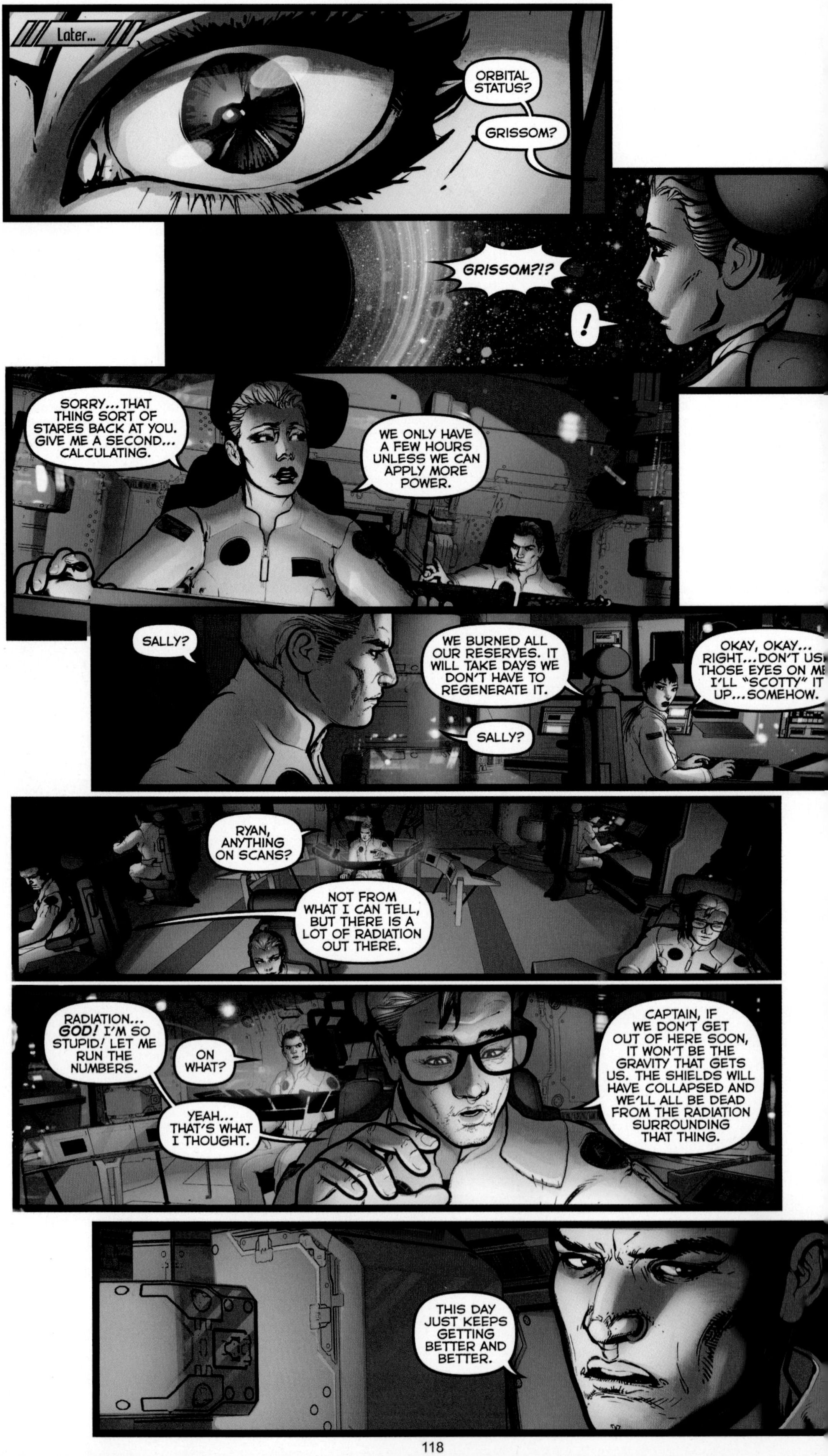
Later...
ORBITAL STATUS?
GRISSOM?
GRISSOM?!?
!
SORRY...THAT THING SORT OF STARES BACK AT YOU. GIVE ME A SECOND... CALCULATING.
WE ONLY HAVE A FEW HOURS UNLESS WE CAN APPLY MORE POWER.
SALLY?
WE BURNED ALL OUR RESERVES. IT WILL TAKE DAYS WE DON'T HAVE TO REGENERATE IT.
SALLY?
OKAY, OKAY... RIGHT...DON'T US THOSE EYES ON M I'LL "SCOTTY" IT UP...SOMEHOW.
RYAN, ANYTHING ON SCANS?
NOT FROM WHAT I CAN TELL, BUT THERE IS A LOT OF RADIATION OUT THERE.
RADIATION... GOD! I'M SO STUPID! LET ME RUN THE NUMBERS.
ON WHAT?
YEAH... THAT'S WHAT I THOUGHT.
CAPTAIN, IF WE DON'T GET OUT OF HERE SOON, IT WON'T BE THE GRAVITY THAT GETS US. THE SHIELDS WILL HAVE COLLAPSED AND WE'LL ALL BE DEAD FROM THE RADIATION SURROUNDING THAT THING.
THIS DAY JUST KEEPS GETTING BETTER AND BETTER.

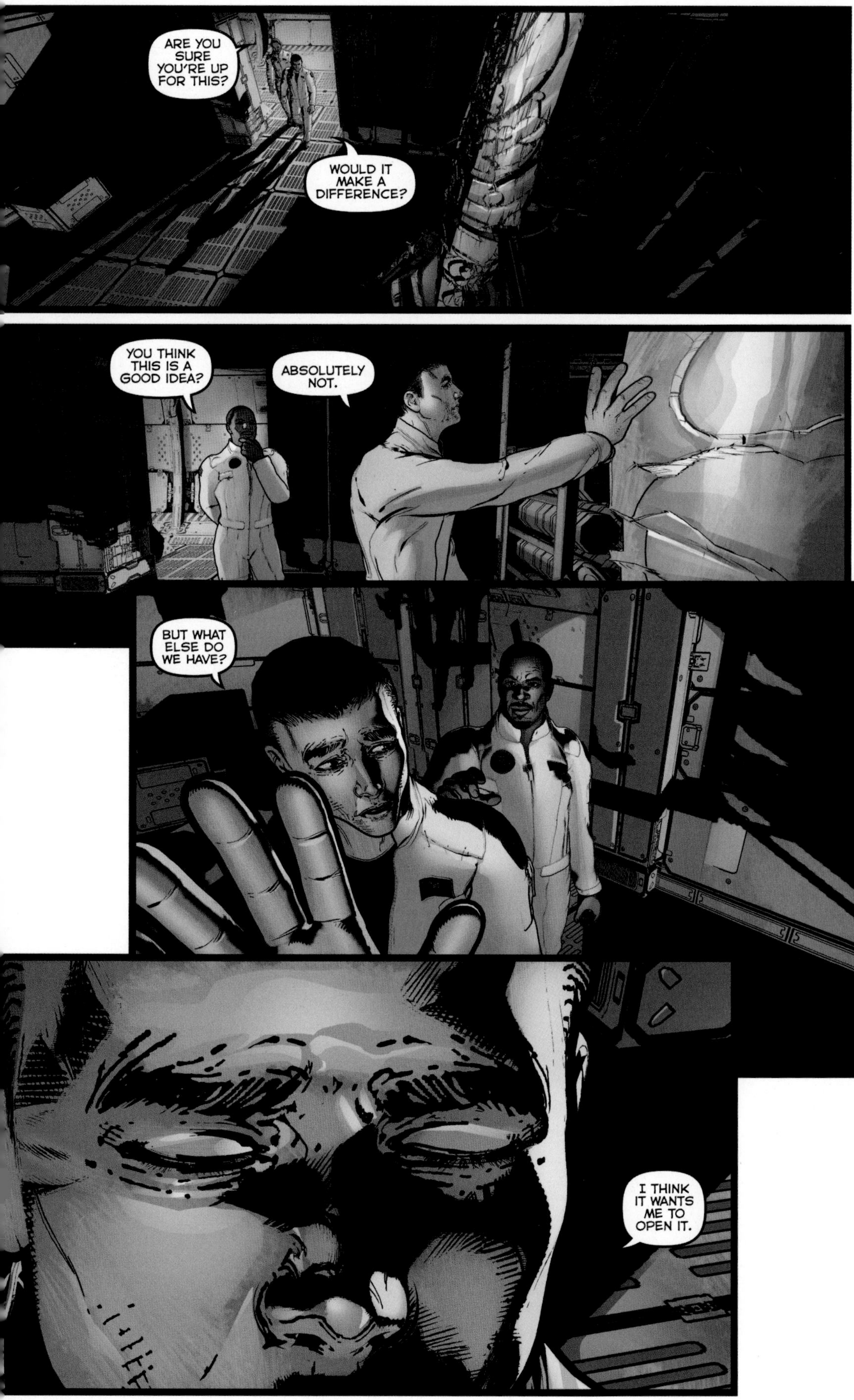
ARE YOU SURE YOU'RE UP FOR THIS?
WOULD IT MAKE A DIFFERENCE?
YOU THINK THIS IS A GOOD IDEA?
ABSOLUTELY NOT.
BUT WHAT ELSE DO WE HAVE?
I THINK IT WANTS ME TO OPEN IT.

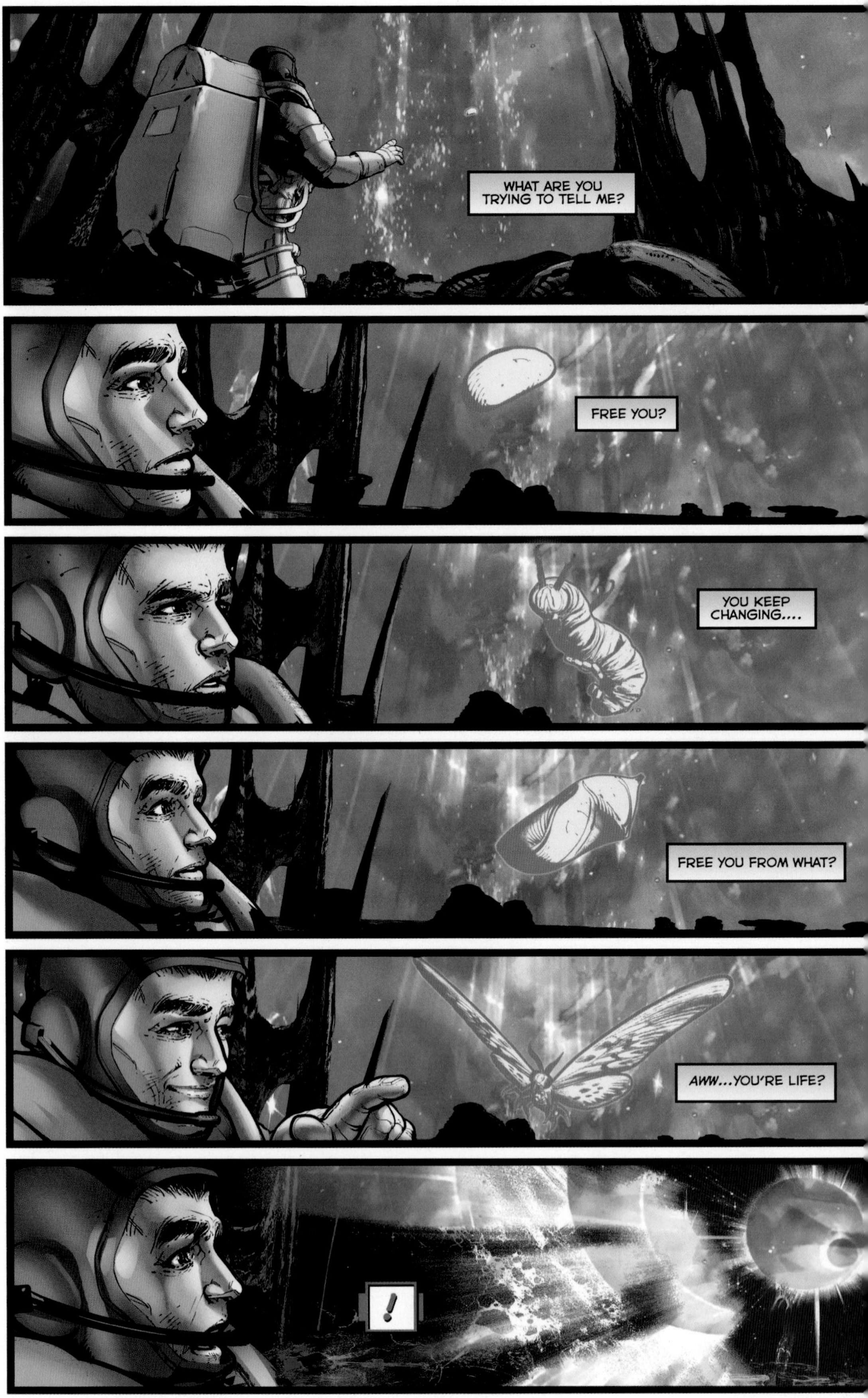
WHAT ARE YOU TRYING TO TELL ME?
FREE YOU?
YOU KEEP CHANGING....
FREE YOU FROM WHAT?
AWW...YOU'RE LIFE?
!

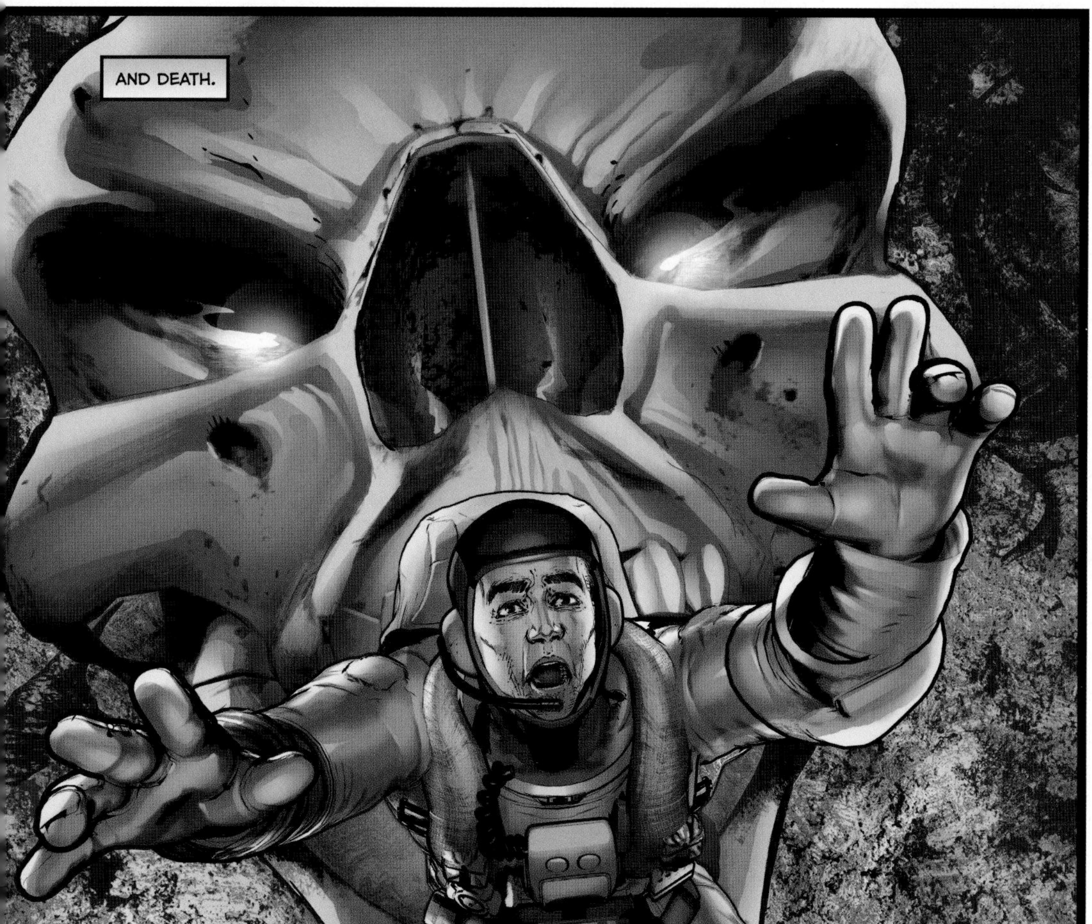
AND DEATH.

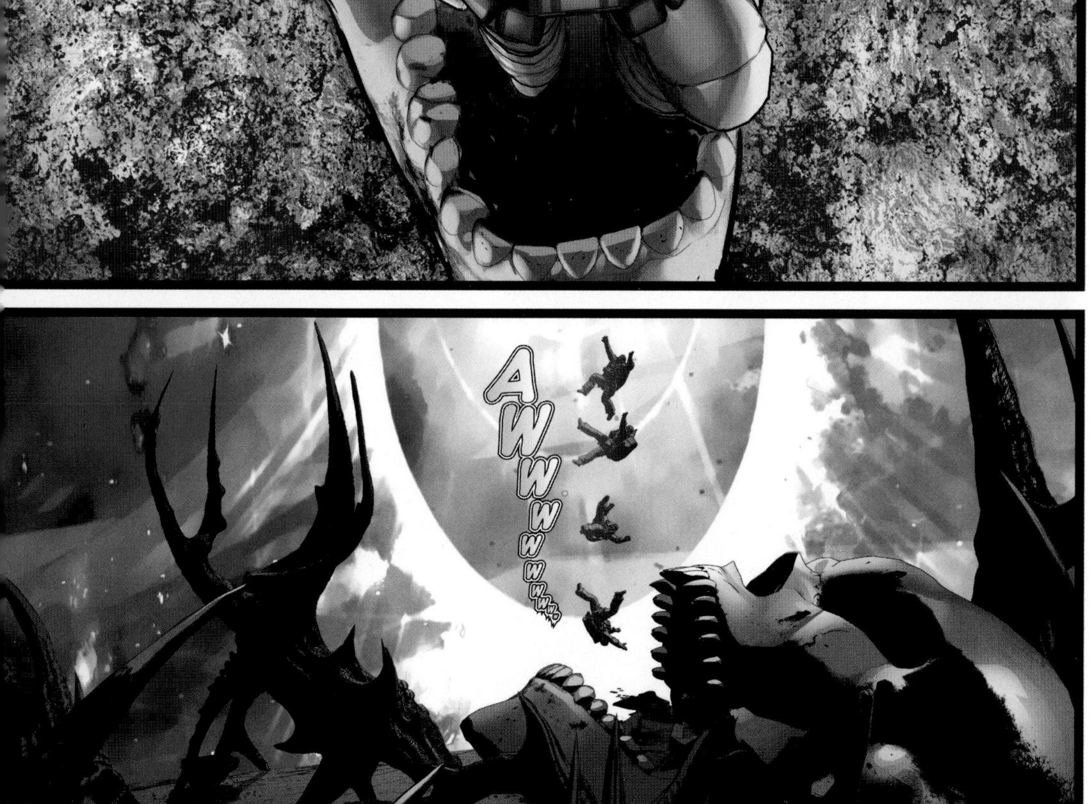
AWWWWWWWW

MAYBE NOT... EMOTIONS AND VISUAL THAT TIME.

HOW DO YOU EVEN OPEN THAT THING IN THE FIRST PLACE?

LA DA DEE LA DA DAA

ARKTUR, I DIDN'T KNOW YOU WERE OUT OF BED. YOU SHOULD...HMMM... I GUESS WITH WHAT'S HAPPENING, IT REALLY DOESN'T MATTER ANYMORE.

DO YOU KNOW HOW TO OPEN THIS THING?

LA LAAAA

I DID...BUT... I—I CAN'T REMEMBER...

YOU SEEM NICE. WHO ARE YOU?

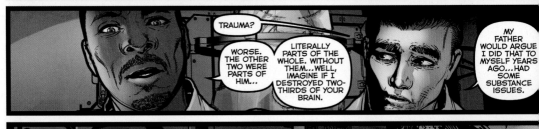

TRAUMA?

WORSE. THE OTHER TWO WERE PARTS OF HIM...

LITERALLY PARTS OF THE WHOLE. WITHOUT THEM...WELL, IMAGINE IF I DESTROYED TWO-THIRDS OF YOUR BRAIN.

MY FATHER WOULD ARGUE I DID THAT TO MYSELF YEARS AGO...HAD SOME SUBSTANCE ISSUES.

WAIT A SEC...WHY IS THIS THING STILL EVEN ON BOARD?

WE...WE WERE GOING TO BRING IT BACK TO EARTH FOR STUDY AFTER OUROBOROS. THAT WAS THE PLAN...HOW DID WE NOT DO THAT?

I THOUGHT WE WERE STUDYING IT.

YOU SAID IT WAS SENTIENT...

I THINK IT'S WAY BEYOND SENTIENT. AND I THINK IT SOMEHOW HAD US KEEP IT HERE ON SHIP.

WHY?

THE BILLION DOLLAR QUESTION. AND YOU WANT TO HEAR THE KICKER? I THINK IT BROUGHT US HERE.

I'M RIGHT, AREN'T I?

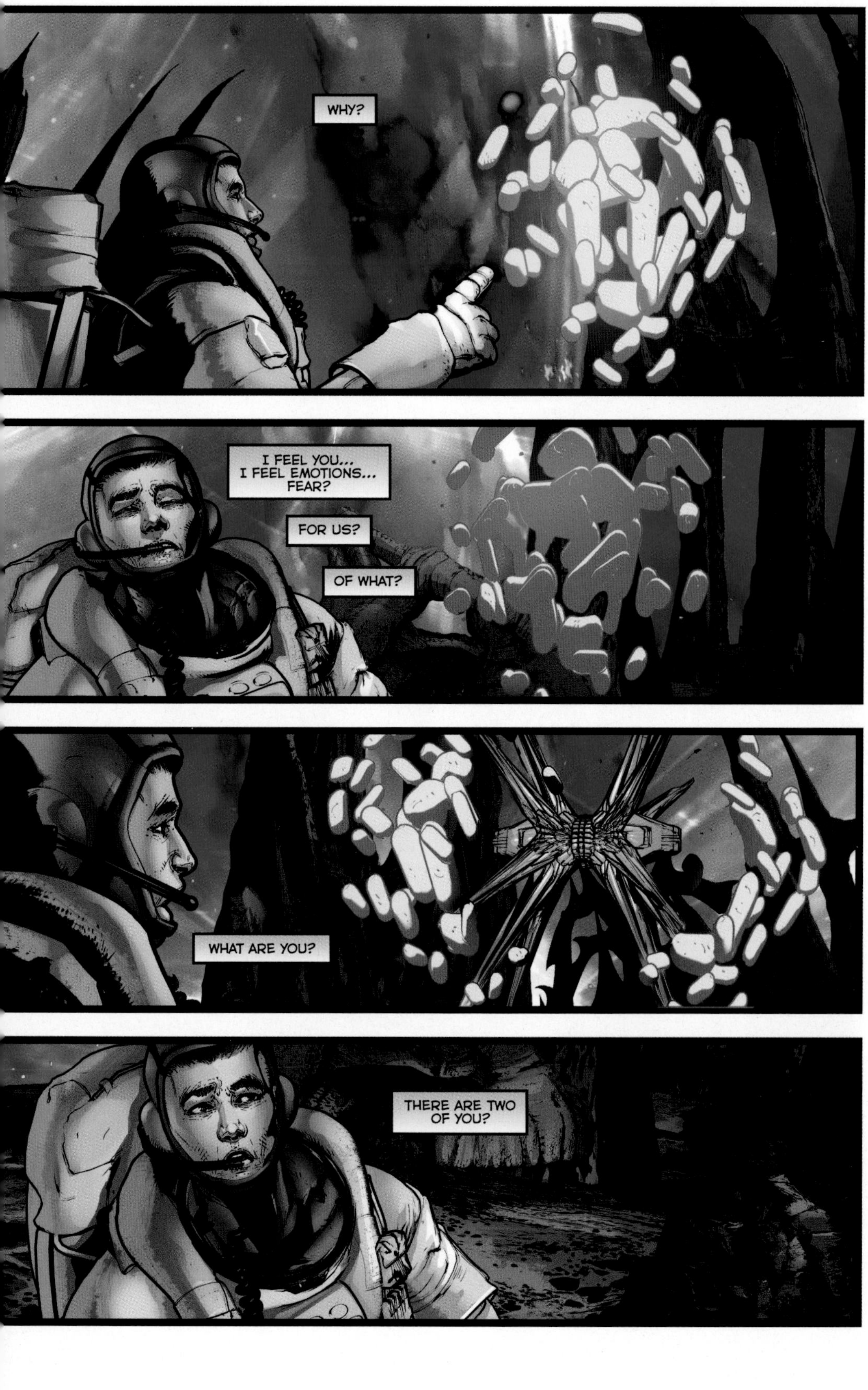
WHY?
I FEEL YOU... I FEEL EMOTIONS... FEAR?
FOR US?
OF WHAT?
WHAT ARE YOU?
THERE ARE TWO OF YOU?

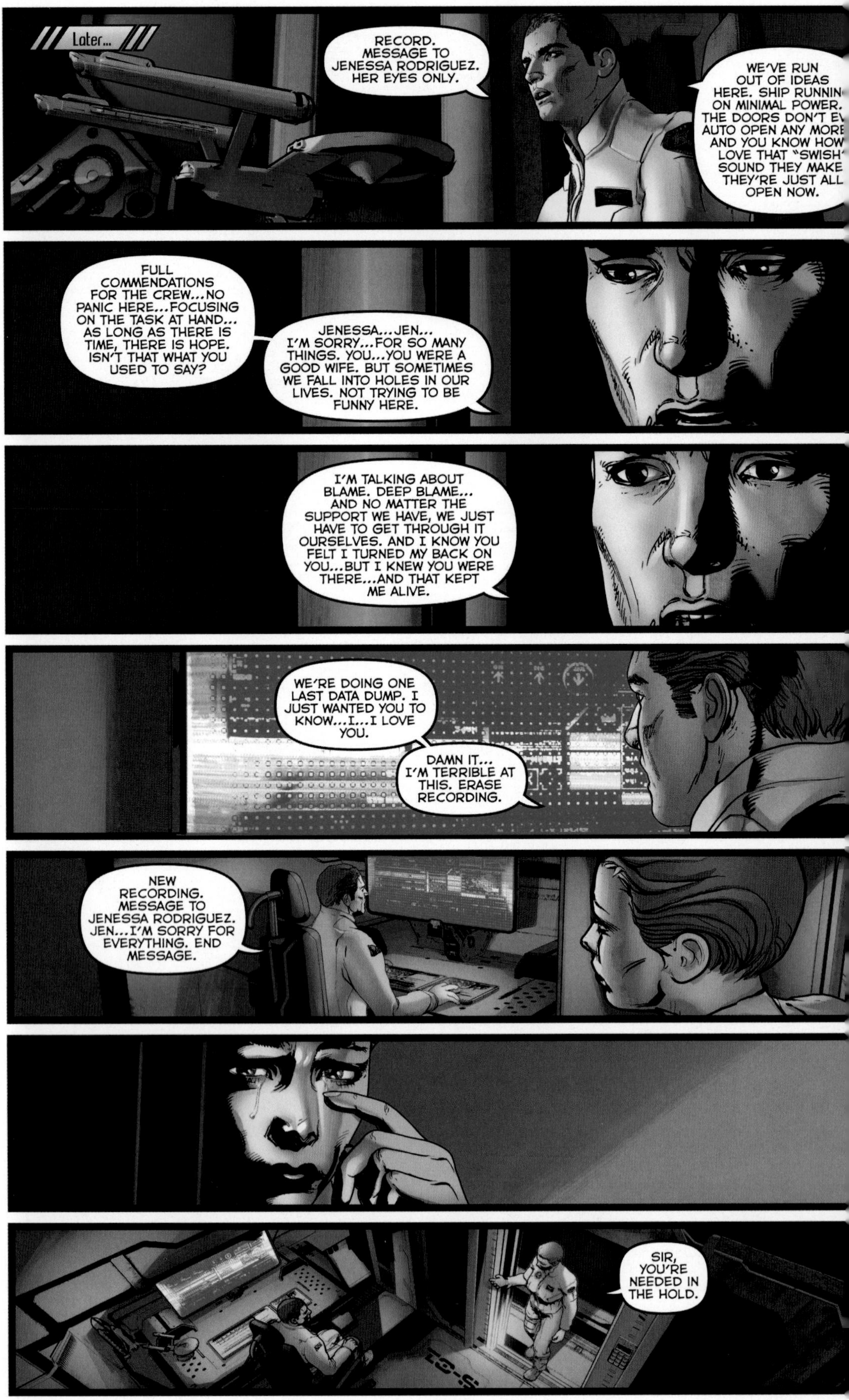
Later...
RECORD. MESSAGE TO JENESSA RODRIGUEZ. HER EYES ONLY.
WE'VE RUN OUT OF IDEAS HERE. SHIP RUNNIN ON MINIMAL POWER. THE DOORS DON'T EV AUTO OPEN ANY MORE AND YOU KNOW HOW LOVE THAT "SWISH" SOUND THEY MAKE THEY'RE JUST ALL OPEN NOW.
FULL COMMENDATIONS FOR THE CREW...NO PANIC HERE...FOCUSING ON THE TASK AT HAND... AS LONG AS THERE IS TIME, THERE IS HOPE. ISN'T THAT WHAT YOU USED TO SAY?
JENESSA...JEN... I'M SORRY...FOR SO MANY THINGS. YOU...YOU WERE A GOOD WIFE. BUT SOMETIMES WE FALL INTO HOLES IN OUR LIVES. NOT TRYING TO BE FUNNY HERE.
I'M TALKING ABOUT BLAME. DEEP BLAME... AND NO MATTER THE SUPPORT WE HAVE, WE JUST HAVE TO GET THROUGH IT OURSELVES. AND I KNOW YOU FELT I TURNED MY BACK ON YOU...BUT I KNEW YOU WERE THERE...AND THAT KEPT ME ALIVE.
WE'RE DOING ONE LAST DATA DUMP. I JUST WANTED YOU TO KNOW...I...I LOVE YOU.
DAMN IT... I'M TERRIBLE AT THIS. ERASE RECORDING.
NEW RECORDING. MESSAGE TO JENESSA RODRIGUEZ. JEN...I'M SORRY FOR EVERYTHING. END MESSAGE.
SIR, YOU'RE NEEDED IN THE HOLD.

WELL, CAN YOU COMMUNICATE WITH IT OR NOT?

THEM... NOT IT.

THE CRYSTAL... AND WHAT'S IN THE CRYSTAL.

THEY'RE BOTH SENTIENT, AND FROM WHAT I CAN FIGURE, BOTH EXTRA-DIMENSIONAL. WE'RE ONLY PERCEIVING THE TIP OF THE ICEBERG.

YOU SAID IT BROUGHT US HERE? WHICH ONE?

THE CRYSTAL. IT LOST FAITH IN OUR ABILITY TO KEEP IT SAFE.

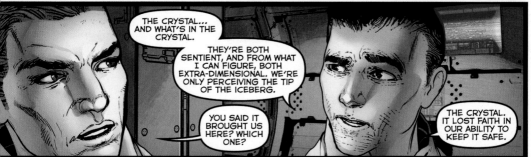

NO...THAT'S NOT RIGHT... I MEAN, TO KEEP IT FROM BEING OPENED. REMEMBER, WE WERE GOING TO TAKE IT TO EARTH TO BE STUDIED...

I REMEMBER. WE DID THAT—

THAT'S JUST THE THING. WE OBVIOUSLY DIDN'T. IT MADE US THINK WE DID...BELIEVE WE DID...I MEAN, WHY WOULDN'T WE HAVE BEEN STUDYING IT THIS WHOLE TIME?! IT MADE US FORGET ABOUT IT...IGNORE IT...IT FELT SAFE. BUT AFTER THE ALIEN ATTACK AND WORD POSSIBLY SPREADING ABOUT ITS EXISTENCE, IT KNEW IT WASN'T SAFE ANYMORE.

THE SINGULARITY...

RIGHT...IT DOESN'T WANT TO BE OPENED. AND IF IT GOES INTO THE SINGULARITY, IT NEVER WILL BE.

WHAT'S IN IT?

NOT SURE. BUT I'VE LEARNED THE CRYSTAL IS OLD. MILLIONS...POSSIBLY *BILLIONS* OF YEARS OLD. SENTIENT TECHNOLOGY THAT WAS GROWN BY A RACE SO ADVANCED THAT TO US...WELL, YOU MIGHT AS WELL CALL THEM GODS...OR SOMETHING CLOSE.

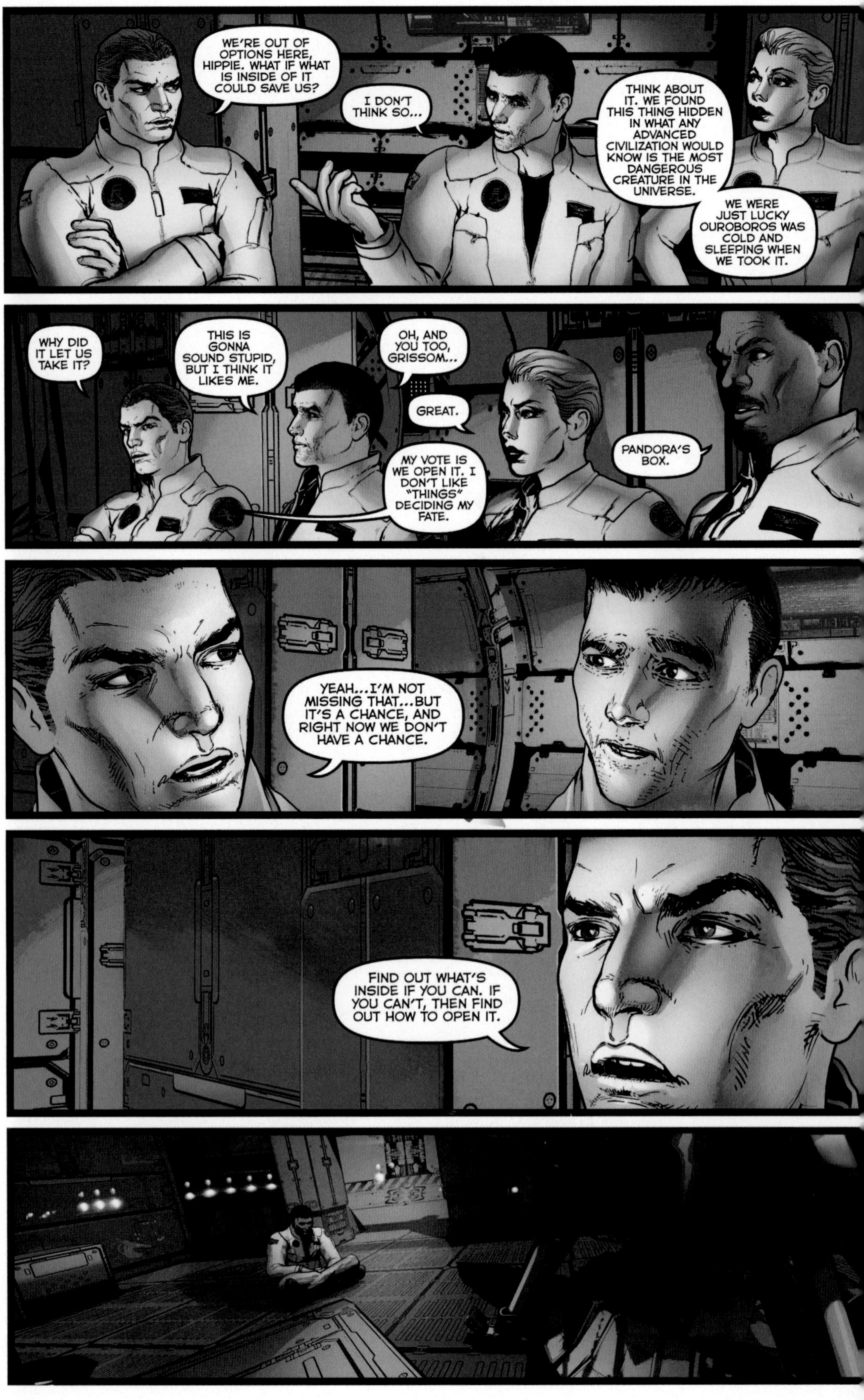

WE'RE OUT OF OPTIONS HERE, HIPPIE. WHAT IF WHAT IS INSIDE OF IT COULD SAVE US?
I DON'T THINK SO...
THINK ABOUT IT. WE FOUND THIS THING HIDDEN IN WHAT ANY ADVANCED CIVILIZATION WOULD KNOW IS THE MOST DANGEROUS CREATURE IN THE UNIVERSE.
WE WERE JUST LUCKY OUROBOROS WAS COLD AND SLEEPING WHEN WE TOOK IT.
WHY DID IT LET US TAKE IT?
THIS IS GONNA SOUND STUPID, BUT I THINK IT LIKES ME.
OH, AND YOU TOO, GRISSOM...
GREAT.
MY VOTE IS WE OPEN IT. I DON'T LIKE "THINGS" DECIDING MY FATE.
PANDORA'S BOX.
YEAH...I'M NOT MISSING THAT...BUT IT'S A CHANCE, AND RIGHT NOW WE DON'T HAVE A CHANCE.
FIND OUT WHAT'S INSIDE IF YOU CAN. IF YOU CAN'T, THEN FIND OUT HOW TO OPEN IT.

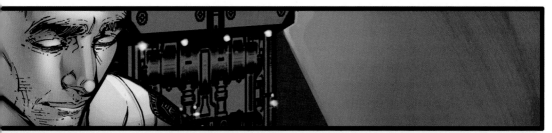

STOP YELLING!

I'M ASKING AGAIN...WHAT ARE YOU?

NO, I GET THAT YOU WANT TO BE FREE AND IT WANTS YOU SECURED. SECURED...NOT IMPRISONED...CONTAINED...

UPGRADE? YOU'RE AN UPGRADE?

OH, MY!

IT'S A BIG BANG... A FRIGGIN' BIG BANG!

SLOW DOWN.

IMAGINE YOU ARE SO ADVANCED, SO POWERFUL A RACE, THAT WHEN YOU SEE THE NEXT BIG BANG COMING, YOU CAN CONTAIN IT. STOP IT. IT'S NOT MALEVOLENT.

IT'S A FORCE OF NATURE... *THE FORCE OF NATURE* IN A BOTTLE!

WE CAN'T LET IT OUT. EVERYTHING WILL BE RESET. IT SAYS UPGRADED...THE NATURAL WAY THE UNIVERSE ITSELF EVOLVES.

BUT WE'D ALL BE GONE. EVERYTHING WE KNOW WOULD BE GONE.

AND THE CRYSTAL DOESN'T WANT US TO OPEN IT, RIGHT?

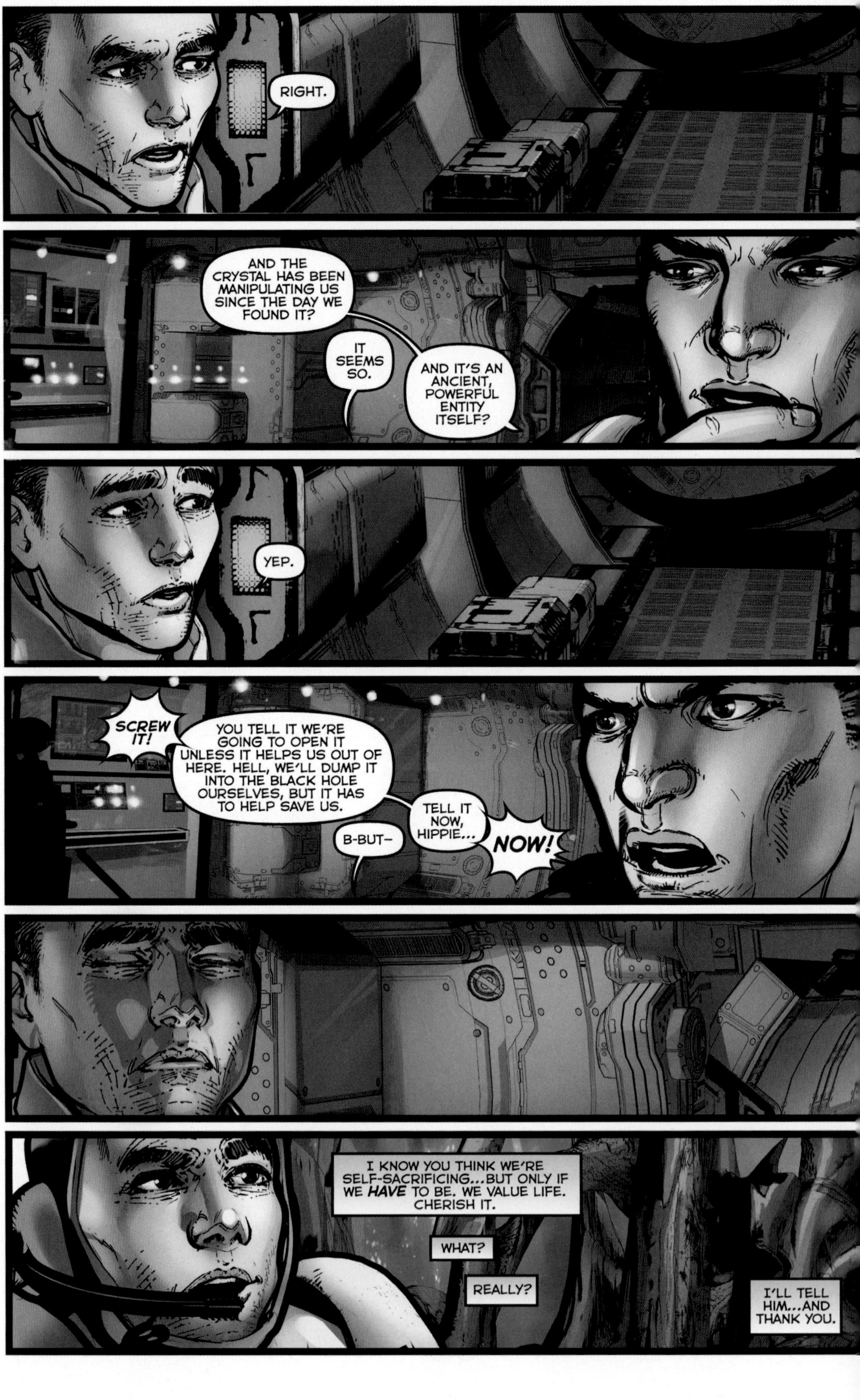
RIGHT.
AND THE CRYSTAL HAS BEEN MANIPULATING US SINCE THE DAY WE FOUND IT?
IT SEEMS SO.
AND IT'S AN ANCIENT, POWERFUL ENTITY ITSELF?
YEP.
SCREW IT!
YOU TELL IT WE'RE GOING TO OPEN IT UNLESS IT HELPS US OUT OF HERE. HELL, WE'LL DUMP IT INTO THE BLACK HOLE OURSELVES, BUT IT HAS TO HELP SAVE US.
B-BUT–
TELL IT NOW, HIPPIE...
NOW!
I KNOW YOU THINK WE'RE SELF-SACRIFICING...BUT ONLY IF WE *HAVE* TO BE. WE VALUE LIFE. CHERISH IT.
WHAT?
REALLY?
I'LL TELL HIM...AND THANK YOU.

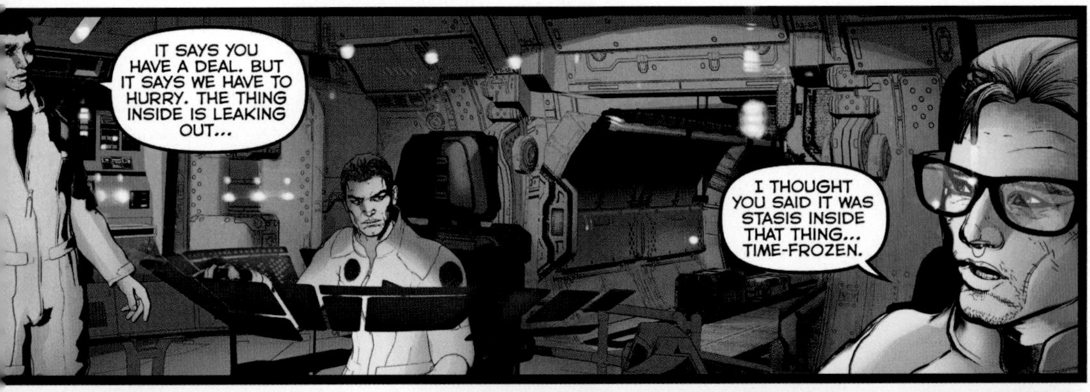
IT SAYS YOU HAVE A DEAL. BUT IT SAYS WE HAVE TO HURRY. THE THING INSIDE IS LEAKING OUT...
I THOUGHT YOU SAID IT WAS STASIS INSIDE THAT THING... TIME-FROZEN.

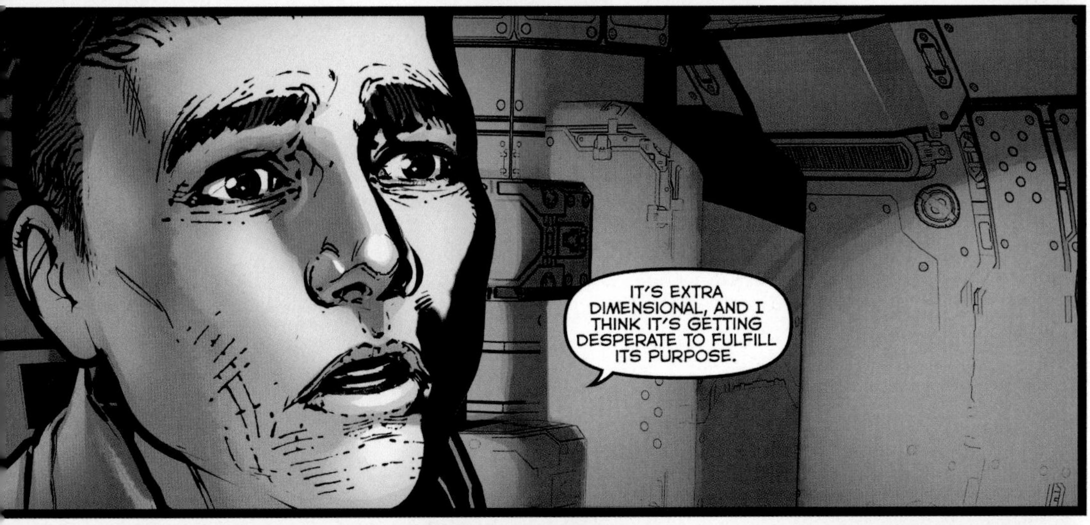
IT'S EXTRA DIMENSIONAL, AND I THINK IT'S GETTING DESPERATE TO FULFILL ITS PURPOSE.

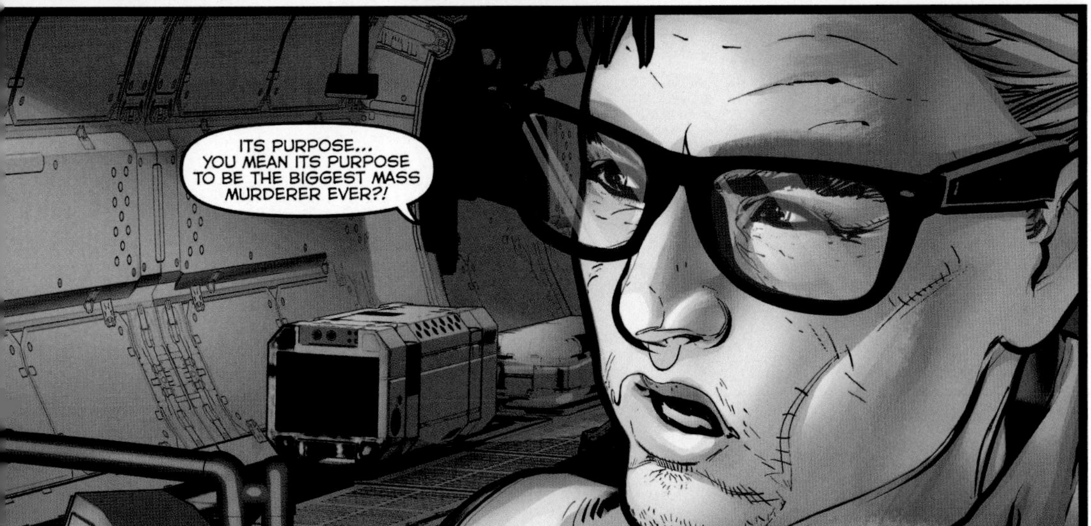
ITS PURPOSE... YOU MEAN ITS PURPOSE TO BE THE BIGGEST MASS MURDERER EVER?!

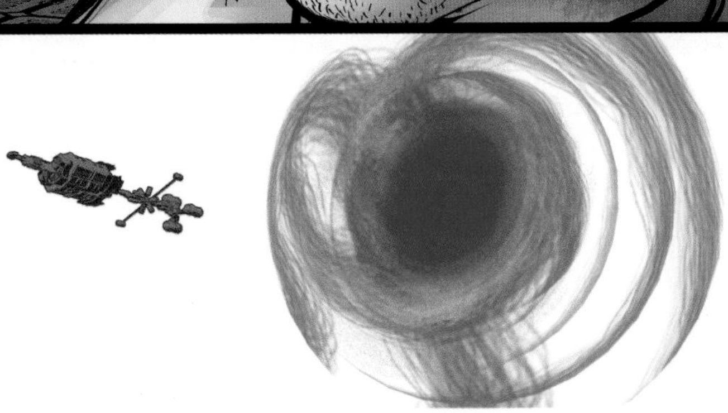

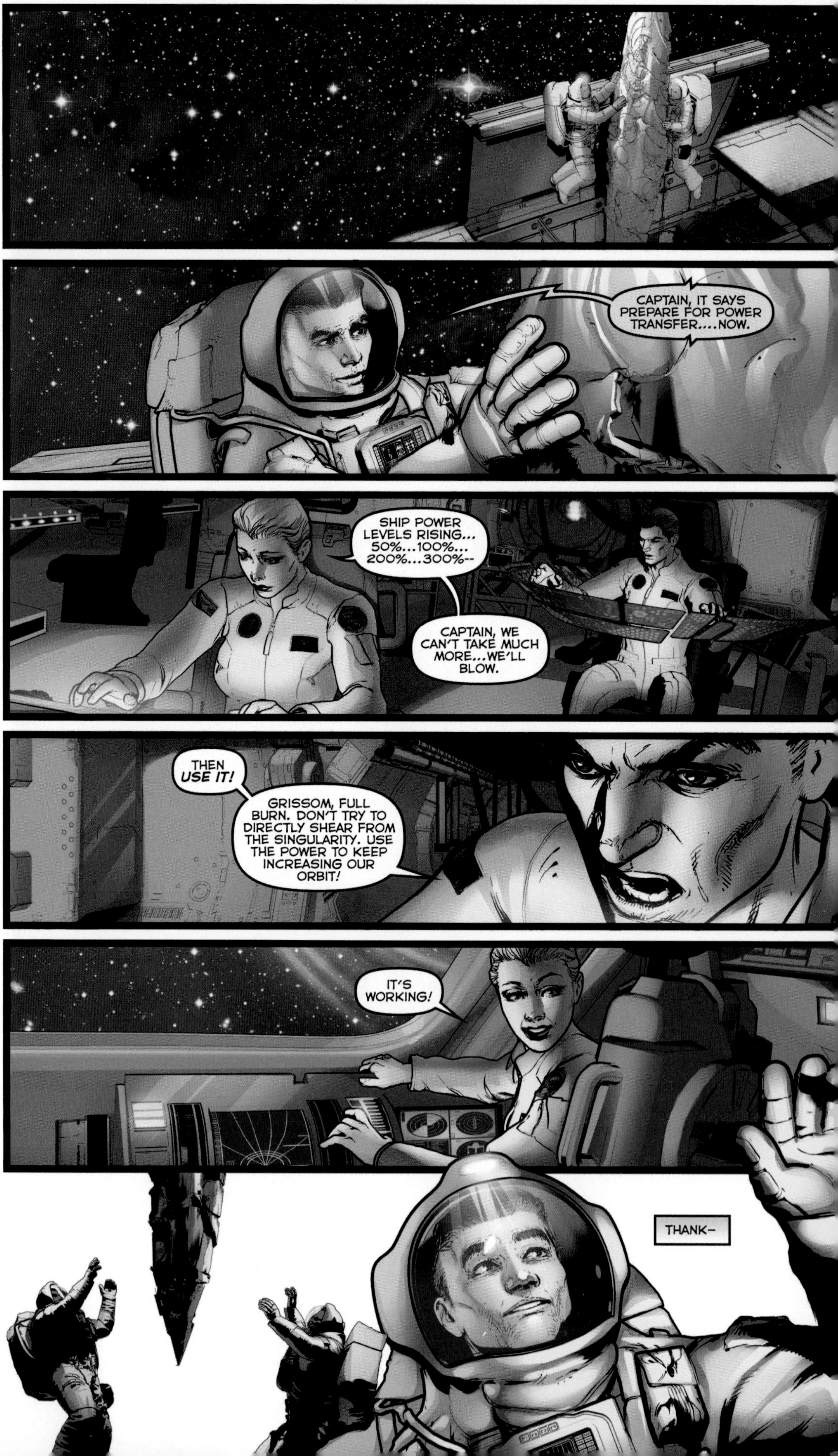

CAPTAIN, IT SAYS PREPARE FOR POWER TRANSFER....NOW.
SHIP POWER LEVELS RISING... 50%...100%... 200%...300%--
CAPTAIN, WE CAN'T TAKE MUCH MORE...WE'LL BLOW.
THEN USE IT!
GRISSOM, FULL BURN. DON'T TRY TO DIRECTLY SHEAR FROM THE SINGULARITY. USE THE POWER TO KEEP INCREASING OUR ORBIT!
IT'S WORKING!
THANK–

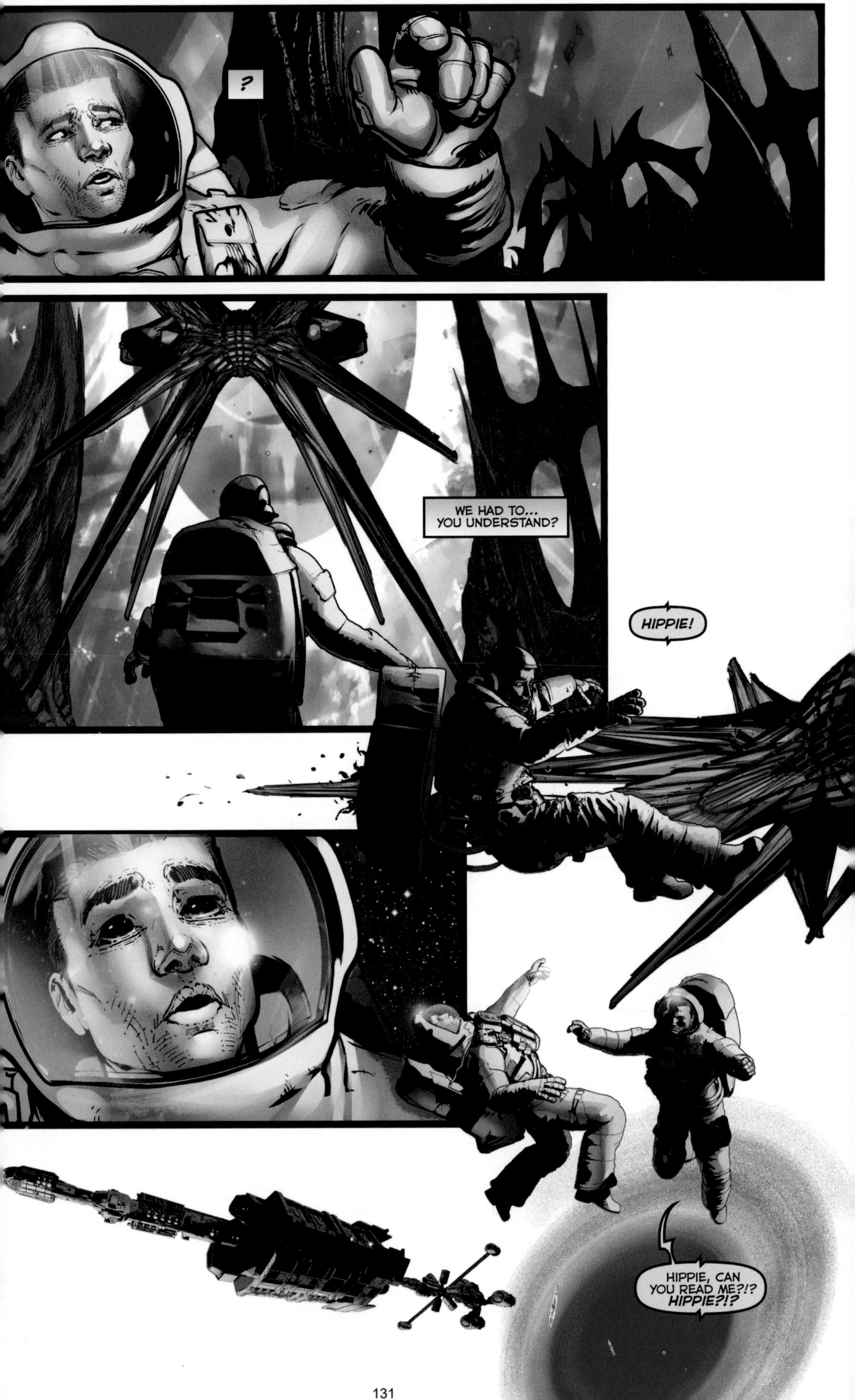
?
WE HAD TO... YOU UNDERSTAND?
HIPPIE!
HIPPIE, CAN YOU READ ME?!? HIPPIE?!?

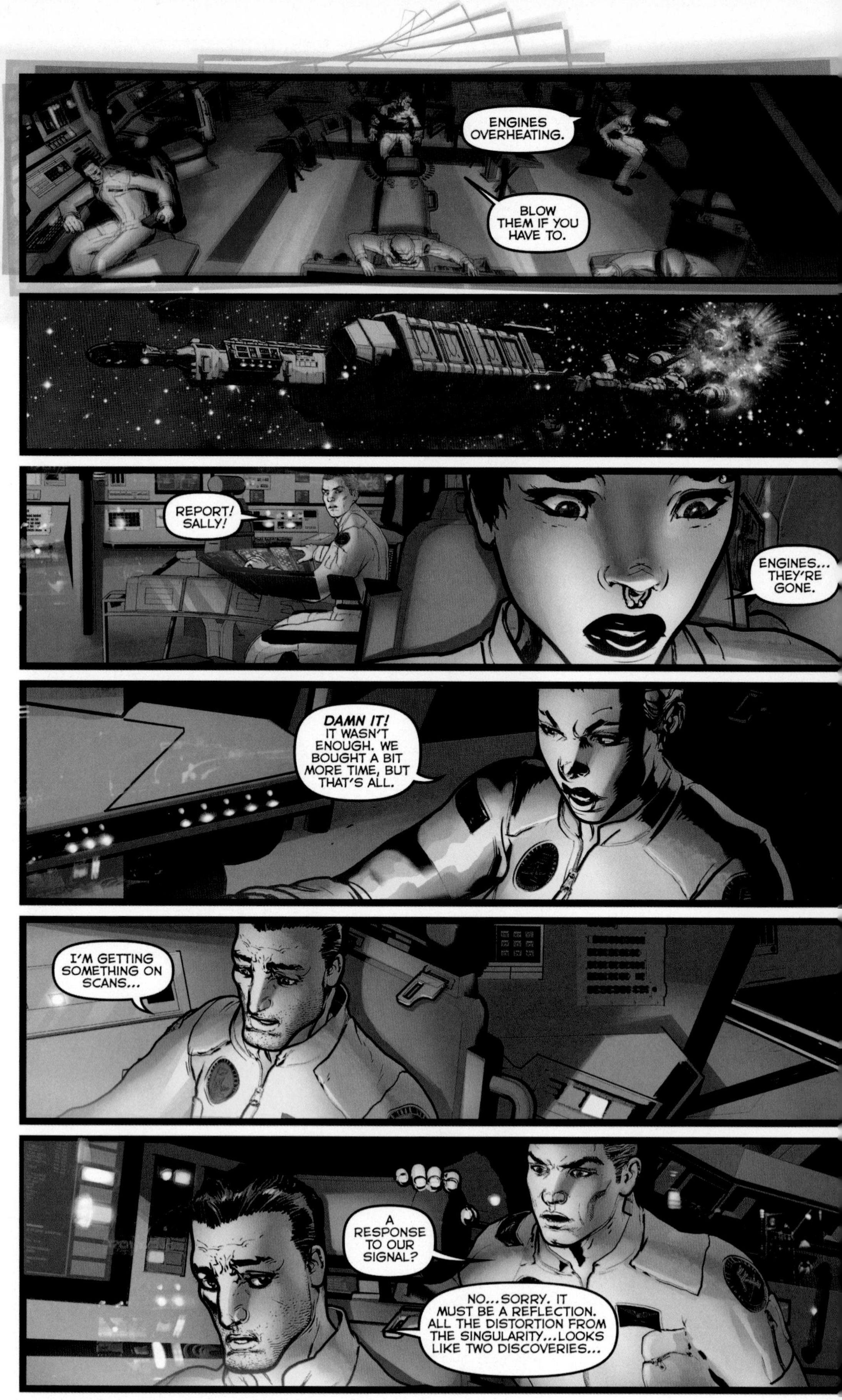
ENGINES OVERHEATING.
BLOW THEM IF YOU HAVE TO.
REPORT! SALLY!
ENGINES... THEY'RE GONE.
DAMN IT! IT WASN'T ENOUGH. WE BOUGHT A BIT MORE TIME, BUT THAT'S ALL.
I'M GETTING SOMETHING ON SCANS...
A RESPONSE TO OUR SIGNAL?
NO...SORRY. IT MUST BE A REFLECTION. ALL THE DISTORTION FROM THE SINGULARITY...LOOKS LIKE TWO DISCOVERIES...

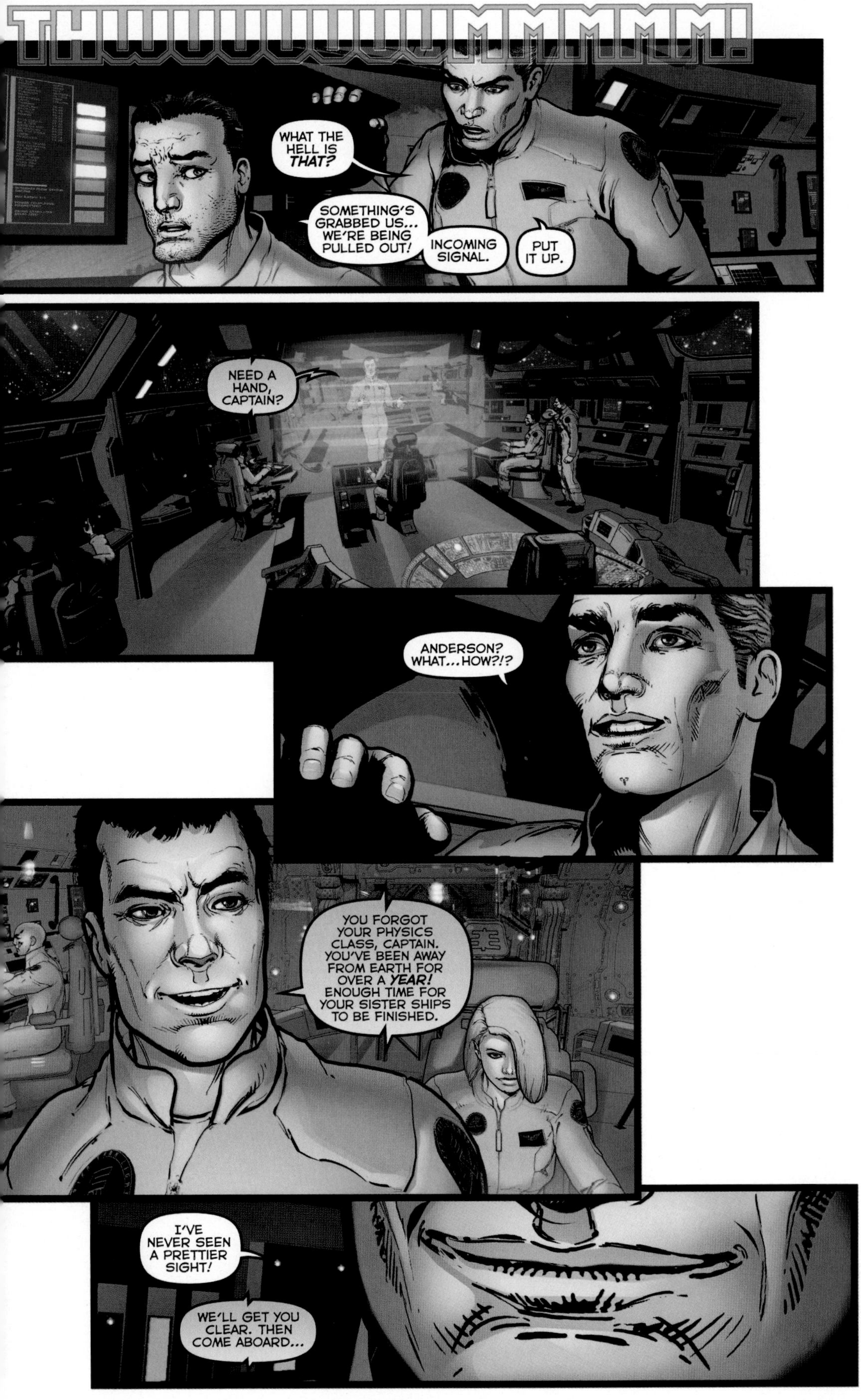
THWUUUUUUMMMMMM!
WHAT THE HELL IS *THAT?*
SOMETHING'S GRABBED US... WE'RE BEING PULLED OUT!
INCOMING SIGNAL.
PUT IT UP.
NEED A HAND, CAPTAIN?
ANDERSON? WHAT...HOW?!?
YOU FORGOT YOUR PHYSICS CLASS, CAPTAIN. YOU'VE BEEN AWAY FROM EARTH FOR OVER A *YEAR!* ENOUGH TIME FOR YOUR SISTER SHIPS TO BE FINISHED.
I'VE NEVER SEEN A PRETTIER SIGHT!
WE'LL GET YOU CLEAR. THEN COME ABOARD...

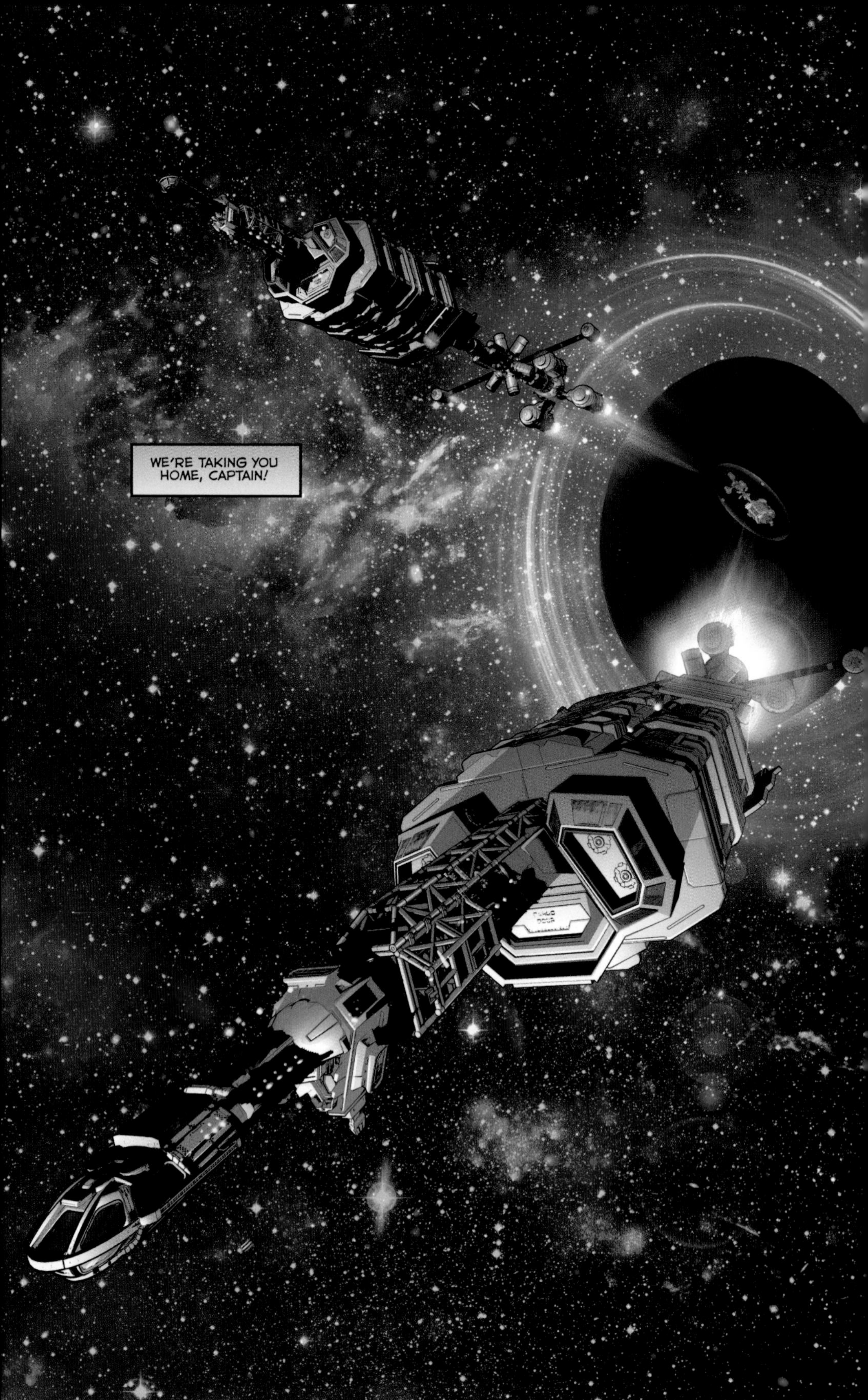
WE'RE TAKING YOU HOME, CAPTAIN!

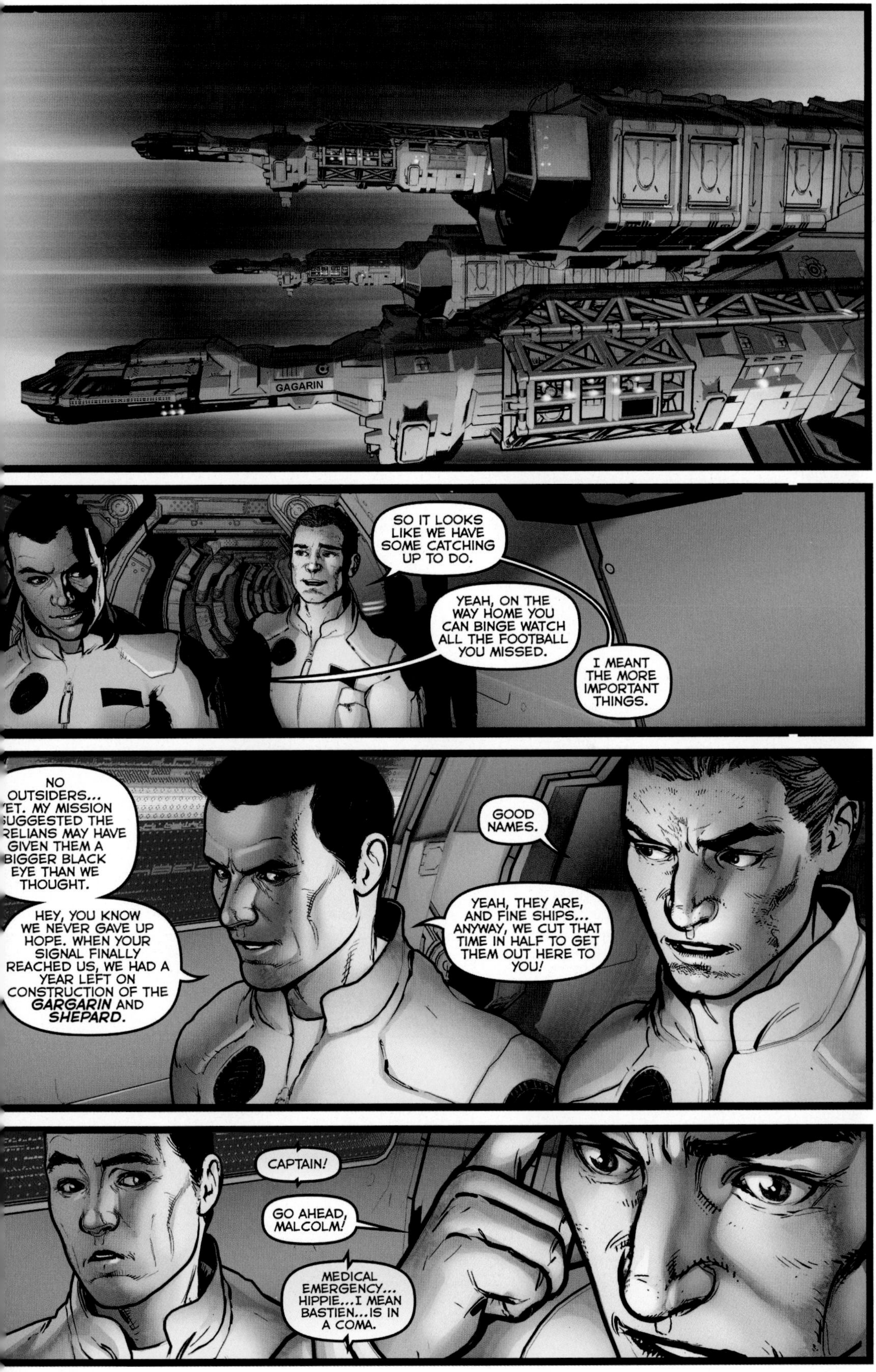

SHEPARD
GAGARIN
SO IT LOOKS LIKE WE HAVE SOME CATCHING UP TO DO.
YEAH, ON THE WAY HOME YOU CAN BINGE WATCH ALL THE FOOTBALL YOU MISSED.
I MEANT THE MORE IMPORTANT THINGS.
NO OUTSIDERS... ET. MY MISSION UGGESTED THE RELIANS MAY HAVE GIVEN THEM A BIGGER BLACK EYE THAN WE THOUGHT.
HEY, YOU KNOW WE NEVER GAVE UP HOPE. WHEN YOUR SIGNAL FINALLY REACHED US, WE HAD A YEAR LEFT ON CONSTRUCTION OF THE *GARGARIN* AND *SHEPARD*.
GOOD NAMES.
YEAH, THEY ARE, AND FINE SHIPS... ANYWAY, WE CUT THAT TIME IN HALF TO GET THEM OUT HERE TO YOU!
CAPTAIN!
GO AHEAD, MALCOLM!
MEDICAL EMERGENCY... HIPPIE... I MEAN BASTIEN... IS IN A COMA.

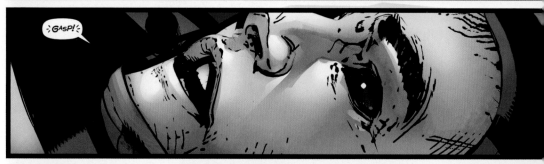

> GASP!

> OH, MY...

> WHAT ARE YOU STILL DOING HERE?

> WHAT DO YOU MEAN, WE?

> OH...I AM SOOOO SCREWED.

FOR MORE FASTER THAN LIGHT GO TO:
ExperienceAnomaly.com/ftlcomic

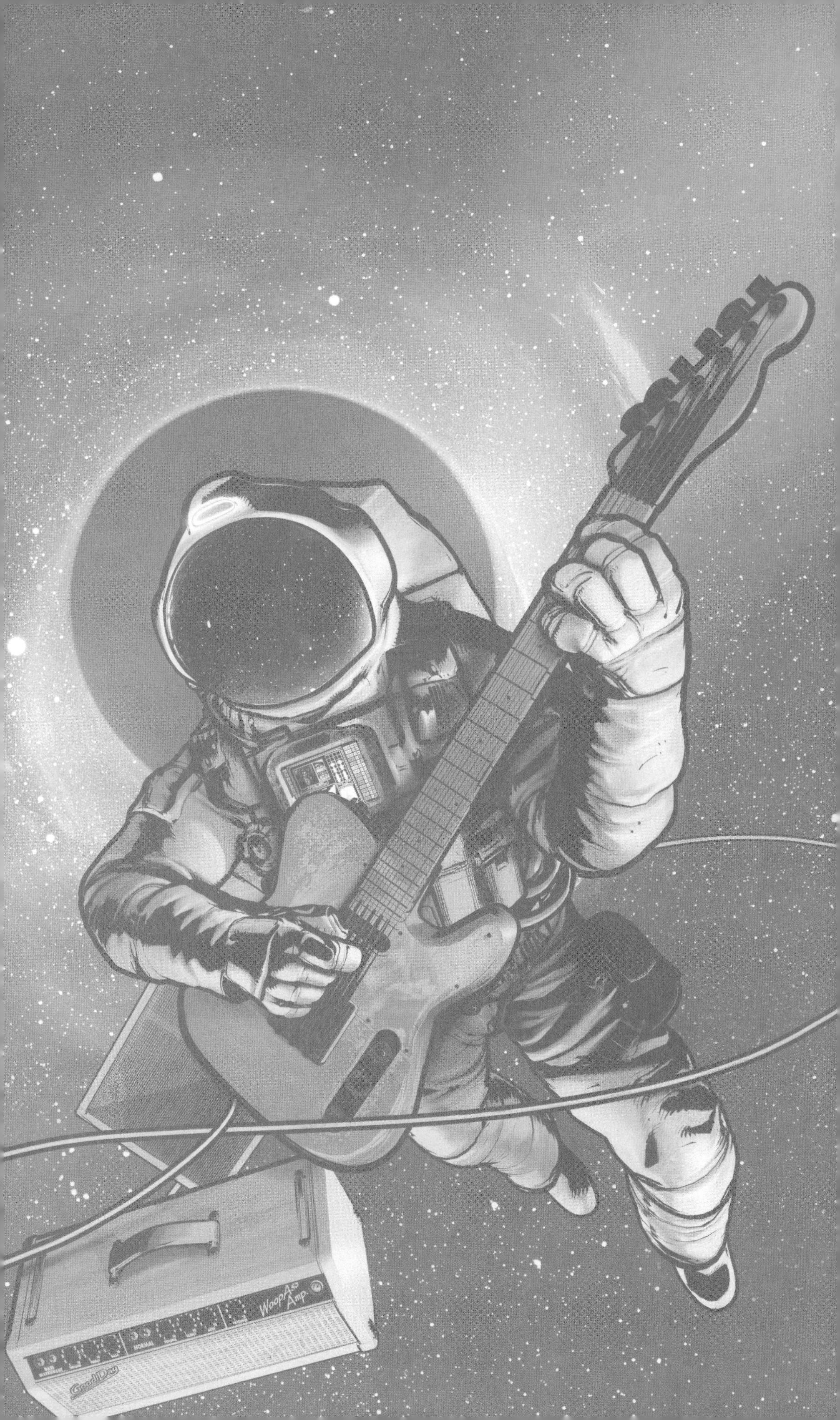
WoopAss Amp
NORMAL
Good Day

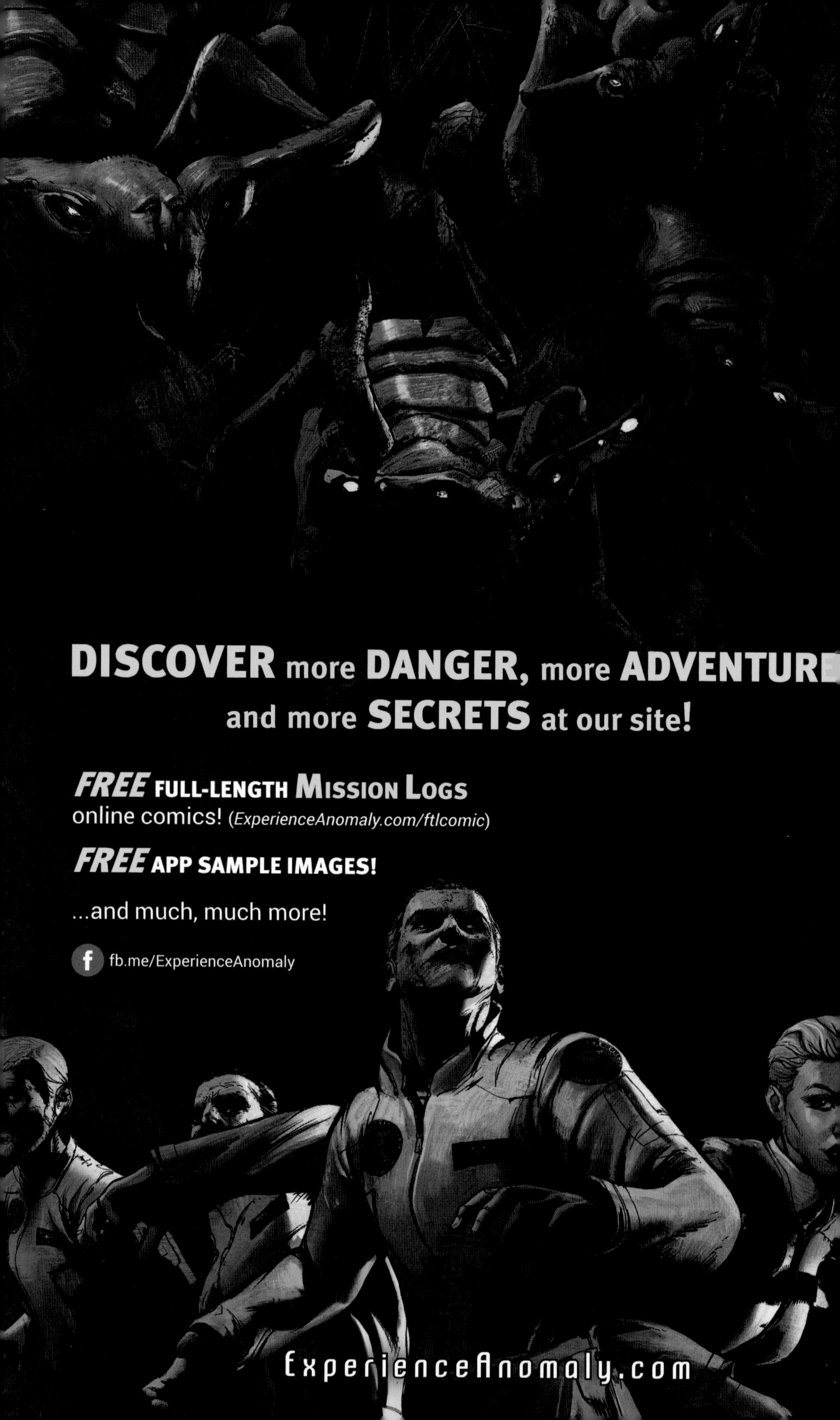
DISCOVER more DANGER, more ADVENTURE
and more SECRETS at our site!
FREE FULL-LENGTH MISSION LOGS
online comics! (ExperienceAnomaly.com/ftlcomic)
FREE APP SAMPLE IMAGES!
...and much, much more!
fb.me/ExperienceAnomaly
ExperienceAnomaly.com

FASTER THAN LIGHT™

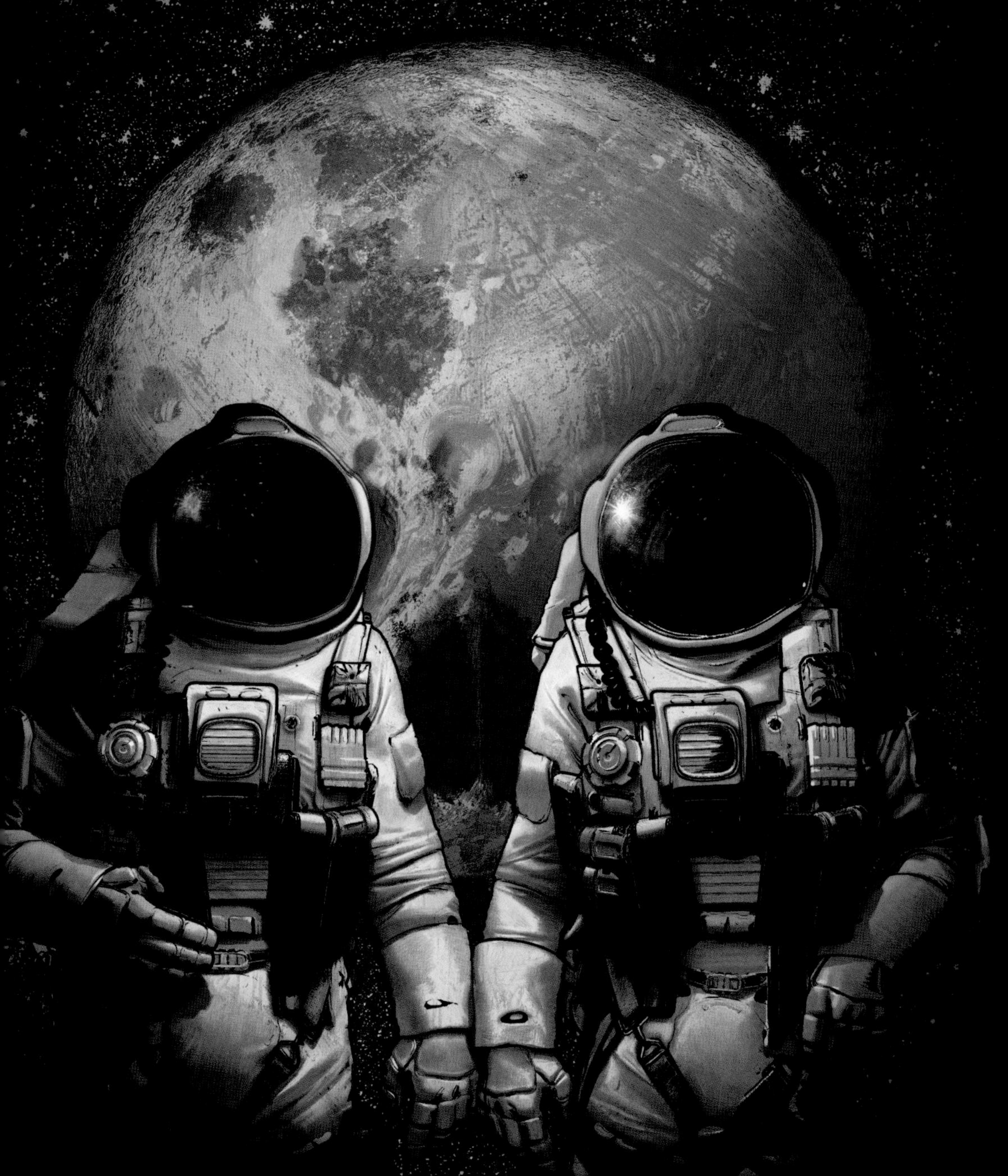

BEHIND THE SCENES

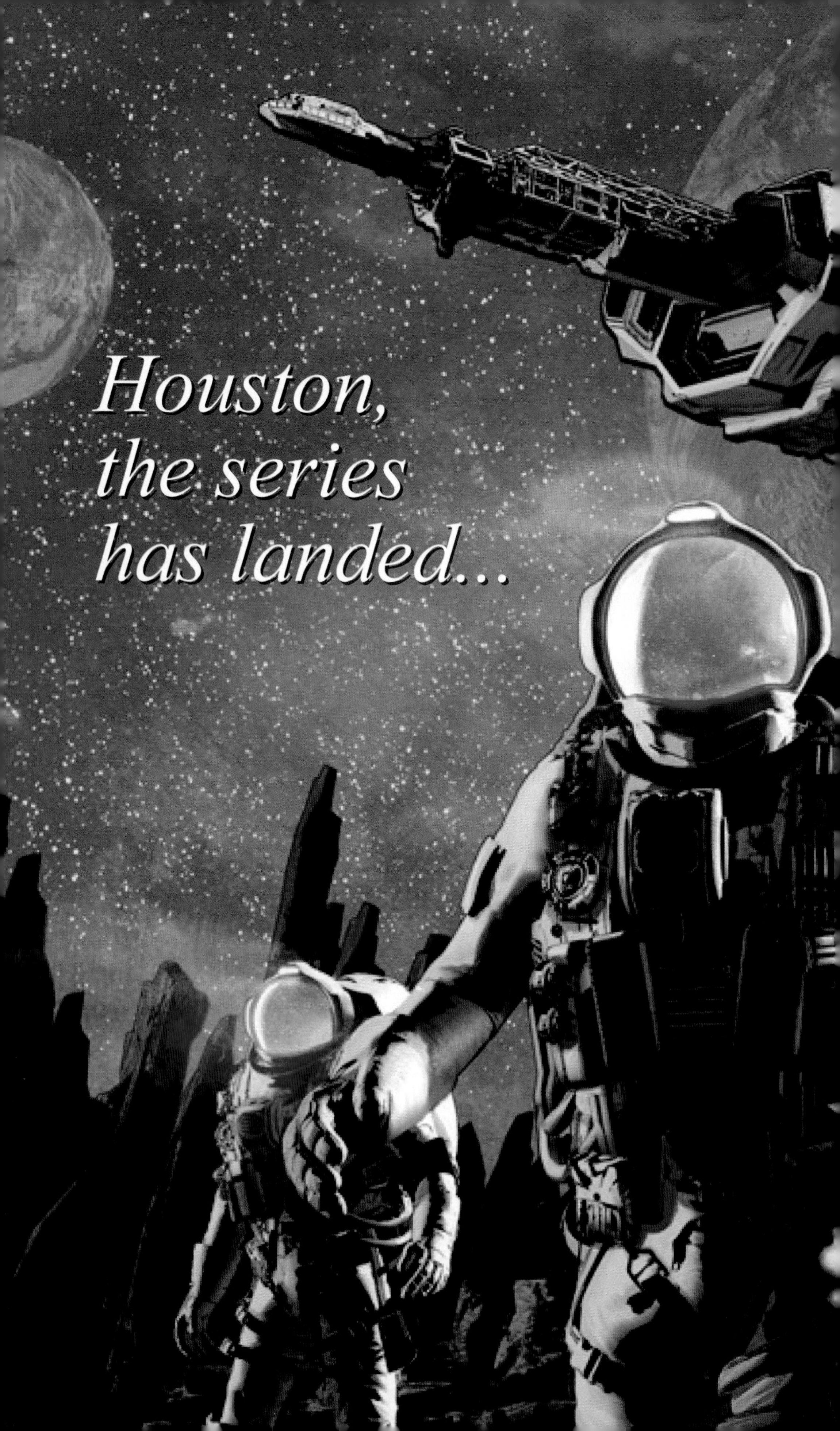
Houston,
the series
has landed...

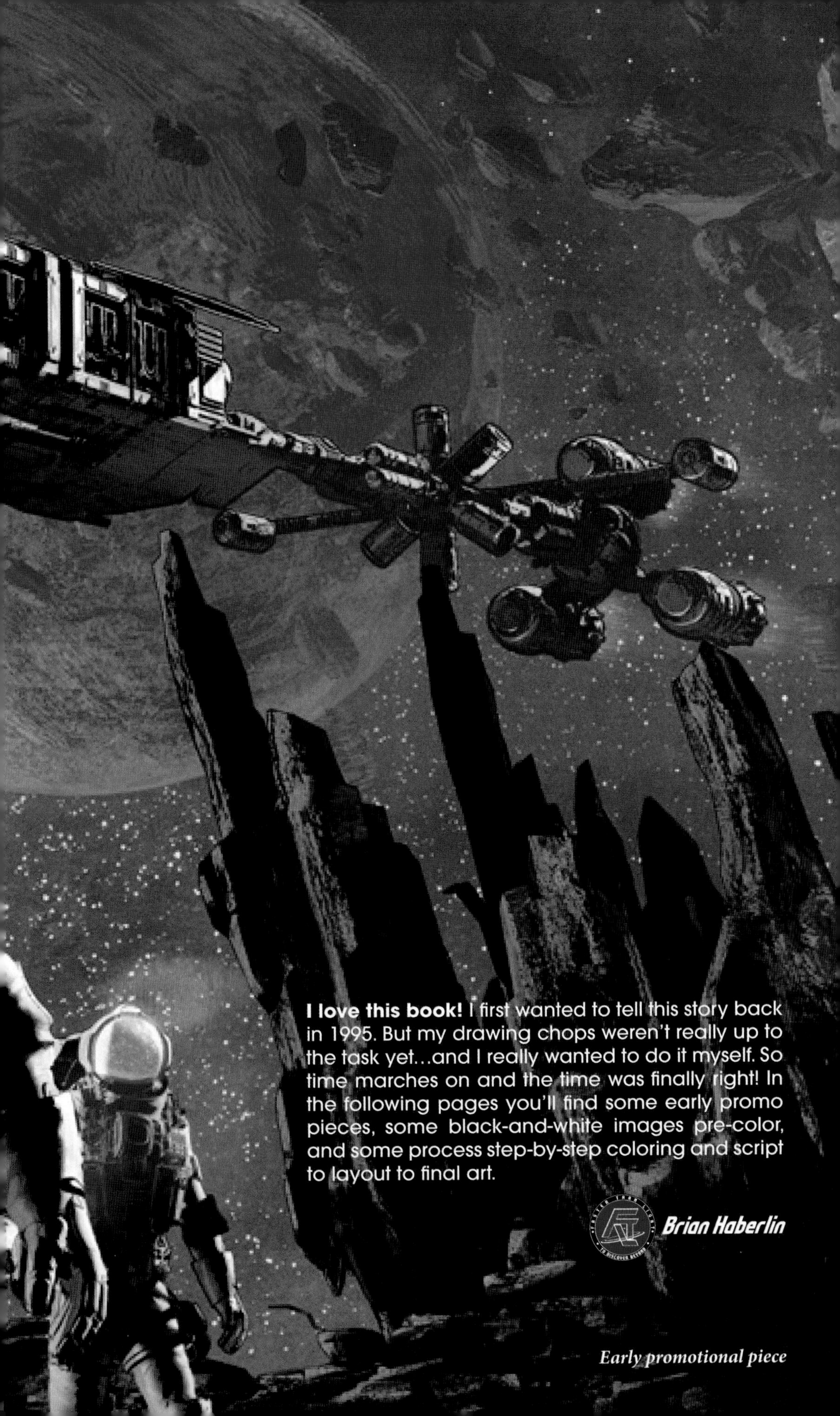

I love this book! I first wanted to tell this story back in 1995. But my drawing chops weren't really up to the task yet…and I really wanted to do it myself. So time marches on and the time was finally right! In the following pages you'll find some early promo pieces, some black-and-white images pre-color, and some process step-by-step coloring and script to layout to final art.

Brian Haberlin

Early promotional piece

FASTER THAN LIGHT ISSUE 6 FIRST DRAFT
PAGE 1

PANEL 1
Caption: EARTH: ICARUS STATION.

PANEL 2
FRENCH COUNCILOR (IN MIDDLE ON FAR SIDE OF TABLE: WILLIAM FOREST, YOU ARE TO BE STRIPPED OF YOUR COMMAND OF THE DISCOVERY FOR REFUSING COUNCIL ORDERS. FURTHER, YOU ARE TO BE BROUGHT UP ON CHARGES OF INSUBORDINATION. DO YOU HAVE ANYTHING TO SAY IN YOUR DEFENSE?

PANEL 3
FOREST: …

PANEL 4
FRENCH COUNCILOR: WHAT DID YOU SAY?
FOREST: I SAID…

PANEL 5
FOREST: HONEY, YOU BET I DO!

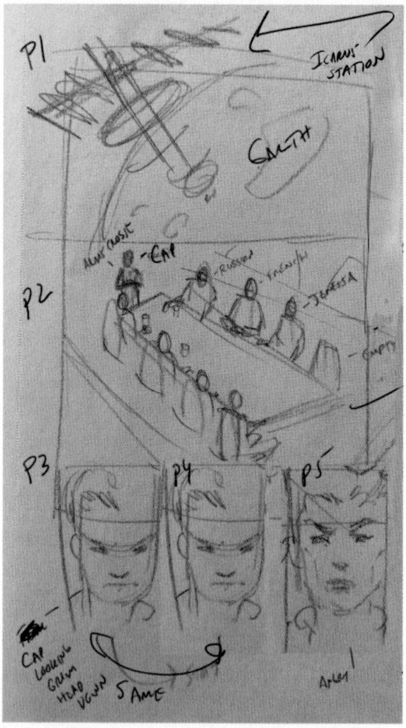
P1
ICARUS STATION
EARTH
P2
P3
P4
P5
CAP LOOKING GRIM HEAD DOWN
SAME
ANGRY

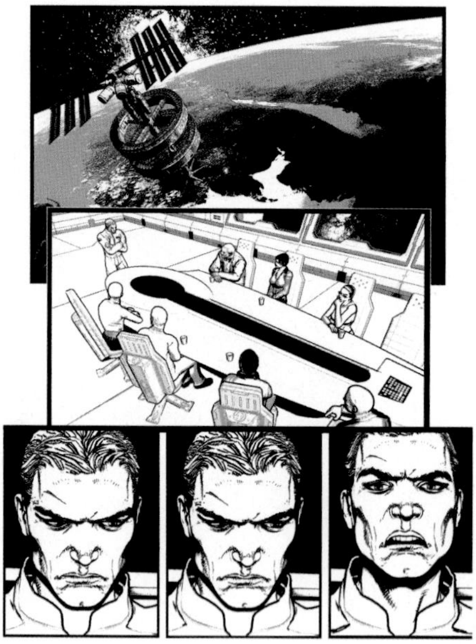

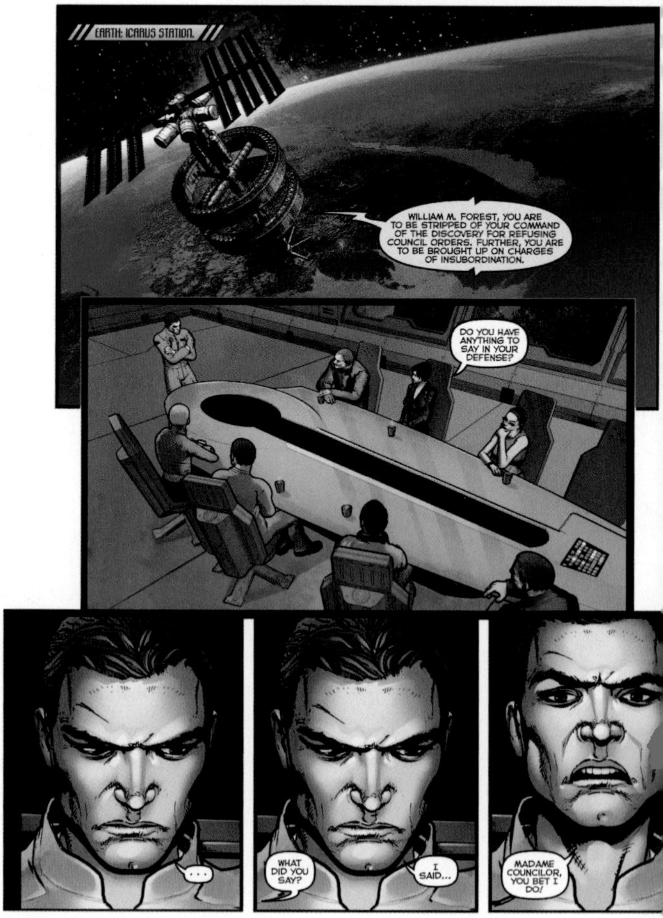
EARTH: ICARUS STATION.
WILLIAM M. FOREST, YOU ARE TO BE STRIPPED OF YOUR COMMAND OF THE DISCOVERY FOR REFUSING COUNCIL ORDERS. FURTHER, YOU ARE TO BE BROUGHT UP ON CHARGES OF INSUBORDINATION.
DO YOU HAVE ANYTHING TO SAY IN YOUR DEFENSE?
...
WHAT DID YOU SAY?
I SAID...
MADAME COUNCILOR, YOU BET I DO!

"Here is the first draft script for issue 6 with my layouts, inks, then final color."

3

LS 1 & 2: NONE

L 3
Y (OFF PANEL): SO…

L 4
Y (NOTICING): WOW…PRETTY GOOD...100
ion... THAT'S A LOT OF LIKES...
: YEAH--WELL...I'm a bit of a ce-
i–

L 5
Y: RIGHT. LOTS OF TV TIME. LET
HOW YOU A PAGE WITH A WHOLE LOT OF
S!

L 6
: !
Y: 100 MILLION IS A LITTLE PATHETIC
ARED TO–

LS 7 & 8
: WHAT!?!
Y: RUGGED GOOD LOOKS AND WAR HERO
P BRAINY GEEK ANY TIME.
Y: DON'T GET ALL SNOOTY UP HERE,
. HERE YOU'RE JUST ONE OF A COUPLE
N OF GENIUSES.

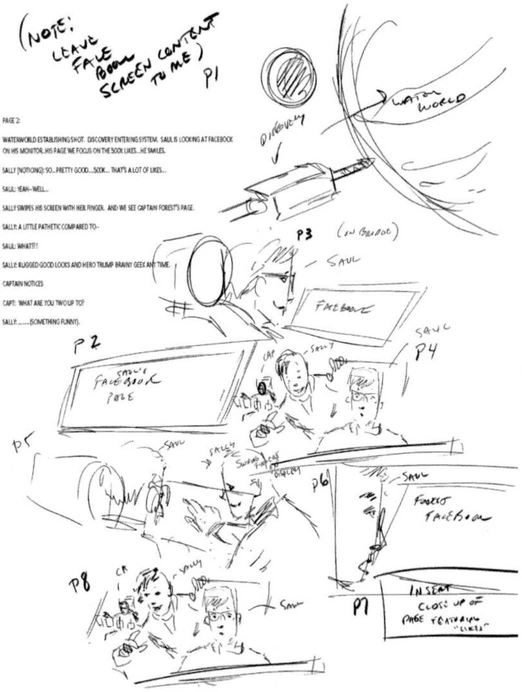

(NOTE: LEAVE FAKE BOOK SCREEN CONTENT TO ME)
P1
PAGE 2:
WATERWORLD ESTABLISHING SHOT. DISCOVERY ENTERING SYSTEM. SAUL IS LOOKING AT FACEBOOK ON HIS MONITOR. HIS PAGE WE FOCUS ON THE 500K LIKES...HE SMILES.
SALLY (NOTICING): SO...PRETTY GOOD...500K... THAT'S A LOT OF LIKES...
SAUL: YEAH--WELL...
SALLY SWIPES HIS SCREEN WITH HER FINGER. AND WE SEE CAPTAIN FOREST'S PAGE.
SALLY: A LITTLE PATHETIC COMPARED TO--
SAUL: WHAT!?!
SALLY: RUGGED GOOD LOOKS AND HERO TRUMP BRAINY GEEK ANY TIME.
CAPTAIN NOTICES
CAPT: WHAT ARE YOU TWO UP TO?
SALLY: ......(SOMETHING FUNNY).
WATER WORLD
P3
SAUL
FACEBOOK
P2
P4
P6
P8
P7

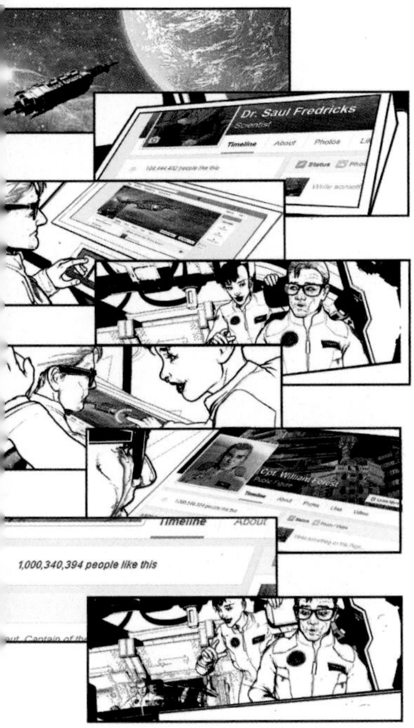

Dr. Saul Fredricks
Scientist
1,000,340,394 people like this

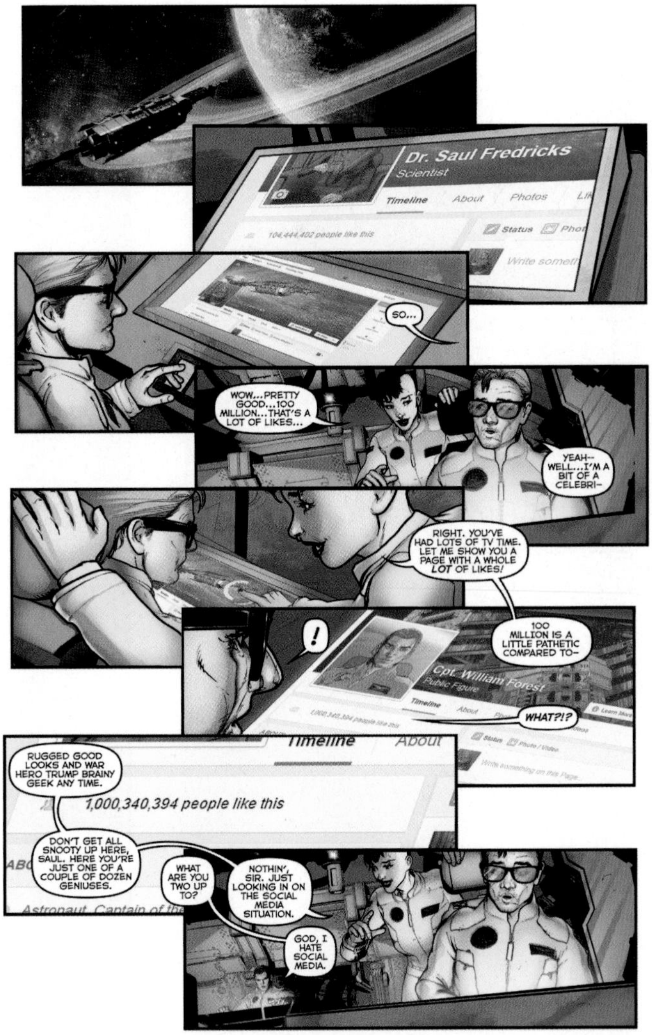

Dr. Saul Fredricks
Scientist
Timeline
About
Photos
104,444,402 people like this
SO...
WOW...PRETTY GOOD...100 MILLION...THAT'S A LOT OF LIKES...
YEAH-- WELL...I'M A BIT OF A CELEBRI–
RIGHT. YOU'VE HAD LOTS OF TV TIME. LET ME SHOW YOU A PAGE WITH A WHOLE LOT OF LIKES!
!
100 MILLION IS A LITTLE PATHETIC COMPARED TO–
Cpt. William Forest
Public Figure
WHAT?!?
Timeline
About
RUGGED GOOD LOOKS AND WAR HERO TRUMP BRAINY GEEK ANY TIME.
1,000,340,394 people like this
DON'T GET ALL SNOOTY UP HERE, SAUL. HERE YOU'RE JUST ONE OF A COUPLE OF DOZEN GENIUSES.
WHAT ARE YOU TWO UP TO?
NOTHIN', SIR. JUST LOOKING IN ON THE SOCIAL MEDIA SITUATION.
GOD, I HATE SOCIAL MEDIA.

PAGE 4

PANEL 1
HIPPIE: WOW...JUST WOW.
CAPT: GLAD YOU'RE IMPRESSED, HIPPIE.
HIPPIE: I CAN'T EVEN SWIM AND THIS IS STILL EXCITING!

PANEL 2
CAPT: LIEUTENANT, HOW'S STRUCTURAL INTEGRITY HOLDING UP? SHE'S RATED FOR UNDERWATER USE BUT I THINK THIS IS THE FIRST TEST AT THESE DEPTHS
SALLY: LOOKING GOOD, CAPTAIN.

PANEL 3
CAPT: GREAT, PROCEED TO THE LANDING COORDINATES THEY GAVE US.
GRISSOM: YES, SIR.

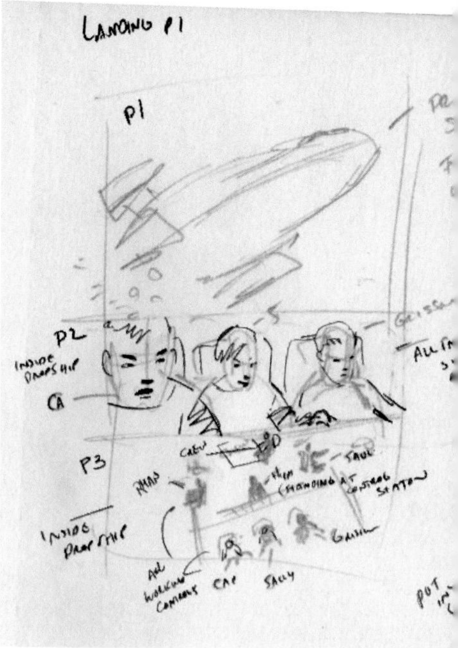
LANDING P1
P1
P2
INSIDE DROPSHIP
P3
INSIDE DROPSHIP
CAP
SALLY

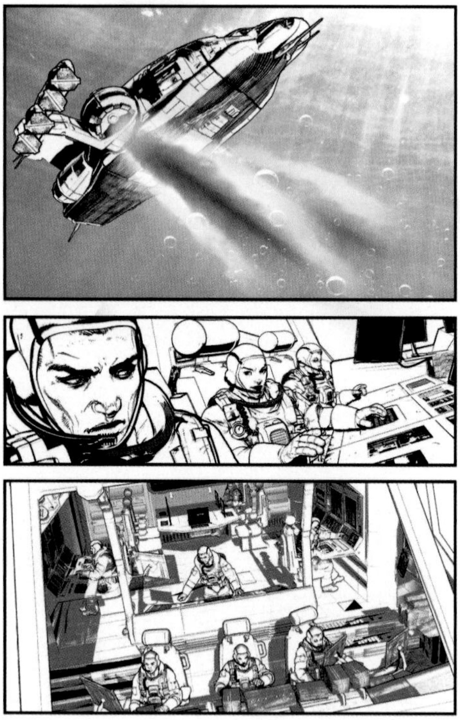

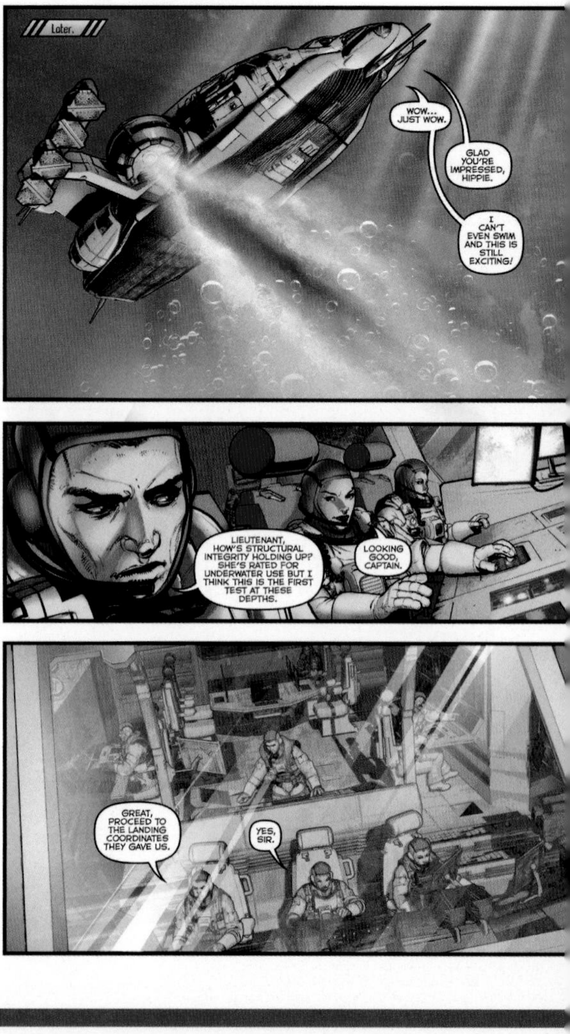
Later.
WOW... JUST WOW.
GLAD YOU'RE IMPRESSED, HIPPIE.
I CAN'T EVEN SWIM AND THIS IS STILL EXCITING!
LIEUTENANT, HOW'S STRUCTURAL INTEGRITY HOLDING UP? SHE'S RATED FOR UNDERWATER USE BUT I THINK THIS IS THE FIRST TEST AT THESE DEPTHS.
LOOKING GOOD, CAPTAIN.
GREAT, PROCEED TO THE LANDING COORDINATES THEY GAVE US.
YES, SIR.

5

L 2
: EVERYONE READY TO GET WET!?!

L 4
IE: THE STRUCTURAL INTEGRITY FIELDS ARE
ING GREAT IN THE SUITS…MY EARS AREN'T EVEN
ING DOWN HERE.
AIN: SHUT UP AND APPRECIATE THE VIEW…IT'S
RDER.

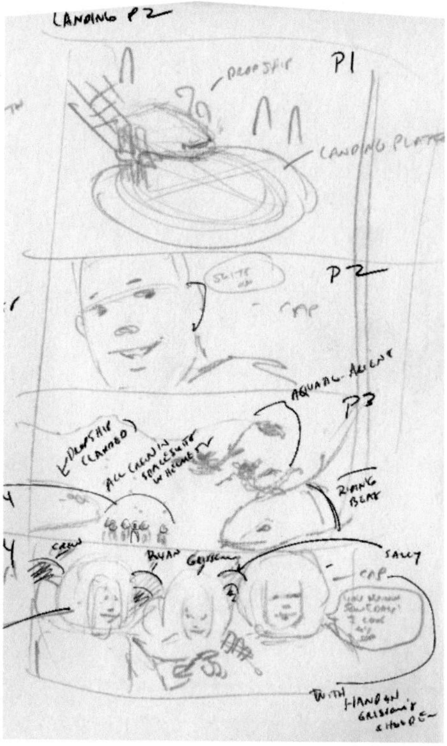
LANDING P2
P1
P2
P3

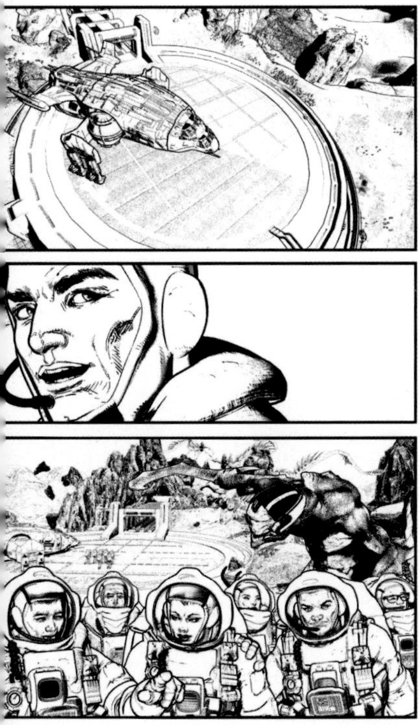

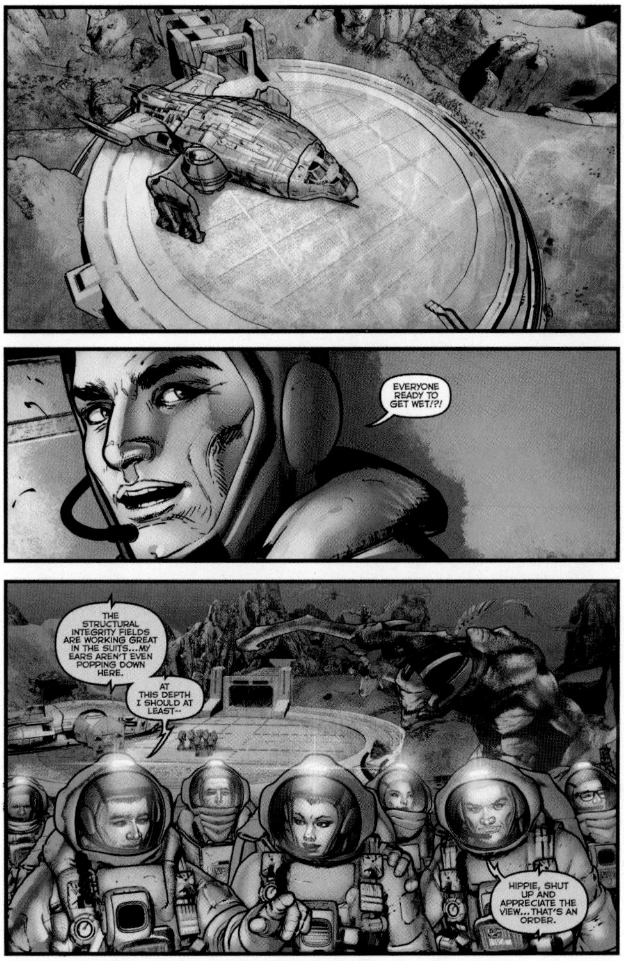
EVERYONE READY TO GET WET!?!
THE STRUCTURAL INTEGRITY FIELDS ARE WORKING GREAT IN THE SUITS...MY EARS AREN'T EVEN POPPING DOWN HERE.
AT THIS DEPTH I SHOULD AT LEAST--
HIPPIE, SHUT UP AND APPRECIATE THE VIEW...THAT'S AN ORDER.

Cover: Issue 2

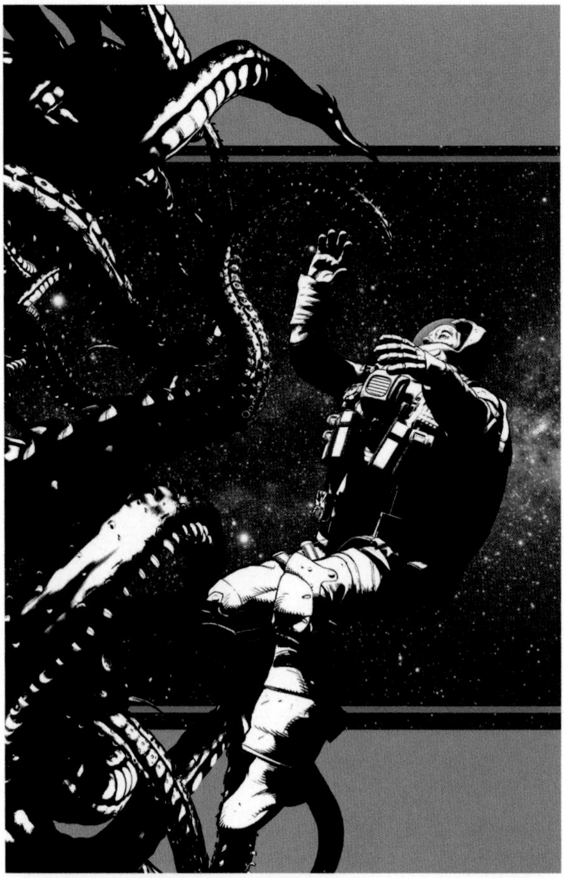

Cover: Issue 3

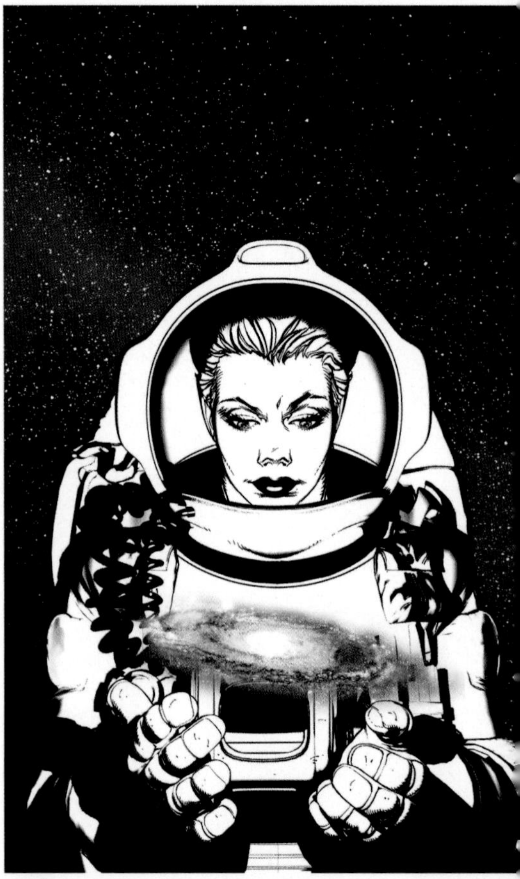

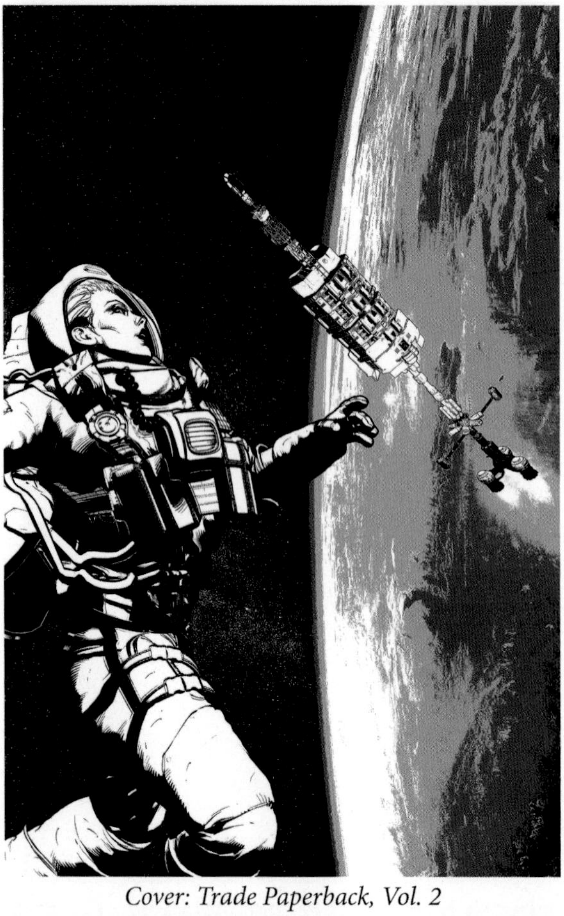

Cover: Trade Paperback, Vol. 2

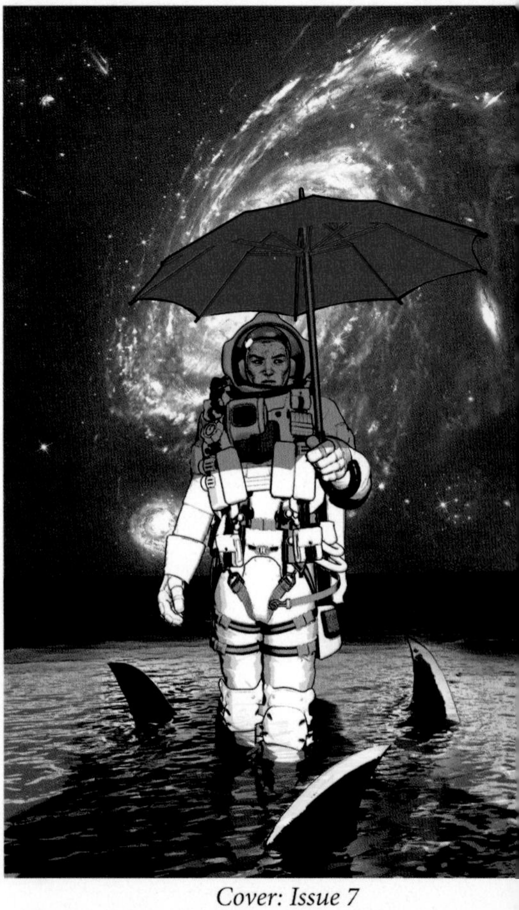

Cover: Issue 7

Cover: Issue 5

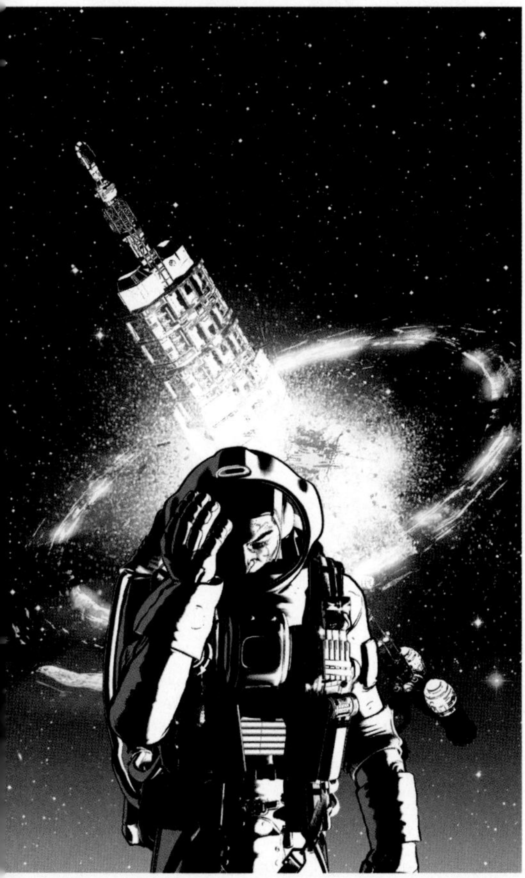

Cover: Issue 8

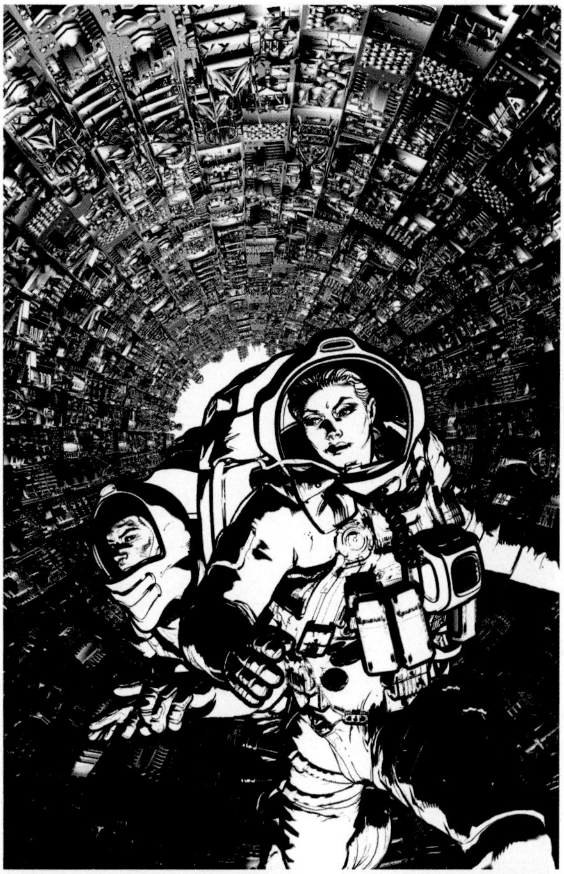

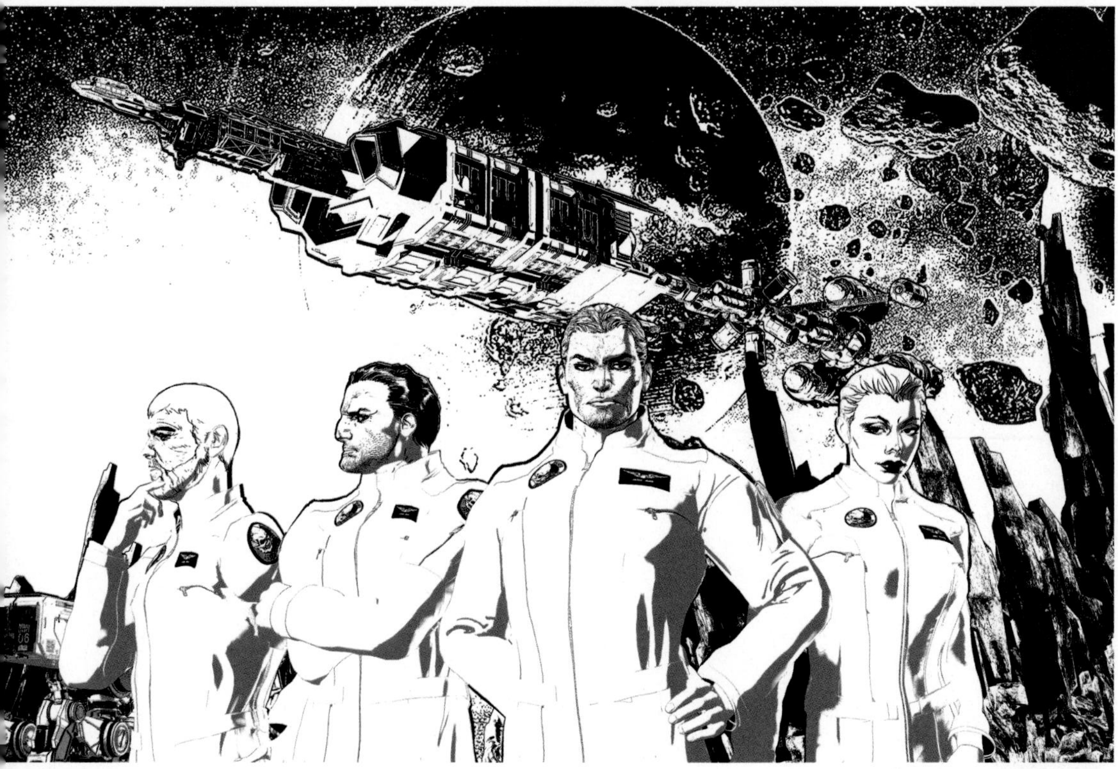

Early promotional image

ie line art from covers and promo
s. Some were just early prototypes
others were actually used."

BLACK & WHITE GALLERY

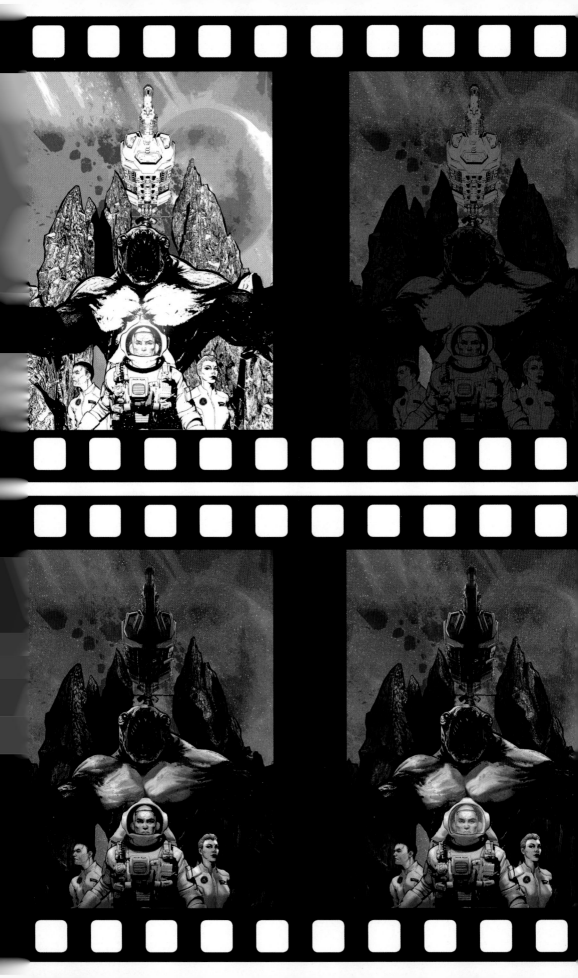

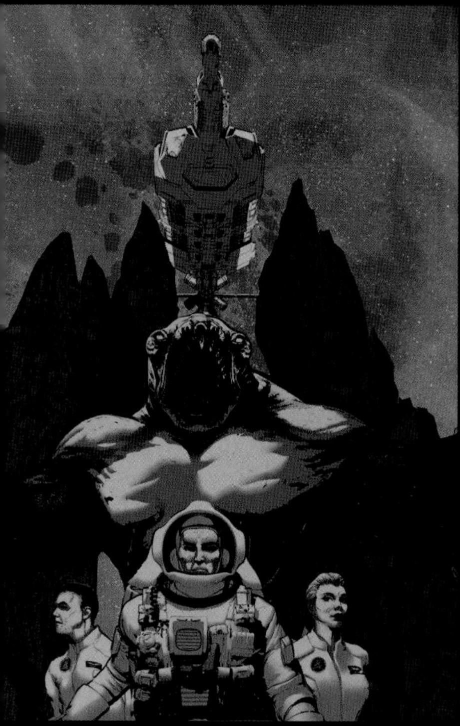

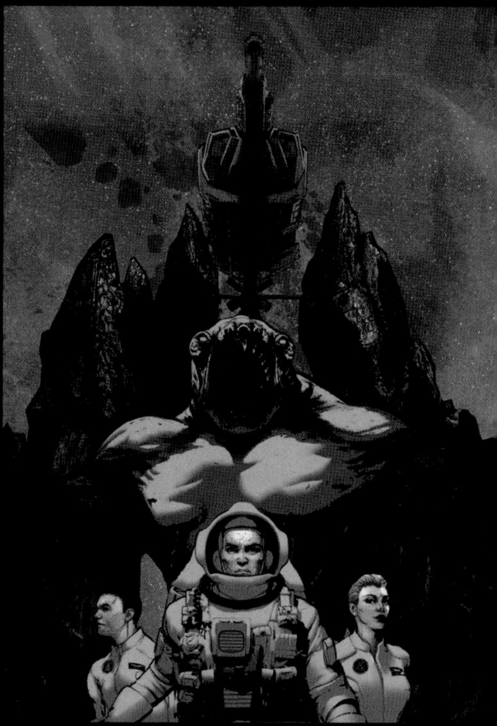

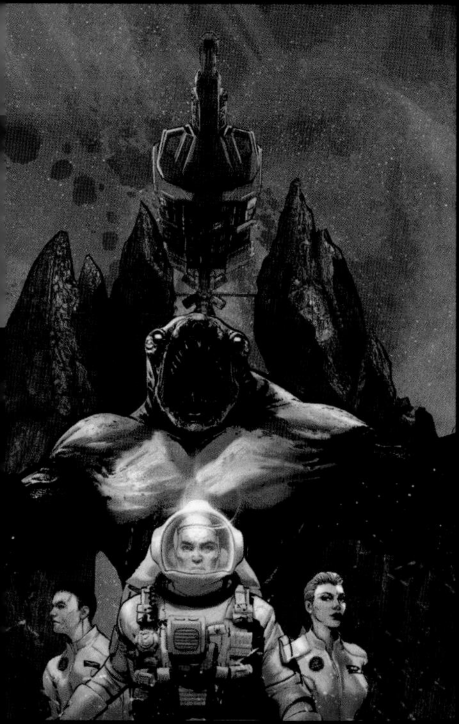

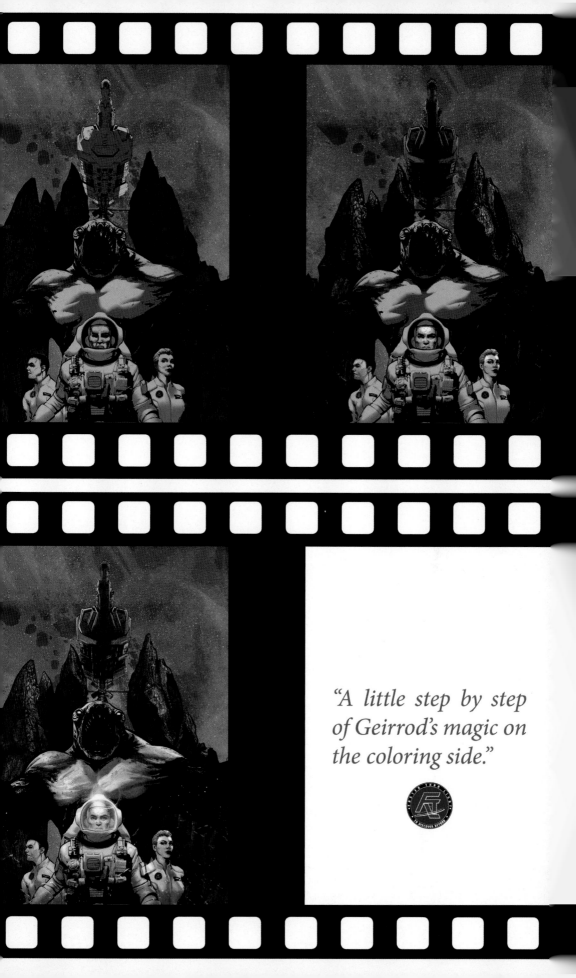

"A little step by step of Geirrod's magic on the coloring side."

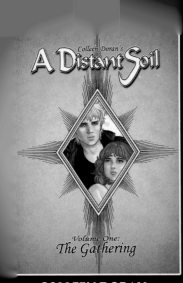

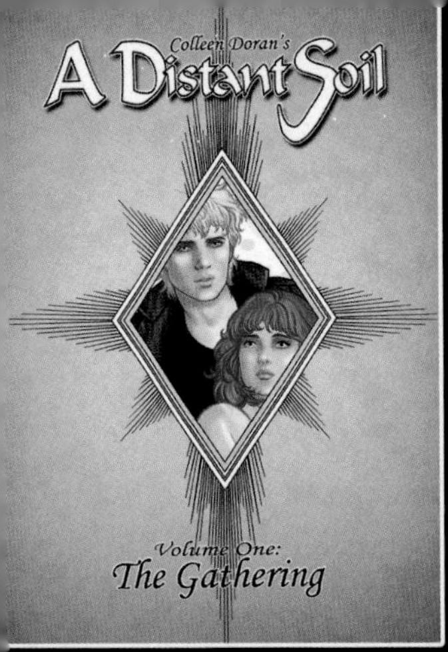
Colleen Doran's
A Distant Soil
Volume One:
The Gathering
COLLEEN DORAN

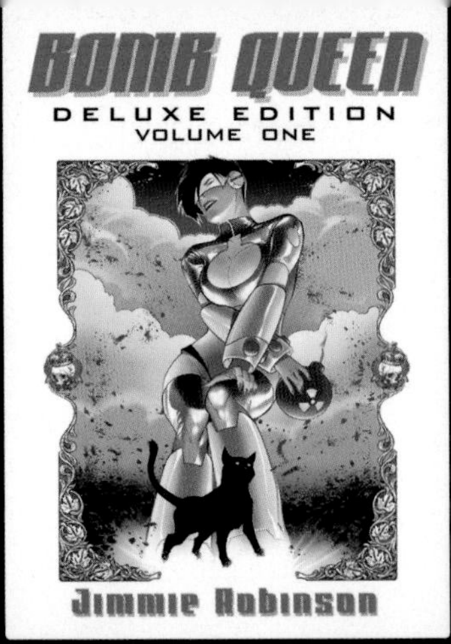
BOMB QUEEN
DELUXE EDITION
VOLUME ONE
Jimmie Robinson
JIMMIE ROBINSON

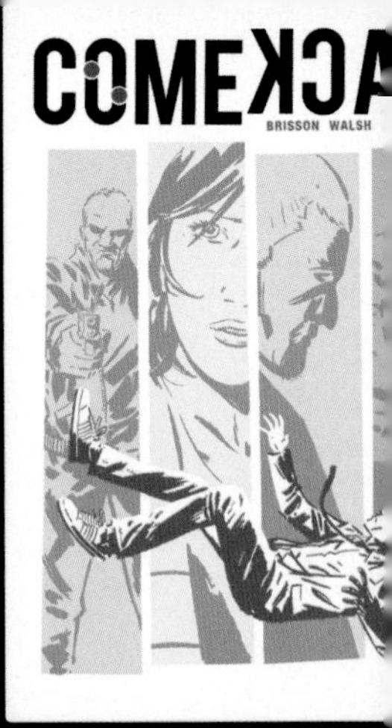
COMEBACK
BRISSON WALSH
BRISSON/WALSH

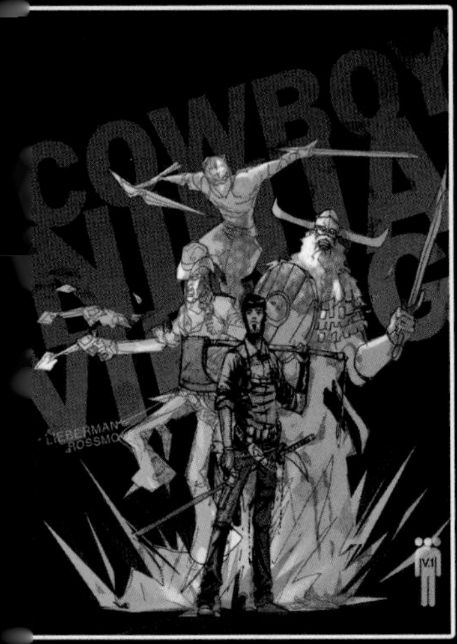
COWBOY NINJA VIKING
LIEBERMAN
ROSSMO
LIEBERMAN/ROSSMO

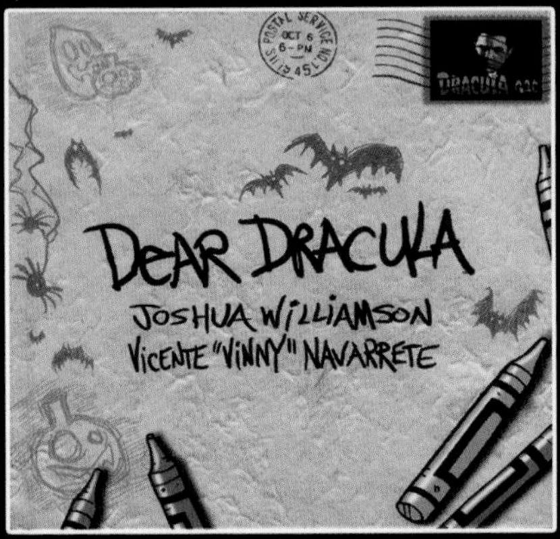
DEAR DRACULA
JOSHUA WILLIAMSON
VICENTE "VINNY" NAVARRETE
WILLIAMSON/NAVARRETE

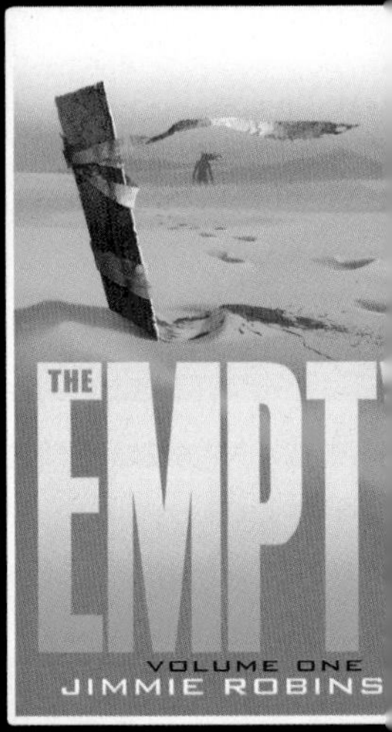
THE EMPTY
VOLUME ONE
JIMMIE ROBINSON
JIMMIE ROBINSON

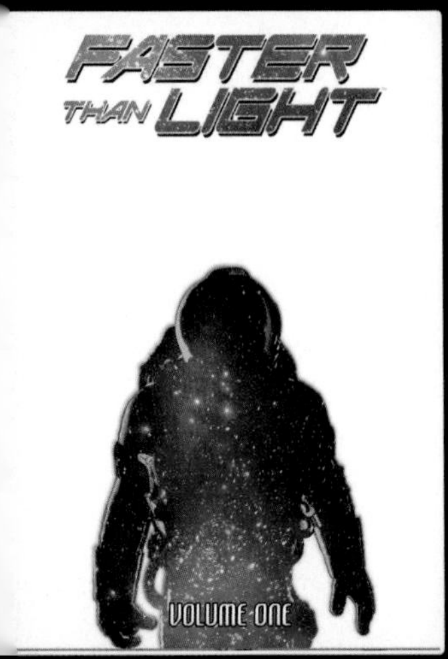
FASTER THAN LIGHT
VOLUME ONE
HABERLIN

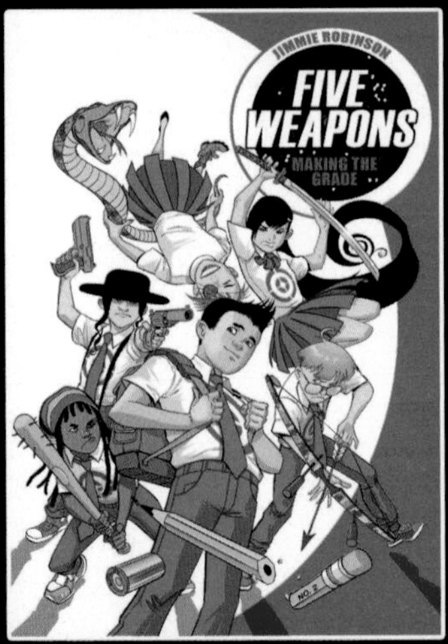
JIMMIE ROBINSON
FIVE WEAPONS
MAKING THE GRADE
JIMMIE ROBINSON

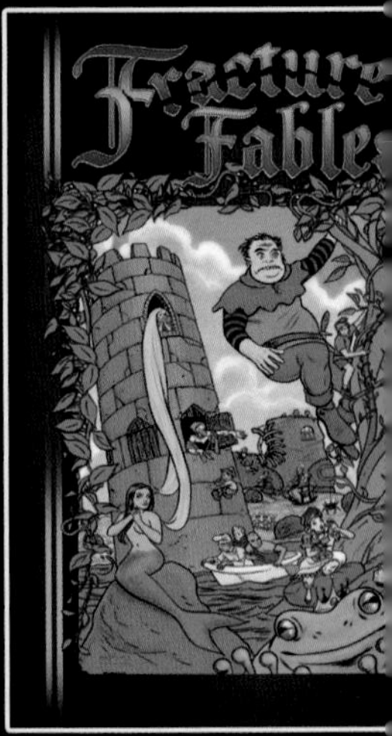
Fractured Fables
VARIOUS ARTISTS

...A Book For Every Taste.

BERMAN/LORIMER

BRISSON/LEVEL

WILLIAMSON/ HENDERSON

TED McKEEVER

PAUL FRICKE

WIEBE/JENKINS

WIEBE/UPCHURCH

TED McKEEVER

JIM VALENTINO